PRAISE FOR Ivan Doig
AND *The Eleventh Man*

"An exciting book with all the right stuff. *The Eleventh Man* might well be the very best thing Doig — an acclaimed and respected author — has done to date. I loved every word."
— *January Magazine*

"Doig incorporates all the elements of a good novel: an intensifying love interest, the drama of war, repeated moments of life-or-death intensity, the complexity of multiple story lines, historical curiosities, seamless prose, and even a winning football team."
— *Rocky Mountain News*

"The strength of *The Eleventh Man* comes in its exploration of larger subjects — the nature of heroism, and of propaganda."
— *New York Times Book Review*

"Doig's book is really about our strong history of storytelling, and the variety of ways we spin out words, especially during and about war times . . . it feels quite right to call Doig's writing a part of Americana."
— *Oregonian*

THE ELEVENTH MAN

Also by Ivan Doig

THE ELEVENTH MAN

★

Ivan Doig

Mariner Books · Houghton Mifflin Harcourt
Boston · *New York*

First Mariner Books edition 2009

www.hmhbooks.com

Library of Congress Cataloging-in-Publication Data
Doig, Ivan.
The eleventh man/Ivan Doig.—1st ed.
p.   cm.
1. Ex–football players—Fiction.   2. Montana—Fiction.
3. World War, 1939–1945—Fiction.   Title.
PS3554.O415E43   2008
813'.54—dc22   2008010046
ISBN 978-0-15-101243-5
ISBN 978-0-547-24763-2 (pbk.)

Book design by Linda Lockowitz
Text set in Minion Pro

Printed in the United States of America

DOC 10 9 8 7 6 5 4 3 2 1

To Becky Saletan
editor extraordinaire

THE ELEVENTH MAN

1943

★

⭐ NEVER MUCH OF A town for showing off, Gros Ventre waited around one last bend in the road, suppertime lights coming on here and there beneath its roof of trees. As the bus headed up the quiet main street toward the hotel, where the lobby served as depot, Ben Reinking saw the single lighted storefront on the block with the bank and the beauty shop. Of course. Thursday night. His father putting the newspaper to bed after this week's press run.

"Here will do," he called to the driver.

The bus driver jammed on the brakes and heaved himself around to take a better look at this final passenger. Using all the breath he could summon, the man let out slowly: "I'll be goddamned. You're him. Awful sorry, Lieutenant, I didn't—"

"I'll live." Most civilians could not read the obscure shoulder patch on his flight jacket, and any camouflage he could get anytime suited Ben.

Right there in the middle of the street, the driver laboriously dragged out the duffel bag from the luggage bay and presented it to him. The man looked tempted to salute. Ben murmured his thanks and turned away toward the premises of the *Gros Ventre Weekly Gleaner*. Well, he told himself as he swung along under the burden of his duffel, now to see whether his father had picked up any news about the repeal of the law of averages, as it apparently had been.

Habit dies hard, even the military variety that never came natural to him; he caught himself surveying these most familiar surroundings in terms of ambush and booby trap, and with a shake of his head sought to change over to observation of a more civil sort. Storefront by dozing storefront, the town still looked as if the world of war had nothing to do with it, yet he knew better. It was simply that buildings don't read casualty lists. He tried to put that thought away and just come to terms with being home. Gros Ventre, he'd learned growing up here, was the same age as the tree rings in the mature cottonwood colonnade along its streets, and altered itself as slowly. Only the season had changed appreciably since the last time he had to do this, early evening unrolling a frosty carpet of light from the front of the *Gleaner* building now as he approached.

He stopped to read the window as he always did. Posted beneath the gilt lettering on the plate glass were handbills announcing a war bonds box supper and a farm machinery auction on lower English Creek. Both were set in the familiar exclamatory typeface his father called Visual Braille. Fooling around as a printer paid for the indulgence of being a small-town editor, Bill Reinking liked to say. Just this moment, Ben spotted him there at the back of the office in the job shop, running the address-ograph himself. As ever, his father looked like a schoolmaster out of place, peering foggily through his bifocals while he fed the dog tag–sized subscription plates into the small machine for it to stamp those names and addresses onto the out-of-town mail wrappers. Ben remembered now: the office help, Janie, had moved to Arizona, where her husband's tank corps was in training.

Past his own reflection in the glass of the door, Ben watched his father at his lonesome chore until it started to hurt. *This part*

*doesn't get any easier either, does it. Two bylines under one roof.
At least we both write with the pointed end, he taught me that.*

With that he stepped inside to the subtle smell of ink fresh
on newsprint, calling out as cheerfully as he could manage: "All
the news that fits, again this week?"

"Ben!" The addressograph made empty thumping sounds
onto wrappers until his father could shut it down. "Surprise the
living daylights out of a man, why don't you. We weren't expecting you until the weekend."

"Well, guess what, the Air Transport Command turns out
to be full of surprises. It's only a forty-eight-hour leave, not the
seventy-two I put in for." He tried to cover the next with a shrug.
"And there's something I have to do out of town tomorrow. Other
than that, I'm the perfect guest."

"Better enjoy you in a hurry, hadn't I," his father said in his
dry way as they shook hands. His face alight, the older man gazed
at the younger as if storing up on him. He was dying to ask what
was behind this trip home, Ben could tell, but doing his best to
be a father first and a newspaperman second. That was fortunate,
because Ben himself did not have the right words anywhere near
ready. In the strange labyrinth of TDYs—temporary duty assignments—that Ben Reinking's war somehow had turned into, this
one was the hardest yet to talk about.

Bill Reinking could see most of this. Not wanting to prompt,
he ventured only: "You've seen a lot of the world lately."

More than enough. England, bombed stiff by the Luftwaffe.
New Guinea, beachheads backed against Japanese-held mountains two miles high. The close call from ack-ack over Palau on
the B-17 ride; the even closer one no one was being told about. Not
exactly pleasant conversation, any of it. Ben got rid of it for now
in mock-heroic fashion: "It was hell out in those there islands."

His father laughed uncertainly. After a moment, the bifocals tilted up in appraisal. "Nice addition to your uniform, by

the way. The Ernies"—Pyle and Hemingway preeminently, but
newsman slang for war correspondents as a species—"don't have
that."

"This?" Self-consciously Ben rubbed the new silver bar of a
full lieutenant on the tab of his shirt collar. Another hole in the
law of averages. The promotion had caught him by surprise almost as much as the blindside orders that landed him back at
East Base yet again. He lacked the time in grade, base commanders were never glad to see him coming, and for its own murky
reasons the Threshold Press War Project did not bother with fit-
ness reports—*So why boost me from shavetail all of a sudden?
What do the bastards have in mind for me next?* For his father's
sake, he forced a grin. "It doesn't amount to that much, Dad, to
outrank civilians."

All during this each looked the other over to see how he was
holding up since last time. Bill Reinking was bald to the back of
his head, but his ginger mustache still matched the color of Ben's
hair. His strong glasses schooled a square-cut face on a chunky
man into the most eager kind of lookout—the newsdigger's close
curiosity that he had passed on to his son. That and the ginger
follicles and not much else. Ben had the Hollywood lineaments
of his mother's people—the bodily poise, the expressive hands.
Those and that unbuyable mark of character: a deeply longitudinal face, neighbored with latitudes of experience—a surprising amount for a twenty-three-year-old—evident in the steady
sea-blue of the gaze. The difference in stature between the two
men was long-standing. Tall enough that he just skimmed under
the Army Air Corps height limit, Ben had an altitude advantage
over his father in a number of ways, although he usually tried not
to press it. Even so, the college education, the football fame, the
TPWP correspondent patch, the bylines and datelines from his
stopovers in the world's many combat zones, those all came home
with him every time, and both men stood back from it a bit.

"How was the trip up here?" Bill Reinking asked, to be asking something.

"Like *Gone with the Wind* without somebody to neck with," his son said and laughed in a way he did not recognize. "Long."

WONDERING HOW MANY more times this could happen in one lifetime, early that afternoon he had stepped out into the familiar blowy weather of Great Falls and pointed himself toward the same old tired bus that again and again had taken him to college and from college, to the war and from the war.

This time around, a person could tell there was a war on from the melancholy wheeze of the bus driver. On easier journeys home, he had been accustomed to forking over his fare to this narrow-shouldered fatherly man—an asthma sufferer, from the sound of it—in the drowsy waiting room of the Rocky Mountain Stageline depot. Now there was a sallow woman in that job who issued "God bless you real good, sonny," along with the ticket, and the ex–ticket agent was puffing around out in the loading area, dragging mail bags and the civilians' suitcases toward the belly of the bus. The war effort, preached on posters everywhere you turned these past two years since Pearl Harbor: it wore on people, without doubt, although that did not seem what the sloganeers intended to convey. Ben tried to slip his duffel into the bus and the seat next to him so he could lean against it and possibly nap during the familiar trip, but the hunched driver grabbed it away and insisted on stowing it for him. "Save your strength for the enemy, Lieutenant," he panted.

Which one?

Keeping that to himself at all costs, Ben boarded. He never liked being last at anything, but the half dozen other passengers, farm people with their city shopping clutched in their laps, long since had claimed specific seats and were giving him the gauging looks that young men in fleece-lined flight jackets tended to draw. *If they only knew.* Swiftly nodding in everyone's general direction the way he imagined someone who looked like a hotshot pilot was counted on to do, he deposited himself nearest the door as always, the coat leather crackling as he folded his considerable height into the worn confines of the seat. In his travels through the world of war, he had learned never to shed the fleece jacket on any means of transport, whether it was plane, train, ship, jeep, or bus, until he had proof the heater worked.

In this case it did not, at least to any noticeable degree, and by the time the bus lumbered away from the depot and rumbled west onto the bridge across the Missouri, he had turned up the coat collar for the full effect of the wool. In more ways than one, he had never really warmed to Great Falls. Scrunched in the perpetual bus seat he felt less comfortable than ever with the thought that this smokestack-marked city—the Anaconda Copper stack there above the Black Eagle smelter dominated the sky of centermost Montana with a constant plume of smoke—seemed to have some kind of unquenchable claim on him.

Three times in a little over a year. How the hell is it possible? How's this for a scene, Mr. Zanuck:

"What did you do in the war, my boy?"

"It's highly classified, but since you asked so nicely—I set the record for making hardship trips home."

There. He had managed to laugh at himself, if nervous laughter counted; maybe he wasn't utterly losing his grip on who and what he was. It still amounted to too much hardship, though. *Compassionate leave. Vic wouldn't have had any trouble laughing over that, poor buddy—I get the leave and he's stuck with the compassion and a folded flag in what's left of his lap.*

"Can't ever get used to the size of that stadium," he heard come his way, the wheeze in that observation alerting him to its source. Always wary of this sort of thing, he kept on staring out his side of the bus, as if the remark was an announcement the bus driver routinely offered up at this point on the route.

"Big old sister, ain't she," the driver persisted. "They don't build 'em like that anymore."

For a few seconds longer, Ben carried on pretending that the remark had been addressed to everyone on the bus, or for that matter, to passengers immemorial. Then, as he had known he would, he pulled his gaze away from the dominating smokestack and turned it to a very different landmark coming up, the mammoth Treasure State University stadium. The other Great Falls industry, football.

He felt his throat dry out. If the pair of years since were any evidence, he was in danger of unwanted conversation about TSU's fabled 1941 team until his last day on earth. But this time, thanks be, he lucked out. The bus driver had given up on him. Better than that, evidently had not recognized him.

Alert all the way to his fingertips now, Ben leaned forward and studied the big stadium and its Romanesque hauteur almost as if he had never played there. The art deco golden eagles, wingtip to wingtip up there around the entire edifice. The colosseum archways that funneled in the biggest crowds in the state's history, to watch the unbeatable '41 team. The perimeter of flagpoles around the entire top of the stadium, like unlit candles on a giant birthday cake. Not for the first time he took in each morsel of detail in writerly fashion, digesting them for the script. *If I can ever get the damned thing written at all.* It had been, what, half a year since he last did this, but he was finding that all of it gripped him as tenaciously as ever. The team's story, his, Jake's, Dexter's, the rest of the unique starting eleven. More than ever now, Vic's story; Quick Vic, most slippery runner in the conference, leaving after practice every afternoon to walk back to the Indian shacktown on Hill 57 over there. Bruno's story, everlasting bastard as football coach; and Loudon's, ruthless bastard as sportswriter. Under and over all the others, Merle Purcell's story, the most famous substitute who never played a game: the twelfth man's story. The story coded somehow there in the white alphabet, those painted rocks arranged into the huge letters TSU, stairstep-style, high on the side of the butte that loomed over the stadium; the Letter Hill. The mental camera in Ben moved across it all with deliberation, panning the scene for the screen, until at last the bus reached the highway and veered northward.

He patted the typewriter case on the seat beside him, which he had refused to yield to the bus driver. Maybe in these next few days he would be able to steal a bit of time in his father's office to work on the script. Although even there, the world of war was always in the way. It was in the way of everything.

BILL REINKING HAD missed out on war—younger than wanted in the first worldwide one, old enough to be ignored in this one—but he knew the caliber of a war story when he saw one.

"Quite the piece you did on those pilots," he was saying with professional gruffness. "It should have people all over the country burning their tongues on their coffee in the morning." He plucked a *Gleaner* off the top of the mailing pile and pitched it to his son. "I gave it three columns of page five. More than I gave myself, I'll have you know."

"I was hoping that'd be in. Christ, they held it long enough." Ben rattled the newspaper open, and the headline his father had put on the piece all but hit him in the face: RAINBOW OF PLANES FROM MONTANA TO RUSSIA.

Hastily he read his lead to make sure it had survived—*The pulse of war can be felt the minute you step onto East Base, a former buffalo prairie on the sunrise edge of Great Falls, where the ground vibrates under you not from eternal stampede but modern 12-piston fighter plane engines*—and skimmed on down, holding his breath. Of all the perplexities that went with a TPWP byline, the most constant was the red pencil of the invisible copy officer back in Washington. Censor, really. Inimical to logic. After a year and a half of this, Ben was as mystified as ever by the inner workings of the Threshold Press War Project, what was let past and what wasn't. He full well understood that the name was meant to invoke the doorstep homefront, the breadbasket America served by mid-size dailies and small-town weeklies such as his father's; the vital breakfast table readership, with its sons and daughters in the war. But it never left his mind for long that a threshold also was where people wiped their feet on something.

Not this time. The cherished name, the bit about the ringless hands at the P-39 controls, all that was still in there. *Foxed the bastard. Can't every time, but—*

His father had been watching in surprise. It wasn't like Ben to nuzzle his own prose. "Maybe I had better go through that piece again myself. What did you sneak in there, an invitation to neck on the bus?"

"Bad business, giving away a trade secret to an editor," Ben intoned, his expression saying he couldn't wait to. "My minder back at Tepee Weepy went for a decoy. I threw in a graf about Red stars over Montana, and he cut that clean as a whistle." He described to his father the East Base paint shop where the giant red stars of the Soviet Union were sprayed on the wings and fuselages of new bombers and fighter planes before they were delivered north. "No way they'd ever let that graf stand, I figured, and maybe I'd get away with the rest of the piece. It worked out."

"Shame on you," said his father, reaching for a pencil and paper. "I don't suppose you'd remember that particular paragraph?"

Ben recited it as his father jotted. When he was done, the older man sighed. "I'll need to be a little careful with this. Probably half the county thinks there's a Red star on me, I wrote so many editorials in favor of Lend-Lease."

"You and Franklin D. got it, you clever devils," Ben's voice imitated newsreel pomposity. "Two hundred planes to our noble Soviet allies last month. Three hundred a month by the end of the year, if East Base doesn't freeze up solid."

Bill Reinking cocked his head. "Should you be telling me all this, Lieutenant?"

Ben wasn't listening. Eyes down into a certain section of the newspaper piece, he was back in the world of pilots.

THE SPARSE CROSSROADS called Vaughn Junction was only the first stop, barely out of sight of Great Falls, but he had piled off right behind the bus driver anyway. This was the one part of the journey home he had been looking forward to.

While the mailbag was being dealt with, he stretched his legs in the parking lot by the roadhouse. A slow little conciliatory smile worked its way onto his extensive face as he thought about the other times here, with her. A laugh helplessly followed the smile. At least there was one thing new about this trip: Cass, coming out of the blue to him.

Checking his wristwatch, he kept scanning the sky to the west. First snow had only brushed the tops of the Rockies yet; a bit of hope there, maybe, that the weather would hold off during his leave. He moved around restlessly, his shadow in lengthened antics behind him as he faced into the afternoon sun. The air was good, out here in the grassland beyond the reach of the smelter stack, and he savored it while he watched the sky and waited. Whether it was football or what, he had always greatly loved these blue-and-tan days of the crisp end of October.

Something else he greatly loved became just visible over the mountains now—at least one military saying turned out to be right, it took a pilot's eyes to see other pilots. Here they came, right on the button. The four specks in the sky, factory-new fighter planes incoming on the hop from Seattle. The unmistakable dart-nosed silhouette of P-39s; Airacobras, in the virulent military method of naming aircraft types.

Ben felt his heart race; another expression that was validated now that he had met Cass. In the month since his fresh set of orders landed him at East Base and the Air Transport Command, he had seen this half a dozen times now, Cass and her WASP squadron ferrying in the sleek gray fighters. Planes poured into East Base from three directions for the Lend-Lease transit onward to Alaska and Russia, but the run from Seattle was all Cass's.

Again this time, he watched hungrily as the Cobras cut through the clear sky, high overhead. From what she had told him, when the flying weather was good this last leg of the route was a snap, the turbulent peaks of the Rockies abruptly dropping behind past the Continental Divide and unmistakable guideposts abundant on the prairie ahead—the Sun River, the grand Missouri, and for that matter, the Black Eagle smokestack. His imagination soared up there with her, her cat-quick hands on the controls, her confident wiry body in the tight-fit cockpit of the lead P-39.

She had not told him this part yet, but by asking around the air base he'd learned Cass Standish also had a reputation for bringing in her flights safely no matter what the weather or visibility. ("She can navigate in zero visibility like a wild-ass Eskimo," a crusty tower officer had provided the apt quote, although Ben had to clean it up.) He stirred up inside just thinking of it. For the life of him, he could not see why the Women Air Force Service Pilots were not allowed to deliver the P-39s, and for that matter the B-17 bombers and anything else that flew, onward north to the waiting Russian pilots in Alaska. In a saner world, where his TPWP minder in Washington wondrously would not exist, his piece about the flying women of East Base would outright say that. Getting something like that across between the lines was becoming a specialty of his.

Still mesmerized, he stood in the parking lot with his hands in the pockets of his flight jacket and yearned up at the fighter planes as only a grounded pilot can. Beyond that, much beyond that, he yearned for Cass. How many kinds of lust were there? The night before last, the two of them had been in a cabin in back of that roadhouse over there, uniforms cast off and forgotten, romantic maniacs renting by the hour. The whispered prattle of love talk, after: "So it's true what they say about redheads." "I'm wrongly accused. It's ginger, not red." "Ginger? That's a spice. No wonder." Now, for one wild instant he wished Cass would peel off out of the formation and buzz the roadhouse and him at an airspeed of four hundred miles an hour in tribute to that night and its delirious lovemaking.

That was hoping for too much. The flight swept over with a roar, the P-39s as perfectly spaced as spots on a playing card. Watching them glint in the sun as they diminished away toward East Base, Ben jammed his fists deeper into his pockets. As quickly as the planes were gone, frustration filled him again. He drew a harsh breath. He knew perfectly well he was thinking about these matters more than was healthy, but it stuck with him day and night anymore, the overriding hunch that for him the war's next couple of years—and, who knew, the next couple after that, and after that—might go on and on as his first two years of so-called service had, yanking him away on noncombatant assignment to some shot-up corner of the world and then depositing him back here for this kind of thing, time after time. And, the worst part, Cass always out of reach. At this rate, he could foresee with excruciating clarity, her letters to him would add up to a string-tied packet in the bottom of his duffel bag. Somewhere in New Guinea there would be a similar packet, wherever her soldier husband chose to tuck them.

Lovesick. Try as he would, he could not clear away the relentless feeling. Whoever stuck those two words together was a hell of a diagnostician. An incurable case of Cassia Standish he was definitely suffering from, its symptoms rapture and queasiness simultaneously. *Vic would think I've gone off my rocker.* Getting himself involved with someone married. Not just married: married to khaki. No surer way to risk loss of rank and beyond that, dishonorable discharge, the Section Eight "deemed unfit to serve" bad piece of paper, him and her both. *Sometimes I think I've gone off my rocker.* "My, my," Cass had kidded him, reaching out naked from bed the other night to stroke that new silver bar on his uniform and meanwhile leering at him as effectively as Hedy Lamarr ever did at a leading man. "What's next, a Good Conduct medal?" *Not hardly.*

"Ready to hit the road if you are, Lieutenant." The bus driver had come up behind him, sounding curious about what kept a man standing in a roadhouse parking lot watching planes go over. Ben clambered back on and reclaimed his seat. He leaned against the window and shut his eyes to wait out all the road miles yet before home. Sometimes he dozed and sometimes he didn't, but either way he dreamed of Cass and more Cass.

"DON'T LET ME interrupt your enjoyment of great literature," the imperative note in his father's voice snapped him out of his absorption in the version of her he had put into newsprint. "But I have to get back at it." Bill Reinking indicated toward the job shop and the table where the addressograph waited. "Had any supper? There's some macaroni salad and fried chicken left."

Ben looked at the bucket supper from the Lunchery down the street, then back at his father.

"Your mother is in Valier," came the explanation. "Play rehearsal. They're doing *The Importance of Being Earnest,* and she couldn't pass up Lady Bracknell, could she?"

"Can't imagine it," Ben conceded in the same deliberately casual tone his father had used. "Let me get some chicken in me, then I'll take over on the addresser, how about."

"No, that's fine," his father spoke hastily, "I'm used to this by now. You can help wrap when I get to that." Turning away, he started up the addressograph again and, a sound his son had grown up on, the name-and-address plates began clattering through like metal poker chips as each alphabetical stack of half a dozen was fed in. Ben left him to it and moved toward the other end of the worktable to put together a semblance of supper. He still felt off-balance about being back amid the comfortable inky clutter of the newspaper office after so much military life. Food would be a good idea, even the Lunchery's.

He was reaching into the meal bucket when he heard a lapse in the addressing machine's rhythmic slap-slap on the wrappers. Out the corner of his eye he watched his father quickly palm a subscription plate off the stack he was working with and slip it into his pants pocket. Ben frowned. His father always chucked aside any discards into a coffee can, there by the addressograph for that purpose, until there were enough to be dumped into the linotype melt pot.

"Hey," Ben called softly. "I saw that." He held out his hand for the discard. "Gimme, gimme, my name is Jimmy."

His father stood frozen there with his hand still in his pocket.

"Dad? What's up?"

A stricken expression came over the older man. "I—I didn't want you to come across this one in the wrappers. Ben, I'm sorry if—"

He handed the flat little piece of metal to his son as if it were a rare coin. Flipping it over to the raised side, Ben instantly spelled out the inverted letters of type. Reading backward was a skill that came with growing up in a newspaper office, and right then he wished he didn't have it.

VICTOR RENNIE CPL. SERIAL #20929246
C CO., 26TH REGIMENT, 1ST INFANTRY DIVISION
C/O U.S. ARMY OVERSEAS POST OFFICE
NEW YORK, N.Y.

CONFOUNDED, HE STARED at his father. "How'd you already know it's Vic? They sit on the names until I—" He gestured futilely.

"I didn't, really." Bill Reinking's face was at odds with his words. "If it turned out to be some other reason you're here, I was going to hand-address this one at the post office."

Ben swallowed hard. Tonelessly he told his father what had happened to Vic Rennie in the minefield in the Sicilian countryside.

Bill Reinking blanched; two years of hardening from handling war news didn't help with this. It had to be asked:

"Everybody else—?"

"All accounted for, Dad, relax. I checked this morning." As he did every morning. Day by day he knew exactly where each one of them was, in the world of war. It was his job to know.

Carl Friessen in New Guinea.

Jake Eisman piloting at East Base.

Animal Angelides on a Marine troop ship.

Sig Prokosch patrolling a shore in the Coast Guard.

Moxie Stamper bossing an anti-aircraft gun pit in England.

Nick Danzer on the destroyer USS *McCorkle* in the Pacific.

Dexter Cariston at the camp that was not supposed to be mentioned.

Stanislaus Havel and Kenny O'Fallon in graves under military crosses.

And Vic, whose chapter of the war had to be put to rest with this journey.

Every soldier, in the course of time, exists only in the breath of written words. The gods that govern saga have always known that. There were times Bill Reinking stood stock-still in this newspaper office, hardly daring to breathe, as he tore open the week's Threshold Press War Project packet and pawed through the drab handouts until he spotted the words *The "Supreme Team" on the Field of Battle . . . by Lt. Ben Reinking*. It awed him each time, Ben's unfolding epic of them, impeccably told. Taken together, they amounted to an odd number—eleven—whose combined destiny began one afternoon in 1941 on a windblown football field, and from there swirled away into the fortunes of war. Montana boys, all, grown into something more than gridiron heroes. One by one, the Treasure State teammates—the much-heralded entire varsity now enlisted one way or another—were individuals rehearsing for history, in newsprint across America. The one with the TPWP patch on his shoulder, with the mandate from somewhere on high to write of them all, now pocketed away the dog tag–sized piece of metal cold in his fingers, as his father wordlessly watched.

The leaden arithmetic was not anything Ben could put away. "Two dead and Vic a cripple, how's that for being a 'chosen' team? If this keeps on, we can play six-man."

Instantly he wanted that choice of words back. *That's what gave us Purcell. Does it all start there?* Not a one of the '41 starters came up out of six-man football, but Merle Purcell had, the newcomer from nowhere who met his doom in eleven-man. Two years hadn't made any of it less raw on the nerves. Fast and skittery as an antelope, Purcell materialized from some tiny high school out in the sagebrush where they played six-man, which was pretty much a cross between football and hundred-yard dash, and given a chance on the scrub team he ran circles around the Treasure State varsity in practice until he would poop out. And subsequently ran himself to death on the Letter Hill trying to toughen up enough for the TSU merciless steamroller brand of football. To this day Purcell was there in Ben's mind's eye, in the script ingredients, struggling up the giant slope to the white rocks after practice and even on his own on weekends; strange jinxed kid who by the miracle of modern sportsmongering had been made to live on as the inspirational "twelfth man" of the perfect season. Ben knew it wasn't fair, he had barely known Purcell, but the interior truth was that he would not have traded a dozen of him, or any like him, for Vic Rennie.

"Son." Bill Reinking did not use that word much in the presence of the tall man in uniform across the table from him. "I know you're having it rough, the whole bunch of you, but—"

"Never mind." He looked over at his father, the shielding eyeglasses, the oblique composure. *This won't do. We skimp past this every time.* "This is getting to me, Dad," he huskily spoke the necessary. "You have anything to do with it?"

"I wouldn't be much of a newspaper editor if I didn't point out that's an indefinite pronoun."

"Don't hand me that, you know as well as I do what I mean. This haywire assignment they've got me on. Anybody you happen to know happen to be behind it, just for instance?"

His father's tone turned dry again. "I assume you mean the Senator. Just because I throw the awesome weight of the *Gleaner* behind him every six years doesn't mean we're in bed together. I would remind you, the Senator didn't want anything to do with this war—the only side he wanted us on is Switzerland's."

"Then is it Mother's doing?" The words exploded from Ben with a force that shook both men. The level of his voice came down but his vehemence did not. "Did she talk some old family friend in Beverly Hills into picking up the phone and calling Robert Sherwood or Elmer Davis or Jesus D. Christ in the White House himself and say, 'Guess what, there's somebody I'd like to see grounded and stay glued to a typewriter for the next dozen years or the end of the war, whichever comes first.' Well? Did she?"

"Ben, will you kindly quit? Unlike you, your mother and I are a bit grateful you're not stationed somewhere getting shot to pieces." His father took off his glasses and polished the lenses clean with the page of a torn *Gleaner*; only window-washers and newspapermen knew that stunt. "To answer you for once and all, though—we know better than to pull strings for you, even if we had any. You made that clear to us long ago." Bill Reinking went on in a milder tone. "I hate to bring up a remote possibility, but just maybe you were picked out for this because you're the natural person for it."

"You don't know how the military works," Ben scoffed. But there was no future in arguing his TPWP servitude with his father, not tonight. "Speaking of that." He reeled off what he needed for his trip out of town in the morning.

"I wish we'd known," dismay took over his father's voice. "Your mother has been putting on the miles, these rehearsals—"

"Dad, don't look like that, it's all right. I know where I can always get it."

His father sighed. "We both know that. Why don't you go tend to it before he closes for the night? Then you can give me a lift home so I can ride in style for a change."

BEN WALKED BRISKLY two blocks up the street and stepped into the Medicine Lodge. The saloon was as quiet as if empty, but it was never empty at this time of night. Inert as doorstops, at the far end of the bar sat a bleary pair of sheepherders he recognized—Pat Hoy from the Withrow ranch, and the other had a nickname with a quantity of geography attached. Canada Dan, that was it. Puffy with drink but not falling-down drunk, the two evidently were winding down a usual spree after the lambs were shipped, when there was half a year's wages to blow. Ever conscious of his uniform, Ben had a flash of thought that except for polar explorers, these befogged old herders off alone in their sheep wagons somewhere would have been about the last people to hear of the war, back in December of 1941. It did not seem to be foremost on their minds now, either, as they and a third occupant expectantly looked down the bar in Ben's direction like connoisseurs of the tints of money.

"Goddamn," Tom Harry spoke from behind the bar. Ben was beginning to wonder why the sight of him made people mention damnation. "You're back again, huh? I thought you'd be up in an aereoplane someplace winning the war single-handed, Reinking."

"Nice to see you again too, Tom." With a ghost of a smile, Ben patted his way along the rich polished wood of the bar as if touching it for luck. The Medicine Lodge was not much changed since his high school Saturdays of wrestling beer kegs and emptying spitoons and swamping the place out with broom and mop. "Saturday night buys the rest of the week, kid," Tom Harry would always say as he paid Ben his dollar or so of wages. Hundreds of such nights produced a saloon that by now had a crust of decor as rigorous as a museum's. Stuffed animal heads punctuated every wall; the one-eyed buffalo in particular was past its prime. The long mirror in back of the bar possessed perhaps a few more age spots of tarnish than when Ben had been in charge of wiping it down, and the immense and intricate oaken breakfront that framed it and legions of whiskey bottles definitely had more dust. Still pasted to the mirror on either side of the cash register were the only bits of notice taken of the twentieth century: a photo of Tom Harry's prior enterprise, the Blue Eagle saloon in one of the Fort Peck Dam project's hard-drinking boomtowns, and a 1940 campaign poster picturing President Franklin Delano Roosevelt so cheerily resolute for a third term that it would have made any Republican cringe.

Taking all this in, for the narrowest of moments Ben could almost feel he had never been away from it. Illusions had to be watched out for. He got down to business, which meant Tom Harry. "Do you still sell beverages in this joint or just stand around insulting the customers?"

The sole proprietor and entire staff of the Medicine Lodge glanced to the far end where the raggedy sheepherders were gaping hopefully in Ben's direction. "Hard to do, on some of them. What can I get you?"

"Whatever's on tap," Ben said before it registered on him that he was home now, he didn't need to nurse away the evening on beer. "No, wait, something with a nip to it—an old-fashioned, how about." *Still in the mood, Cass.* The other night in the roadhouse when they were priming themselves by playing coma cola roulette—each buying the other some unlikely concoction off the mixed drinks list before adjourning to the cabin for the night—she'd wickedly ordered him up one of these, saying it might put him in the mood for an old-fashioned pilot like her. Now he dug into his wallet. "Give the choirboys a round. Catch yourself, too."

"Thanks, I'll take mine in the register. Save you the tip." Schooners of beer flew down the bar, the whiskey and paradoxical bitters and sugar were magically mixed, Ben watching fascinated as ever at the skill in those hands. Tom Harry could never be cast as a bartender, he decided. He overfilled the part. The slicked-back black hair, the blinding white shirt, the constant towel that swabbed the bar to a gleam. The peerless saloonkeeper scowled now in the direction of the sheepherders, which seemed to make them remember their manners. In one voice they quavered a toast to Ben: "Here's at you."

With that tended to, the man behind the bar put his towel to work on the trail of the glass after he slid it to Ben. "Just get in?"

"Hour ago."

"Been places, I hear."

"They ship me around, some."

"Gonna be anybody left on the face of the earth when this war gets done?"

During this the sheepherders conferred in mumbles. Celebrating their largesse of beer, the two were counting out their pooled small change, pushing the coins together with shaky forefingers. "Barkeep?" Canada Dan cleared his throat importantly. "You got any of them jellied eggs?"

"Jesus, gourmets," Tom Harry muttered, carrying the briny crock of preserved boiled eggs down the length of the bar along with his disgust. While the egg transaction dragged on, Ben quietly sipped and gazed past the reflections in the plate glass window to downtown Gros Ventre at night. The civil old trees. His father's newspaper office, still alight down the street, another timeless pillar of the town. On the next block beyond the *Gleaner*, the Odeon theater where teenaged Ben Reinking every Saturday night of his life stayed on through the second show—the "owl show" at nine that repeated the feature movie for a tardy gathering of drunks, late-arriving lovers, and insomniacs—to dissect how the makers of movies made them. Centralities of his growing up here, those, along with the one where he sat now. He knew there was no denying the influence of bloodline, but by quite a number of the readings he could take on his life so far, Gros Ventre and the Two Medicine country, out there in the dark, served as a kind of parentage too. Whatever he amounted to, this was where it came from.

The keeper of the bar returned, still wagging his head over the jellied egg binge. Ben twirled his glass indicatively on the dark wood. "Any more of this in the well?"

"The war must be teaching you bad habits," Tom Harry grumbled as he mixed the refill.

"Speaking of those." Ben watched for a reaction, but could see none. Standing there swishing the towel, the saloonman showed

no sign he had ever been acquainted with practices such as providing working quarters for prostitutes, bootlegging, and, now
with the war, operating in at least gray margins of the black market. "Here's what it is. I need a car and a bible of gas coupons."

"Where you think you're gonna drive to with those—Paris,
France, to get laid?"

"You ought to know. Probably all over hell, but I'll start at the
Two Medicine."

The uncomprehending look on his listener was a reminder
that not all of the world knew about Vic, at least yet. He again
told what the minefield had done.

"What a hell of a thing to go through life like that." Eyes reflective, Tom Harry wiped slowly at the bar wood after Ben told
him. "Known that kid since he was a pup." He flicked a look at
Ben. "Weren't you here for funerals the last couple of times?"

Ben gulped more of his drink than he'd intended, unstead-
ied by having something like that attached to him. O'Fallon's
and Havel's, those were. The mouthy mick left guard and the
taciturn baby-faced center. Tepee Weepy wanted every drop of
drama from the Supreme Team; it had sent the Pulitzer judges
his piece about the Butte slum wake held for O'Fallon. He hadn't
even liked O'Fallon.

How much does history rehearse? he had to wonder. The first
funeral of all was Purcell's. The entire team in that tumbleweed
hometown cemetery. Coach Bruno piously delivering the eulogy
into the radio microphone at graveside. Didn't it set the pattern,
the team's every movement on the airwaves and in the headlines
from then until—

All at once he realized Tom Harry still was eyeing him
speculatively.

"There's a war on," he managed to say evenly. "Things happen to people."

"Must get kind of old, is all I'm saying." The bartender slung the towel aside. "Drink up. The Packard is out back."

The long black car, its grandeur a bit faded from ten years of imaginative use, seemed to fill half the alley behind the saloon. Ben circled the streamlined old thing as Tom Harry stood by, proprietorially. "How are the tires?"

"What do you think?" the Packard's beset guardian barked. "Thin as condom skin. Here, throw these in the trunk." He rummaged in the shed room piled high with amazing items that Medicine Lodge customers with more thirst than cash had put up as collateral, and rolled two spare tires toward Ben.

"Reinking." Tom Harry tossed him the keys to the car, then the packet of gas ration coupons. "Tell Toussaint for me I'm sorry his grandkid got it that way. If you can find the old coyote."

2

⭐ *How did you ever stand it out here in hermit heaven, Vic?* Looking around from the height of the river bluff at the silent miles of prairie in three directions and the mute cliffs of the Rockies in the other, Ben reconsidered. Make the question, how did his best friend ever stand being crammed into Army life after an existence populated only by wind, buffalo grass, and a wraith of a grandfather? Military routine could tie a person's guts in knots; he knew the feeling himself.

Impatiently he checked his wristwatch again; half the morning was gone just getting here. Cass was curious, the other night, why this had to be circled in on, phony days of leave and the bus ride home and all, and he couldn't blame her. In between kissing him silly she had asked why he couldn't just requisition a motor pool car for a day and get back in time to attend to business in bed. The answer was not a damn bit more satisfying now than it was then: because that wasn't how Tepee Weepy did things. *There's the easy way and their way.*

Leaving the Packard on what passed for a road along the rocky upper gorge of the Two Medicine River, he picked his way on foot through the braid of ruts that led down to the Rennie ranch buildings huddled at the river's edge. The log house did

not show any activity as he approached, although all too plainly
a visitor was a rarity.

There was a bad sign, literally, the moment he stepped into
the dooryard, a blotch of something written in red on the rusty
weathered door, like lipstick on a witch. Walking up to it with a
sinking feeling, he found it was a shingle tacked to the doorwood
and lettered on it in barn paint the message: ELK SEASON.

Incredulous, Ben squinted west, met there by half the mountains in North America. Hunt a hunter in one day, in all that?
It was too much, this whole deal of Quick Vic and a roving
grandfather old as the hills. Toussaint Rennie must be crowding
eighty-five. He didn't have any business going after elk alone.

While Ben stood there stewing, the silence of the dried-up
little ranch seemed to reprove him. Out where weeds took over
from the yard, the pole corral stood empty except for one broom-
tail pony, and the barn looked like it would fall down if a person
blew his nose in its vicinity. All right, he conceded, maybe pursuit of elk was the only business Toussaint did have. But where
in this rugged upper end of the Two Medicine country would the
old reprobate have a favorite hunting ground?

For a moment—more than that, actually—he was tempted
to give this up and concoct whatever he could, from football
times together, for the TPWP piece about Vic. Give it the Loudon
treatment for once. Loudmouth it, as the Treasure State team
had learned to refer to the guff put out week by week by the
sportswriter climbing to fame on their backs in '41. Ted Loudon's
coarsest lead followed Vic's four-touchdown game: *Wyoming was
scalped on its home field today by a halfback marauder from the
northern plains named Vic Rennie.* Ben would have given plenty,
then and now, to see the copy Loudon handed in and verify
whether the sonofabitch had actually written *half-breed halfback*
and a queasy editor struck it out, or if Loudon had chosen to let
it just smirk there in the shadows of *marauder* and *scalped.* He

and Jake Eisman and most of the rest of the team had wanted to go to Bruno and tell him to shape up his mouthpiece buddy Loudon, but Vic only said he was used to that kind of crap.

Conscience makes tough company, Ben found again. Concocting would not do—this was Vic, and the last time he would be written about, possibly ever—and besides, in the zipper pocket of the flight jacket was what he was supposed to give to the old man who had raised his friend; he would have sworn he could feel the weight of the thing in there, featherlight though it was. No, at the very least he had to ask around. *This is such a famously friendly neighborhood, right, Vic?* He trudged back up to the Packard, patted it in apology, and navigated it across a barely wide enough stringer bridge to the reservation side of the river, to look up Toussaint's Blackfeet relatives. In-laws, rather, and that proved to be the problem.

"That skunk fart—why would I keep track of him?" was the extent of the answer at the first ranch of the Rides Proud clan that he tried.

Ben had been afraid of this. It was notorious throughout this Blackfoot end of the Two Medicine country that the Rennie bloodline was from away—some adamantly mysterious route that seemed to take in hazy tribal background to the east and the Métis rebellion in Canada to the north and very likely a French trapper named Reynaud somewhere along the way— and Toussaint Rennie reveled in perching just outside the edge of the reservation, knowing everyone else's business and never showing his Blackfoot neighbors any of his own hand except the back of it. He conspicuously never got along with his Blackfoot wife, Mary Rides Proud, while she was alive, and to judge by how good a job her blood relations were doing of keeping up hostilities in memory of Mary, even long after. Twice more Ben underwent it, amiable leather-faced men emerging from corral or barn in greeting, then turning away when he mentioned the name Toussaint. *Goddamn it, you'd think they were the Germans and the Russians going at it.* As he pulled in to the last ranch on that stretch of the river, he was watching cautiously for the next Rides Proud man on the prod.

This time, though, a Blackfoot woman came out on the front steps, her hands in the folds of her checkered dress, and told him in the flattest of voices her husband was up on the bluff fixing fence.

Something in her features reminded Ben of Vic. He gave it a try: "I'm looking for Victor's grandfather."

"Victor," the woman tested the name and ignored the rest. "His mother was my cousin."

Ben gingerly fished into the tangle of family. "The relative who'd raised Victor by the time I knew him was his grandfather. It's important that I find him. Where would he go to hunt elk, do you think?"

The woman kept her gaze on Ben for some seconds, then came down off the steps. She turned her back to the mountains and pointed. "Likes to say he has his own herd."

Totally surprised, Ben stared east into the deep V of the river valley and the distant patches of prairie captured between the outline of the bluffs. He had never in his life heard about any elk herd in the Two Medicine bottomlands. *She's putting me on. What do I do now?* Then it sank in on him. The woman was pointing all the way east, to the horizon. To the Sweetgrass Hills, rising like three mirage islands on the earthbrim where the sun came up.

Back at the car, he took another sighting on the ghostly trio of distant hills. He figured the trip at a hard two hours' drive, but he didn't mind that as much as the direction. He still could not shake the creepy feeling that the law of averages was not working, something was cockeyed; every point on the compass since this set of orders caught up with him in New Guinea was *east*.

EAST BASE HAD changed beyond sane recognition when he'd alit there, the month before. Only the Black Eagle smokestack stood the same as ever on the transformed prairie—the military in its inexplicable fashion having chosen to install an airfield almost under the shadow of the highest man-made obstacle between Seattle and Minneapolis. Who would have thought Montana was destined to become a staging area for the war in the first place? But the world of war shifted massively when Hitler invaded the Soviet Union, and with the task of conveying thousands of aircraft to the forces of America's new ally Joseph Stalin, the Air Transport Command had snatched up this base since the last time Ben landed here. Up until now he had not paid much attention to the ATC, something of a stepchild in the military scheme of things, other than the jeer he'd heard in fighter pilot school that the initials stood for Allergic To Combat. Never mind, he tried to tell himself, hadn't he pulled temporary duty at out-of-it outfits before?

Reporting in, fatigued from bucket-seat flights in C-47 transports, he presented his paperwork in the same tired routine as he'd done countless times, countless places. This time the processing clerk, a bald corporal, furrowed up over the orders before stamping them and handing them back with a dubious "There you go, Lieutenant"—they all did that—then jabbed a finger to the base map on the wall. "Here's your next stop, the clap shop."

"Cut the crap, okay? I don't have anything." In no mood for dealing further with a cynical paper-pusher, Ben was trying in vain to pick out the bachelor officers' quarters on the map; whatever else the Air Transport Command transported, it brought buildings by the dozens.

"That's what all the boys say, sir," the clerk sang out. "Commander's orders. He's on a tear about VD. All incoming personnel have to be checked out, first thing."

Drawing on his annoyance to plot how he might get away with *infectious* in a piece on the level of enthusiasm here, Ben stepped out into the world of East Base. Now that he had a chance to take a good look around, there wasn't a trace of the tar-paper infirmary he remembered before, nor anything else from his last quick TDY here. Mammoth hangars yawned open onto the longest runway he had seen yet in his war travels. Deep inside the hangar nearest him, swarms of mechanics on platform ladders squirmed into open bays of fuselages. Fresh new bombers and fighter planes had to undergo shakedown here after being flown in from factories on the West Coast and before being handed over to Russian pilots waiting in Alaska, he understood that much of the Lend-Lease operation. But he puzzled over the relatively empty flight line, no clusters of aircraft rolled out and sitting ready to go. Instead, great batches of unpainted planes were lined up on an apron behind the hangars, like shorn sheep trying to get out of the weather. A sudden wild gust that had him grabbing at his crush hat made him laugh in spite of himself. *Think about it, Reinking. You're in Great Falls, home of the seventy-yard punt when the wind is up.* Those planes were tied down to mooring rings back there so they wouldn't blow over.

At least the wind was something familiar. He had not paid enough attention to where the irksome clerk pointed on the map. Casting around for directions, he wandered into the huge hangar and over to the nearest P-39 where a lone mechanic was up on a wing and head-down in the engine compartment. "Hey, buddy, which way to the clap shop?"

The figure in coveralls withdrew from the engine and a fetching brunette hairdo and hazel eyes with temper in them came with it. "Cozying up to strange women," the voice was feminine but oh how it carried, "is usually a good start toward it."

Ben stood there wondering if he looked as mortified as he felt. All over the hangar other heads popped out of other planes: a set of blonde curls here, a hairnet there, and everywhere chest-high indications in the coveralls. The place was all women. A majority of them, it seemed to him as he tried not to gape, were devoting full attention to him and this vixen high over him on the airplane wing.

Trim as a terrier within the folds of the coveralls, she was wiping her hands on a grease rag while she eyed Ben up and down. If looks could kill, she did not need a fighter plane on her side. Squinting up as she glared down, he parked his hands in the pockets of his flight jacket, hoping a casual approach might simmer her down. "Don't get the wrong idea. I'm only checking in. Which means I have to be checked out, they tell me. Look, miss, I'm not trying to be fresh."

She did a little something to the collar of her greasy coveralls, and an insignia flashed out. "Try 'Captain,' why don't you."

Too late he caught sight of the ready-bag sitting in the cockpit hatch, with WASP wings and a squadron commanding officer's striped star stenciled on it. *Just my luck with this base, I light in here and brush up against a queen bee.* "Next time I'll be sure to, Captain. Steer me to the infirmary and I'll have my IQ checked along with the rest, how about?"

"Three buildings down from Ops, where the control tower is, and ask for the short-arm inspector. If your IQ is where I think it is, you can have both done at once." She finished him off with a last dismissing look. "Crew chief!" she was moving on to her next victim even before he turned away. "Who looked over this engine, Helen Keller? The points are burned. I want them filed down and reset before I take this crate for a checklist run."

Glad to get out of there with his hide on, Ben went and presented himself at the infirmary for the evidently important process of dropping his pants. A clean bill of health promised to be his only gain for the day, however. At his next stop, the BOQ clerk did not even make a pretense of looking up an empty bunk for him. "You're billeted downtown, transient basis. The Excelsior Hotel."

A memory clicked from college days; the Alka-Seltzer was one of the wino flophouses on First Avenue South. "How the hell come? I'm here TDY, not transient."

"Because it says so here. Orders from headquarters, sir."

Ben resisted the impulse to whip out his higher set of orders and wipe the smirk off the clerk with them. He didn't want that reputation until he knew more about what this damn base had become. Stoically he listened to the clerk recite the daily schedule of the shuttle bus between the base and downtown Great Falls. Meanwhile a fresh-faced private with an armband marking him as the runner from the orderly room had come in, and was hovering nearby. He broke in:

"Lieutenant Reinking?"

"I was when I got here."

"General Grady wants to see you."

"Who?"

"The commanding officer of the base, sir. Wants to see you."

"As in, this minute?"

The runner nodded nervously.

Ben slung his duffel behind the desk where the clerk had no choice but to watch it. Before turning to go, he asked: "Do you have a Lieutenant Eisman bunked here?"

The clerk showed a sign of life. "Sure do—the football All-American? Ever see him play? I bet he didn't even have to run, he could just walk through the other team."

"Tell him the moving target is back." Ben glanced at the orderly-room runner waiting edgily to escort him to the head-quarters building. "Lead on, Moses."

As if some signal had been given, East Base began to hum with activity while the runner led him through the military maze of buildings. Fire engines trundled to their ready spot near the end of the runway, followed by the medical corps ambulance, known on every air base as the meat wagon. Next, the flight line went from empty to maximally busy in a matter of minutes. A spate of P-39s took off one after another and headed north, leav-ing their chorus of roar behind. Other fighter planes, likely the checkout flights, were being rolled out of the big hangar he had blundered into. Ben watched it all; another day in the war, of the six hundred and some he had been through. Back here, he could tell time by the sun, and he aligned the other zones around the world with it now. The clock of war was in his head every waking minute. It was close onto noon here, so in England the day was drawing down and Moxie Stamper would be in a supper chow line on a secure bomber base if he was lucky. Carl Friessen would be in a foxhole listening to the night noises of the New Guinea jungle. On the destroyer zigzagging in the Pacific, Nick Danzer already was in tomorrow; Danzer, with his taste for any advan-tage, would like that. Member by member of the Supreme Team, Ben memorized anew the time difference from here to there, adjusting himself toward the schedule of teletype messages that followed him from base to base.

The one-star officer in charge of East Base evidently had been building up a head of steam while waiting for the TPWP inter-loper. Base commanders generally did. Ben sometimes wondered if that's why they were called generals.

Ben's salute still was in the air when this one, an obvious old ranker with a face like he'd been eating fire, started in on him. "So you're here to make us famous. I'm not sure I like that."

Nice even-tempered base you run here, General—everybody pissed off all the time. Ben stood his ground by standing at attention until the personage behind the desk was forced to say, "At ease, shit's sake, man." The general peered at the lieutenant down all the rungs of rank between them. "Well? Why us? Why can't we get on with what we're doing without your outfit, whatever it is"—he glanced with abhorrence at the Threshold Press War Project patch on Ben's shoulder—"poking its nose in?"

"Somebody cut me the orders, sir. Confidentially, I'd prefer to be doing something else in the war."

The *confidentially* did not go down well with the general. "Then tell me this. Are you here to play up the women pilots?"

The presence of WASPs and the hangarful of female mechanics had come as definite news to Ben when he blundered into it all. The commander's resistance sharpened his instinct some more. "It depends, sir."

The commander dug a finger in his ear. "On what?"

"What you mean by 'play up.' Just so you know, General"— Ben had a moment of panic; he had been in front of so many of these one-star lifers in charge of obscure bases that he'd lost track of the name here—"General Grady," he picked it up from the nameplate on the desk and plunged on, "I'm an accredited correspondent as well as a soldier. Those hats don't always fit the way other people would like to see them, but I'm stuck with wearing both. You have to understand, sir, I'm assigned to write about things of interest to—"

"These females were wished onto me, and so were the Russkies," the commander blared; for a moment Ben wondered if the man was deaf from too much prop wash. "That doesn't mean everybody and his dog has to read about them." He shot a non-negotiable look across the desk. "Those Supreme Team write-ups of yours, bunk like that, that's all right. Good for the war effort. Lieutenant Eisman has a wild hair up his ass whenever he's on the ground, but he's a good flier—write your brains out about him for all I care. As long as I'm in charge here, that's the kind of thing I want to see, due tribute for my men who fly these planes to Alaska. Is that understood?"

"Duly noted, sir. I'll be doing a piece on Jake Eisman as soon as—"

"That's all, Reinking," the commander swung around in his chair to peruse some imagined event out on the flight line. "Go see the adjutant," came the imperial drift of order over his shoulder, "he'll fix you up with desk space somewhere."

Where does the military find these types, central casting? Ben let silence do its work before he cleared his throat and uttered: "But sir?"

The general's chair grudgingly swiveled in his direction again.

"The situation is," Ben stated as if he had been asked, "I'm under orders to do other stories, too, wherever I see them." He had been in front of enough base commanders to have perfected a polite stare that nonetheless underlined his standard message: "Orders from Washington, sir."

"Lieutenant, shit's sake, we're all under orders from Washington!"

Not like mine, Buster. He reached to the zipper pocket of his jacket. "May I?"

Eyeing him more narrowly now, the general reached for the folded orders. He opened them with impatience and read at top speed. Then went back over the words, evidently one by one. Sucking in his cheeks, he handed the paper back to Ben. "Why didn't you say so?" he rasped. "Carry on, Lieutenant, it sure as shit looks like you will anyway."

On the way out, Ben had taken a closer look at a base map to locate the ready room where the WASPs would be waiting for takeoff.

EAST BUTTE, THE farthest of the Sweetgrass Hills, was keeping its distance as Ben drove the undeviating dirt road from the map-dot town of Chester where he had gassed up again; every time he looked, the rumpled rise of land ahead added another fold of steep ridge, another tuck of timbered canyon large enough to swallow an elk herd and an old hunter.

The geography definitely did not budge in his favor while he had to change flat tire number two, in a wind doing its best to blow the hubcap away. Off to the west where he had started this day, the Rockies were a low wall on the horizon. Ben glanced up at the midafternoon sun and cursed with military fluency. *Toussaint, you old SOB, I can about hear Vic laughing at what you're putting me through. I thought I liked hunting, until today.*

While he grunted over the lug nuts and the bumper jack and the lug nuts again, that other time of hunting came back to him, the Christmas vacation—in 1940 before the war meant much in America—when Jake Eisman and Dexter Cariston and Vic rode home from college with him to go after deer. So ungodly much had happened to the Treasure State teammates since, but what a benign autumn that was. Bruno's coaching had not yet turned apocalyptic as it would the next season, and they could feel reasonably good about the team's seven-and-three record, topped off by beating Butte Poly in the Copper Cup game. Ben searched closely in his memory as he tightened the tire on. Did he have it right, were he and his hunting companions already breathing the heights of the next football season, their senior year of crazy glory, there under the mind-freeing palisades of the Rockies? Time colors such occasions. By then the draft was somewhere on their horizon, but so was the knowledge that the previous time the world had gone to war, America sat out most of it. So, as far as the four of them knew then, in some not distant future they would victoriously hang up their cleats, Ben would take a newspaper job until he mastered the art of movie scripts, Dex would go on to medical school and save the human race, Jake would return to the Black Eagle smelter but in a spotless office where his engineeering and metallurgy degree hung on the wall, and Vic would play basketball for the barnstorming Carlisle 'Skins from one end of the continent to the other.

You could dream those types of dreams when the rifle in your hand was of civilian make. The whole batch of them tramped their legs off in the rough country there below the mountain reefs for a couple of days, never even seeing a deer but honing in on one another in high spirits. When Vic and Dex stopped to catch their wind on a sharp slope, Jake, who was mass and momentum combined, blew them a fart in passing and went on up the trail telling the world two halfbacks did not add up to a fullback. How lucky, the puffing pair agreed between themselves, to have someone the size and mentality of a horse along to pack out all the meat the two of them were going to get. It was Ben's country, there along the continent-dividing upthrusts west of Gros Ventre, and he was content to guide and grin until his face ached and try to stay on the lookout for deer. The last afternoon, a fine four-point buck strolled out of the timber on the ridgeline above them, nicely silhouetted but at extreme range. The other three looked at Vic, who had grown up on rifle-taken venison. Dex Cariston in particular stood back; his family, pioneer Helena merchants risen to various kinds of financial dominance, could have bought the Rocky Mountains as a hunting preserve, and he went out of his way never to appear presumptuous. "I'll give him a try," Vic accepted the general vote of confidence and flopped down to settle his .30-06 across a downed tree. But he was rusty—a man can't spend his autumns playing major college football and keep his shooting eye up too—and after he fired, the buck simply turned its head, antlers tipped a bit to one side, as if quizzical about all the noise. Ben and the others crouched waiting for Vic to touch off a second shot, but instead he clicked the safety on his rifle and looked up at them, poker-face serious. "Isn't that the damnedest thing you ever saw? A dead deer standing there looking at us." They all were laughing so hard they could not get their rifles up before the deer bounded off into the jack pines. *We'll never get him now, will we, Vic, old kid.*

BEN THREW THE flat tire on top of the other one in the trunk of the car and dusted off his hands. Some night soon, he knew, he and Jake would meet at the Officers' Club to do their best to drink away what had befallen Vic, and the next morning they would put on their unbloodied uniforms the same as always. He winced at the next thought: Dex was another story.

Right now the puzzle was geography. Stumps of a mountain range that they were, the Sweetgrass Hills sat wide on the prairie and Ben knew he could not afford to waste miles circling East Butte the wrong way. He guessed west—traveling by wagon, Toussaint might have come cross-country from that way—and aimed the Packard in that direction on the loop road around the sprawling butte, hoping. This time the first place he asked at, a wind-peeled farmhouse, paid off. The farm couple, the Conlons, were acquainted with Toussaint Rennie, not necessarily by choice; for as long as they could remember, he passed through their place at this time of year, nodding politely and heading on up to elk territory. If they had to guess, they would say he might be somewhere up the old mining road to Devil's Chimney. Something tingled at the back of Ben's neck: east again.

He jounced the car up the steep rocky road, praying for the tires with every jolt, as far as he dared, then set out on foot. He skirted timberline above a creek that dropped with a pleasant-sounding rush down through a coulee filled with tall grass and wild roses. He had never seen a more likely place for elk to browse, and there wasn't a one in sight. Nothing wanted to cooperate today. Dreading the moment when he would have to abandon the oldest etiquette and shout out a hunter's name in the possible presence of game, he scanned farther up the slope toward the gloom-gray chimney of rock at the forested summit, turning an ear to the wind in one last attempt to conjure the sound of an elk herd on the move somewhere out there in the timber. What he heard came into his other ear from not ten feet away.

"Looks like Ben."

Ben nearly levitated out of his flight jacket.

When he spun and looked, at first glance he still couldn't pick out the man in the shadowed patch of juniper and downed trees. "Saw the car," the old voice came again, a chuckle entering it. "That Packard. Stories it could tell." A swag of juniper branch lifted, not quite where Ben expected, and the walnut crinkles of the aged face came into view.

"Christ, Toussaint, they could use you in camouflage school. Room in there for one more?"

"Make yourself skinny."

Ben eased in from the back of the hunting blind and found himself in something like a man-sized thatched nest. Toussaint had bundles of long-stemmed sweetgrass stacked all around the interior of his lair; the place smelled like a sugarcane field, and no passing elk would get any scent of man. Ben tried to get used to the confined space in a hurry, shaking hands with Toussaint as he inched past him. Sitting there potbellied on a rickety kitchen chair, in faded wool pants and a mackinaw that had seen nearly as many years as he had, the old hunter peering up at him put Ben in mind of a Buddha that a pile of grubby clothes had been tossed on. The rifle propped against the side of the blind showed a catalogue shine of newness, however. Toussaint chuckled again. "Sold a cow to get the gun to hunt elk. Don't know if that's progress."

He gestured hospitably. "Pull up a rock, Ben." Ben settled for a log end. Dark eyes within weathered folds of skin were contemplating him as if measuring the passage of years. "Haven't seen you since Browning," Toussaint arrived at. "You were catcher."

Ben smiled. "It's called 'end' in football, Toussaint."

"Did a lot of catching, I saw."

A dozen catches, in that final high school game against the reservation town; good for three touchdowns. Gros Ventre always pounded Browning into the ground in football, just as Browning always ran up the score sky-high against Gros Ventre in basketball. That game, though, Ben and his teammates had a terrible time handling a swift Browning halfback named Vic Rennie. "Vic damn near ran the pants off us."

"He knew how to run."

Ben's heart skipped when he heard the past tense. Had word reached Toussaint already? It couldn't have. He bought a bit more time with an inquisitive jerk of his head toward the far-off Rockies. "The last I knew, the Two Medicine country had elk. Why hightail it all the way over here to hunt?"

"Those buffalo."

Toussaint spoke it in such a way that Ben nearly looked around for shaggy animals with horned heads down in the high grass.

The old hunter swept a hand over the farmed fields below the Sweetgrass Hills, the gesture wiping away the past seventy years. "It was all buffalo color then, Ben. Too thick to count, that herd. I was just yay-high"—a veined hand indicated a boy's height—"and mooching my way to that Two Medicine country. The Crows gave me a horse, let me ride here with them—don't know why. All the tribes came here for those buffalo. Too busy hunting to fight. Even those Blackfeet." The dark eyes, a spark of mischief in them, held on the visitor again. "Could be some leftover luck here, so I come hunting."

"I'm glad I asked," said Ben.

"You are not here about buffalo. Elk either."

"True." Softly but swiftly to get it over with, he told what had happened to Vic.

When that was done, Toussaint looked out past the old contested country of the tribes, off somewhere into the swollen world of war. His voice turned bleak and Ben wondered whether a chuckle would ever enter it again.

"They blew up my boy?"

"He was pretty badly torn up by the land mine. They had to amputate."

A grunt came from the grandfather, as dismal a sound as Ben had ever heard. Quickly he reached to his jacket pocket. "I don't know if it helps, but I brought you a letter from Vic."

The old man held the pale blue sheet of paper at arm's length to read it. Watching this, Ben felt uncomfortably responsible for its contents, whatever those were. He'd had to move military heaven and earth—Tepee Weepy, which amounted to the same thing—to get word to Vic and then speed the resulting letter through top channels. The courier, a sleek young Pentagon officer exuding importance, had stepped off the plane at East Base disdainfully looking over Ben's head for the almighty TPWP officer in charge. "I'm him," Ben had announced, and the courier's expression only grew worse when the briefcase handcuffed to his wrist was unlocked to produce a single slim envelope that looked like ordinary mail. Ben wished him a nice flight back to Washington and tucked the letter in his jacket. Now Toussaint lowered the piece of paper and refolded it carefully.

"Vic writes he can't get a new leg. All the things they can do these days, they can't get him a new leg?"

Ben shook his head.

Neither man spoke for a while, Toussaint still creasing the letter, until at last he asked the question his visitor had been dreading most:

"Why don't they send him home to me?"

Ben hoped it wasn't because a one-legged hero did not fit with TPWP plans. He could hear the strain in his voice as he tried to put the secretive hospital in the English countryside in the best light. "There's a facility—a place there where they help people pull through something like this. It's an estate." It was for depression victims. Mangled Royal Air Force pilots. Commandoes wrecked in body and mind from the disastrous Dieppe raid. And, Tepee Weepy had seen to it, a Supreme Team running back with an empty pantleg.

He left all that last part out; from the look on the man who had raised Victor Rennie, bringing the letter maybe was bad enough. After a bit Toussaint said absently: "Vic says it's awful green there. Hedges."

"Toussaint, you better know. I'm supposed to write something about Vic. It's my job."

"Funny kind of job, Ben, ain't it?"

You don't know the half of it, Toussaint, not even you. He tried to explain the ongoing articles about the team, the obligation—if it was that—to tell people what had happened to Vic while he was fighting in the service of his country.

"Country." Toussaint picked up that word and seemed to consider it. He gestured in the direction of Great Falls. "Hill 57," he let out as if Ben had asked for an unsavory address. "You know about that." Something like a snort came from him, making Ben more uneasy yet. After a long moment, he held up the letter. "Here's what's left of Vic, that I know of." He handed it over. "Take down what it says."

Nonplussed, Ben unfolded the piece of stationery and read it through. He chewed the inside of his mouth, trying to decide. It had been offered and he couldn't turn it down. "You're sure?"

Toussaint shrugged as if surety was hard to come by.

Ben took out his notepad and jotted steadily. When done, he handed the letter back and put a hand on the rough shoulder of the mackinaw. "I'll get word to you when they give Vic the okay to come home, I promise." Drawing a last deep breath of sweetgrass, he started to get up. "You know how to put on the miles. I have to get back to Gros Ventre yet tonight."

Toussaint nodded. "Say hello. Your father is good people."

"Ask a hard question when you have one foot out the door," that father schooled into every cub reporter, including his son, who passed through the *Gleaner* office. *"A person turns into an answering fool to get rid of you."* Ben hesitated. Toussaint Rennie was never going to be an answering fool or any other kind.

The question did not wait for him to reason it out. "Help me with something if you can," he blurted, turning back to the seated figure. "Did Vic ever say anything about that kid on our team? Merle? You know the one I mean."

He watched the eyes encased within wrinkles; something registered there. "The one that died on that funny hill?" the voice came slowly. "With all the white rocks?"

"That's him."

"That one. Nobody ought to run that much." Now the old man scrutinized him in return. "Vic comes home, you can ask him."

"I want to. It's just that he's never brought it up."

"That's that, then." Toussaint glanced away, then back again. "Better look up that aunt of his."

Ben's hopes sagged. He had knocked on the door of that Hill 57 shack any number of times, trying to reach the elusive relative Vic had lived with during college. "She's never there."

"Downtown, drunk," Toussaint grunted as though he could see the woman from where he sat. "Catch her sober, after she gets over the shakes. That's the trick with a wino. Wait until allotment money's gone."

"End of the month, you mean?"

"Middle. She's a thirsty one."

"I'll give her another try." Ben touched the bowed shoulder again as he edged past.

"So long, Ben." The old man shifted his weight, settling deeper on the spindly chair. "See any elk, shoo them this way."

IT WAS FORMING in his head by the time he reached the car. He could have kicked himself for not having brought the typewriter. He ransacked the glove compartment and came up with some old whiskey invoices billed to the Medicine Lodge. The backs of those gave him enough to write on. First he carefully tore out the notepad pages the letter was copied onto and laid them in order on the car seat, reading them over a couple of times. Then he began to scrawl, sheet after sheet, more like scribbling than writing, things crossed out often, but the words that survived felt right to him. He worked like fury at it, and the piece grew under the pencil.

In the hills he had made his own, the grandfather heard from the world of war only by farthest echoes. Little Bighorn. Wounded Knee. San Juan Hill. Montana boys, neighbors' sons, at a place from Hell called the Argonne Forest. Pearl Harbor. He knew death did not send a letter, but harm was likely to. He opened this hand-delivered one past the return address of the grandson he had raised— *Cpl. Victor Rennie, somewhere in England.*

"Old man, the friend who will bring you this will tell you what happened. All I will say is that it was like dynamite going off under me.

"No more hunting for me. My left leg is gone, almost to the hip. These doctors treat me the best they can, but they can't bring back the leg.

"You will want to know what this place is like. There is a green lawn as big as our horse pasture, and hedges as high as the corral. It rains here. Days are all the same. You remember my folks' funeral. This is like being at my own, every day. They say I will adjust, whatever that means. I can't see it, myself. The crazy thing is, it reminds me of going to a movie with my friend Ben. We got a kick out of the Westerns, a stagecoach always going around and around those big buttes in Monument Valley while the Indians chased it. Time after time, same butte, stagecoach and Indians going like hell around it again. Grandfather, you are going to have to know—when I come home, my life will be like that, nothing but the same, over and over."

Vic's chapter of the war ends there, but not his story. When this war has its valley of monuments, in the tended landscape of history, they will not all look alike. One will be what we call in Montana a sidehill, a slope populated with shacks at the edge of a thriving American city. The nickname, Hill 57, speaks to the variety of hard luck there—poor, Indian, jobless—and it was from Hill 57 that Victor Rennie each day walked to college and, one farther day, into the world of war. His Army unit was in hard fighting in the invasion of Sicily. Vic survived that, as he had survived so much else. Then came the bivouac outside Messina in a stretch of country the German forces supposedly had retreated through too fast to set land mines. The routine patrol led by Vic set out at first light . . .

Football never entered into the piece.

✪ "Cass? Are you in, Captain ma'am, or folding like a sane person would?"

Walled in by the drone of the cargo plane and the din of her own thoughts, Cass Standish forced her attention back to the cards in her hand. Pair of jacks, deuce, trey, ten. *Could be worse, but just as easy could be better.* The flight plan of the C-47 gooney bird, monotonously circling in bumpy air for the last half hour, could have stood improvement, too. *I'm not in charge of that, at least.* Just the lonely one-eyed jacks staring her in the face. Across from her, Della teased a finger back and forth across the edge of her cards as if sharpening them for the kill. Glancing right and left, Cass caught up to the fact that Beryl and Mary Catherine had already thrown theirs facedown on the makeshift table of parachute packs, bluffed out. It was a shame Della was not as good a pilot as she was a poker player.

"I'll see you in Hell first, Maclaine." Cass took a dollar bill from her depleted stack and tossed it into the ante.

"Tsk, Cassie. That's one for Mother." Reaching across, Della plucked up another wrinkled bill from Cass's pile of ones and dropped it aside into the cuss pot, which they always divvied after the game.

"What's the program here," Cass said crossly, "to get rich off my vocabulary? That's chickenshit, Della."

The others eyed her. They knew Cass had the best cockpit nerves in the human race; when she was not at the controls, things could fray at the edges now and then. Beryl, ritual elder of the group, was about to say something but thought better of it. This time, Della only crept her fingers a little way toward Cass's pile, asking as if it was a matter of etiquette: "Another for Mother?"

Knowing that she needed to get a grip on the situation, Cass theatrically fanned at her mouth as if shooing off flies, then forked over another dollar for swearing during the game. As everyone laughed, she sneaked another glance at the nearest window port and still saw only fog; Seattle was socked in tighter than she could ever remember—that was saying a lot—and there were mountains out there. Even she, who had to have faith in instrumentation, was ready to divert to sunny Moses Lake. She caught the eye of Linda Cicotte, her B flight lead pilot, and pointed urgently toward the cockpit. Linda nodded, teetered to her feet, and felt her way forward to talk to the pilot. The rest of the dozen women, all in the baggy flying gear called zoot suits, slouched in sling seats along one side of the aircraft; the majority of the cabin was taken up with bulky crates. TARFU Airlines, these numbing transport trips in the equivalent of a boxcar with propellers were known as: Things Are Really Fucked Up. Circling in grade A fog this way was worse than usual, on these trips to the Coast, but there was nothing to do about it but go with the routine. Linda's team of fliers as usual were curled up as best they could, trying to catch some sleep. C flight, Ella Mannion's, did crossword puzzles and read books. Cass was not sure she wanted to know what it said that hers always sat on their parachute packs in the tail of the plane and played cutthroat poker.

Right now, Mary Catherine palmed the deck in cardsharp fashion, ready to keep dealing. "Cards, sisters in sin?"

"Honey"—Della was only from somewhere in southern Ohio, but when she poured it on, she sounded like Tallulah Bankhead on a bender—"I couldn't possibly stand one more good card."

Cass flinched inwardly. *What am I getting myself into here? A lot of that going around lately.* Saying "Hit me twice," she slid the deuce and trey to the discard pile. The new cards might as well have gone straight there, too. *Lucky in love doesn't seem to count in poker either, Ben.* Even so, when Della upped the ante, she stayed with her. Della raised her again, which mercifully was the limit. Cass met the bet and, fingers crossed, produced the jacks.

"Pair of ladies." Della laid down queens and scooped up cash. "Thank you for the money, y'all, it'll go for good causes, widows and orphans and the home for overmatched poker players."

Cass looked at Mary Catherine, and Mary Catherine at Beryl. Simultaneously they reached to their piles and each flung a dollar into the cuss pot. "Piss in the ocean, Della!" they chorused.

"My, my," Della drawled, cocking a delicate ear. "Do I hear a whine in one of the engines?" Cass had to hand it to her; shavetail latecomer or not, she was sharp as a porcupine on most things. The full lieutenants, Beryl Foster and Mary Catherine Cornelisen, had earned their wings in the very first contingent of WASPs, as Cass herself had. The three of them together had endured the bald old goat of a flight instructor at Sweetwater, Texas, who claimed women pilots would never amount to anything because they couldn't piss in the ocean—the Gulf of Mexico, actually—from ten thousand feet through the relief tube like the male pilots. If that had been deliberate motivation toward every other kind of flying skill, it worked in their case. Sometimes the aircraft they ferried from the plant were finished products and sometimes they weren't. Mary Catherine once had been going through a cockpit check on the factory floor when the engine of the shiny new fighter burst into flames; pure textbook but against all human inclination, she rammed the throttle open and blew out the fire. And Beryl knew what it was to land at East Base with nothing but fumes left in a leaky auxiliary tank. With scrapes enough of her own, Cass would not have traded their cool heads for reincarnations of Amelia Earhart. Della, though. Nearly a year behind them in flight school and immeasurably more than that in experience, Della still showed signs of thinking of herself as a hot pilot. Hot pilots tended to end up dead pilots. Cass knew she had her work cut out for her with Della.

Starting about now; Della was shuffling the cards in such a fashion that they purred expectantly, but she did have the smarts to check with Cass before dealing out another hand.

Cass shook her head. "That's it, officers. Time to ready up." She climbed to her feet, stiff from all the sitting. "M.C., where'd you put those newspapers?" They had grabbed up a pile of the *Great Falls Tribune* before takeoff; the article about them and the picture of the squadron proudly posed on the wings of an Airacobra had brought whoops of tribute to the inquisitive war correspondent in the fancy flight jacket. *And they're not even in the sack with him.* Cass tried to stifle that thought and keep a straight face as Mary Catherine uncovered the newspapers from under her gear and began passing them out. "Here you go, read all about our classy squadron commander and her Flying Women. How many does everybody want? Cass?"

"Oh, a couple." *One to send to Dan. What a case I am. Show the hubby the nice things the other man I love writes about me.* Dry-mouthed, Cass hoped she was better at a straight face than she was at stifling.

Linda Cicotte came weaving her way to the back of the plane. "We're in the hands of a hero, Cass." She jerked a thumb toward the cockpit. "He still says he's going to get us on the ground in Seattle."

"He didn't happen to say, 'Or die trying,' did he?" Cass asked in exasperation.

Linda simply rolled her eyes. "Are we going to fly out in this, do you think?"

"Too soupy for good health." Cass herself didn't mind instrument flying, bracketing the radio beam and the rest of the things you did to let the machine navigate itself through limited visibility. But she couldn't risk her fliers; Della in particular tended to trust her own instincts over the instruments, a good way to meet a mountain. "You know what a hard-ass this dispatching officer can be," Cass shared her thinking with Linda, who had flown the Seattle run nearly as many times as she had. "I'll work on him unmercifully. Tell your bunch and Ella's we're going to try to RON this one." Remaining overnight, when they were supposed to be picking up planes and heading back, would not be popular with the higher-ups at East Base. It also threw off tonight with Ben. Briefly she felt better about herself for not letting either of those get in the way of her decision.

Beryl looked up from the newspaper she was holding. "Cass? I didn't know that about the ring. Mine won't come off even if I wanted."

The line in there about the ringless hand, nothing between it and the controls of an Airacobra: *Damn it, Ben, you don't miss much, but I wish you'd been looking the other way that time.* They'd started off deadly stiff with one another when he showed up to interview her and the other WASPs, as was to be expected after that run-in in the hangar. The atmosphere started to thaw as soon as he discovered she gave a straight answer, no matter what the question, and she found out he knew his business about flying. He'd done his homework on P-39s, was familiar with the Cobra's reputation as a tricksome aircraft, with the engine mounted in back of the cockpit creating a center of gravity different from more stable fighter planes. And he had looked into the Lend-Lease lore that what was gained from the radical design was ideal room up front for a 30-millimeter cannon poking out of the propeller hub like a stinger; the Russians were said to adore P-39s for strafing, just point the nose of the plane at German tanks and convoys and blaze away. Cass drew a grin from him when she agreed it was a *flighty* aircraft, one you had to pilot every moment, but she confessed she didn't mind that about the Cobra; weren't you supposed to pay total attention when you were in the air? As to the funeral ticket always there in that big engine right behind the pilot's neck, she offhandedly said the answer was to not get in a situation where you had to make a belly landing. That drew somewhat less of a grin from him. The true tipping point came, though, when she climbed into a tethered P-39 to show him the cockpit routine, automatically slipping off her wedding band as she slid into the seat and he wanted to know what that was about. Somehow willpower—*won't power, too,* she ruefully corrected herself—went out of control from then on.

"My husband is too busy to mind about something like a ring, he's in New Guinea."

"With the Montaneers? So is one of my football buddies—I was there a little while back."

"You were? Is it as bad as they say?"

"I'll bring you the piece I wrote there, you can decide."

All that. Then before they knew it, nights at the roadhouse or his room at the Excelsior. She had done anything like this only once before, during the spree in Dallas after winning her wings, when that well-mannered tank officer as viewed through a celebratory haze of drinks looked too good to resist. That was strictly a one-nighter, and she had no illusions that Dan Standish refrained from similar flings when he was loose on leave in Brisbane and Rockhampton among the Sheilas of Australia. Supposedly it was different for men, their urges painted as almost medical, "the screw flu"; to hear them tell it, nature was to blame. But what about the strain of being a woman in singular command of a squadron of nerve-wracking planes and pilots both, and Ben Reinking happens into your life, nature's remedy for desolate nights if there ever was one? In the world of war, turn down such solace just because chance made you female? It had started off as only friendly drinks, Ben still asking her this and that as he worked over his piece about her squadron, the two of them sudden buddies over the topics of planes and New Guinea, until all at once he was revealing to her that he'd been wounded during his correspondent stint there. Every word that followed had stayed with Cass ever since:

"Where?"

"Place called Bitoi Ridge. Kind of a jungle hogback, in from the bay at Salamaua."

"Modest. I meant on you."

Ben paused. "I don't generally show it off."

She bolted the last of her drink, but there was a challenging dry tingle in her mouth as she spoke it: "Never make an exception?"

And ever since, the part she hated: if she wanted to hang on to her marriage and officer's rank, they didn't dare get caught at it. Tell no one. Show nothing. Staying casual as you hid a lover was a surprising amount of work, but now she managed to shrug at Beryl's remark. "I've just always done it, Bear. Dan and I knew a mechanic who slipped off a ladder, caught his ring on a bolt head. Pulled it right off."

"The ring?" Della was deep in admiration of the newspaper photo, where the flip of her blonde hair showed to advantage. "So what?"

"The finger, fool."

"Yipe. Guess I better stay single, keep on playing the field."

"Is that where you head out to with that warrant officer who has the jeep," Mary Catherine wondered, "the nearest field?"

"Nice talk, Mary Cat. I don't see you around the nunnery." Della tucked the newspaper into her ready-bag. "Maybe I ought to set my sights higher, a war correspondent. Anybody find out, is he up for grabs?"

"He's engaged," Cass made up on the spot. "Head over heels for the lucky girl, from the sound of it. Everybody, strap on those chutes in case this moron pilot isn't any better at reading a fuel gauge than the weather."

Mary Catherine couldn't resist a last dig on Della. "You're losing your touch, Delly. You might have known that dreamboat of a correspondent is taken." She spoke with the air of one who had been through enough men to know. "The good ones always are."

"LIEUTENANT REINKING, sir? I've been looking all over for you."

Not again. Doesn't that damn general have anything else to do, like run the base? On edge anyway, Ben had intended to slip into his office only for a minute before heading to the communications section and then checking the flight board again. The last two times, the board showed NTO ZV—no takeoff, zero visibility—for Cass's WASP 1 squadron. It spooked him—possibly more than it should, but it spooked him nonetheless. Fog induced crashes. That 1,200-horsepower engine situated directly in back of the pilot seat, like a cocked catapult. *Seattle wrote the book on fog, surely to God they'll scrub the flight, won't they?*

Along with fretting about Cass and trying to wind down from leave, he had spent the afternoon with his typewriter in a back room at the base library, wrapping up the piece on Vic. The war did not recognize Sunday, but somehow it was the slowest

day of message traffic and his intention was to send in the piece
while the sending was good. In the way of that stood a squat
broken-nosed hard case in rumpled uniform, nervously fiddling
with his cap. Ben eyed him distrustfully until he realized there
was no armband of an orderly-room runner on this one.

"All over is the right place to look for me," Ben admitted.
"What's on your mind, soldier?"

"Didn't they tell you, sir? I'm your new clerk."

Caught off-guard, Ben shot a glance at the desk in the corner;
it had been swept clean of everything except the typewriter and
the Speed Graphic camera, making his own chronically overloaded desk look even more like a dump. "What happened to
Wryzinski?"

"Nobody told me that, sir." The anthem of the enlisted man.

Ben had just been getting used to Wryzinski. "Right, why did
I even ask. Tepee Weepy taketh away and Tepee Weepy giveth."
He offered the new man a handshake. "What do I call you?"

"Jones, sir."

"Nobody's named that," Ben responded, grinning to put him
at ease. "It's taken."

"I don't quite catch your meaning, sir."

This was going to require some care, Ben realized. "Let's do
this over, Corporal. First off, I'll try to remember to wiggle my
ears when I'm making a joke and you try to pretend there is such
a thing as a joke. Second, drop the 'sir' when there's no one here
but us, and that's all the time." The makeshift office that had
been tossed to Ben—in earlier life it was some kind of overgrown
storage bin, for onions from the smell of it, at the rear of the
mess hall—at least provided seclusion. "Maybe then we can get
along reasonably well, okay?" The plug-ugly face indicated it was
determined to try. "So, Jones, enlighten me—what did you do in
civvie life to condemn yourself to being assigned to me?"

"College. Religious studies, ahead of seminary."

Ben examined him. Jones looked as if any study time he had put in likely would have been with Murder Incorporated. "No kidding. At any place I ever heard of?"

"Out at the university." This drew him closer scrutiny from Ben. "I was a freshman in '41. Yelled my head off at every game, Lieutenant. What a team you guys were."

"Then you know what this is about," Ben indicated the overloaded small office. "Go ahead and move into that desk. I'm just on my way over to the wire room and—"

"Sir—I mean, Lieutenant? I was just over there. Figured I could at least check on things until you showed up." The incipient clerk looked uncomfortable. "There's a slew of messages, but they said for your eyes only. They told me to, uhm, get lost."

They told you to go screw yourself six ways from Sunday, didn't they, Parson Jones. Welcome to the East Base version of close combat. "I'll have a word with them about giving you confusing directions like that. Just so you know, I need to sign off on all messages. Don't ask me why, I don't write the regulations." The war clock ticking in his head, he suddenly asked: "Any skinny about where these came in from?"

Jones pursed his lips as if calculating where gossip fell on the scale of sin. "Uhm, I did pester the teletype operator until he'd tell me that much. Pacific theater, Lieutenant."

Friessen and Animal Angelides and Danzer. Rest camp in Australia and troop ship in convoy and destroyer on noncombat station. Those should be okay; routine reports this time of day. Relieved, Ben grabbed up the materials from his desk that he had come for and turned to go. Jones still stood there fidgeting.

"Lieutenant, I better tell you, I don't have the least idea what I'm supposed to be doing here. I never heard of this TPWP outfit until I was assigned to you."

By now Ben could have recited it in his sleep, the same spiel he had given Wryzinski, and Torvik before him, and Sullivan before that, that the government was in the habit of setting up special projects for certain war priorities. There was one for lumber production, and one for the artificial rubber called guayule, and a rumored strange one going on out in the desert at Hanford, Washington, that no one would talk about officially, and who knew how many others. "In ours, we produce boilerplate for the newspapers, to put it politely. You do know how to handle a typewriter and a camera, right? Where is it you were stationed, before?"

"The Aleutians. I was on the base newspaper at Adak, the *Williwaw*." A mistily nostalgic expression came over the thug face. "They really had the weather up there. It was great for Bible study."

"I'll just bet." If the Aleutian Islands were known for anything, it was sideways rain. That remote Alaska outpost was about as distant as possible from Montana and any logical assignment to this office. Another of those chills blowing through a gap in the law of averages crept up Ben's spine as he inspected the unexpected corporal again. The war tossed people like scraps of paper to far corners of the world, except those who happened to have attended Treasure State University in '41; those it was busily sifting back to Great Falls. Jake Eisman, first. Then himself, and now this clerk with nothing standing out on his record except piety. Would coincidences never cease: the tangled situation with Cass, and all of a sudden a Ten Commandments officemate who would definitely know which number the one against adultery was.

"Tell you what, Jones, things are kind of slack at the moment and it's late in the day," he resorted to, wanting time to think over this latest circumstance, "so why don't you just get settled in the barracks. I'll collect the messages and we'll start work in the morning—with any luck, the two of us will have the war won by noon."

Jones cleared his throat. "Sir? We have company."

Another soldier was standing in the office doorway wringing a cap. This one wore an armband.

"I HAVE BEEN reprimanded," the base commander set fire to each word. "Because of you, Lieutenant Reinking."

Standing at attention in the same old spot at eye-chart distance from the desk nameplate that read GENERAL GRADY, Ben mentally tried out "*I was just trying to do my job, sir,*" and decided silence sounded better.

The general continued, at volume. "A certain United States senator from here read your article on the WASPs. Ordinarily that wouldn't matter a shit's worth, but he's a busybody on a committee the Pentagon has to get along with. It seems he wants to know why, if women have the training to fly these airplanes of ours in American air, they can't cross a meaningless line on the ground called the Canadian border and do the Alaska run. The interfering old fart."

"Sir?" Ben risked. It drew him a glare, but also a nod for him to speak if he dared. "Could you maybe fill me in as to why the WASPs can't fly north?"

The general said sardonically, "I thought you were supposed to be bright, Reinking. I use the Alaska run to weed my pilots. It's the next thing to combat flying."

He whirled in his chair and slammed a hand to the wall map behind him. "Shit's sake, man, just look at the terrain! The hop from here to Edmonton, anybody in ATC can fly that with one eye closed. But then comes the real flying, every goddamn Canadian mountain there is and then the Alaskan ones. That flight is long, the weather is bad half the time and worse the rest, the Fairbanks airport is no cinch—do you see what I'm driving at? Those who can hack it on the northern hop"—the general reached high to resoundingly slap the Alaska portion of the map—"I see to it that they have a good shot at transferring over to be fighter or bomber pilots. Those pilots, perhaps you have noticed, Lieutenant, according to United States Army Air Corps regulations need to be m-e-n." The general spelled it out for him ever further: "Letting the goddamn WASPs onto that run would get in the way of that."

"I see, sir." *Does the Senator?*

General Grady slumped back in his chair as if under the weight of that thought. "Not that it matters, now that I have to screw the mongoose on this"—Ben did not let his face show how much he savored that description—"but what do I have to look forward to next from you, Reinking? I am supposedly in charge of all personnel on this air base, yet you have orders from somewhere on high that lets you flit around here doing whatever you damn please. Exactly who is behind this kink in the chain of command?" The general leaned far forward. "The President? Joseph Stalin? God?"

A COLONEL WITH a Gable mustache, actually.

Ben's war then had not yet become an endless maze of map-plastered base offices and florid commanding officers discomfited by his existence, but it was about to. That last spring morning in 1942 at the pilot training base outside Nashville, reporting as ordered but so mad he could barely see straight, he stepped into the briefing room the visiting colonel had borrowed. He still was reeling from the epic chewing out inflicted by his training squadron CO, minutes before. "So, Reinking, is your father possibly a Congressman? He's not? Then where the hell does your pull come from? I'm supposed to produce fighter pilots. I get somebody who looks like the second coming of von Richthofen, and ten days from graduation he chickens out. First thing I know he's detached to the goddamned puzzle palace in

D.C. A colonel flies in from Washington just to fetch you—if that isn't pull, Reinking, I don't know what is. Have a nice safe war, and get out of my sight."

Torn between outrage and trepidation, Ben approached the waiting colonel prepared to plead this as a case of mistaken identity. His rigid salute went unanswered, the officer waving him to stand at ease. That and the way the Pentagon man casually perched on the edge of a desk instead of requisitioning it said he was not a military lifer, Ben deciphered. Instead he looked like someone off the cover of *Time,* the slicked-back hair, the dapper pencil-thin mustache, the executive attitude; there was always a smokestack or an assembly line over the tailored shoulder on the magazine cover.

Colonel Whoever-he-was meanwhile had given Ben an equal looking-over and now said, as if it was the first of many decisions, "Light one if you've got one. Or try one of my Cuban 'rillos?" He held out a pack of thin dark baby cigars.

"I don't smoke, sir."

"Still in training, good." The colonel flipped open his lighter and puffed a cigarillo to life. His sudden question caught Ben off-guard. "Did you happen to hear the Ted Loudon show last Saturday?"

Loudmouth? You couldn't pay me enough to listen to that creep. Ben stuck to, "Can't say that I did, sir."

"Too bad. You were prominently mentioned. Here's a transcription." He held out a fold of yellow teletype paper for Ben to take.

THRESHOLD PRESS WAR PROJECT PICKUP FROM CONTINENTAL BROADCASTING SYSTEM, the slugline read. And beneath in the familiar staccato spatter of wire-service copy:

Good evening, America, and our fighting men and
women everywhere. This is Ted Loudon with the latest

Sports Lowdown. And have I got a super-size scoop for
you tonight." *(Ben could just hear that rat-a-tat-tat radio
patter. Not for the first time, however, Loudon's brand of
spiel went beyond anything that could be expected.)* "On
the gridiron of life, champions now are taking the field
in a game for all the world to see. Every true follower of
football will remember the war cry of the Golden Eagles
of 1941. That Treasure State University team gallantly
rallied to the memory of its 'twelfth man,' the teammate
whose heart tragically gave out on the practice field, and
went on to an undefeated season. Now those Golden Eagle
players have heroically committed themselves to victory on
a field as large as the world. Every starting player of that
unforgettable Treasure State team—now get this, fans—
those eleven players all are now in the service of their
country.

"I have searched the records high and low, folks"
*(—Ben would have bet most of it was low, wherever Loudon
was involved—)* "and with the natural exception of the
military academies of West Point and Annapolis, no college
football team has ever before offered up every member in
simultaneous service to our country. Count on it, friends,
Hitler and Tojo are in for some rough tackling from these
fellows. The roster of this Supreme Team is quite amazing:

Moxie Stamper, the slinging quarterback.

Jake Eisman, the Iceman, cool head at fullback who
always delivered in All-American fashion when vital short
yardage was needed.

Quick Vic Rennie, as fast as a halfback gets.

Dexter Cariston, deceptive as a ghost at the other
halfback spot.

Then the outstanding line, beginning with ends Nick
Danzer and Ben Reinking, two of the catchingest receivers
this side of Don Hutson."

On down the list. The one surprise to Ben was Dexter Cariston, who always claimed the only blood he intended to be around any time soon was in med school. Dex must have decided not to wait for the draft.

Ben passed the transcription back to the colonel, wishing he could wash Ted Loudon off his hand. "All due respect, sir, I already knew most of that." Swallowing hard against the possibility that he was going to throw up, he managed to croak out: "Could you possibly tell me why was I yanked out of pilot training to read a wire story?"

"For one thing," the colonel said mildly, "because you know what a wire story is. Two summers with the United Press bureau in Helena ripping and reading the teletype, am I right? And you know how to meet a deadline, as well. 'Letter from the Hill' every week for, what, three seasons?"

Staring at the man, Ben felt a rush of blood through his head, although he couldn't have told whether it was draining from his face or coloring it up. His football diary had run in only the college newspaper; what was the Pentagon doing reading the *Treasure State Nugget*?

"An upbringing in your father's newspaper office on top of that," the colonel was going on, as if he was ordering parts for something he wanted built, "and you were sharp in class, your grades always up there on the dean's list. Plus that famous football season. Quite the pedigree." Abruptly he shifted ground. "Was it a pact? The eleven of you talking it over and deciding to go into the war sooner than later, one for all and all for one, that sort of thing?"

"No, sir." All for one, one for all? However much else this Pentagon whiz knew, he didn't know Stamper and Danzer. Nor, for that matter, Dex. "Sure, a few of us went to the enlistment office together right after Pearl Harbor. But other than that it was strictly one by one, guys trickling in as they felt they had to, from what I hear."

"Pity. But that doesn't change the essential story, fortunately."

The colonel sprang it then, the Supreme Team coverage for the duration of the war, that Ben's background singled him out for. He listened in a daze as the colonel brought it all home to him. "Naturally we will accredit you as a full-fledged correspondent. You'll be on detached duty to TPWP for the duration, and there are a few ins and outs that go with that. But you'll learn the ropes quickly enough." Then the brief one-sided joust, with Ben heatedly asking whether he had any choice in this and the colonel replying, "Not really. Your orders already have been cut. In fact, I have them here." The man patted an attaché case of an elegance that had nothing to do with military issue.

Heart thudding, knowing this would take endless sorting out between the writing chance of a lifetime and the loss of flying, Ben ended up blurting what he had to:

"Sir, begging your pardon. But following the team all during the war that way, what are we supposed to do"—*what am I supposed to do*—"if not everybody makes it through?"

A sharp nod from the colonel. "Good, let's get that contingency out of the way. We've had the casualty figures from other wars run," he said as if Ben had asked that as a favor. Another cigarillo appeared in the manicured hand, another flare of the lighter. The colonel appraised Ben through a puff of smoke before going on. "You aced your statistics course in college, so you'll be interested in what our stix section came up with. An American male of military age had a greater chance of being killed or maimed in, say, a logging camp or a deep-shaft mine than in the front lines of either the Civil War or World War One. Does that surprise you?" He tapped the slightest dab of ash into the ashtray on the desk. "It did us, but not unduly. The size of veterans' groups from both wars indicated that many, many more soldiers survived than people think, and our figures merely back that up. Statistically speaking, in this war we are looking at a nine

percent mortality rate for active combatants such as your teammates. Rounding that off to a whole man, as we must"—Ben
stared at a human being who could use the law of averages to
measure dirt on a grave—"that is one in ten, isn't it. That unfortunate formula of fate or something very like it would occur
whether or not we"—he gestured with the cigarillo as if striking
that word—"or rather you, Lieutenant, do this."

No uniform of authority Ben had come up against in the many
months since held a candle to that. Now he looked at the red-faced
East Base commander and informed him he was not at liberty to
divulge who was behind this kink in the chain of command, as
the general called it. In the same dead-level tone of voice he added:
"General Grady, since you ask, my next piece is about a teammate
of mine wounded in action. He has one leg left."

    Warily the base commander took another look at Ben. "That's
a shame, I'm sure. What about the article you said you'd do on
Eisman?"

    "His turn is coming. Will that be all, sir?"

The flight board still was not doing Cass or him any favors.
Chalked slots swarmed with on-time departures and arrivals
across the entire vast trellis of routes into and out of East Base,
every B-17 and P-39 and all the birds of the air evidently having
enjoyed a day of fine weather for flying, with the lonely exception of squadron WASP 1 still sitting in murderous fog in Seattle.
Swearing to himself, Ben banged out of the Operations building.
He hit the communications section next, to send off the piece on
Vic, remembering to threaten the wire clerk with certain demotion and possible dismemberment if he didn't keep a civil tongue
toward Jones.

    Back out in the dusk breeze where the runway yawned empty,
he stood there so sick with the mix of worry and love he felt in-

capacitated. Nothing prepared a person for this. The way he and Cass had fallen for each other was as unlikely as a collision of meteors. But since it had happened, as hard to sort out, too. The hunger of love. There was no limit to it. Finally he decided there was nothing to be done but call it a day until further word on her flight. His body agonized that there was little hope now of seeing her tonight, even if her squadron lifted off before sunset in Seattle; his brain tried to fight down the wave of desire and encourage the fog to hold so Cass would bunk there for the night instead of flying blind into murk and mountains.

Jake Eisman wasn't bunked in anywhere, he could count on that. Halfway up the whitewashed walkway to the Officers' Club, Ben caught the sound of his penetrating baritone—in their playing days, Jake was restricted to whispers in the huddle lest he be heard the length of the football field—in the mob of song emanating from within; the O Club always tuned up drastically when a planeload of pilots returned from the Alaska run. Ben never ceased to marvel at how fertile the war was for songs. He intended to write about this someday, just for the havoc to be created at Tepee Weepy by lyrics such as Jake was enwrapped in at the moment:

> Oh, the Russians are drinking in Fairbanks,
> While we fly through snow, ice, and shit.
> When we land they shout out, "Thanks, Yanks!
> Now watch us bomb Hitler,
> And Himmler,
> And Fritzie,
> And Mitzi,
> While you fly through snow, ice, and shit!"

Central as a vat in the bibulous bunch ganged around the piano and hoisting another drink at the end of each chorus, Jake jerked his head toward the bar as soon as he spotted Ben. They hadn't seen each other for a week and the ATC's largest and

possibly most boisterous pilot always came back from the far
north with more Alaska tales than Robert Service. Tonight Ben
was more than ready to let the conversation flow from that direction. Ordering a beer for himself and another as reinforcement
for Jake, he drifted to their usual corner table while the bass-and-
baritone crowd around the piano roared through a final chorus
like sea lions.

Tense as he was about Cass, he didn't manage to have the
best face on things when Jake showed up at the table. Jake plainly
had been here indulging in beer and song long enough to be jus-
tifiably somewhat askew. His dark hair flopped to one side—on
him it looked good—and his tie was loosened. His breast pocket
nametag was a radical number of degrees off angle; a hand-
lettered last name only on everyone else, his as ever notified the
world in full: LT. JACOB EISMAN.

"What's eating you, scribe?" The big man roughed Ben's shoulder with a mitt of a hand as he went around to a facing chair. "A
three-day leave don't agree with you? Send the next one my way,
and you can freeze your ass over the Yukon while I party."

"Why would they hand me an airplane when they barely
trust me with a pencil?" Ben roused himself and got busy de-
flecting the topic of his leave. "No substitutions allowed anyway,
you ought to know that. Grandpa Grady himself told me within
this very hour you are the pride of the ATC—"

"Only because I slipped him tickets on the fifty-yard line for
the Homecoming game."

"—so there you go, who'll mush the flying dogsleds north if
not you? The serum must reach Nome, Nanook."

Jake snorted. "Alaska runs on vodka these days, ain't you
heard?"

"War is heck," said Ben, cracking a smile in spite of himself.

"I'll clink to that." Jake tapped Ben's beer bottle with his own,
drained what he had left, and reached for the next bottle. "Been

meaning to ask you, Ben friend. If I'm so all-fired popular, when do I get my moment of fame again?"

That particular question had more behind it than Ben wanted to deal with. Juggling the Supreme Team pieces into some kind of monthly sequence was always tricky, even without what had happened to Vic and what waited in the file after his. Now this. He said shortly, "Dex is next. No cutting in line."

Jake leaned in, covering the table like a cloud but grinning as he came. "Where is he, Ben? C'mon. Where's the dexterous one putting in his war?"

"Goddamnit, Ice, will you lay off that? I still can't tell you. They'd have me cleaning latrines from here to eternity if I did." *And you wouldn't like knowing.*

"That rich sneak," Jake was saying appreciatively. "He's in something like the OSS, isn't he. Greased his way in there with the other blue-blood daredevils. The glamorous war, that'd be his. Parachuting into Krautland in the dark of the moon with a knife between his teeth. That it?"

"Have another beer, Jake."

With lazy grace Jake signaled to the bar for another round apiece. "Top secret, huh? Tell Dex to bag a few of the bastards for me."

Just then the hubbub in the club went up several more notches as yet another flock of pilots came rollicking in. Several of them were shorter guys, fighter plane jockeys who looked even more compact beside the brawn of the bomber pilots, and their particular reason for celebration, Ben could overhear, was that they hadn't had to bounce through the air to the cold of Alaska, only Alberta. Edmonton was the first hop for P-39s, with their limited fuel tanks, and Canadian reserve pilots in need of flying time sometimes ferried the planes onward up the long chain of bush-country airfields to Fairbanks. These flyboys swarming the bar were home from an easy day's work before dark. Glazed, Ben

stared past them out the club's picture window to where the de-
fining lines of evening were making the buttes across Great Falls
stand out like oldest earthen fortresses. Sundown would reach
Seattle in less than an hour, on top of fog. Consumed with fret
about Cass, he tried not to hate the lucky fighter pilots elbowing
to the bar.

During this there had been a distinct lack of words from
across the table, and he realized Jake had been studying him
critically. A different kind of grin sneaked onto Jake now. "Benjamin, you've been holding out on me another way. But I found
out about it, ho de ho. Can't fool Yukon Jake."

Ben's insides lurched. He and Cass had tried to be as hard
to spot as chameleons; how did they stand out all the way to
Alaska? "You don't want to believe everything you—"

Impatiently Jake wiped that away with a paw: "I have it on
good authority. Shame on you, earning yourself a purple one in
your spare time over there in the paradise of the Pacific. What
are you, some kind of incognito hero?"

"You're too swift for me," Ben exhaled in some relief, although Tepee Weepy did not want it made known that its supposedly unarmed correspondent had a combat exploit and a scar
to show for it. "Where did you pick that up?"

"Carlo the Friesian, who else." Jake sat back, folding his fire-
log arms in satisfaction. "Probably comes as a surprise to arty-
farty ends, but tackles can write and fullbacks can read. Letter
from Carl the other day says you and him got a New Guinea
welcome from the Japs and you came out of it with the wound,
the Purple Heart, the commendation, the whole schmear. How
come you didn't tell me about it?"

Ben started to hide behind a swig of his beer, but was afraid it
would come right back up. "It was just a graze." It was everything
beyond that for the infantryman an arm's length away from him
and Friessen. *And the Jap.* The memory churned in him. The

grotesque hand-to-hand struggle on that jungle trail. His three weeks of impatient mending on the hospital ship. "Don't look at me like that, Ice. I'd have told you about it sooner or later." *Maybe.* "It's not something I'm particularly proud of. Correspondents are supposed to stay out of the way of metal objects flying through the air."

"That your next piece?" Jake pressed. "After Dex? Hell, I'll give up my spot to read about it. Carl said it was pretty hairy."

Ben made a zipper motion across his lips, hoping it would end this.

Jake gave a huge sigh of exasperation. "Then I might as well give you a bad time about something else while I'm at it. I read in the newsypaper you went calling on Grady's Ladies. So tell me, how's the hunting there?"

Minimum honesty sounded innocent enough here. "Too many of them are married."

"That's a sonofabitching shame, you know that?" Jake let out over the increased noise, the piano gang lustily singing a filthy tribute to Daisy in the grass. Ben squirmed and wished they would work their way to something that did not rhyme with Cass and the rest.

"I mean, can you imagine a marriage like that?" Jake looked askance at the very idea. "The old lady gets up in the morning, puts on her flying suit and straps on her .45 and goes off to war. Wow."

"Jake, something like that happens these days more than you might think." In the Excelsior Hotel some mornings, for instance.

"I know you," Jake bridged right over that, pointing the neck of a bottle at him, "you were too busy scribbling things down to sniff out the needy bachelor girls for us needy bachelors. Myself, I never get a crack at our sisters in arms. I fly out, they fly in, round and round we go."

*Good thing, too. That's all I'd need next after Jones, you link-
ing up with that she-wolf blonde in Cass's flight.* "Airships that
pass," Ben philosophized hopefully.

"Besides, I don't need any of your hotshot WASPs," Jake
stated with startling primness. Then leered goofily. "I've got
something of my own going. Tell you about her sometime." Ben
was surprised. It wasn't like Jake to be mysterious about any female conquest.

"You made them sound pretty good, you know." This time
Jake spoke soberly, and Ben went back on guard. "Like maybe
they could handle the Alaska run, Ben buddy?"

"All I say in the piece was some of them, all right, a bunch
of them have as much flying time as any of you and if they were
handed a map could quite possibly find their way to Fairbanks.
But I didn't mean—"

"I'm for it," Jake broke in. "Let the WASPs fly that run and
send me after Germans. Sooner the better."

Ben sat up. "Jake, serious a minute. Bombers over Germany
get the guts shot out of them—when I was at St. Eval doing the
piece on Moxie I saw them land with holes the size of boxcar
doors. You really want in on that?"

"If that's what it takes, hell yes. I don't like what Hitler has in
mind for me if the crazy little dipshit wins the war."

"Plenty of those bomber pilots end up bailing out over occupied territory," Ben said slowly. "POW camps are no picnic." His
throat was tight as he tried to find a right way to say it. "What I
hear is that the first thing they do is check dog tags to sort people
out. No telling what they'd do to you, Ice."

"You think that's not on my mind?" Jake replied in the quiet-
est tone he was capable of. "But I figure it this way," the voice took
on a calculating timbre, "those ack-ack assholes have to single me
out from a lot of guys dropping bombs on them, first."

Goddamn it, don't count on that. Half in despair, Ben stood ready to point out that the law of averages had not been any suit of armor for certain Supreme Team members so far, but Jake knew as much about that as he did, almost. It was always a mistake to see the workhorse fullback known as the Iceman, the sportswriters' consensus pick for All-American at that position in hallowed '41, as mainly a physical specimen. Jake stood 6'3" in stocking feet but the upper several inches were brain. The chips in his grammar from smelter work were deliberately maintained, Ben understood; in Black Eagle, the melting pot under the smokestack, someone like him had to make his words register on people high, low, or in between, as needed. Drinking with Jake was treacherous, but in any other human endeavor Ben would have trusted him with his life. Seven years they had been friends, since the high school all-star game that put them together on a team for the first time. Then hundreds of TSU football practices, banter, bull sessions, a long winning streak of camaraderie. Joshing arguments were nothing new between them; this had turned into something far beyond that. Ben felt he had to pierce the matter:

"That's why you wanted me to hurry up and do the piece on you, isn't it. So you could wave it at somebody who might have some influence and say, 'Hey, I'm a famous guy, wouldn't it be great to have me over there bombing the balls off the Germans?'"

"Couldn't hurt, could it?" Jake responded defiantly. Then just as quickly looked sheepish. "Sorry I asked. Sonofabitching war, I don't know what gets into a guy." He set about working himself toward normal with a boost of beer. "I mean it, though, about getting over there somehow. Ben? I'm not saying you got any pull, because if you did, you'd be up, up, and away like the rest of us, wouldn't you. But if you ever stumble across any, remember

your poor deserving teammate, okay?" The old grin came back.
"Who's gonna look out for me if not you? What's that poem"—
Jake pronounced it *pome*—"'*O Captain! My Captain!*'"

Relieved, Ben responded in the same vein: "You're looking
for pull from someone who took a demotion from civilian life,
are you? Good thinking, Ice. Didn't I help you crib your way
through the logic course any better than—"

Jake was holding up a hand for silence. He cocked an ear at
the preliminary commotion from the piano. "It's bad luck not to
sing this one. Everybody in." Swinging his beer bottle to the beat,
Jake joined in mightily to the swelling roar of music that filled
the building:

> Bought the farm, bought the farm!
> Crashing the plane leads to harm!
> There was blood on the cockpit,
> and blood on the ground.
> Blood on the cowling,
> and blood all around.
> Pity the pilot,
> all bloody with gore,
> For he won't be flying
> That airplane no more.

After the last chorus tailed off into drinking, Jake looked
across at Ben. "You're not singing these days?"

"Frog in my throat."

"You really are off your feed. C'mon, Ben, it's just a song. Lets
off the steam."

"I know what it lets off, for Christ's sake." He shoved back
from the table and popped to his feet. "Just remembered, I need
to check something in Ops. A VIP flight I'm supposed to keep
tabs on in case there's any brass worth interviewing. Be right
back."

He sprinted to the Operations building, slowing only as he walked into the room where the flight board covered one wall, hoping the clamor of his heart was not loud enough for the night Operations staff to hear. As ever, he whipped out his pad and stood there jotting random flight information, scanning the entire board like a good working reporter, but the chalked entry for WASP 1 midway down instantly had told him what he needed to know. Since meeting Cass he had never imagined looking forward to a bed without her in it, but the three white letters—RON—up there for blessed REMAINING OVERNIGHT did the job.

Back at the Officers' Club, he veered to the bar. "Fill the tray," he told the barman.

The bartender crowded beer bottles onto the round serving tray until there were ten or a dozen, Ben didn't bother to count. He picked it up and steered toward the table.

Jake surveyed the forest of bottles on the tray. "What's all this?"

"Anesthesia. I have something to tell you about Vic."

4

⭐ "I interrupted the greatest movie never made, didn't I," Cass's murmur came from the region of the hard-used pillow.

"Immortality will just have to wait," Ben's came from where his head blissfully rested on her.

"How many *t*'s in that?"

"You are a merciless woman." Still hazed over with the spell of their lovemaking, he lay clinging to her in the wreckage of the sheets, every part of the two of them bare except for wristwatches—they hadn't taken the time to unstrap those. Hers, the type with luminous numerals that was issued to pilots, showed she had slipped into the room at the Excelsior merely twenty minutes ago. Before he could even get up from the typing table to greet her she'd slid the bolt home on the door and turned to him saying, "I guess we have some catching up to do." In the next breath they were at each other, kissing every direction, and here in the aftermath the creaky room with its flung clothing and kicked-off bedcovers looked like the muss after a spirited rummage sale; the one spot their mess hadn't touched was the portable typewriter with the page of script Ben had been pecking away at, and he couldn't help knowing half of that was crossed out untidily as usual.

"Bulletin for you." She was stroking the back of his head with a motion tender and tense at the same time. "This'll have to be another short night. I fly out again at 0600."

"Why didn't you say so? I'd have moved the bed closer to the door."

She chuckled and swatted him behind the ear. "Fool."

"Probably."

Mustering strength enough to lift himself onto one elbow, he gazed down at this woman he should not be with as if committing her every feature to memory. The attentive cheeky face that a few years back could have been of the calendar kind but now could serve on a recruiting poster; Cass was dramatically weather-tanned, a trace whiter around the eyes where the goggles masked her while flying. Dark brown hair naturally wavy, which she kept authoritatively short off her shoulders; she'd told him she cut it herself with a razor blade, there wasn't ever time to command a squadron and visit a beauty shop both. The invitation of her snug peach-perfect breasts, and the tomboy thrift of her body on down. Already he was hungry for her again, in a way beyond what they had just been doing in bed. Fresh from the night before, when his imagination had given her up for lost, the ache with her name on it cut through to his bones. Life without Cass? Last night had shown that wasn't life, it was barely existence. What kind of a passion pit was the dark of the mind, where he had struggled every way he knew and still ended up so far gone on this woman? *And if they catch us at this, we're goners of another kind. Double jeopardy, Cass. The law of averages isn't doing the two of us any favors either.*

Watching his mood turn, Cass headed off whatever he was about to say. "Save it for the chaplain, okay? We're not the first ones who ever caught the screw flu and—"

"This is more than that, Cass, you know goddamn good and well it's more."

"—call it what you want to, it always comes down to one of two things, doesn't it. We either quit with this or go at it like crazy while we still have the chance. Right now we don't seem to be much good at quitting, I'd say." She flicked him the urgent smile that showed the irresistible tiny gap between her front teeth, and he melted like a schoolboy and knew it. Deeply and rigorously they kissed again, running their hands silkily here and there, as if keeping track of everything in the book of hotel-room romance. "Welcome back, by the way," he murmured when their heads were clear enough. "I never knew I hated fog so much."

Her voice rose from where she lay. "Those shiny-pants lame-brains last night couldn't make their minds up to scrub that flight when they couldn't even see to the control tower." Cass disposed of the Seattle military hierarchy while flat on her back. "They held us in the ready room until full dark, the chickenshits. What did they think, we'd be able to see better in the fog at night, like bats?"

She rolled sharply up onto an elbow, facing Ben from so near he could feel the warmth of her breath on his face. "While I'm at it. Know what, Scar?" she resorted to a mock growl as her free hand lightly traced along the groove in his skin where he had been wounded. "You need a thicker hide in more ways than one. You'd be better off not checking the flight board when I fly."

"Doesn't matter. I'd be worried to death that way too."

Something like a wince came to her hazel eyes. He saw her start on a word, then draw it back.

Finally Cass wrinkled her nose at him. "Hopeless man, I guess there's no cure for what ails you then. Hey, that reminds me"—she pushed off him, and slick as a seal, flipped herself over and around, instantly onto her feet at the side of the bed— "before we got distracted, I was going to offer a guy a drink. One thing about Seattle, the Navy commissary is never short on scotch." Not bothering with clothes she padded across the room, evidently oblivious to the cold linoleum and all else, to where her ready-bag had been dropped by the door.

Ben sat up to take in the sight of her on parade. Stripped, Cass was as slim and wiry as a jockey, medium height for a woman, a perfect fit for the notoriously snug plane she flew; the P-39 carried the reputation that the aircraft company's president, a little guy, had scooted into the mock-up of the cockpit not realizing it wasn't full-scale, declared it just right, and started production that very day. The consequence supposedly was that male air cadets had to have their butts measured to see if they could fly the thing, and when that proved to be too much trouble, the P-39s were Lend-Leased off to the Soviet Union where 5'6" Laplanders flew them. Ben was journalistically skeptical of any of that, but he could not argue with the fact that Captain Cass Standish's trim but shapely behind was a commanding one, in or out of a Cobra fighter plane.

Cass knelt at the bag, triumphantly plucking the pint of scotch out. "That's funny," he called over as he appreciatively took in her and the bounty in her hand, "they didn't teach me naked bartending in officers' candidate school."

"Man's world," Cass retaliated. "Women always have it tougher." She picked up the single cloudy tumbler from the dresser, looking around. "Does this dump have two glasses?"

"I keep one in the bottom drawer. For visiting royalty."

"Flattery will get you," she purred.

"I'm not so hot on the rest of my manners. I forgot to ask— survived the USO one more time, did you?" He knew she had been stuck with one of those extraneous duties that are slapped on when an officer isn't looking, East Base liaison to the United Service Organizations at the downtown Civic Center. The USO did such things as hold theoretically chaste dances where servicemen could meet young ladies from the leafy neighborhoods around and bring entertainment acts to town; since General Grady in his perpetual tear against venereal disease and other debilitations had put thirty Great Falls whoopee establishments off limits, the Civic Center outfit had no lack of customers. By Cass's telling, the goody-goody nature of the USO just about drove her up the wall. On the other hand, it was the perfect chance for her to sneak the few blocks to this skid row hotel. *They ought to see her now,* bare as the day she was born while she excavated the absent glass from amid the underwear he'd forgotten he dumped in that drawer.

"I just smiled until my back teeth hurt," she was reporting of the earlier part of her evening. "Luckily they don't miss me at all. Joe E. Brown is over there making faces at them right now."

"You passed up Joe E. Brown for me?" Ben's voice rose mischievously. "Where's your sense of humor?"

"Yuk yuk," she obliged. "He has his audience, I evidently have mine." He watched as she poured double wallops of scotch, then driblets of water from the chipped enamel pitcher: Cass could fly with the boys, Cass could drink with the boys.

He made room for her now as she slid in and propped up against the bedstead next to him, each being careful with the precious scotch. Nonetheless Ben snuggled in on her. Do illicit lovers snuggle? He decided hell, yes, they do in this case. The war was away for the night, even if it was going to be a short night.

Cass, though, interrupted his attentions by clinking her glass against his.

"Hey you, Mister Busy. We need to have a toast. To General Grady, our poor ass-chewn commanding officer."

Very slowly Ben took a sip, eyeing her. "How'd you know he hauled me in to his office yesterday because of that?"

Her turn to be surprised. "I didn't. We just heard tonight about Grady getting reamed out good, along with the change of orders. Mary Catherine's sister is a WAVE clerk back there"— *there* always meant Washington—"and she phoned M.C. to say it was all over the Pentagon, how the prissy old Air Transport

Command got turned every way but loose over a dozen WASPs in Great Falls."

He took a stronger swig of his drink. "What change of orders?"

"We get to fly on the Alaska run, Ben." She looked at him proudly. "The first leg of it anyway, up to Edmonton. That's a big, big start—WASP 1 crossing the border just like the big boys."

"The hell you say." It took him no time whatsoever to put it together. "The Senator kicked until they gave in." *The old wire-puller reads a line or two I put in that piece, and Cass and her pilots get Canada handed to them? Tepee Weepy and me, that deadly a combination?*

Cass grinned. "Maybe Mrs. Senator did some kicking of her own."

"Could be. Anyway, screw Grady, let's drink to Luther and Sadie." With that, the state's senior senator and possibly just as senior spouse were accorded their due in scotch.

Cass belted hers down while his was barely to his lips, and scooted to the dresser to fetch the bottle. This time Ben saw not only a lovely, lively woman who happened to fit into a Cobra cockpit, but a destined ace pilot of some kind. Captain Cassia Standish and her squadron given the go-ahead to fly in wartime airspace outside the U.S., even if it was only across a couple of Canadian provinces so far: who knew where that would lead? War correspondents read other correspondents, and he was well apprised from Russian dispatches that the Red Air Force already had women flying in combat, surely some of them in the same P-39s—the Laplander legend notwithstanding—that had hop-scotched all the way from East Base. It went through him in a chill mix of clarity and dismay: if the powers that be were ever to begin miraculously handing out assignment orders according to abilities shown thus far in World War Two, Cass and her WASPs might as well go all the way to the Eastern Front and take on the

Luftwaffe, while groundpounders like him stirred the Kool-Aid at USO dances.

Cass luckily broke in on his tumble of thoughts. "I've been so wound up, I haven't even asked how leave was. Fun?"

"The opposite." He told her the story of Vic.

"That's rough." Without being asked, Cass bolstered his drink. "A leg off—I think I'd rather be dead, put out of my misery."

When Ben didn't say anything, she shifted around on the covers to face him more directly. In bed and out, he was unbeatable company, bright as a mint silver dollar, funny when he wanted to be, but deep-down serious about life; any way she looked at him, he amounted to a first-class passion ration. And while maybe she was stuck with wearing a wedding band, he was the one trapped in a wartime marriage of inconvenience with the shiny-pants Washington outfit with all the initials. *It's going to happen one of these times like that, isn't it, Ben. That Tepee Creepy outfit will yank you off somewhere to chase after another one of your team buddies and make you keep going, no more East Base, no more me. No more us, except pen pals. And that kind of ink never lasts.* Asking, she carefully confined it to: "What's next?"

Sensing treacherous territory, Ben answered with equal care: "Just more of the same, a catch-up piece on one of the guys on the team. He's—someplace I can't tell you about or why."

Cass let her puzzlement show. "Then how do you write about somebody like that?" Jake Eisman the other night had asked the same thing: "How in the hell do you show off Dex without blowing his cover?"

"Goddamn carefully," Ben recited the same answer. "Don't give me that look, you with the airplane. I know better than anybody that what they've stuck me doing in this war is a strange business, stranger some times than others."

"Touchy. All I was going to ask is, are you going to be away? To wherever this mystery gink is?"

"I find that out tomorrow."

"Ben?" Cass swirled the last of her drink, gazing into the bottom of the glass as if fortune-telling. "Something you better know."

At her tone, he braced back a bit against the bedstead. "Ready on the firing line, I guess."

"I'm a wingwalker."

He looked at her cautiously. "The county fair kind?"

"Fairs, air shows, rodeos, you name it. Anywhere people would pay to see somebody swoop over them hanging on to the struts and guywires of a biplane. If it was a woman, so much the better for the take." She tossed her head, as if the whipstream of wind from back then was in her hair again.

"I, ah, more figured you for a stunt pilot."

"That, too. We—"

Her voice caught on the word, Ben waiting unmoving until she could get hold of herself enough to go on. She had told him how she'd haunted the airfield outside Missoula when she was a kid, brassed her way into the Civilian Pilot Training course when there was a tiny opening for women, and in the end linked up with a smoke jumper turned aircraft rigger for the Forest Service; the wedding ring there on her finger told the rest of that.

"—Dan and I," she managed to get the words out, "talked about barnstorming across the whole country. Turn into flying gypsies, kind of. We weren't much more than punk kids, it sounded like heaven to us. Off we went, weekends, holidays, giving it a try wherever there was some kind of two-bit show. I'd loop the loop and all that, and for the finale a buddy of ours who flew for the smokies would take the controls and I'd waltz out onto the wing. We were hot stuff on the fairgrounds circuit there for a while. Then right away with the war, Dan's Guard unit was called up—you know all that."

Choosing between perils, Ben turned the topic back to wingwalking: "Uh huh, well, that's quite a talent."

"Know what the first rule of wingwalking is?"

He could tell this was not the time to guess *Don't sneeze?* "I'm here listening."

"Never leave hold of what you've got, until you've got hold of something else."

He covered her ring hand with his own, the ache for her now a sharp pain.

"That goes for guys as well as guywires, am I to understand? Husband kind of guy?"

"For the duration, Ben," Cass said levelly, "like every other damn thing. Even if I wash out of the war somehow or who knows what happens"—he understood that meant even if something took him out of the war in more or less one piece—"I couldn't do it to Dan, leave him while he's out there getting shot at. If I did, you would always wonder what sort of tramp you'd ended up with."

Her next words stumbled a bit but they came.

"We're loco over each other, but that can't change the fact that I am as married as a person can get." She poked him in a rib, trying to change the mood, her eyes saying she was desperate to. "So, football hero—why aren't you? It might have saved us a lot of trouble."

Ben thought. "I didn't ever have time to."

"Ben!" Cass couldn't help laughing. "It only takes two minutes in front of a Justice of the Peace, believe me."

"Two minutes is a long time for a football player." He wanted out of the dead end of conversation as badly as she did. "The wingwalking. You're, ah, not going back to that, are you? After the war?"

"Don't know yet. A lot depends."

He shook his head, resorting to mock rue, some of it not so mock. "A woman who flies a fighter plane with a ceiling of thirty-five thousand feet, and as if that isn't enough fooling around with altitude, she wants to get out and stroll along the wing of some crop dust clunker. I have to inform you, Captain Standish, that's the long way around to get your kicks. A nuthouse doctor would definitely call that a promiscuous acrophiliac tendency."

Cass's smile crept out and grew impish. "Know what? You make it sound dirty."

"A guy can hope."

She peeked down. "I see he can. And there's still some night left."

THE TELETYPE CLERK looked up nervously when he strode into the wire room, early if not bright, the next morning. Ben was used to causing dismay this way. He knew he was hated by innumerable men around the world who had never laid eyes on him. Public affairs officers required to keep close track of the doings of whatever member of the Supreme Team they were unfortunate enough to have in their unit. Code clerks who had to make room for the priority dispatches to some destination known as TPWP. All of them wondering, what in the name of brassbound military rigamarole was this about? Hell, he wondered that himself too much of the time. Resolutely trying to clear his head of the lingering effects of the scotch and Cass, he grabbed the nearest message pad—it happened to be the jittery clerk's—and wrote down in block letters:

ODD MAN OUT STILL OUT. WHAT DO?

As the clerk took it to code and send it, Ben added an instruction guaranteed to further mess up the man's day: "Let me know as soon as the reply hits that machine. Not a runner. You."

Ben had barely settled into his desk chair to try to look busy and Jones was assiduously sorting old piles of accumulated paperwork into new piles when the clerk stuck his head in the office. "It just came in, sir."

What there was of it. Standing over the teleprinter as the clerk fed in the decoded version, he frowned at the sole word that chattered out:

PUNT.

Very funny, you bunch of sadistic deskwarmers. Actually he had no idea whether Tepee Weepy's cryptic messages emanated from an entire bureaucratic swarm or from that mustached colonel single-handedly thrusting pieces of paper at some frazzled wire clerk. Either scenario, it came to the same: orders were supposed to be orders. In the face of that, Ben pulled the message pad to him again and wrote out:

FIELD SLIPPERY HERE, PUNT INADVISABLE. GO TO CAMP?

He didn't even make it back to the office before the clerk chased him down. The reply awaiting him this time was anything but brief.

DO NOT REPEAT NOT GO TO CAMP. MAKE STORY LOUD ON BACKFIELD ANGLE. IMPERATIVE.

Ben's groan alarmed the clerk. *Sonofabitch.* Loudon, of all damn people to be expected to imitate. *If they want the Loudon approach*—twelve hundred overripe words about the glory days of the Treasure State backfield, the cloud-of-horseshit kind of sportswriting Ted Loudon could produce in his sleep—*then why don't they just put the jerk in my uniform and be done with it? Let him phony it up about Dex.*

Ben crumpled the message into his pocket and stalked out. The more he thought about it, the more fed up he got. The likes of Ted Loudon and Grantland Rice and other bards of sentimental slop about sports notwithstanding, the One Great Scorer was not visibly awarding touchdowns to the TSU backfield in the game of war. A misty-eyed glance backward to the season that ended with Pearl Harbor would do no justice to any of the four teammates. Jake would puke. Moxie Stamper would snicker. Vic above all deserved a decent cloak of quiescence over his running days. And Dex, whatever he had become, was no soap-slick half-back anymore. Ben reached the office with his mind made up.

"Jones, old lad, how would you like to go for a little ride tomorrow? Fill us out a motor pool requisition. Under REASON put down: *dogs of war*. And you better fill your pockets with puppy biscuits."

THE PODS OF parachutes opened prettily, one blossom of silk after another, cloudflowers against the blue field of sky overtopping Seeley Lake and the Mission Mountains beyond. Ben had just joined the large circle of jumpsuited men craning their necks upward; even so, his uniform and flight jacket drew slanted looks from corners of eyes. He knew he had to hold his temper against the automatic hostility here; guys in the situation of these had plenty to watch out for. A groan went through the group as a billow of dust whirled across the landing strip, where strips of canvas were crisscrossed—tent-pegged down so as not to blow away, Ben could not help but notice—into a prominent X. Carrying its mischief higher, the gusty wind caught the dozen chutes, dancing the dangling men sideways across the air as if they were dandelion seeds. The first jumper managed to land with a neat tuck and roll, which could not disguise the fact that he had missed the X by fifty yards. The chutists after him, sawing desperately at their lines, landed progressively farther and farther off the mark, until the last few were blown into the chokecherry bushes at the far end of the airstrip.

"God damn it," the grizzled foreman of the parachutist squad hollered at the windstrewn legion, "if you can't come any closer to the God damned target than that, you might as well have stayed in the God damned airplane!"

Wincing at the language, the camp director made his way through the canvas-clad younger men and steered Ben off to one side.

"Tough way to get to a spot," Ben spoke the measure of sympathy he felt for the jumpers. More than once on New Guinea he had seen fliers bail out of flaming planes and be swept behind Japanese lines by tropical easterlies. It seemed to him an unfair fate even for war.

The camp director smiled thinly. Solemnly hatted, with silver showing at his temples and everlasting wrinkles in his thrush-brown suit, he looked like a parson. As Ben knew he was, of some kind.

"The U.S. Forest Service prefers to believe it can prevail over wind," there was a bit of pulpit in the voice. "Not to mention fire and terrain." The man was gazing at Ben as though he could see into him if he only were given time enough. "Their belief and ours have been made to coincide here, as we tell all our visitors."

Ben looked around. The Seeley Lake smoke-jumper camp was a mix, right enough, old Civilian Conservation Corps buildings together with fresh woodframe ones that somehow appeared more ecclesiastical than governmental. An obstacle course at one end of the layout was balanced off by a restful chapel at the other. The whole place did have the feel of discipline, but not the military kind. Here, he was uncomfortably aware, a war correspondent was the odd man out. Every man at this camp—aside from profane exceptions like the parachutist foreman in a forest ranger hat—was a conscientious objector. "Enlistees in alternative service" by official jargon; "conchies" by rougher account. Somewhere in their number, conscientiously aloof from the fate-willed military brotherhood of the rest of the TSU football team, was Dexter Cariston.

Remember that hunting trip, Dex? I'd be ashamed to tell you, but I've thought many times how that could have come out different, and then this would have. If your rifle had gone off while we were climbing around up there in the rocks, the kind of thing that happens. Shot yourself in the foot—hell, just one toe—that would have done it. You'd have been safely out of the war and on into med school with nothing said, and I wouldn't be here trying to figure out how to lie about you in a couple of thousand newspapers.

The truth itself, in what he was seeing around him here, was strange enough. A pacifist camp born of wartime needs. Whoever ordained it, here the paradoxical project was in the tall woods of Montana, where the historic peace churches—Quakers, Mennonites, Church of the Brethren—were providing their able-bodied young men in place of other able-bodied young men conscripted for combat. And still were belittled for their pacifism; he regularly heard these rigorous noncombatants with parachute packs on their backs sneered at as draft-dodging yellowbellies, notwithstanding that they were volunteering to tumble out of airplanes into the worst mountain country to fight forest fires.

But where was the familiar husky form of Dex, in any of this? Up there in the jump plane doing wind calculations? Or hiding out when he saw the jeep with the stenciled U.S. ARMY AIR CORPS/EAST BASE pull in?

Ben's silent perusal of the camp was brought to a brisk end by the director. "What can I do for you, officer? I don't mean to be inhospitable, but the military is supposed to leave us alone."

"Preacher"—Ben had no idea on earth how to address a minister of these plain-collared denominations—"nothing would make me happier. I'm the palest imitation of 'military' you're ever apt to see, though. Only a pencil-pusher, sent around to write up several of my college buddies doing what they think their duty is. One of them thinks his is here with your bunch." *I will now lead thee into temptation, Parson.* "You wouldn't mind seeing his standpoint splashed across most of this country's newspapers, would you?"

"Mysterious are the ways," the camp director granted, again smiling marginally. "Which member of our 'bunch' is this?"

Ben spoke the name, still searching the faces of the sixty or so smoke jumpers arrayed on the airstrip as if Dex's familiar one had to be there.

"Ah, our Dexter," the ministerial timbre resounded. "He's in the boneyard, of course."

Everything within Ben, body and soul, turned over. Dex, dead, here in conchie Valhalla? How? There weren't odds steep enough to cover such a thing. The war killed O'Fallon and Havel a predictable way, on the battlefield, and claimed Vic Rennie's leg in the casual accounting on the margin of combat. But this lightning strike straight through any reasonable order of life onto Dexter Cariston in these peaceable woods—through the shock Ben tried in vain to make his voice work.

Nothing marred the camp director's. "You probably ought to hustle across there," he pleasantly indicated to the other side of the airstrip. "His shift is about over."

Then Ben saw it beyond the clustered smoke jumpers, the low businesslike building with the mandatory red of a first-aid cross painted on its eave: the "boneyard," right. Broken ankles from hard landings, busted fingers and hands from banging into trees on the way down, those doubtless were the constants of an infirmary at a place like this. Relief pumped through him. *Why didn't I guess, Dex? Follow the trail of bandages toward anything medical and there you'll be.*

Taking quick leave of the director, Ben climbed back into the ragtop jeep Jones had requisitioned. He still felt somewhat guilty about dropping Jones outside Helena, all by his lonesome, to do the dreary photo shoot on military sled dogs and their earnest trainers, but not overly. Jones and everyone else had to be left out of this. The last thing in the world Tepee Weepy wanted made known was that one of its Supreme Team heroes was sitting out the war at a pacifist camp. For that matter, it was the last thing the others on the team, up to their necks in the armed

struggle, would want to find out. As he drove around the end of
the airstrip and pulled up to the infirmary, Ben found himself
half hoping Dexter Cariston, marked down from dead, was in
there on crutches with a fractured something-or-other; INJURED
IN TRAINING CAMP was a story he could fiddle around with and
not have to say just what kind of camp.

A cowbell clattered above the door as he stepped into the infirmary. Medical clutter was everywhere, shelves and tables of it.
Over by a rack of crutches a single shabby desk sat unoccupied.
Through a doorway toward the back, however, a sandy-haired
figure could be seen bent over a microscope. "Be with you in a
jiffy," came the glossed voice, as incongruous here as it was in a
football huddle, "quick as I dispose of this strep culture."

"Take your time, Dex, it's looking like a long war."

Dex's twiddling of the microscope ceased for a bare instant,
but his head did not budge from the eyepiece. "They all are,
Ben."

Ben watched him deal with the glass slide beneath the lens,
step out to the sink, and soap up and wash as exquisitely as a
surgeon—Dex had only to come into a room and the air grew
rarefied—then with just a hairbreadth of hesitation arrive across
the board floor with right hand extended. *Handshakes are the
last to go,* Ben thought as their palms met. "Something tells me
you're not here to fish famous Seeley Lake," Dex was saying in
his easy way. Next, though, a held-in expression twitched across
his sturdy Scotch face. "Hated to hear that about Vic. Always has
had more than his share of hard luck, hasn't he."

The roar of engines drowned out anything Ben might have
had to say about how luck was distributed. Landing briskly, a
Ford Tri-Motor blasted up dust as it trundled along the airstrip
toward the next set of parachute trainees. Dex moved to the window to watch as if it were his sworn duty, leaving Ben to join him
or not. After a moment, he went over. *What do I know about how*

*they run this preachy outfit, maybe this is some kind of rite—they
all worship the Tin Goose every takeoff.* Whatever the foreman
was hollering now at the chutists ducking aboard was lost in the
plane's racket, but Ben would have bet significant money these
next practice jumps would be closer to the mark. He turned and
asked:

"I'm curious—how come you're not out there leaping into
thin air with the rest of the smokies?"

"Don't think I didn't," Dex answered tightly, eyes still glued
to the shuddering aircraft filling with jumpsuited men. "Twice.
Both times I threw up in the face mask. Ever try to steer a parachute into a forest of hundred-foot ponderosa pines with a faceful
of vomit, Ben?" Consciously or not, Dex rubbed his mouth with
the back of his thumb before managing to say: "They washed me
out of jumper training. All the years of football and Bruno and
his Letter Hill, and five minutes of bumpy air does me in. Isn't
that a corker?"

That needed no affirmation. Dex had been the team's best
natural athlete, elastic as a circus performer, comfortable on the
field as a cavalier at a lawn party. And here he was, handing out
crutches without even earning one. Ben glanced around the infirmary. "You're it, here? Doesn't this kind of setup need a medical staff?"

"The Rochester doctor I didn't get to be, you mean."

They both laughed in their old way, briefly.

As if remembering his manners, Dex sobered and spoke as
he turned from the window. "The way things are, doctors can't
even begin to be everywhere they're needed. Not in the war, not
here either. I'm the equivalent of a medic. I can splint a man up,
shoot some morphine in him, until we can get him to the hospital in Missoula. If it's something besides bones and bruises," he
shrugged, "there's a registered nurse here in town, comes in twice
a week. Don't grin at me like that, Reinking. She's married."

Ben's grin went out like a light. He looked away, across postcard-perfect Seeley Lake to the summer cabins and rowboat docks spaced the distance of a flycast apart. The maintained forest along the shoreline stood sumptuous as fur trim, and even the hackles of brush looked scenic. *Peaceful sonofabitching place. Skipped over by the clock of war.* Cass with a dozen red-hot pistons gobbling combustible aviation fuel at the back of her neck this very minute. Jake Eisman freezing his bodacious butt at the controls of a B-17 while wishing the Alaskan caribou far below were Germans in his bombsights. Carl Friessen in the utmost swamp of Hell that was New Guinea, dug in for another night in a stench-filled foxhole that he didn't dare leave even to take a crap. Every one of the team members in the actual war, those who were left, ticked through Ben's mind like split seconds on a stopwatch. He realized he was breathing harder than he should and tried to steady down, the antiseptic air of the infirmary not helping. What bugged him so much? Conscience wasn't priced by the pound; Dexter Cariston could have found simpler ways to stay the warless one of them all—the purr of money in his family could have taken care of that. Even so. "This does it for you?" the question shot out before he had time to tame it any. "Watching guys hop out of planes into trees? I'm really asking, Dex."

"I'm doing what I can to keep blood in people," the words came clipped, "instead of letting it out of them."

The superior tinge in that answer did it. Anguish went through Ben like a convulsion. *There's more to know about blood than shows up in a microscope, you medical Jesus conchie!* He stood there unsteady, momentarily mindblind, wondering whether he had screamed that in the frozen face of Dexter Cariston.

THE NEW GUINEA jungle, a few months back. Everyone warned him the place dripped voracious insects when it wasn't oozing rain warm as monkey piss, and by the time he tracked down Carl

Friessen in a rear-echelon tent encampment along the Sanananda road, the crisp new combat fatigues he'd been issued were
wringing wet and he was trying hard not to scratch numerous
bites that itched like crazy. *At least nobody's shooting at me. Yet.*
Standing there smacking mosquitoes with one hand and then
the other, he peeked in through the bug netting that served as a
tent flap trying to make sure he had the right man. In their football years Friessen had been rangy enough to plug more than his
share of the line at left tackle. Now he was rawboned, worn down
to sheer frame. Deliberate as ever, though, he hunched there on
his bunk wearing thin black Jap pajamas—Ben thought he had
seen every conceivable form of war souvenir, until now—while
cleaning his carbine with an old toothbrush.

"How's the hunting been, Carl?"

The lantern jaw that had tempted football opponents to mention the word "horseface"—invariably to their regret—swung
around from the rifle-cleaning task. "Lefty! They let just anybody in this bugger of a place, do they?" The same dromedary
grin, even if its wearer was a barely passable imitation of the
Friessen of old in any other way Ben could see. The nickname
he so seldom heard any more twinged in him a little. He was
not left-handed, not even close. Back there on the football field,
that mattered not a bit to Friessen and the other four; the TSU
middle linemen, the brawn brigade, always had their own slant
on things, all of them calling him Lefty because he was the left
end. The right end, Danzer, they just called Danzer.

Now, as if remembering his manners, the pajama-clad soldier
left off work on the carbine and ceremoniously came to unloosen
the netting. "Quick, step inside out of the skeeters."

They whacked one another like kids and talked without letup.
One by one, Ben caught him up on the other team members, Carl
deliberating over each report. "In on something secret, huh?" he

said to Ben's quick passing over of Dex. "He would be, the sonof-agun." The good-natured grin appeared again, but not for long. "This's been all kinds of fighting, Lefty," he sounded veteran far beyond his years. "Three months nose to nose with the dinks to get this"—he sent a heavy look around the pulverized jungle of the Sanananda battle perimeter—"though I don't know why anybody'd want it." Morale did not stand much of a chance here, Ben had to acknowledge. New Guinea notoriously was a back door of the war, everything about it shabby and short shrift while the bulk of Allied military effort was addressed to the battle for Europe. Yet a continent was at stake here, too, the Japanese army almost within touch of Australia as long as it clung to outposts on the New Guinea coastal plain. The patchwork force of desperate Aussies and scraped-together National Guard units were assigned to root the enemy out pillbox by pillbox, sometimes sniper tree by sniper tree. The regiment here was called the Montaneers, hardy Montana Guardsmen given the task of spearheading the fighting against the Japanese from the beachheads on up into the over-grown tropical mountains. Even if Ben had not seen the battle reports on the savagery of this death struggle in the jungle, it could be read in the lines of Carl Friessen's face. "We're nowhere near done, either," the bony infantryman was saying. "The hot rumor is a landing up around Salamaua." He estimated Ben with a flat gaze. "You come all this way to go in with us?"

"Alongside you, Carl," Ben replied more calmly than he felt about it, "that's the idea. Although they only let me carry paper and pencil."

Friessen deliberated again. "Suit yourself, Lefty. We've tried all other kinds on the Japs, why not pencil lead?"

A week later, the two of them were on a slippery trail in the head-high grass on the ridge above the Bitoi River, with the other seven men of Carl's squad. Ben intended to called it quits as soon as they made it back to the invasion perimeter. His pad was full with the past days. The predawn scene in the landing craft as it broached in a big wave and seasick soldiers had to dodge a sliding jeep that broke loose from its fastenings. The Australian commandoes guiding them ashore with blinking signal lights after wading in from behind enemy lines through a swamp and swimming to the assault beach, the winks of brightness showing each man of them standing in the sand proudly naked except for his Digger hat. The steady advice from Carl during the endless crawl for the shelter of the tree line as Japanese bullets flew over them: "Keep your head and butt down. Remember gopher hunting? We're the gophers here." By now, abundantly shot at but not shot up, Carl's unit was dug in inland from the beachhead and everyone agreed they had lucked out so far. The Japanese line had bent back up the height of ground overlooking the Bitoi River and the plan was to let the artillery plaster them there for a while. Sent on patrol before daybreak to sight out a forward observation point, the squad had mapped and azimuthed a good spot and, job done, were heading gingerly back down the trail, the scout out front with a tommy gun, followed by the buck sergeant in charge, then Carl with Ben tagging close behind, the rest of the column bringing up the rear. When something plopped in the mud at the heels of the scout, it took a split second for them all to realize it hadn't dropped from his pack. That left very little time before the grenade would go off.

"Down!" the buck sergeant screamed. Carl hit the ground, Ben an instant behind him. The grenade's explosion heaved the trail under Ben's belly. He heard somebody cry out, hit by fragments. The trailside grass tore open, Japanese in camouflage uniforms pouring out, five, six, *will they never stop coming,* eight. Carl reared onto his knees and shot one before his rifle was clubbed out of his hands by a Japanese mortarman madly swinging the mortar barrel like a sledgehammer. The American on the other side of Ben was being bayoneted by a surprisingly large enemy soldier. Fumbling for the only weapon he had, a trench knife, Ben rolled that direction and slashed the tendons across the back of the Jap's legs. As Ben scrambled to his feet above the shrieking, flopping enemy soldier, a shot came from someplace—he never knew where—and tore a piece of meat off the tip of his left shoulder. It missed bone and bicep by a fraction of an inch, but the impact and pain sent him reeling. Around him the trail had turned into a muddy trench of men clubbing, grappling, firing. Another American went down, then two Japanese blown away by the buck sergeant's .45 pistol. Carl was kicking at the maniacal mortarman who in a final wild sling hurled the mortar and grabbed for a grenade on his belt. Carl swarmed onto him and the two went down in a pile together, the Jap's arm outstretched and the grenade twitching in his hand as he tried to dislodge its pin. Wound and all, Ben flung himself, desperately pinning down the struggling arm, his blood dripping over the tangle of the three of them, until Carl clambered astraddle of the enemy soldier and with no other weapon at hand beat the man to death with his helmet.

"WHAT'S THIS, THE poor man's Hemingway green around the gills?" Dex's tone turned unmistakably medical and concerned. "Something wrong with you?"

Trying not to let the effort show, Ben forced himself back to the task that had brought him to Seeley Lake.

"Sick of what we're all going through, isn't that enough?" he evaded with another modification of truth. He had led the camp director to believe Dex's decision not to fight could be read between the lines of whatever he wrote about the smoke-jumper camp; try as he might, people would need something stronger than Dex's microscope to find anything of the sort, Tepee Weepy would see to that. He had told poor Jones before leaving him to the dogs that he was going into Helena to spend the day covering a war bonds bingo marathon; half an hour had taken care of it, then he'd headed here. *Big day for the one-man liar's club.* He was starting to feel like he needed a bath. Something had to be said, and he put all he could into it:

"Dex? Guess what, it's your turn to be written about and I'm up against it."

"I thought so." The well-bred Cariston face smiled the slightest bit. "Isn't there a saying from one of your movie moguls, 'Include me out?'"

Ben brought the TPWP patch on his arm around under Dex's nose. "The outfit I'm assigned to believes in all or none, and they're not interested in none."

"Can't they count better than that? I'm only one man out of eleven and—"

"Nine, now. Counting Vic."

Dex winced. "Ben, all right, I am the only one without his rump on the firing line somewhere." He eyed his listener speculatively. "Even yours on occasion, if I don't miss my guess. You have the look of someone who wants 'at them.'"

I've been at them. They've been at me. My shoulder hurts, thinking about it. "Let's don't argue about each other's reasons, Dex. Pearl Harbor and Hitler invading everyplace are signs enough to me they're out to get us, and I don't like being got."

"Granted. But I believe several million others are 'suited up for democracy'"—Dex took a meaningful look at Ben's flight jacket—"to forestall that. There will never be a shortage of people to fight wars, will there. Would the eleven of us be missed if it wasn't for this mysterious menagerie you write for?" He arched his head to one side as if a thought had just come to him. Ben was remembering the time Dex had stopped football practice cold by asking Bruno why football-field lines always were laid out in skin-eating lime instead of talcum. "Take that further," he was formulating now, "what if all of us together had said no to induction—"

"You'd have had to hog-tie Animal."

"—and instead—"

"And coldcocked Stamper and Danzer because they wouldn't get to show off at parades."

"—shut up a minute, will you; and volunteered for something like this outfit instead? The team that followed its conscience away from war instead of toward it." Dex's gaze at him had grown as intense as it could get. "You're the writer, Ben, what's wrong with a story like that?"

"You want my two-bits' worth? First, we wouldn't be known as the famous Golden Eagles of '41 anymore, we'd be called the Golden Chickens. Maybe that'd be a relief, I don't know."

"Not necessarily," Dex put in caustically. "There's still a reputation attached. When we hitchhike to town from here, the local yokels try to run over us." Somewhere overhead the Ford Tri-Motor droned around and around, no doubt dropping little weighted windage test chutes. Dex glanced up. "We even have to watch our step around our Forest Service trainers. Some are okay about us, some aren't."

"I imagine. To answer what you asked, though. If the rest of us pleaded conscientious"—he tried to glide nicely over the *conchie* sound in that—"alongside you, I figure we'd all add up to a footnote in some philosophy book someday. A one-paragraph kiss on the cheek from Bertrand Russell, tops. One thing sure, the United States military wouldn't be demanding a piece on you peachy-keen gridiron heroes from me every month."

"We're nothing but trophies, you're saying."

"No, on top of that you're a friend and a pain in the ass." Ben checked his wristwatch and made a face. "Dex, listen, I only came here because I have to know. This is it for you?" He swept a hand around at the camp. "For good?"

The uncommon furrow across Dex's brow showed he took that as an affront. Before he could say anything, Ben spelled out:

"For the duration. For however long this damned war takes. If there's any chance you're going to change your mind, get tired of people trying to run you over and decide to waltz off into a medical deferment from a friendly doctor your family might happen to be acquainted with"—he locked eyes with Dex and kept them there—"I need to know now. If I wiggle hard, I could skip writing about you maybe a month or two yet." He paused. "What I can't do, you better understand, is some piece that out-right says you're a conscientious objector. They'd throw that away so fast it'd set the wastebasket on fire." Ben shifted from one foot to the other, as if adding body English to what he was about to say. "But I'm not the only scribbler in existence, Dex. If that's the story you want out, you could put it out yourself. The *Chicago Tribune* loves anything that shows up Roosevelt and his crowd. Or go the other direction, the parson who runs this place likely would have some ideas about how to show you off to the world as pacifist Exhibit A."

"Don't think he hasn't brought it up." Now Dex was the one who looked anguished. "You want to know if I'm here until the last shot is fired. All I can tell you is, I made the hardest choice of my life to be here and I *am* here. Believe me, I've lost sleep over it. Most nights." Ben read his face in a way he had never had to before; Dex was not the confessing sort. "You aren't able to write the plain truth about me," he could hear the cost in the words, "and I don't dare make it known either. One guess why, Ben. Cariston Enterprises. I have two brothers-in-law in the war. I'm the direct heir, but there'll be a family fight for control, down the line. The gaffer"—Ben wondered just how much wealth one had to grow up with to call one's father that—"is backing me, so far. But he doesn't want it shouted around that the last male Cariston refuses to shoulder arms for his country." Dex broke off, offering a bleak smile. "There. Secrets of the rich."

"One size fits everybody," Ben said thinly.

"So, you have to hide me in plain sight." The idea seemed to intrigue Dex. "I'll be interested to see what you come up with."

So will I, Dex, so will I. Before turning to go, there was one more thing he had to tend to. "I'll bet an outfit like the Forest Service would have a jerry can of gas they could loan to a man. Particularly if they didn't know about it."

"Stuck your neck out to get here, did you?"

"Only about a hundred miles."

Dex clapped him on the shoulder. "Come on, there's a back door to the fuel shed."

THE NEXT DAY, his conscience objecting every word of the way, he wrote Dexter Cariston into undesignated war duty, a medic repairing men who parachuted into fields of fire, the type of fire not specified.

5

⭐ *You're hard to keep up with, Ben. First time I've ever been on a date on an obstacle course.* The painted stones spelled the way down the steep sidehill, the enormous lettering ghost-white in the bunchgrass. "I've flown over this rockpile a hundred times," Cass said over her shoulder, trying to watch her footing on the path pocked with gopher holes, "and always wondered, What goofball did this?" She and Ben were in civilian clothes, gabardine slacks that cheatgrass and other pestiferous plants theoretically could not penetrate, and good warm canvasback jackets, and battered fedora and granny scarf which they teased each other looked like missionary throwaways. He carried the heavy picnic basket and she had the blanket over one arm.

Shaking his head at the countless chunks of sandstone amassed and laid out side by side into a blocky 5 and 7, Ben answered: "A pickle salesman with time on his hands." Together the numbers took up what looked like half an acre of hillside, sitting prominent enough on the prow of the butte that the dubious eminence of Hill 57 could be read from several miles off. "One guess on how many varieties the guy peddled."

She laughed and skidded a little at the same time.

"Hey, careful," he chided. "I don't want to have to pick you out of somebody's junkyard down there."

"It's your fault, Romeo. I'm usually in a cockpit when I'm up this high."

The view of Great Falls stretched below them, the squarely laid-out city with the renegade river winding through where it pleased, the smelter stack like a monstrous chess piece at the farthest city limits, the university cozy amid its groves of trees at the closer edge of the street grid, and nearest of all, the stadium cuddled at the base of the butte across the way, with game-day flags flapping brightly in the breeze. "How do you like Homecoming so far?" he asked with a solicitous grin as he gave her a hand around a patch of prickly pear cactus.

"My hunch is, it'll never replace poker." Cass stopped short, staring ahead. "Ben?" she murmured. "Are you sure this is such a hot idea?"

"Let's find out what our hosts think about it."

There were twenty or so of the Hill 57 residents on hand as spectators, mostly ragged-looking men but a couple of families with kids in charity clothes, all sitting with their backs against the pale curve of rocks that made the bottom of the 5 and now all looking over their shoulders at two unexpected visitors. Ben tried to read the line of Indian faces, but the scatter of rough-built shacks and even more miserable lean-to shanties farther down the hill said enough; tar paper and gabardine would never meet comfortably. He clutched Cass by a tense elbow and they stood waiting a minute. Finally a chesty man at the near end of the group lurched to his feet and faced up the slope toward them. Tottering alcoholically or arthritically or both, he rumbled out: "You folks a little lost?"

"We came to watch the game, if you wouldn't mind some company," Ben called back. He gestured toward the stadium in the middle distance. "I played football with Victor Rennie, down there. Then we went in the service together."

"Are you that Ben friend of his?" The tone had changed markedly. "From up the country, at Gros Ventre? Vic talked about you plenty. Come on down." As they approached, the big-chested man swept a hand around the tan grass-covered slope. "Grab some ground. Want a Shellac?" A case of Great Falls Select beer sat open and obviously in use.

"The lady prefers whiskey." Ben tapped the lid of the picnic basket.

"Smart lady."

Wasting no time, Cass moved off to spread the blanket in a snug spot against the rocks and wink at the shy kids clustering in curiosity. Ben took the chance to steal a look around. The site was right. From up here, the bowl of the stadium was a green swatch amid the prevailing gold and silver of the Homecoming crowd; the band members at midfield blaring out the TSU fight song were the size of toothpicks and faceless, as he and Cass would be to anyone bored enough with football to gaze up here at the denizens of Hill 57. He could relax about that, but he felt keyed up every other way possible. *Game day. Weren't they all, one way or another, with that bastard Bruno?* The other paint-marked sidehill stood almost directly across from him, steeply rising out of the broad coulee where the facing buttes drew back to let the wind into Great Falls: the Letter Hill. He could not take his eyes off the chalky stone insignia there, the broad splay of the T, the coil of the S gripping its stem, the hanging swoop of the U. Every book on scriptwriting warned against the seductions of the sweeping overhead shot—Sam Goldwyn supposedly said that anyone who wanted to spend his money to go that high to look down ought to take the free elevator at the Empire State Building—but the conjured scene coaxed insistently into Ben's movie eye: a long line of figures in football uniforms, strung out on the trail up the Letter Hill as haphazardly as a caravan in distress, toiling toward the interlinked letters high above. Fade to dusk, and one lone runner still struggling against gravity.

The sound effects were not of his choosing. "Treasure State University is proud to welcome its special guests to Homecoming, 1943!" The announcer's voice on the stadium public address system sounded tinny and spectral as his spiel wafted up Hill 57. The Governor, the Senator, the alumni president—ritual tributes echoing from two years back. Ben's mind fastened on the thought of the team then waiting in the maw of that stadium tunnel to trot onto the field, Vic on two good legs, Havel and O'Fallon with breath and soul still in them, Dex and Jake smacking one another on their shoulder pads in jolly superstition, he himself fresh as a colt, the entire eleven of them magically unacquainted with defeat.

He wrenched himself back to present surroundings. Not far down the junk-cluttered slope of Hill 57 stood one shack that appeared more dilapidated than the others, if that was possible. Glancing toward it, he asked their Indian host in a low tone: "Whatever became of Vic's aunt? I keep trying to catch up with her, but she's never home."

"You mean Agnes? Went back to the reservation to mooch a while, last we knew. Got a daughter there."

"If you see her, would you tell her—" Ben broke off. Tell her what? Say he had been pointed to her by an old hunter, nearly as elusive as herself, who despised her and her drinking ways? Pass word to her that he could not get Vic, in despond somewhere in England, to answer his letters? *I'm afraid you were right when you said "That's that," Toussaint.* "Just say I have a mailing address for Vic I can bring her."

The chesty man lifted his shoulders. "If you want. She don't much know how to read, though."

Cass impatiently was motioning that she required the picnic basket. Ben went over. No sooner had he set it down than she reached in and began handing around opera glasses. "I want these back, lords and ladies." In no time the Indian kids were in fits of giggles as they peeked at one another through the wrong end of the lenses, and by kickoff time their elders were dividing their time between beer and binoculars.

Settled onto the blanket beside Cass, Ben nudged her. "I wondered why that basket was so hellishly heavy."

"Might as well get some benefit from having to make nice to the damn USO at the Civic Center, I figured. The Gilbert and Sullivan bunch won't miss these until tonight." She checked to make sure all other eyes were on the football game, then leaned against him and kissed his ear. "I was starting to get lonesome. What were you doing so long with our buddy over there, negotiating a treaty?"

"Just agreeing that Custer had it coming." The petite binoculars nearly lost in his hand, he watched a Treasure State pass fall flat against the Colorado team. It looked like a long game; he nestled closer to Cass. "I forgot to ask. Do you even like football?"

"I like a certain football guy."

Ben smiled; that was good enough. Among women of his acquaintance only his mother evinced understanding of the contrary grace he'd found in playing the rough-and-tumble sport. "I can hardly ever say so, but you take after me in that, Ben. I loved that same feeling in ballet lessons"—girlhood in Beverly Hills had its advantages—"it stays with you, the right muscles still know the rules. Even square dancing with your father."

Cass was scrabbling in the picnic basket. "Here, Jim Thorpe, have a sandwich. There's Spam or Spam."

"Yum."

"I know, but it's the best I could do." They munched on the

manufactured meat and had nips of scotch as the game went along. Cass scanned elsewhere half the time, often to the planes taking off from East Base in the distance, but Ben was not really conscious of that, lost in his private tunnel of vision back to the scrimmage where everything began in the season of 1941.

THE PLAY WAS whistled dead before the ball could be snapped, the shrill echo in the empty stadium halting the practice game sooner than usual, and varsity and second-stringers alike uncoiled from their stances reluctantly.

Animal Angelides spat toward the sideline. "Here it comes. Why the hell can't he stay over there playing pocket pool with Loudon instead of frying our nuts?"

The other interior linemen groaned along with him and Ben at left end held in his own with effort. He watched with the others as their coach and chief tormenter came striding onto the field as if he personally owned Treasure State stadium. In his camel-hair topcoat and snap-brim hat Lionel Bruno could strut standing still, so when he added some swagger to it as he did now, he was practically parting the grass like the Red Sea. It was times like this when Ben wished he had been elected, say, water boy instead of team captain.

Hastily he checked over his shoulder to see how the backfield was taking this development. Moxie Stamper smirked unmercifully behind his quarterback privileges, about as expected. At the left halfback position, Vic sent Ben a private look as if he couldn't believe what was happening to this season either. At right half, Dex was coldly watching the coach's progress onto the field. Bulking between the pair of them, Jake had yanked his helmet off and stood tapping it in agitation against his thigh pads.

As if scripted, Bruno marched straight to the football. He plucked it off the ground and walked back and forth through the players, holding the ball in front of their faces as if all twenty-two

of them were nearsighted morons. Ben couldn't even guess which
speech it was going to be this time, there were so many.

"If the bunch of you would pull your heads out of your butts,"
the coach started in on them, "and put aside the lesser things of
life to concentrate on the basic game of football—"

Oh oh, that one.

"—then you just possibly *might* have the makings of a genuine team." At the word *might*, Bruno squeezed the ball so hard
it threatened to pop. "Forget nights on the town. Forget dessert and the cigarette after. Forget about trying to get into your
girlfriend's pants," he preached with rising intensity. "This"—he
brandished the football higher—"this is the one and only object
of your desire from this moment forward, people. You have to
want this ball. You have to lust for this ball. You have to *love*
getting this ball and handling it as if you are the only ones on
the face of God's green sod it is entrusted to." Pausing for emphasis or maybe it was breath, Bruno nursed his disgust in front
of them for all it was worth.

There was more than one audience for this. Ben risked a
glance toward the near sideline where Ted Loudon, Bruno's pet
sportswriter and nobody else's, was taking in the coach's every
word hungrily. *Why? He'll keep making up whatever he wants
to about "the team that can't find itself" anyway.* Loudon even
trigged himself up in camel-colored topcoat and snap-brim hat
in imitation of Bruno but fell short as a fashion plate due to
newspaper pay.

"Listen up, people," the coach intoned, as if they had any
other choice, "do you know what you want to be as a team? Slick.
Operating together smooth as shit through a goose. I want team-
work from you so slick the sissies across from you won't be able
to see straight, you hear me?"

Nearest across the scrimmage line from Ben, Purcell uncomfortably did. The lanky sophomore was blushing red-hot at the

coach's choice of language. *Where the hell was he raised, in a Sunday school?* A walk-on from six-man nowhere, Merle Purcell had been turning pink since the first day of practice when he stepped into the locker room wearing a droopy high school sweater that showed he had lettered in football, basketball, and track. Instantly he became known as *the three-letter man* and crude suggestions were made as to what those letters stood for. He wasn't necessarily hazed any harder than any other sophomore scrub, but on him it seemed to stick. On the field the freakish kid could outrun anything said about him—Ben, who was quick, comprehended the cosmic difference between that and fast—yet when he wasn't in motion he lapsed into a sitting duck. Purcell was a handful in more ways than one, but right then Ben had everyone else on the squad to worry about.

Bruno paused again, then resumed like a thunderclap:

"There is not, I repeat, *not* an opponent on the schedule that the Treasure State University Golden Eagles of nineteen hundred and forty-one can't beat the living piss out of, if you will merely play this game my way. *If!* Do you hear that word? *I-F!* And now that I have your attention, may I point out to you something there is no goddamn *if* about. It is one week from today to the season opener. *One week!* That gives you seven days to pull together into a team that devotes itself heart, soul, and fart hole to this ball."

Now—Hollywood could not have cued him better, Ben had to admit—the coach put the football down gently as an egg. By then varsity and second-stringers alike knew Animal indeed was prophetic, here it came. "People?" the coach addressed them as if dubious about that. "To help you concentrate on the loving care of this miraculous object, you are now playing under the Golden Rule."

Despair followed those words like jackal tracks behind a caravan. The only thing biblical about Bruno's Golden Rule was that

it was blunt-edged and carried the whiff of Hell. The dreaded
maxim was actually a catchall for his wrathful coaching can-
ons—no fumbling the football, no missing a tackle, no messing
up a play, no time-outs to fix shoulder pads, no anything else
that could conceivably offend the exacting eye on the sideline—
but what sane person in a football uniform was going to stand
out there arguing singular and plural with the gridiron lord and
master?

Not Ben, not quite yet. *Not in front of everybody. He'd run
the legs off all of us up to those big white sons of bitches just to
show me.*

His involuntary glance toward the butte looming out there
beyond the end zone stands was not the only one. The Letter Hill
was roundly hated. Of all Bruno's raging innovations this year,
trickier drills, tougher calisthentics, full-length slam-bang practice games that pitted the varsity against the scrub team twice a
week, the punishment runs up to those pale letters halfway into
the sky were the hardest to take. Penalty laps around the field
were a custom as old as football cleats, but nobody had signed on
to clamber up a junior mountainside any time a volcanic coach
blew off steam. Dex would be his bet, for the first to shove the
Golden Rule in Bruno's face and walk off the team, followed immediately by Animal and Jake. Today could be the day. Even the
Butte hard case at left guard, Kenny O'Fallon, looked mutinous.
Sig Prokosch, the other guard, built like an engine block and
usually as imperturbable, showed similar signs. Stan Havel would
stay; hiking the ball was the one thing he was fluent at. Moxie
Stamper and Nick Danzer were Bruno's cubs, they couldn't be
driven off this field by any means known to mankind. Carl Friessen could tip either way, easygoing but with a razor streak of sen-
sibility underneath. Ben himself—*God damn it, this isn't football,
it's Russian roulette.*

Still looking supremely disgusted at what he had to work with, the coach gathered himself to go. "All right, Stamper"—another mark of Bruno was that he did not acknowledge the existence of first names—"show us something that resembles football."

Instantly Moxie yapped at the varsity, "You heard the man, huddle up, everybody get your ass in gear." In his ornery pirate-captain style as quarterback, he had in his favor a quick slinging way of passing that made it hard for the defense to see the ball coming. On the first play now, he hit the right end, Danzer, with a screen pass for ten yards. Right away he caught the scrubs by surprise with the same play again, good for a dozen yards this time. The second-stringers, no slouches, did not like being patsies on such calls and Danzer didn't help the matter any. Physically flawless as a swan, the lithe receiver preened past them with an exceedingly leisurely trot back to the huddle. Ben by contrast, with no action on his side of the field but to block the daylights out of Purcell, was starting to feel like a paying spectator; his hands itched for the ball but he couldn't argue with first downs.

It did seem to cross Moxie's mind tangentially that there were others in the backfield besides him, and on the next play he handed off to Jake for four yards up the middle. Then, though, like a roulette player repeating his bet on one lucky number, he called yet another screen pass to Danzer.

"Christ, Mox, again?" Animal panted. "What the hell you trying to prove?" The tackle, guard, and center had to check-block on the play, then muscle their way downfield to form a blocking wedge in front of the pass receiver; this meant Animal, Sig, and Stan were pulling double-duty on every one of these right-side trick plays. "Is Danzer the only guy who gets to handle the precious little old ball besides you?"

"I'll do the play calling, Angelides, you just do the blocking," Moxie snapped. Ben could feel the tightening circle of tension in the huddle. Stamper and Danzer were the only ones on the team who weren't fed up with the Stamper-to-Danzer aerial circus in these practice games. But he couldn't say anything without looking like he wanted more catches for himself. Which was true enough.

Animal muttered something to Sig and Stan as they left the huddle. When Moxie took the snap, all three blocked no harder than feather pillows and scrambled on through, leaving the line of scrimmage wide open. Barely did Moxie have the football in his hands before he was smothered under a gleeful avalanche of scrub-team players. Interestingly, the whistle on the sideline stayed silent over this, and Animal sent Ben a wink of triumph. Moxie got up slowly, wiping at a trickle of blood out the corner of his mouth and glowering at the right-side linemen as everyone shambled into the huddle. But this time the play he called was "Reinking, left-side slant pattern long."

Precise as the moment the center snapped the ball to Moxie, Ben feinted and broke free as though catapulted. The exhilaration of momentum took him over, the field flying under him so instinctively sure that he knew to the instant when to veer past the scrambling pass defender, and at top speed aim himself to the unknowable but sure spot where he and the airborne ball would intersect. He looked back only then, the looping pass coming to him as if in a recurrent dream, from backyard lobs by a bespectacled father when he was ten to the Gros Ventre high school field's skyful of leather pluckings to this supreme stadium's ordination of sure-handed catches, another one now. How miraculous it always seemed, then and when the war trained him into the beginnings of a pilot, the grace of gravity that kept a propelled object aloft; the substantiality of air that some first human eye surely mused on with lasting wonder at a leaf floating by. It all gathered into him, half-known half-sensed, with the conclusive feel of the ball finding the skin of his hands. The pass secured, he raced final yards and was in the end zone.

Still whooping after that and the extra point, the eleven of them lined up across the green field to kick off to the scrub team. And in that permanent moment, time previous going to shadow and all else now lit from what they were about to become, Vic boomed the kick high and far, and the Treasure State University varsity raced down the field.

By chance the kickoff sailed to Purcell, and everyone bayed a warning and went into high gear to head him off. Vic himself managed to nail the scrub-team speed demon at about the thirty-yard line, and they all exhaled in relief.

Eyes downcast as the second-stringers broke their huddle and flooded to the line of scrimmage, Purcell lined up opposite Ben. As ever, Ben felt like he was looking across at wasted evolution. Reedy, long-limbed, big-eyed, Purcell resembled some creature Nature shaped for speed but forgot to give fang or claw. Bred to flee, but not to block and tackle in the flatten-'em-into-the-ground manner preached by Bruno. No coach could resist that tantalizing speed entirely, so he stuck Purcell in at right end on the scrub team. Until the varsity wised up in a hurry, the wispy speedster caught a few passes in the open and gained so much yardage it began to look like mileage. But from the very first pass that the kid juggled and dropped, Ben divined what was going to be Purcell's problem: he heard footsteps. When a defender closed in on him, Purcell would flinch—maybe infinitesimally, but that was enough. It was a matter of guts: the one necessary requirement for an end was to hang in there and catch the ball first, however much of a hit was coming at you. Anybody, Ben included, could look at Purcell's leggy insubstantial build and sympathize, but sympathy couldn't make up for a leak in fortitude.

True to form, Purcell flitted all over the field on the next series of downs, but the scrub quarterback played it safe and let his backs pack the ball. Ultimately the scrubs had to punt and managed to contain Dex on the runback. Moxie was impatiently ragging the varsity into the huddle when the whistle blast from the sideline cut in.

Now what? As startled as everyone else on the field, Ben swung a look toward where the coach was standing. Bruno kept to game conditions when the Golden Rule was in force, and that meant no substitution except for injury. But as they watched, Purcell was imperiously waved in to the sideline by the coach. Bruno jawed hard at him for a minute, Loudon hovering right there lapping it up. For the life of him, Ben was unable to understand why Bruno constantly went so rough on the sophomore. That speed of his alone qualified as true talent. Why wasn't the kid being brought along with encouragement, as Ben and Danzer had been before Bruno ever entered the scene, to groom him for one of their positions after the only thing left for them to catch was their diplomas? *What is this, pound him into the ground to make him grow? What if he shrinks instead?*

At last Purcell, head down, jogged back onto the field and crossed the scrimmage line to the varsity huddle.

Puzzled, Moxie watched him approach. "Look who's here from Cow Pie High. You trying to set a record for being farthest offside, Purcell?"

"Coach sent me in for Danzer," Purcell reported bashfully.

"The hell you say." The quarterback's face clouded. As Ben read them, though, most other faces in the huddle showed no dismay.

"I could use a rest," Danzer said languidly if unconvincingly and sloped off to the sideline.

"Let's get to business," Moxie snapped out. "Our fancy sub on a fly pattern." Purcell's Adam's apple bobbed for everyone to see, but he looked determined as he took his stance at right end.

On this pass play to the other side of the field Ben was to knock the defensive end opposite him off balance, which he thriftily did, then Carl Friessen rotated onto the man, springing Ben loose into the secondary to block as needed when the catch was made. From the corner of his eye he saw Purcell already was twenty yards downfield. The kid did travel like a flash.

Moxie's pass was one of his patented flings, not that much on it but it somehow sailed and sailed to give the receiver time to get under it. Almost. Purcell not only got there but had to pull up a bit and, off balance from broken momentum, he juggled the catch, the ball bouncing on and off his fingertips, those phantom footsteps distracting him just enough. Racing toward him from the opposite direction Moran, an ambitious scrub, snatched the ball before it could settle into Purcell's hands and lit out up the sideline for the end zone seventy yards distant, the entire TSU varsity strung out behind him like barnyard puppies trying to catch up with a coyote.

If Bruno whistled the play dead, no one heard it. But before everyone had even stopped running, the coach had stormed the middle of the field, his jowly head swinging back and forth as if trying to clear away what he had just witnessed.

Unexpectedly, when he spoke there was clemency for some. "Second-string, head for the showers, you at least have earned it." Then, though, he turned ominously to the varsity.

"The passing game, people, only works if the receiver hangs on to the ball." Bruno was enunciating now like a coroner giving a tutorial. "Can you grasp that, Purcell? Along with the football, perhaps? Purcell, I did not hear your answer."

"Yup, Coach, I—I'll do better."

"You will also do the Hill," Bruno decreed, "you heard me invoke the Golden Rule. In the meantime, get your dropsy butt over there to the bench and wait for me. The rest of you," the coach swept a hand as if to get them out of his sight, "head for the locker room and while you're there, see if by any chance you can talk each other into playing some actual football next week. *Seven days,* people!" he flung over his shoulder as he stalked toward the sideline.

The team, half of whom had flubbed chances to teeter Moran out of bounds, stood rooted in surprise that Purcell was the only victim among them, Ben more caught by it than any. Then and there, he gave up on waiting for the right moment, there did not seem to be such a thing around Bruno. Of course Loudon had been absolutely sopping all this up on the sideline. *Just what we need, a slobbering columnist spending the next week ranting about the sputtering TSU football machine and its noble mechanic of a coach trying desperately to fix it.* Sportswriter be damned, Bruno and his Letter Hill had to be dealt with somehow, the faces of the team were saying as much to Ben.

Four-fifths of them, rather. Already jogging to the locker room, Moxie Stamper looked piously murderous, while Purcell, the object of that, went slinking off the field in the opposite direction. The other eight teammates hung on around Ben. "Purcell got the shaft on that," Carl Friessen stated the case from the linemen. "Could have been any of us on any old thing."

"Moxie underthrew that pass," Vic said quietly.

"Maybe not by accident," Dex fitted on to that.

Jake and Animal were not saying anything, worse than if they had.

"All right, I know. I'll try my goddamnedest to make Bruno hear us on this," Ben promised. "But I want to do it out of range of Loudmouth."

"That'd be good." Sig Prokosch seldom spoke up, so when he did everyone pointed an ear. "Coach has got his hand up Loudon's butt, he operates him like a puppet."

All around Ben the expressions moodily backed up that assessment. "I'll be a while, guys." Everyone else filed off the field, and he trudged over to speak with the gesticulating coach in one-sided conversation with Loudon.

"Off the record for now, Ted, but what does it take? You heard me lay into the entire bunch of them to shape up or else and look what—" Bruno broke off his grousing to the sportswriter when he became aware of Ben approaching. Up close, the coach was thickset and biscuit-faced, but there was always that slick hat and concealing coat. Now he brushed a dark speck, probably a gift of the smelter stack, off a camel-hair sleeve and looked up, farther than he seemed to want to, at the taller younger man. "Look who's honoring us with his presence. Reinking, I was just discussing the mob you are unlucky enough to be the captain of. Can't you do anything to jack them up?"

"I need to talk to you about some of that, Coach." Ben glanced at Loudon and stepped away a few paces. "All the way off the record."

"Excuse us, Ted," Bruno adjusted to that in the bat of an eye. "Catch me in my office later." He jerked his head at Ben and strode to the middle of the field, out of earshot of the sideline just in case the sportswriter was slow to withdraw. At the fifty-yard line, the stocky coach halted and gazed around the stadium as if he couldn't get enough of it. "So what's on your mind?" he asked Ben in a narrow tone. "It better have to do with how to win football games."

It did and it didn't. That always seemed to be the case where Purcell was involved. Resolutely Ben indicated to the troublesome figure slumped on the bench waiting for his Letter Hill fate. "It's him. That was his first play on the starting team, remember, and he didn't have any time to settle down. Besides, Moxie didn't get quite enough zip on that ball." He watched the eyes that should have seen that, but the coach yielded nothing. "The guys pretty much think you ought to go easy on Purcell this once."

Bruno's scowl gave off cold. "Is that what they think." He looked at Ben oddly. "I'm surprised at you, sticking up for Purcell. You're a grab-ass buddy of his, are you?"

"Not so as you would notice. The Hill is on everybody's nerves, Coach, we all think you should lay off it now. You've made your point." *And made it and made it.*

"That again." Bruno managed to sound put upon. "Your touching concern for Purcell is misplaced. The dumb damn kid comes out and runs the Hill himself Saturdays and Sundays, you know that."

This was true enough. Gawky Purcell trying to build himself up with a struggling solo run to the base of the letters was a common if sad sight. Ben stuck to the obvious. "That's different from doing it when he's pooped out after sixty minutes of a practice game, and with full pads on."

There still was something strange in Bruno's expression as he faced around to Ben. "You're an interesting case, Reinking." The impression was he could have said vastly more on that score, but that was not what came out: "It's getting late, and I have to deal with a rube three-letter man. You can tell your friends in the locker room they needn't worry about themselves so goddamn much." The coach spun away in a manner that warned off any impulse to follow him. Ben watched his receding back as he stalked toward the gangly figure on the bench, but not needing to see more than that, did his own angry pivot toward the locker room and the task there.

"No go, Purcell's still going to get it," he reported tightly as all the faces in there turned to him. "Maybe not the rest of us from here on out—I think I got through to our esteemed coach that we've had enough of that Hill crap."

In the lateness of the day, everyone showering and clearing out in a hurry, it was not noticed that Purcell never showed up in the locker room.

He was found the next morning almost all the way up the Letter Hill, at the stem of the T. Word raced through the dorms, and instead of breakfast the team went to the locker-room meeting hastily called by Bruno. White-faced, he reported that he had watched Purcell make his run to the base of the letters and head back down, before he himself quit for the day and went to his office. Never dreaming, he vouched, that Purcell would take further punishment on himself and keep running the Hill, evidently time after time, until his heart gave out. The funeral was to be on Wednesday, just three days before the opening game and most of the way across the state, but as though it was the most natural thing in the world, the coach announced the whole team had been named honorary pallbearers and would attend.

And out there in a dried-up homesteader cemetery with tumbleweeds banked against a wire fence, they climbed off the team bus and gathered at the grave, outnumbering Purcell's relatives and townspeople. Ben sensed something as soon as he spotted the metal call-sign initials on the radio microphone at graveside: KOPR, statewide coverage. What unsettled him more was the sight of Ted Loudon instead of a radio newsman stepping to the mike before the funeral service got under way. In a rapid-fire patter he obviously been practicing, Loudon reeled off phrases of pathos: "Not since the sad demise of Notre Dame's George Gipp in the prime of his playing life has football seen a tragedy such as this. . . . Now in the eternal annals of the game, The Gipper is joined by The Ghost Runner, for that is what Merle Purcell's teammates called him for his fleet-footed elusiveness on the gridiron. . . . Every lad of the TSU team is here today to do him honor . . ."

Having grown up around journalistic boilerplate, Ben knew beyond the shadow of a doubt Loudon's same words would show up in tomorrow morning's sports column in virtually every daily paper across Montana. The copper company owned those as well as the statewide radio network. For whatever reason, Purcell was getting a send-off from the powers that be.

Stepping up to the mike, Bruno dramatically cleared his throat and the ears of countless listeners. "We at Treasure State University, and indeed this great state for which it is named," he boomed his words out as if to make sure they reached from border to border, "have suffered a loss before the football season of record has even begun."

Dex and Jake and several others of the team stirred uneasily with Ben at equating a death on the Letter Hill with losing a game played with a ball. Vic, who knew all about treacherous slopes from his daily ascension of Hill 57, listened cold-eyed. Moxie Stamper, in a suit coat and pants that didn't match, was trying to adjust his slack face to the posthumous promotion of Purcell to The Ghost Runner.

The coach of them all swept right on. "But valor can rise from a field of loss. That is the lesson we must take from this tragedy. Merle Purcell was among us for too brief a time on the patch of earth he loved above all other, the football field. What better site, then, to remember him on."

Now Bruno sprang it.

"I have gone to the president of Treasure State University. Mr. and Mrs. Purcell"—he inclined his head solemnly their direction; it proved to be the first of pauses emphatic as bullets—"are to be our honored guests at every game, home and away. As shall Merle, present in spirit. In our commemoration of the undying valor of giving his life for the sport he sought to excel at. There will be eleven men on the field each Saturday, but by the presence of his memory among us, he will be there too. I ask every member of the Treasure State team in their endeavors on the field, and all TSU alumni and supporters in your cheers in the stands and beside your radios, to dedicate this season to Merle Purcell, our twelfth man!"

Notepad pages flipping, Ted Loudon was writing it all down like a mad monk.

Afterward, Ben could look back and see the team had been trapped. By the trappings draped all over TSU home games from then on, if nothing else. The stadium-shaking stomping roars of "*Merrrle!*" led by the student section as Twelfth Man pennants flew in their hands. Purcell's awkwardly dressed-up parents unmissable in the guest seats of honor. While up there in the KOPR booth, inflated to sportscaster by the heady vapors given off by his prose back there at graveside and the days of headlines after, Loudon rattled on about the uncanny inspiration driving the team to destiny.

Did the eleven of them buy into it? Not fundamentally. But there is always a *but*. Among themselves they tried not to feel the pull of the so-called season of the Twelfth Man, seized upon by Bruno and Loudon and their helper bosses to make a football saint out of a yokel kid who blew a gasket on his heart doing something he shouldn't have. There were times in the huddle when Moxie, having had to motion the crowd to settle down so his signals could be heard, would crack something like "Never knew Purcell had lung power like that" and draw cynical laughs. Yet as the victories piled up, something unaccountable had to be credited. Even Ben, their elected skeptic, could feel it. They all, every one of them, were playing every minute as if their lives depended on it. This season was like no other; it was that simple and that complicated. They could try to ignore each weeklong buildup of expectation or joke past the game-day din all they wanted, but Purcell's fate up there on the hill over them sobered their talent to a certain purity. Death was death, no matter how you cut it. Ben did not quite have the words for it yet, but somewhere deep he came to understand that for these inexplicably singled-out young men he was among, one short of a dozen, what had happened to that remindful twelfth man was like an

alarm clock going off murderously early in someone's room next
to yours.

"Hey." Long thoughts left him at halftime as Cass passed
the scotch bottle back and forth under his nose like smelling
salts. "Better revive yourself, your team could stand a shot of
something, too."

"Nothing a wholesale bunch of touchdowns couldn't cure."
He'd have felt better about the shellacking TSU was taking if
Bruno still were the coach. Naturally the bastard had parlayed
the '41 season into the job at a California football powerhouse.
Scum always rises.

A covey of waist-high Indian boys blasted past, tussling and
trying to tackle one another. Ben glanced down the line of white-
rock seating to see how his and Cass's welcome was holding out.
Opera glasses clapped to their eyes—somewhat unevenly in the
case of the most serious beer drinkers—the Hill 57 grownups were
engrossed in the gyrations of the marching band and the cheer-
leaders. He did justice to the scotch and passed it back to Cass.

She had been watching him. "Old times getting you down?"

At her words, emotions rose up in him like contending crea-
tures and the nearest one won out. He slipped a hand to the back
of her slacks. "New times don't have that problem. You want to
see the rest of this travesty of football?"

"Gee, do I have a better offer?"

"Not much of a game, I hear. Ain't civilization declined since
we hung up our jockstraps? Whup, I saw that, don't wear yourself out reaching for your dough—this round's on me. Here's to
bolshoya semnadtsi." Jake tapped the first Officers' Club bottle of
beer of the night against Ben's and swigged enthusiastically.

Ben didn't lift his. "Call me suspicious, but I don't drink to
anything I can't savvy."

"Where's your linguistic skills, Benjamin? It's Russian for 'big seventeens.' Uncle Joe's gang in Fairbanks goes around yakking that every time we hand over those nice shiny new bombers to them." Beer in hand, he leaned back like a Murphy bed going up and angled a look across at Ben. "There, now that I've educated you, how's the war treating you these days?"

"Same as usual. Dodging bullets from the teleprinter."

"I've got the cure for that." Jake could hardly wait to get it out. "Whyn't you come along on the Alaska hop tomorrow? See what a real airplane is like instead of those puddle jumpers you flew."

Surprised enough that he didn't trust his tongue—*Do you actually sit up nights thinking of ways to complicate my life?*—Ben waited a bit to respond. "I thought the ATC drill is you always fly with a full crew, no hitchhikers."

"Yeah, well, my bombardier has had enough practice at not pulling the trigger on trapper cabins. Fact is, he feels like he's coming down with three-day flu. Twenty bucks' worth. I figured you could take it out of petty cash from that oddball outfit you work for."

"Short notice, Ice, I'll need to get busy and run this past Grady—"

"—who like a sane general thinks this is the perfect chance to grab off some long overdue notice for his star B-17 coolie, the modest but capable Lieutenant Eisman. I already cleared it with him. C'mon, Ben, Dex got his rah-rah for slapping splints on guys somegoddamnwhere. Moxie gets his for shooting off ack-ack in some English cow pasture. How about mine, what're you waiting for?"

HE HAD TO RESIST yanking his feet off the floor of the Plexiglas nose cone as the bomber shuddered across acres of unforgiving concrete in what seemed to be a never-ending takeoff. Then, like

an elevator going up, the B-17 Flying Fortress lifted, turned its
tail to the smelter stack, and began the long climb north.

Beneath and on all sides of him, old known earth mapped
itself on the underside of the plastic shell where he huddled
in fascinated suspension. Wheatfields winter-sown and fallow
stretched below like checkered linoleum laid to the wall of the
Rockies. There to the west he could pick out the long straight
brink of Roman Reef and its dusky cliff, and the snake line of
watercourse that would be English Creek. Gros Ventre, though,
held itself out of sight beneath its cover of trees. The four big
engines drummed loud enough he regretted he had not brought
earplugs. However, that would have denied him the company of
Jake and the crew via the earphones.

"Everybody copacetic? Navigator, the fake bomb jockey still
with us? Make sure he doesn't touch anything that can go off."

"I'll slap his hands, skipper."

Ben was pretty sure they were kidding. On the other hand,
twin half-inch guns poked up from the cheeks of the plane just
on the other side of the plastic from him and he made a hurried
inventory of switches not to bump.

Jake got back to business. "Sparks, how's that weather by
now?"

"Clear at Edmonton. It starts to heavy up after that. Cumulo-
nimbus to thirty thousand, the whole ball of horseshit."

"Hear that, Ben? Arranged a ceiling flight for you."

Christ and a bear, that's seven miles up in one of these things.
"Just don't drop me, Lieutenant Eisman."

"Haven't lost a scribbler yet."

Soon the Sweetgrass Hills crouched beneath the plane, their
three ancient summits the only sentinel points in uncountable
miles of prairie. For a fleeting moment aligned with the bomb-
aiming panel of Plexiglas directly in front of Ben, Devil's Chimney looked like the front sight of a rifle zeroed in. He thought

back to Toussaint Rennie and hoped a dressed-out elk was hanging in that windsprung barn on the Two Medicine. Scanning the passing geography and jotting frantically, crystals of detail for the Tepee Weepy piece, snatches to write to Vic, his thinking as ever quickened with the vantage point of defied gravity. *Maybe I was meant for thin air. Or is that birdbrain logic?* Either way, he had the giddy feeling of being on top of it all. The colossal modern warp of time claimed everywhere below him; only a man's puny lifetime ago, the swiftest things on this shoulder of the planet were buffalo and Indian ponies. B-17s annihilated every pace of the past and along with it substituted sky for high ground. "Space is the bride of time." Elemental Gaussian physics, weirdly brilliant even back there in the stolid print of the college textbook, the blindered genius Carl Friedrich Gauss sitting in Gottingen unaware of the Napoleonic Wars going on around him while he figured out basics of the universe. The goddamn Germans, too bad they were born with brains.

The intercom broke in. "Friendlies at three o'clock, skipper."

"I see them. Our sisters in arms."

"Not in mine," moaned another voice on the intercom.

Ben reached behind him to the airframe and grabbed binoculars out of their wall pouch. Sleek as the four points of a prong, the formation of Cobras was overtaking them as if the bomber was a lumber wagon. Flying tight and right. He knew, he just knew. Cass in her element.

"BRUISER AT NINE o'clock, Captain, fifteen hundred yards, same heading as ours."

There could not be a better wingman than Beryl. Cass radioed back, "Roger, over. Hold course, everyone, there's plenty of elbow room." *And our route just as much as theirs, now.* She grease-penciled this portion of the Edmonton hop onto the flight plan map strapped to the right thigh of her flying suit; the

Canadian border stood out down there like the edge of a new jig-
saw puzzle, the patterns of its fields contrasting with the American side. Automatically she checked how the rest of her pilots
were doing. The other wingman, Mary Catherine, was hanging
in perfectly, smooth as a mirror reflection. Even Della, bringing
up the rear, matched up with the formation without wandering
today. *Damn. You just get something going good and it starts coming apart.* She was going to hate to lose Beryl if her transfer came
through. Couldn't blame her, wanting in on the Wichita factory
run, closer to her husband. And getting to ferry B-17s like that
one, now that the high brass had decided women of a certain
height and heft could possibly handle the controls of a bomber in
the most wide-open airspace in the country. Cass had to laugh.
There wouldn't be all this half-step stuff if it had been the Wright
sisters at Kitty Hawk.

As THE FLIGHT OF P-39s pulled away to the north, Jake's voice
crackled on the intercom again. "There they go, Grady's Ladies
into the Great Canadian Beyond. You happy now, newspaper
guy?"
    "All God's chillun got the wings they earned, Ice."

FROM EDMONTON on, the flight was a relay race from one bush-
country airstrip to the next, with malicious weather in the way.
Between Watson Lake and Whitehorse, Ben had to abandon the
nose cone; he hated losing the vantage point, but riding there had
become too much like being the hood ornament on a snow tractor. Shaking with chill, he retreated to the table corner offered
by the navigator. Then through the earphones came the further
numbing news that the aircraft's heater had frozen up and quit.
He'd thought it might be a prank back there in sunny Great Falls
when Jake made him put on double layers of long underwear,
three pairs of heavy socks, a fur-lined hooded flying suit over

his flight jacket, and a chamois face mask. The Yukon climate was not impressed. The cold, some perverse apex at this altitude, went through fur, fabric, and skin alike. It seemed possible his blood had turned to slush. He not only couldn't take notes, he could not even make a fist. Time seemed frozen to a standstill. What the hell did Jake want missions over Germany for? This was bad enough. Hunched there helplessly in the refrigerated body of the bomber, he could not get beyond wishing he had something to thaw out with. A blowtorch, maybe. When Ladd Field at Fairbanks at last presented its snowy self, he was hoping the frigid chamois would not take his face off with it.

IN THE WARMING hut that seemed tropical, Jake drew him aside. "So, Benjamin, the transport from Nome doesn't pick us up until morning. How do you want to celebrate the layover?"

"Thawing out."

"Wallflower." Jake delicately fingered a frost-abused ear as if to make sure none of it had dropped off. "Got a little something I better tell you." He took a circumspect look toward the other end of the hut where the rest of the crew was loudly stomping and rubbing warmth into themselves, then leaned in close to Ben and whispered:

"I'm getting Russian tail."

Still numb enough that he was not sure he had heard right, Ben checked the lusty expression on Jake and saw that he had. "Are you." If his enterprising friend had come across some Muscovite hot number in an Alaskan whorehouse, so what? "They owe you some, I guess."

"Yeah, wouldn't the Cossacks just cream their britches?" Jake grinned proudly.

"Who's the unlucky woman?"

"She's a pilot."

Ben stared at him.

"Well, was a pilot. She's missing a few parts—got all the right ones, though. But a couple of fingers." Jake waggled a hand with the last two digits down out of sight. "Those pissant Nazis like to shoot back. Now she's a bug driver."

This, Ben found nearly as stupefying as the pilot part. The runway they had just come in on was pulverized ice, gray banks of chips spewed up by metal grippers in countless plane tires, with furrows that were more like ruts to land into. Buzzing around out there in thirty below, on one of the little tow tractors called bugs, sounded to him like a job for only the hardiest Eskimo. Or a madwoman. Or worse.

"Jake, or should I just say Bonehead—"

"Ben, Ben, hold it down, okay?"

"—get your mind up from between your legs and think about this a little, will you? What the hell are you doing, bucking for a Section Eight? Anybody the Russians trust enough to station here is apt to be a Red, like those big stars on the sides of these planes, remember? And the United States government does not look kindly on the Communist Party."

"What are they going to get me for, consorting with an ally?" Ben's point did cause Jake to reflect. "I wouldn't be surprised if she diddled a commissar or two along the way to get here. She knows her diddling."

"Will you listen a goddamn minute? You and Tractor Woman—"

"Katya. Katya Gyorgovna Zhukova. The Russians really go in for names."

"Jake, we're heading to the mess hall," the copilot called. "You two coming?"

"My scribe and me have got matters of national importance to attend to. You're in charge, Charlie, see you at breakfast."

The copilot gave a wave and was on his way. "What happens when you get famous."

Ben was furiously fumbling out of the last of his layers of flying gear. "Do you have a lick of sense left at all? Maybe you're living on love, but I need chow."

"You're going to get it, don't worry," Jake soothed. "The Russkies have their own mess hall and they like to talk shop with B-17 pilots. C'mon, you're gonna meet Katya."

HE WONDERED IF he was imagining, but the crowded mess hall smelled to him straight off the pages of Dostoyevsky. Cabbage, dank wool clothing, copious boot grease. Feeling as if he was in another world, he spooned up the formidable soup and devoured hunks of bread while Jake alternately ate and banked his hands through the air in testimony to the maneuvering capabilities of B-17s. Across the table, Russian pilots who looked like either plowboys or middle-aged pirates—the generation between had largely been wiped out by the Germans' demonic sieges from Leningrad to Sevastopol—listened monastically. Amid the bulky men, a woman who was not at all what Ben had expected—trim, keen, authoritative; she reminded him alarmingly of Cass— translated Jake's effusions and Russian spatters of questions.

"Yakov, they say, how big bomb pile?"

"Bomb load, right, three tons," Jake made an expansive gesture, "do you have those back home?"

"*Tonna*," Katya reported and translated the tonnage, drawing the first smiles from the Russian airmen.

At first Ben had been relieved to see other American uniforms in the roomful of brown drab, a plump major and a couple of shavetail aides sitting with an ascetic-looking Russian major- domo of some sort. The major proved to be the liaison officer, which meant he was there only under obligation, and in a matter of minutes had sent over the more diminutive of the aides to inquire why they were not in their own mess hall with everyone else. *Awful good question, shorty.* Jake pulled out all the stops, citing Ben as a big-shot correspondent chronicling Lend-Lease and the peerless pilots of both nations. When the underling relayed that, the major gave them an edgy look, but he directly departed and so did the thin-featured political commissar or whatever he was. The entire room sat at attention until the man was out the door. The moment he was gone, Katya relaxed and turned to Ben. "You are from *gazeta*?" Her voice was throaty and adventurous, and in spite of himself he could imagine how smoky it would sound in bedroom circumstances.

"Gazettes of all kinds, right, Ben?" Jake trumpeted. "He's as important in our country as your guys on *Pravda*."

"Thanks all to hell for the comparison," Ben snapped. The Russian airmen were getting to their feet, taking their leave with stiff nods. As the mess hall began to empty out, a contingent dressed like Katya, male and female alike in thick-ply ground crew coveralls, drifted over curiously. She rattled out something and they sat down. *Wonderful, Ice. Now we're the main attractions at the zoo.* Of all there was to worry about in this, he figured he might as well start way up the list. Katya was watching him bright-eyed. "You have the same name as a very famous person," he speculated.

She burst out laughing. "No, no! Marshal Zhukov is not my family. He is great man, we are no ones."

Ben wanted that to be true. Zhukov was the titan of the Eastern Front, reputedly able to stand up even to Stalin's midnight military whims, and with geography on his side he had held out until he could start bleeding the German invaders to a slow death. The glut of war on Soviet soil seemed beyond sane comprehension. Two years now since Hitler made Napoleon's old mistake and turned thousands of miles of Russian snow into the blood of both sides; Ben had access in the correspondents' pool reports to the riveting dispatches of the Red Army frontline daredevil

Vasily Grossman and discerned from Grossman's crafty coverage that survivors of the struggle had been through hell from both the enemy and their fanatic rulers. His eyes slipped to Katya's right hand and the sacrificed fingers. The million-dollar wound, a piece of body exchanged for a grant of existence. Before he could ask her what kind of aircraft she had flown—he had a spooky feeling it was a P-39, but that very well might have been Cass on his mind—Jake interjected. "They use this place as a canteen after it shuts down. Get ready to toast Mother Russia, Benjamin my boy."

Vodka made an immediate appearance. Glasses were splashed full and hoisted in accompaniment to a unison cry of "*Na zdrovya!*" Jake winked across at him. "That much Russian I know. 'Good health,' buddy." Wary from Cass's coma cola elixirs, Ben tested what sat so innocently clear in his glass. It tasted like springwater that had been tampered with by a moonshiner. While the Russians tossed theirs down he took a medium swig and clamped his fist around the glass to hide the fact that he hadn't emptied it. Nonetheless the bottle was making the rounds again and another toast was necessary, this one Jake's "To *bolshoya semnadtsi!*" The Russians banged the table in homage to big bombers and gulped down. Here came the bottle again. *Holy damn, they inhale the stuff.*

Katya leaned toward him as if what she was about to say was vital. "Kheminveh. You have meet in the war?"

The Ernie question. He'd had it dozens of times. *You'd think Hemingway invented the written word.* "I met him once, yes." He did not say it had been in the bar of the Savoy in London. He hiked his shoulders up and huffed out his chest to show the Hemingway mien. "Built like a bull. He was on assignment for *Collier's*—"

"Coal? Kheminveh write about stove thing?"

"It's a magazine." Ben pantomimed flipping pages.

"With us *magazin* is on gun." Katya was impatient to reach her point. "Question. Kheminveh famous in Soviet Union, we all read. Hero in *The Sun Up Again*. Is he steer, not bull?"

Jake woke up to the topic. "Wait a minute. I read that. The guy lost the family jewels? Where'd it say so?"

"That's Hemingway for you," Ben sought to explain and realized the vodka wasn't helping. "He doesn't outright *say*—"

Jake shook his head in disbelief. "Weird. Did you ask him?"

"Of course I didn't ask him, the whole point of the goddamn book is—"

"Whoa. How can that be, the guy has lost his valuables and we're supposed to read it between the lines? I'd say that's news, it ought to be spelled out in black and white."

"Kheminveh is kid us, *da*?" Katya contributed. She shook her head censoriously. "We have saying: 'What is write in ink, axe cannot cut off.'"

It hit him then, along with whatever shot of vodka the count was up to by now. He chortled and couldn't stop, laughing himself silly while others around the table tittered in anticipation. Finally he caught enough breath to say it. "That character's name is Jake! Get it, Ice? He's a *Jake* and his working part is missing in action and yours is present and accounted for and—" Jake guffawed and vowed to write Hemingway a complaining letter. Katya reddened and grinned foxily, translating in a rapid low purr to the other Russians. They caught on and roared.

Wiping his eyes—a bit of a sting there; he crazily wondered whether vodka could reach the eyelids—Ben focused as best he could on Katya. "Question for you." Her expression froze at a degree of politeness. "You flew. Tell me about that, please?"

"*Nachthexen.*" Katya rapped her breast sturdily, then fluttered a hand through the air while giving out an eerie high-pitched whistle. It was the kind of sound you could feel on your skin, and Ben tried not to twitch.

"It stumped me at first, too," Jake broke in. "But they've got great big mothwing biplanes called Polikarpovs that just about float through the air. Our darling here flew one of those. Two-seater, so what they'd do, she and a woman bombardier would go out in the middle of the night and get up a little altitude, just behind the front lines, then cut the engine and glide over the German side," his outsize hands tracing that out in the air. "The bombardier had the explosives in her lap, she'd toss the bomb package out, blow up some Germans, and Katya would rev the engine back on and they'd haul ass out of there." Jake nearly bent double in fealty to the next episode. "Here's the best part. The Germans are down there scared shitless, all they can hear is the wind in the wingstruts as Katya and her chum come drifting over. They run around yelling '*Nachthexen!*' Night witches!"

"Was good, flying," Katya said quietly. She pantomimed steering a tow tractor. "Day witch now." Shrugging, she reached for the latest vodka bottle with the remnant of her hand.

Dazed, Ben sat out the rest of the evening that stretched toward morning. He felt he had to, he was Jake's alibi for consorting with allies who happened to be Red as their crimson flag. The conversation whenever toasts weren't being made crashed along in two languages and in between. At some point Jake volubly told the joke about the dude who was invited to a fancy barbecue and worried whether he would be able to tell cow pie from caviar and which fork to use with which. Katya's back-and-forth lingo had turned giggly, but Ben was numbly aware she could hold the tongue-tangling booze better than he could, they all could. In the haze of alcohol, muddled images kept coming to him. Cass wingwalking amid the struts of a whopping biplane with a grinning Katya in the cockpit cutting the engine, on and off, on and off. *Sonofabitching war. Women didn't start it, why does it have to drag them in?* He tried to ward it off, but New Guinea replaced Alaska at terrible intervals, the grassy ambush, gashed bodies everywhere mingling with a teletype ticker absurdly chattering in the middle of the trail.

He pinched himself in hidden places to drive off those blears. Sick with longing for Cass—*shame to waste all this drinking without her*—he endeavored to concentrate on the troubling matter of Katya. Suppositions were not in shortage. Suppose she had a husband somewhere? Suppose she had a Communist Party commissar somewhere? Suppose she actually was the daughter of the great general Zhukov, performing whatever patriotic duty it was to hang out with clueless Yanks? No, wait, the clues simply were different, each to each. Jake's forebears had two thousand years of periodic murder directed at them. If anything, it had given Jake immunity from common fear. Jake didn't have to back up for Mother Russia or anybody else.

Determinedly he took stock of his massive friend across there amid the merry Russians, and that did it. The broad Slavic faces around the table all at once reminded him of Havel from football. And along with Havel, O'Fallon. Vic with greatly more cut off him than a pair of fingers. The others, out there in the treacherous time zones. He felt like sobbing. The team and its mortal dangers were a mere handful compared to the innumerable slaughtered in the vaster jaws of war, no question there. But they were his handful. God damn Jake and pulling *Pravda* out of the air. He was more than just a mouthpiece for a government propaganda organ, wasn't he? Had to be. Tepee Weepy only had him in its custody, it didn't own him. His mind lurched to the piece waiting to be written about Jake and this polar oasis where big bombers were handed off. *Good old ink, get it down with just enough between the lines, can't even cut it off with an axe, right, Ernie?* He wished he had a typewriter then and there, to capture all that was going to seem incredible in the sober light of day. Jake and him, up near the top of the world, frozen though it was, thrust out of the lives they'd thought they would lead and into the company of a female warrior who proudly answered to the name of Night Witch.

A COUPLE OF time zones to the east, Bill Reinking rolled out of bed, careful as always not to disturb his wife. Cloyce was a notably late sleeper. Not many of those in a town like Gros Ventre, and he reflected on the distant passion that had brought this particular woman from satin bedcovers to the quilts they had shared for nearly two dozen years. She was all for any manner of bedding at the time. *As was I.*

This time of year first light detached itself from night in stubborn gray, and he put on his glasses to track down his clothes and shoes. Padding across to the window that gave a glimpse of horizon through the giant trunks of the cottonwoods, he checked the sky as usual, not that the weather of the moment meant anything in Montana.

The day ahead of him began cumbrously sorting itself out as he crept down the stairs—the county agent's session at the high school on food production for the war effort, all afternoon given over to typesetting the gleanings sent in by his rural correspondents, a Ladies' Aid potluck supper nominally nonpartisan where the Senator would just happen to whip through and speak his mind about the condition of the nation. By now he could forecast those indignant sentiments almost ahead of the words coming out of the Senator's formidable mouth, and the Senator no doubt could parrot off his dogged editorials before they were written. *We're as bad as an old married couple.*

That stray thought stung. He tried to yawn it away, stoking up the kitchen stove in the semidark to hurry the coffee. It was a terrible habit for a newspaper editor, rising at dawn after late nights. Yet he had always done so and figured he always would. *The early bird gets the worm, but is that a balanced diet?* Fumbling for a pencil and pad on the sideboard, he wrote that down to use as a column-bottom filler.

While the coffee perked, he put on his mackinaw and hat to go out and scrape the frost off the car windshield. Another bit of headstart that did not gain a soul much in the long run, but it was something to do. Besides, the dawn air brought him a little of Ben now that he was stationed at East Base once more. That rainbow of planes to Alaska and then Russia: any amount of time Ben put in where virginal aircraft instead of bullets were flying was to be prized. *Praise be, Franklin D. I knew Lend-Lease was worth the abuse I took every week for being for it.*

He paused bent over the whitened windshield, taking in the silence that ushered the slow change of morning light. As a newspaperman he had to hew to the necessary enlistment of all men's sons in this war against the evils of Hitler and Tojo, but as a father he could privately covet any interval of amnesty for Ben.

Scraping off another peel of frost, he paused again to listen. East Base started up even earlier than he himself did. It was an added habit now, delaying out here in the daybreak until he could hear the first distant sound of planes in transit.

HIS BUNK WAS shaking and he wanted it to quit. Any motion made his head feel on fire, approximately to the roots of his hair.

When he finally unclenched his eyelids, Jake was standing over him with one big mitt of a hand rocking the bunkframe. "Another day, another dollar, buddy. How you feeling?"

"Next thing to dead, if you really have to know."

"The more you sleep, the less you sin," Jake said cheerily as he opened the blinds and let in sunlight harshly magnified by snowdrifts. "You ought to be pure as a daisy."

Ben shielded against the brightness with an arm. Groggy as he was, it occurred to him to ask: "What time is our plane back?"

"It's gone." Jake busied himself at his ready-bag. "The other guys went with it, but I got us a better deal. We are now the captain and crew of our very own bush plane, Benjamin."

Ben woke up entirely. "Bush plane?"

"Sort of, yeah. You'll see. Weather people up here use it. Needs a little fixing up, so they're sending it south. It'll get us there, don't worry."

"When?" He wrenched up in bed, with something like congealed panic oozing past dizziness and hangover. "Have you gone even more crazy than usual? I've got to get the piece on you done and in to Tepee Weepy on time or the bastards will never let me live it down."

"You're on assignment, ain't you? So assign yourself a nice leisurely flight and relax. You can write in the air as good as you can on the ground, I bet."

"Jake, square with me a minute, okay? Am I in a bad dream or something? Won't it take goddamn near forever to make it to Great Falls in the kind of kite you're talking about?"

"That's the whole point," Jake explained with magnanimous patience. "Hours in the air, Ben—guys like me have to live by 'em. This'll put me up on anybody else in the East Base group by twenty or more hours of flying time. That much closer to the real war, my friend."

"Let me catch up here." Ben wobbled his head to try to clear it, which proved to be a painful mistake. "This field just lets you walk off with one of their planes to go home in?"

Jake rubbed his jaw. "It took a radio message to Grandpa Grady. He said he could spare me for a couple extra days. Said he could spare you indefinitely."

"I'M TRYING TO decide whether to commend you or bust your nuts in my report, Eisman." The Fairbanks operations officer petulantly kicked the tire of the parked aircraft as if shopping the last jalopy on a used-car lot. "At least it gets this thing off our hands. But when you said your friend here has his wings you didn't bother to tell me he hasn't used them since, did you." His eyes bored into Ben. "I've never let a paper-airplane pilot be a copilot before."

"He's just along as sandbag, sir," Jake soothed, "strictly a glorified hitchhiker."

"That is precisely what he needs to be. Reinking, is that your name?" The ops officer appeared dubious about even that. "Unless Eisman goes deaf, dumb, and blind, or has some other kind of shit fit, you are not to touch those controls. Do you hear me?"

"Loud and clear, sir. I am to sit at the right hand of flying ace Eisman and be inert bodyweight for the next two or three days." Ben's answer drew heavy gazes from both men. "Does that about sum up my heroic role in the war effort?"

Jake piously stepped in. "Don't mind him, Major, he rolled out of the sack on the wrong side this morning. I'll throw him out the cargo hatch if he tries to wrest the controls from me."

"With my blessing." The ops officer walked away as if the pair of them might be contagious. "Hand in your flight plan and vacate my airfield, lieutenants."

Skeptically Ben studied the aircraft again. "All right, Ice. What did you say this piece of junk is?"

"A Grumman Widgeon. Quite the rig, ain't it?" Jake was going through the motions of his inspection walk around the plane, although they both knew he was going to give it a clean report unless a wing dropped off and brained him.

Exhausted as the Widgeon OA-14 looked, Ben considered that a possibility. A spiderweb crack across half of the cockpit window—on the copilot's side, naturally—lent it a walleyed ap-

pearance. Perhaps fittingly for a weather plane, most of its paint
from nose to tail had been swiped away by Alaska's vicious moods
of climate. Dents in the struts of its wing pontoons indicated it
had encountered more than occasional tree limbs while docking
at inlet weather stations. Ben felt doubt in his gut. He had flown
in amphibious aircraft before, but this one seemed designed to
dither between sea and land. Beneath the cockpit and the passenger seats was a belly hull for it to float on, and spraddle-legged
landing gear with narrow tires called bicycle wheels poked peril-
ously out of that hull, barely holding the craft up off the concrete
runway. Not since the most rudimentary biplane, back in earliest
pilot training, had Ben seen aircraft wheels like these, and the
rubber was so aged and bald it looked to him as if it very well
could have been the same weary set of tires.

He could not help eyeing the low belly of the semi-seaplane
and the accumulated runway glop. "Will this thing clear?"

"Just," Jake said as if were a sure thing. Coming around the
nose of the plane, he lobbed a bundled flying suit, which Ben
instinctively caught. "Ready to go for a ride?"

WITH JAKE APPLYING considerable body English to make up
for two fewer engines and a couple of thousand fewer horse-
power than he was used to, the Widgeon crawled into the air
above Fairbanks. After the B-17, which was like traveling in a
submarine in the air, to both men the floatplane felt like a flying
raft, fickle every time it met a new air current. Slowly, slowly,
it wafted over the tin rooftops of Fairbanks, its shadow lagging
and shrinking behind it as if reluctant to leave the safety of the
city limits. While Jake was busy coaxing the engines to smooth
out, Ben peered out his side window at the glistening ice of the
Tanana River and the curd of war materiel along its banks, instantly reaching for his pad. The supply dump, as it was aptly
called, consisted of an infinite number of crates of aircraft parts,

heaps of tires, long ranks of belly tanks, runway equipment of every sort; some of it tarped over and some of it not, the Lend-Lease mountains of supplies resembled an otherworldly tent encampment, strangely peopleless, strewn beside the frozen river for miles on end. Ben jotted as fast as his hand could go, adding the scene to others of untold weaponry stacked on Pacific atolls and Atlantic docks. He had read that the weight of impounded water in gigantic dams, Fort Peck and Dnieperstroi and their serpentine ilk, in theory added up to enough to affect the rotation of the earth. Looking down at the enormity of the random arsenal piled up on one Alaskan riverbank, it could be readily imagined that the depots of war were pooling into a mass force certain to make the world wobble on its axis.

"Pilot to copilot," Jake intoned from two feet away. "Say farewell to Fairbanks, it's all bush from here on."

Ben glanced up and out over a sunlit wilderness seemingly unmarred by anything but the frail cracklines of the cockpit window. Sky, land, perimeter of the earth, all seemed to enlarge as the plane throbbed out into the circle of blue morning. To his astonishment, winter gradually gave way as they headed southeastward toward Yukon Territory. Fairbanks was caught in some isobar that had slipped from the North Pole, but snow had only seeped into the highest elevations along the upper Tanana. The river threaded ahead of them, marked as far as the eye could see by the gold of birches captured in its valley.

Expansive as the outdoors around them, Jake grinned over at him. "Not bad, huh? Feel like Jack London yet?"

"Trapped this way in a tiny cabin with White Fang for days on end, yes, I do."

"My, you are cranky today. We'll purr into Northway in time for lunch, you'll see."

Time slowed, attuned to the stately beat of the engines. Half-hypnotized by the ceaseless tapestry of scenery, Ben sat back and

let his mind drift. First of all to Cass, the situation with her always up in the air, an apt locution right then but one that made
his lips draw tight. Off sideways to the piece he'd done on Dex,
legerdemain he couldn't maintain forever for Tepee Weepy and
was not at all sure he should. Back around to Jake, sitting here
hoping to ride written words and padded flying time to the air
over Germany. Afloat over a corner of the world the war had not
found, Ben uneasily traversed such thoughts as though they were
air pockets, unbidden but there.

The plane was droning along at 4,200 feet—he would forever
remember that altimeter reading—when Jake announced:

"I feel a pimple coming on my butt and therefore deem myself incapacitated. Take over."

Ben made a derisive noise. "Thanks anyway, Ice, but it's been
too long since—"

"Bullshit, Ben. Once a pilot, always a pilot. Get busy and fly
this heap."

"Knock it off, will you?" Unearned favors did not go down
well with Ben, never had, never would. "That prissy ops officer
had it right, I *am* a paper-airplane pilot anymore, and nothing—
hey, where're you going?"

"To take a leak in the jug, what does it look like?" Jake vacated the pilot's seat and turned sideways to edge past Ben, patting him on the head as he did so. "Better fly the plane, kiddo,
somebody has to."

"You damn fool," Ben hurled over his shoulder, his hands
clamping onto the controls. Maybe he was imagining, but the
Widgeon seemed instantly restless as Jake's weight moving toward the rear of the cabin altered its center of gravity. His hands
managing to tame that without any conscious help from the
rest of him, Ben scanned the infinite banks of dials, switches,
and gauges of an instrument panel that now seemed the size
and complexity of a cathedral window. Flight school had never

included this peculiar breed of aircraft in the first place. He could hear Jake back there humming loudly to himself while peeing, which did not help. Still inventorying the instrumentation, he kept coming up one short. Precisely now, of course, the Tanana River chose to turn cockeyed, twisting away in fresh directions, glinting like a silver snake. Alert in every corpuscle, Ben could see wirelike trees down there on its banks, he could see the carpet of yellow leaves on the ground, he could see the bald tops of hills regularly passing under the wingtips. What he could not spot, somewhere right under his nose, was the most basic aeronautical instrument.

While he was trying to navigate without it, the Widgeon gravitated below four thousand feet and he hurriedly dropped the flaps for some lift. Just then Jake returned to the cockpit, gyrating into the pilot's seat as the plane bounded upward. "Ride 'em, cowboy. I will say, you fighter jockeys fly livelier than us old bomber drivers."

"Funny as a crutch, Ice," Ben gritted out, hands and eyes busy in several directions. "Here, do something with this airplane."

"Just when you're getting used to it? Wouldn't be fair." The big man sat back comfortably to spectate. "Don't worry, Uncle Jake is here to hold your hand."

"Then get busy and do it." Ben squirmed, feeling his face redden as he had to put the question the rawest rookie pilot would hate to ask. "I give up—did they forget to put the compass in this turd bird?"

Yawning, Jake squinted into the glare of the morning sun. "What, you don't know east when you see it?"

That again. Isn't there any other direction anymore? "Goddamn it, Jake, I mean it. If I can't get a compass bearing I'll eventually have this thing headed off the map somewhere. Let's don't fool around in the middle of Alaska, all right?"

Jake was unfazed. He sat there loudly humming the chorus that went "Some people say there is no Hell, but they're not pilots, so they can't tell" until finally, when Ben had run out of swearwords, he rolled his eyes.

Ben's gaze ascended along with his, to the front ceiling of the cockpit where the compass hung like a bat.

"That maybe is one of the things they're gonna modify in this clunker," Jake speculated as Ben sheepishly adjusted course to the compass setting. "Now then, you ready to fly like a sane person?"

"Damn you, you know I am."

Bursting into laughter even though he still was struggling to tame the Widgeon's twenty-eyed dials and sluggish wings, suddenly Ben had never felt better. It ran through him like the thrill when he first soloed, the magic of being lightly attached to the sky. With Jake there beside him to coax and scold and to master any of the alchemy of the cockpit he erred on, the plane was his until they reached the barrier mountains and tricky downdrafts, perhaps half an hour yet. In that window of time, he hoped with all he was worth that Cass right then was flying too, the invisible musculature of the air supporting them both at once.

Eventually Jake took over and thriftily landed at the dirt runway at Northway at noon, and by late afternoon they were far into Yukon Territory. They overnighted in a cold Quonset hut at Whitehorse, then kept to the pattern the next day, Jake handling the plane in and out of dirtpacked Canadian refueling fields and then Ben's exultant turn at the controls whenever the terrain was not producing choppy air or something else insidiously murderous. His flying intervals became less as mountains grew, and he believed even Jake was relieved when at last they crossed the Rockies and ahead lay the hill country around Newbride, the final refueling stop before the big base at Edmonton.

"Circle a few times so they can get a good look at us," Jake unexpectedly turned the plane over to him when they were a few miles out from Newbride. "The radio's on the fritz, let me work on that." Slipping his own earphones on, Ben heard static and a voice that sounded a lot farther off than the airfield in the middle distance. Treed hills and straggles of the town penned in the field, but it appeared to be a more substantial runway than the dirt patches they had been putting down on farther north. Ben was ready to be on the ground. The air turned bumpy, and he concentrated on holding the altitude while Jake fiddled with the radio as if profanity was the sure cure. After many oaths, a particularly lurid outburst got through and he turned toward Ben and winked. "Sorry about that, tower. Requesting permission to land. Over." When the radio back-and-forth was done, Jake checked the altimeter and throttle settings and everything else Ben had conscientiously been trying to mind, but made no move to do more than that. "Want to brush up on your landing skills?"

Temptation nearly overwhelmed Ben. "Love to, but the air has more lumps in it than I like. You take it."

Jake sighed. "Okay, if you don't want any fun out of life. Looky there, nice gravel runway and everything, and you chicken out. I just don't know about you sometimes, Ben buddy." Taking the controls, he aligned with the runway, and as if showing how it was done, waddled the plane down to a perfect touch.

Abruptly the runway seemed to devour the Widgeon. With a sickening lurch the plane nosed over and skidded along on the belly hull at high speed, metal screeching hideously on the runway surface.

Ben shouted, "Put the wheels down!"

"The sonsabitches are!" Jake shouted back. "It's *fresh* gravel!"

The hair-raising grating sound continued to fill the cockpit, both men tossed in their seats by the rough ride, as the plane plowed along. Eventually it ground to a halt.

There was a moment of sickening silence, then the strange wail of the Canadian version of a meat wagon reached them.

"I thought you were going to land it, not fly it into the ground, Ice. You all right?"

Jake rose out of the pilot's seat as if it had offended him. "Never mind me, how's the frigging airplane?"

They scrambled out as the ambulance crunched to a stop a little distance away and a Royal Canadian Air Force officer came leaping off its running board. The back doors flung open and a couple of teams of medics poured out, stretchers ready. They all halted at the sight of Ben and Jake standing nearly to their ankles in the runway gravel, gazing at the furrows made by the Widgeon's thin wheels in the loose surface and cursing violently together.

"Tch, tires of that sort," the Canadian officer said with a mild frown when things settled down. "We've had your P-39s and our own planes through here, no trouble. If it's a hard surface you're looking for, though, you're a bit preliminary." He gestured toward heavy equipment parked at the side of a hangar. "We'll have it tarmacked by this time next week, we figure."

Jake looked pale as he turned toward Ben. "I'll miss the next bomber run to Alaska. Grady will have my ass."

And your flying time will be just what it was. And Tepee Weepy will turn me inside out for missing a deadline. "Try it in the morning?" Ben came out with, not knowing what else to say, as a bulldozer coughed to life and clanked out to tow the Widgeon to the paved apron outside the hangars.

THEY WERE OUT on the flight line in the Canadian dawn. Like odd postulants, the two of them knelt under the Widgeon's scarred but intact hull and almost prayerfully began to let air out of the narrow tires on the landing struts. When the tires squished down to nearly flat, Jake proclaimed: "Let's see if that gives the damn things enough surface."

They strapped in, and Jake taxied out, revved the engines to an alarming roar and started down the runway. The entire airfield personnel clustered outside the hangars to watch, and the meat wagon had its motor running.

Shuddering and rattling, the Widgeon struggled mightily to free itself of the ground and there was a brief moment when Ben thought it had. But the more power Jake fed it for takeoff, the more the acceleration of force on the skinny wheels drove them down into the coarse gravel, even as deflated as they were.

As sharp as if it were on their own skin, both men felt the first scrape of the underside of the plane coming into contact with the runway. There was another interminable hideous screech of aircraft metal against rough surface until the Widgeon skidded to a stop, stranded there in the middle of the airfield like a fish on land.

Jake killed the engines.

"Damn," he said, barely above a whisper. The bulldozer lurched out and towed them back to the parking apron.

Before getting out to face the Canadian contingent, Jake sat in the cockpit chewing his lip. "I hate to start taking the plane apart. Grady will—"

"—have your ass, and rightly so. But maybe only half your ass," Ben told him with more hope than he felt, "if we can get what's left of this thing back to East Base more or less on time."

Looking over his shoulder, Jake took inventory of the interior of the plane and conceded. "Okay, okay. Let's see if our hosts would like some nice plane seats for their canteen."

ONCE THE GROUND crew had unbolted the passenger seats and lugged them off merrily as scavengers given a shipwreck, Jake lined the lightened plane up with the waiting runway and gave it the gas. Glued to the side window as the twin engines raged and the plane shuddered against the drag of the wheels in the gravel,

Ben saw they were past their previous skid marks and thought they might make it this time. Then, agonizingly, they heard the telltale scrape again and in no time the friction of another skid slewed the Widgeon to another dead stop in the middle of the airfield.

"This is starting to get on my nerves," Jake spoke first in the quiet of the cut engines.

Ben indicated toward the bulldozer operator climbing back onto his big yellow machine. "Think how bored that cat skinner is getting."

While they waited to be towed back to the hangar apron again, Jake softly tapped a big fist against the steering column. "Got one more trick up my sleeve. It takes some doing, old buddy. By you."

"As long as it doesn't take buckets of blood," Ben answered, "let's hear it."

He listened without saying anything more until Jake laid out the whole scheme. This time he indicated toward the forest at the end of the runway. "If it doesn't work, don't we end up with a plane in those trees?"

"The damn thing isn't any good to us the way it is," Jake provided in all reasonableness.

That much was unarguable, and the rest came down to the skills the two of them could muster in what they had been trained in. Ben took another look at the trees and swallowed hard, but got the words out: "Go for broke, Ice. You're the pilot, rumor has it."

Jake clapped him on the shoulder. "And you're the sandbag, so here's how I want you to do it."

Back at the hangar apron, they ran through the maneuver in the silent plane a number of times. The Canadian ops officer puffed out his ruddy cheeks when Jake told him what was intended, but the truth was, he wanted the high-and-dry floatplane off his airfield as badly as they did. "Have a go," he bestowed ultimately and went off to alert his ambulance crew.

Ben climbed in behind Jake, keyed up and as ready as he could ever make himself be. No sooner had Jake put on his headphones than he motioned to the copilot's seat as if it was an easy chair.

"Sit down and relax. We need to wait half an hour, the sissy in the tower won't clear us for takeoff until they get here."

"Who?"

"The volunteer fire department from town. They're particular about their trees up here."

Ben settled in the seat, put up the collar of his flight jacket and tried to nap. The world of war marched through his head, ridiculous incongruities on parade. Years in uniform dwindled to this, two men trying to get an aging floatplane off a gravel runway some thousands of miles from the nearest combat. Survival perhaps dependent on a meat wagon and a fire engine in somebody else's country. The contradiction that an airplane amounted to anyway, a machine nominally too heavy to stay airborne due to the colossal engines needed to keep it airborne. Cass, all her P-39 flights with those hundreds of pounds of mechanism in back of her ears. A miracle every time. How long could miracles go on?

Jake was shaking him. "Here we go."

Ben snapped to. This time, he saw, the Canadian officer had positioned the medical rescue squad near the far end of the runway, with the firefighting equipment added.

"All right, Ben my boy." Jake sounded reconciled or ready, it was hard to tell which in the start-up throb of the Widgeon engines. "Third time is the charm."

"It beats 'Three strikes and you're out,'" Ben had to grant. He squeezed Jake's shoulder as he edged up out of the copilot's seat. "See you in the wild blue yonder, Ice."

He went to the rear of the cabin and crouched. Up front, Jake fed the throttles even more and started down the runway at full force again, the squishy plane wheels doing their determined best to plow into the gravel. Imagination ran rampant in a situation like this, but with his weight back there shifting the center of gravity toward the tail, it did feel to Ben as though the plane poised itself a trifle higher, at a more elevated angle, up there at the nose.

Noise poured over him and the ride was so rough he had to brace himself with both hands on the floor; otherwise, he stayed in football stance, ready to go at Jake's signal. He could tell they were nearly to the point of the runway where the drag of the wheels drew the plane into the gravel on previous tries. The part of the mind that deals with such things considered whether the battered metal of the hull would hold up through another high-speed skid or whether it would split open and he and Jake would smear against gravel at seventy miles an hour.

"Now!" Jake roared, his hands busy with the controls and the throttles, and Ben leaped catlike toward the cockpit, grabbing onto the crank that controlled the wing flaps. As fast as his hands could go he dropped the full flaps, and an instant later, hoping Jake's brainstorm had something to it, yanked the lever that pulled the landing gear up.

Its support gone from under it, held barely above the runway only by a sudden upthrust of air from the flaps, for a terrible moment the Widgeon seemed to hover in defiance of gravity, like a leaf on a last breath of breeze. It then gave a slight lurch upward as if startled. *Don't stall!* was the single thought in both men's minds. Jake did something, although Ben wasn't sure what, and the plane stabilized. They were airborne, at least at the elevation of a few feet. Now the line of trees was approaching fast. Delicately Jake fingered the controls and yelled, "Sandbag!"

Ben flung himself to the back of the cabin, half-rolling into his crouched position again, trying to make himself heavy. As he did so, the nose of the plane lifted with the shift of balance, but he still could see green spears of treetops everywhere in the cockpit window. "Hang on!" he heard the shout from Jake.

Instead he gave a little jump from his crouched position, and when he came down the front of the plane teeter-tottered a bit higher, still staggering toward the treetops.

He did it again, the Widgeon's nose once more bobbing up ever so slightly. By now the wall of dark green branches was rushing at them so close and hard the effect was hypnotic. This was it, he knew, that daylight nightmare of Cass's engine hurtling forward to crush her but in this case two engines to rip loose and plow flesh, one each for Jake and him. His mortal organs getting busy with their last task, Ben braced himself into the back corner of the cabin for the crash, staring uncontrollably at the ridiculous agency of his oncoming death, the tops of evergreens as serene as Christmas trees.

Then sky.

It took some moments for this unexpected lease on existence to register on him. He huddled there not daring to move lest any twitch of a muscle disturb whatever equilibrium the Widgeon was struggling itself into. Its engines still at full throttle, he could feel the floor of the plane lurching drunkenly under him, but along with it was what could be construed as—*Jesus, is it? Is it?*—the sensation of lift.

Then the engine noise settled to a guttural effort and Jake was calling over his shoulder in a shaky voice: "Nothing to it. You can come out of hiding now."

Ben stumbled his way forward and dumped himself into the copilot's seat. Trees still were not very far below, but the Widgeon laboriously kept on rising above the branches' reach.

He saw Jake was wearing a grin big enough to eat pie sideways.

"Kind of puckers a guy up, down there in the seat of the pants, don't it? Better get busy writing all this up, scribe, so they'll give us medals for getting this tub off the ground."

"Right, Ice. A piece of gravel pinned on with a Band-Aid. How about if I just sit here and let my insides catch up with me?"

They flew giddily, men given wings, for the next little while. Canada's immense share of the earth spread around them in the clear autumn morning in timber thick as fur and pocket mirror lakes and rivers flowing north.

Fondling the controls, Jake was chortling and calculating aloud how long it would take to fuel up in Edmonton and then the flying time to reach East Base for suppertime beer at the Officers' Club, when one of the engines went rough, smoothed out, sputtered a time or two, and quit.

"Now goddamn what?" Jake indignantly checked the instrument panel. "Take a look, it's the one on your side."

Before the words were out of Jake's mouth, Ben had craned around to give the stilled engine a looking-over. It only took an instant. Aviation gasoline was whipping away behind the engine in a fine mist. "It's slobbering fuel like crazy," he reported hoarsely.

"Then I guess we do without that one, don't we." Jake feathered the propeller before the words were out of his mouth. "We'll have to limp on in to Edmon—"

The other engine quit.

—"aw, shit," Jake finished his sentence.

In the vacuum after that, the only sounds the wind in the struts and the creaks of a gliding plane, the pair of men stared the question at each other and made the same guess without having to say it. The Widgeon's repeated rough treatment on the gravel runway must have ruptured the fuel lines, and the gravity-defying takeoff over the treetops had encouraged leakage. By now Jake was striving to maintain altitude with every stunt he could think of with the controls and the flaps, while Ben twisted in every direction in search of water they could set the plane down on. Off on the horizon a lake gleamed, but too far for any sinking airplane to reach.

"This thing glides like a dump truck," Jake said with strained calm. "How about we belly in on that clear patch down there?"

With gas all over us? Shielding the sun from his eyes with his hands, Ben scanned the stretch of forestless terrain coming under the plane, like a shaved-away spot on a mammoth pelt. He had to grit to give Jake the news that a windstorm had done the clearing. "It's full of downed trees, Ice. Tangled all to hell."

"That changes things. Raise Newbride, quick"—as Jake spoke, Ben already was on the radio chanting their position—"then grab the chutes. Toss me mine and the bivvie bag and you go first."

Having no choice, Ben clambered into jumping position, aware of the tail and other portions of the plane that he did not want hitting him when he went out the hatch. *Jump plenty far out when you jump, at least I remember that from flight school.* He gripped the rip-cord ring. Great gulps swept through him as he attempted to blot out Dex's experience of puking in mid-air. Clinging in the hatchway, he stared past the toes of his flight boots, trying to judge. The Widgeon was losing altitude like mad, he could see individual stumps and logs down there; wasn't the ground too close for jumping?

"Get out! Now!" Jake's bellow and the sickening shift of the plane as he abandoned the cockpit sent Ben out into the air.

Two opposed things happened almost simultaneously, the sensation of floating as the parachute opened and the uprush of a monstrously large downed evergreen directly beneath him, its

root-ball splayed toward him like a natural mantrap. With everything he could muster, dangling and falling at the same time, he
tugged at the parachute's lines in an effort to miss the log. At the
very end of his mid-air dance of trying to twist aside, a limber
root end raked up his body, swatting him under the side of the
jaw and taking some face skin with it.

The next thing he knew he was on his side on the ground.
The tree, as prone as he was, was close enough he could reach
out and touch it. Still foolishly gripped tight in his hand was the
rip-cord ring.

Raw-faced and wincing from the sideswipe by the tree root,
he lay there testing himself for anything broken. Except for his
breath, nothing seemed to be. He was gasping his way toward
normal intake of air when he heard, somewhere off across the
mess of downed trees, the nasty sound of a crash. *Too big for
Jake. Had to be the plane.* That started his thought process whir-
ring. Before he even was onto his feet he was calling at the top of
his voice:

"Jake! Jake?"

It took several shouts, but then a voice not all that far away
answered. "Tone it down, Ben. I don't want my ears hurting too."

"Where are you?"

"How the hell do I know? Over here."

Using the root-ball as a rough ladder, Ben managed to climb
high enough to see across various logs to where a white drape of
parachute indicated Jake's location.

"I'm on my way. Doctor yourself till I get there, can you?"
The optimistically named bivouac bag, containing a medical kit
and other emergency essentials, was with Jake.

"Who said I need doctoring?"

To Ben, that response did not sound particularly convincing.
Wasting no time, he bundled up his own chute in his arms like
dirty laundry and began picking his way through the maze of

downed trees. Mostly the forest here had been tipped over by a big wind, roots and all, like a spill of wooden matches. A good many tree trunks, though, had been snapped off, leaving stray splintery snags tall as totem poles. Here and there stood survivor trees, incongruous loners with their kilts of evergreen branches above it all. The muskeg footing was laborious. Ben was sweating by the time he rounded the last big log and there was Jake, upright but wincing as he stood there flexing the ankle in his unlaced left boot.

"How bad?" Ben asked.

"I feel beat to hell, about like you look."

Another spasm chased across the big man's face as he put weight on that foot. "Think maybe it's a sprain, not a break. Not gonna take the boot off to find out, the way the damn thing is swelling."

Jake's eyes met Ben's. "Tell you what really hurts—I dropped the bivvie bag coming out of the plane. Piss-poor time to fumble. Sorry about that, Ben."

"Don't worry," Ben spoke it with effort. "We've still got our chute packs. Can you walk?"

Jake hobbled around to test that out. "More or less. We're not going anywhere for a while anyway, I guess." Both men turned and gawked south where a pillar of smoke marked the burning aircraft. After a bit, Jake said: "That was a sad-ass aircraft, you know that?"

"Never mind that, let's see what we're supposed to live on." Ben knelt to unzip the pack portion of his parachute for its emergency items, and Jake did the same. Each reached in and pulled out the first thing they found. They stared at the short machetes in their hands.

Next to come out was a tiny fishing kit, followed by rocklike pieces of chocolate called tropical bars.

"Jungle issue," Jake said tonelessly. "Goddamn sonofabitching goddamn supply depot bastards—"

"Quit," Ben ordered. "Eat. We've got to keep our strength up." He tried the chocolate and nearly broke a tooth. "Petrified."

"Must be what the machetes are for," Jake muttered.

They sawed their way through the chocolate and sucked on it while they spread out the white parachute canopies as a marker for any search plane. Around them hung the ear-ringing silence of the Canadian forest. It was at the forefront of both their minds that in country this far north, it was always about five minutes to winter.

"Man oh man, this is not so good," Jake eventually observed out loud. "Where are the Canucks with all their rescue regalia when we want them?"

Wondering that himself, Ben said, "Takes a while to fly here, you know that. We'd better get busy, just in case. Firewood. Come on, let's get to whacking with these daisy cutters."

They had amassed a woodpile of the driest branches they could find to cut and were digging in the muskeg trying to reach water—none too successfully—when they heard the sound of a plane.

A small spotter aircraft of some kind, it looked about the size of a moth as it puttered through the air, in over the forested edge of the windfall and ever so slowly toward them, an arm waving out the copilot's window in good cheer as it made a pass over them. No airplane created could land in the jumble of trees, snags, and logs, so both Ben and Jake knew what to expect, the drop of a bag of survival gear. Around again came the plane and again the cheery wave, but no bag was dropped.

"I wish he'd hurry up," Ben muttered as the small plane buzzed off to circle in for another try. "Puddle jumpers like that don't carry all that much fuel." Jake simply fixed a solid glare at the visiting aircraft as if the emergency bag could slide down on that.

One more time, here the frail aircraft came, propeller whirling like a child's pinwheel, and a sizable soft object was lobbed toward them. It blossomed out in a little parachute all its own, then decided to ride the breeze, straight toward the topmost branches of one of the taller standing trees nearby which Ben and Jake had paid no particular attention to, until now.

The chute neatly snagged on the worst of the high branches, tangled itself, and dangled the bag sixty feet above the cursing pair of men.

They bayed obscenities at the rescue bag festooned in the treetop like a Christmas trimming, until better sense kicked in. Meanwhile, the light plane wagged its wings—in the circumstances, it seemed more like a regretful shrug—and flew off in the direction of Newbride.

It was Jake, sounding almost pensive, who remarked, "That guy wasn't waving for exercise, was he. He wanted us out away from this shit-eating tree."

Taking stock of the situation, they could tell it was impossible to climb an evergreen that tall and spindly; the upper branches would break off under the weight of a man and so might the whole crown of the tree. On the other hand, the base of the tree looked appallingly substantial when the only thing you had to chop it down with were machetes meant for jungle vines.

The first half hour's worth of excruciatingly careful chopping, so as not to break the blades, produced a notch about as big as a beaver could chew in minutes. Panting and arm-weary, they had just resigned themselves to another hour or so of chipping away, when the sound of a more powerful aircraft engine reached them.

They looked up. This one was arriving from what they figured was the direction of Edmonton and coming like a streak.

Ben identified the silhouette and wondered if he could be imagining.

"VIP treatment this time around, Benjamin." Jake shaded his eyes. "We rate a P-39. Hope the guy is bringing us long woolies and his aim is better than that last prick's."

There were thousands of Airacobras in the sky of war, hundreds of pilots gunning a twelve-piston engine to a full four hundred miles an hour at any given time. This one roaring in on them had no business being flown by her, Ben knew in the deepest reasoning part of himself; Cass could be on the Seattle run, or on the ground at East Base, or anywhere between. But reason did not stand a chance as he craved her into creation there in the sun-glint of the rapidly oncoming cockpit. As he watched, afraid to blink, the P-39 lowered its nose and dove toward them. Jake, waving both arms, froze into semaphore position as the plane skimmed into the clearing in the forest, low as a crop duster and fast as an artillery shell. Facing into the madcap flyover, Ben no longer knew whether to pray it was Cass or not at those controls.

The P-39 tore past so close over them they could feel the prop wash. Now he was sure it was no one but her. He felt queerly responsible: Cass only would have flown a circus stunt like that to see what condition the crash left him in.

"That," Jake declared in the corridor of dwindling roar as the fighter plane climbed sharply, "is one shit-hot pilot." Both men watched the Cobra's ascent as fliers do, as if counting contour lines of elevation.

At around fifteen hundred feet the plane pulled up and settled into circling over them.

"What the hell now?"

"Writing a message," Ben somehow was sure. "Come on, let's get way out in the middle of this mess, we don't want the drop bag to end up in another tree."

Clumsier than vertical bears, they plunged through the
fallen-timber maze until they reached a marginally more open
patch of muskeg. They planted themselves in anticipation there,
and Jake took up waving again. "The goddamn guy doesn't have
to check his spelling," he complained as the Cobra kept to its
droning orbit over them for the next some minutes. "Just tell us
how they're gonna get us out of here."

"He will." Ben had nearly admitted *She.* "Next pass, watch for
the drop bag."

Both of them tensed, ready to chase down the weighted leath-
erine bag, like a long yellow stocking, wherever it landed.

What came sailing out of the P-39 was the size of a bulging
mail sack, so accurately aimed it very nearly hit them.

Jumping back until they were certain it was through rolling,
Ben and Jake needed a further instant to realize it was a duffel
bag. Together they pounced and opened it. They pawed through
like pirates at a treasure chest. C rations. Wool socks and gloves
and watch caps. A down mummy bag. Matches. Two canteens
of water. Two thermoses of hot coffee. Four cans of beer. Nestled
amid it all, the message drop bag, and inside, the scrawled note:

> Flyboys:
> Happy to see you up and around. Proceed five miles,
> compass heading S/SW, to nearest lake. Bush plane will be
> waiting for you tomorrow—sorry I can't, but WASPs and
> Cobras don't swim.
> Only room for one sleeping bag in the duffel, you'll
> have to share. Don't snuggle any closer than I would.

Jake looked up from the note as the P-39 cut another perfect
tight circle over them, as if they were the bull's-eye of a target the
size of Canada. "Bitch, whoever she is," he said in admiration.

The only acknowledgment Ben could think of was to throw
up his hands in the possible direction of Edmonton—*Go! Go!*

Jake looked at him for a moment, then commenced rummaging through the duffel bag. "Here's a dilemma—coffee or beer?"

"Save the beer." Ben watched the fighter plane go. "It's going to be a long night."

THE FIVE MILES took them all the next day. Jake peglegged the distance, his twisted ankle splinted with halved tree branches, while Ben humped along with the precious duffel and picked out their compass route. At noon, barely halfway and their energy depleting fast, they made the decision to cram down all the C rations to give their bodies something to work with. Ultimately both men were staggering, but always in the direction pointed by the compass needle in Ben's hand, as they lunged out of the forest to a lakeshore just before dusk. Half a mile away at a mooring buoy, a floatplane revved its engine and began to cruise across the surface of the water. In terror that it was taking off, the two of them futilely tried to outshout the roar of the engine. Then the skimming floats beneath the plane cut an arc on the lakewater like skates curving on ice, and the aircraft slowed to a chug, aiming in to shore exactly at them.

TWENTY-FOUR HOURS later, with Jake unhappily tractioned in a hospital bed by the Canadian medical authorities, Ben mustered himself as the C-47 shuttle from Edmonton touched down at East Base. He ached in every possible part of himself and his face looked like he had been in a fight with a bobcat and he still had the entire slew of writing about the bomber journey to Alaska to be done. *Am I imagining, or am I losing ground faster than I can type?*

Jones was waiting for him on the runway, faithfully rumpled and homely as a mud fence. "Welcome back, Lieutenant. I spent yesterday going over the regulations about escorting a coffin, but I'm glad it's you instead."

"Jones, you say the sweetest things." Even as the wind added its pesky greeting, Ben had to admit East Base looked like an oasis after where he'd been.

"Tepee Weepy radioed," Jones reported, awed at having heard the voice in clear air. "They want your first-person story of the crash right away. 'Soonest,' they said—I didn't know that was a word."

"It is with them."

"Uhm, Lieutenant, I'm supposed to tell you. Commander's orders, you're to report to the infirmary before you do anything else."

"If Grandpa Grady thinks I've had time to bring a dose of clap in from Canada—"

Jones surveyed Ben's black-and-blue jaw and skinned-up face. "Somehow I don't think it's that." He leaned in as if giving solace to a parishioner. "My guess is, he considers you a hero and wants to make sure you're all right."

"I'm touched," Ben growled.

"You maybe want to look at this while you're getting checked over—it came yesterday, highest priority." Jones handed him a wax-sealed packet. "The courier didn't want to give it to me, but I told him it was that or he could go find you in the Canadian wilderness."

"You're getting the hang of this, Jones." Throatily Ben pushed the words out past the choke hold of apprehension brought by the packet, the kind his transfer orders to another base ordinarily came in. He didn't want to open it with Jones watching. "Meet you back at the office."

"Don't forget the—"

"—clap shop, I won't, thank you very much, Jones."

Ben stood there at the edge of the East Base runway buffeted by the wind, his thoughts whirling wildly. *If they yank me out of*

*here now . . . How will I ever see her . . . When will the war ever
quit . . .* He trudged toward the nearest hangar—it happened to
be the one where he had first laid eyes on Cass—and ducked in
out of the wind. Not a P-39 in sight; a B-17 bomber, clean-skinned
and somehow the more ominous for that, was being worked over
from nose to tail by a swarm of female mechanics. A hairnetted
crew chief more muscular than Ben immediately slipped over to
him. "Help you with something, Lieutenant?"

"Something sharp, chief, to open this with?"

The brawny woman pointed to a workbench strewn with
tools. Ben went over and picked up a chisel. He lightly gouged
the wax, the clock of war turning in him. How many time zones
away from Cass Standish could a man stand to be? Her husband
was seventeen away, if that was any guide. *And look what's happening to him.*

He reached in and instead of orders pulled out a P-file, the
standard military personnel folder, with the name, rank, and serial number inked in the upper right corner. In the opposite corner the file bore a red KIA tag, denoting Killed in Action. Carl
Friessen was dead.

Stunned, Ben took in the words—"On patrol to secure the
Hollandia perimeter in the New Guinea campaign . . . enemy ambush . . ." No million-dollar wound nor any other kind short of
lethal for the laconic lineman he had played next to, in the faraway
of two years ago. Somehow Friessen's number had come up on the
wrong side of the law of averages with the earlier two—so much
for Tepee Weepy's goddamn statistical measurement—and a sick
fury at the merciless twist in arithmetic filled Ben. Making a fist,
he crumpled the envelope to hurl it in the waste barrel at the end
of the bench; something inside resisted. He shook the envelope
onto the worktable. Another file fell out, also with a KIA tag.

This one was Vic Rennie's.

1944

★

6

★ THE WEATHER EVER since Christmas had not been able to make its mind up, thawing and then turning cold, and candles of ice hung silvery on the otherwise darkened eaves of Gros Ventre. Now snow flurries and the breeze courting them waltzed across the surfaces of light spread onto the hardened ground from the front windows of the festive house, lit up in more ways than one this last and most celebrated night of the year. All evening long Cloyce Reinking had reminded her husband to keep the drinks flowing, people in this town soaked it in in a fashion that would have put a Beverly Hills crowd under the rug. She appraised the heightened conversations filling the living room from corner to corner and took as much satisfaction as she would allow herself in how the party was going.

"Unfair." Carnelia Muntz materialized at the buffet table as Cloyce was trying to deploy the buffet remnants to better effect. "How am I supposed to top this when I have the canasta club over, spike the angel food?" Carnelia was the banker's wife and always regally aware of it. She sighted over her glass to the circle of guests around the prize of the evening, the Senator and his wife and daughter. "You're a hard act to follow, Cloycie."

"You sound like Bill. He accuses me of a pagan passion for New Year's Eve."

"Your night to shine. I see Ben finally made it."

"The bus was late. This weather."

Carnelia negligently nibbled a crumble of the colorless cheese from the local creamery which neither woman would have stooped to if it hadn't been for wartime rationing. "He's quite the hero one more time, isn't he, walking away from that plane wreck."

Cloyce held her tongue, not wanting to further sharpen Carnelia's. She looked across the jammed room past the medleys of the socially positioned of the town—doctor, lawyer, mayor, school superintendent, county agent, on down to postmaster and druggist, and their wives in holiday best—to the kitchen hallway where her son's ginger hair overtopped her husband's. What now? she wondered with a frown as the pair of them in their nook stayed oblivious to the wall-to-wall guests. Midnight was not that far off, and Ben still had not been in general circulation.

"So we won't be seeing much of you for a while." Bill Reinking's knuckles whitened on his bourbon glass.

"Mine not to reason why," Ben responded, tired through and through from trying to do exactly that. "I'll let Mother know tomorrow." What his latest set of orders, courtesy of Tepee Weepy, had in mind for him in the weeks and months ahead passed for creative in the military, but that didn't make it any less daunting to handle. All during the bus trip from East Base, calendar and map of war blended together into a twisty scroll he could see no end of, and arriving home under these circumstances further blurred the proportions of the existence being asked of him. Even the favorite old civilian clothes he had slipped into felt unfamiliar. The rising and falling crescendoes of party hubbub seemed otherworldly, echoes from some everlasting spot of time

when mead and feasting greeted a solar change of fortunes. Yet
this year's version held one prominent difference from his mother's other annual extravaganzas, there across the room where the
Senator was holding forth about something and everyone around
him was nodding as if keeping time. "Our hostess with the most-
est hit the jackpot tonight, didn't she," Ben acknowledged. "The
big sugar himself. How'd you drag him in on this?"

"The incalculable power of the press, of course," came the
puckish answer. Bill Reinking elaborated that the lawmaker was
in town on the start of a swing to sprinkle reclamation appro-
priations down the Continental Divide watersheds where his big
voting majorities lay county by county. In short, the Senator had
his own way of celebrating the onset of an election year. "When
his press mouthpiece—sorry, his spokesman—phoned wanting
to know if the Senator could get together with a few people while
he was here, all I said was, 'How about half the town?'" The proprietor and opinion-setter of the *Gleaner* sighed. "Now I have to
give the old boy a hard time in a couple of editorials to show he
doesn't have me in his pocket."

"The fun and games of dealing with Washington. I'm going
to have to take lessons from you." Ben did not smile as he said it.

"Don't I wish I had the formula to give you," came the swift
response. "How hard did TPWP kick about your piece on Vic?"

"Enough to smart for a while," Ben had to admit, the hard-
edged teletype messages back and forth still with him. "I finally
had to dig in and point out to them they got all the goddamn
combat angle they could possibly want in the one I had to do on
Friessen."

A cascade of laughter from the contingent surrounding the
Senator caused Ben to pause and look over there, then back at
his father. "It was just Tepee Weepy's view of the war against
mine, Dad. I'm over it." He wasn't. The whole thing with Vic still
haunted him. Escorting caskets had that effect. When Corporal

Victor Rennie was interred with full military honors in the cemetery up on the hill, the scene drew everlasting lines in the sod of memory. Toussaint ancient and alone on one side of the grave, the Blackfeet relatives at a little distance on the other side. Jake thumping around on his cast served as a pallbearer; Dex sent word he could not. Ben withstood it all except for the final three words in granite. *I managed to wangle out of my story what the lying bastards wanted in, buddy, but I couldn't keep it off the gravestone for you.* He glanced out the nearest window-well of light at the flurries lacing the bases of everything with whiteness; the stone-cut line KILLED IN ACTION soon would be covered until spring, at least.

Bill Reinking shook his head. In his time he had thrown away bales of news releases less fanciful than the Threshold Press War Project version that bestowed a heroic death in combat on a one-legged hospital patient confined to a wheelchair. "What've you been able to find out," he asked low and close, one journalist to another, "about the honest-to-God circumstances?"

"It wasn't pretty," Ben began tightly, "but it wasn't that different from what England has been put through all the time, either." Once more he imagined Vic there in the green and gray countryside where distant skytrails of smoke marked the ongoing battle between the Royal Air Force and the Luftwaffe. "Officially they called what happened a bombing raid on the hospital—that's how they tagged it 'combat' because it's a military installation of a kind and maybe somebody there did take a shot back at a plane." He lifted his shoulders, the universal *who knows*? In the scene in his mind, what counted was the amputee on wheels suddenly left to himself, his perch on the rolling lawn forgotten in the general scurry away from the approaching sounds of bombs. "Since no buildings were hit, my guess is it was some Jerry dumping his load before scooting back across the Channel and a few bombs strayed onto the hospital grounds."

The next words he organized with slow care, not wanting them to be too theatrical. "There's one of those old canals they have everywhere in that part of England, at the bottom of the slope from the hospital, where they used to haul supplies in by barge. During all the commotion, Vic's wheelchair went in the water. They didn't find him until the next day."

Ben stopped there, although he need not have. He was certain as anything that while the hospital attendants were ducking for cover, Vic had taken one last sharp look around and given the wheelchair a running start down the slope toward the deep-sided waterway, his chosen exit from a life that no longer held anything for him.

"Not quite like the official handout, was it," Bill Reinking summed that up in the arid tone of a veteran editor. Uneasy with what Ben had to contend with, he asked: "Who makes a decision like that, how they classify that kind of a death?"

"Someone who wants every dead soldier in any uniform of ours to be a shining hero." *Four for four, so far. The Supreme Team stays perfect with a little help from Tepee Weepy and in spite of me. Or Vic.*

Just then Chick Jennings, the postmaster, reeled past on his way to the bathroom. "You sure know how to throw a party, Bill. And how you doing, Ben?" he delivered with a passing clap on the shoulder. "What do you think, this the year the boys will whip the Japs and Krauts and get to come home?" It was common knowledge Chick's son was a Navy quartermaster safely tucked away in Pascagoula, Mississippi.

"Not all of them," Ben said through his teeth.

"Ben," his father began, "people say things they don't—"

"I know, Dad, it's okay. I lost it there for half a second, is all." *Don't get on your high horse,* he chided himself, *this is just the Officers' Club of the home front.* He knew he ought to rouse himself to the business of festivity even though he had no stomach for it

away from Cass. "Any chance to be home, do it," she had urged
him to take the holiday pass, a case of use it or lose it. "Get away
from this military madhouse. I'm on standby that weekend anyway, you won't be missing any ton of fun here. Go, palooka."

SHE AT THAT moment was nursing her one lonely scotch in the
back area of the Officers' Club known as the "orphans' corner."
It felt odd to be there with the handful of male loners—for some
reason, they tended to have tidy little cookie-duster mustaches
like department store floorwalkers—who sat one by one staring
out darkened windows as they toyed with their drinks. However,
it was the safest territory around. A woman sitting alone anywhere else in the building invited the interest of every brass type
with a touch of the screw flu. Here Captain Cass Standish was
just another withdrawn officer trying to drink slow and write a
letter. Besides, at midnight she had to go back on standby in the
ready room; unless Germany or Japan directly attacked Great
Falls, that meant another stint of killing time until 0800. Nineteen forty-four did not look like anything to celebrate yet; she
hoped Ben was having better luck where he was.

   Out of sight of Cass although definitely not out of hearing,
the throng around the piano player gleefully spotted a target of
opportunity as Della Maclaine and her date frisked in from outside. If they were somewhat mussed from fooling around with
each other on the way over, in the overriding smudge of cigarette smoke and pall of alcohol no one was paying attention to
personal tidiness. What caught the combined choral eye was the
sassy tilt of the crush hat on Della's blonde flow of hair and, of
course, the pilot's insignia prominent on her chest. The piano
bunch was instantly inspired.

   Oh, don't give me a P-39,
   The engine is mounted behind.

> She'll tumble and spin,
> She'll augur you in,
> Don't give me a P-39!
>
> No, give WASPs the P-39,
> Let them cuss the design.
> There'll be medals in baskets
> For flying those caskets,
> Give WASPs the P-39!

Della gamely lingered and took it, the motor pool officer she was with nervous at her side. The song done, she sent a honeyed smile to the serenaders and gave them a thumbs-up. No, wait. It was a different digit. Passing the hooting piano gang as her date broke trail toward a table at the quieter far end, she could not help but notice the big pilot with a rakish flop to his dark hair giving her the eye as she went by, but she was not in the market for the glee-club type. Better someone with a jeep or classier wheels.

On past the singing drinking coterie, she spotted Cass holding down one of the spots for the socially backward. Captain Standoffish, too occupied with herself to join in the celebration along the bar. Seizing the chance, Della cooed an excuse in the ear of her date and promised him better things to come, then headed for Cass.

"Care if I join you, Captain ma'am?"

Cass looked up in surprise from her writing paper. "What the hey, Lieutenant Maclaine, sit yourself down."

BEN FELT A HAND, loving but firm, at the crook of his elbow. "Time to break it up, you two. I need to borrow my soldier." Words warm as toast, and the crust there for emphasis. His mother's diction made her a standout in amateur theatricals, the loftier the dialogue the better. Certainly she looked like the leading lady tonight, with her hair freshly fixed and her aqua-marine party dress on, and both men self-consciously shrugged around in their clothes a bit as if that would help to approach her level. "Bill, I think people are ready for another round."

"Next year I'll just hand out bottles instead of glasses." As his father went off to liquor duty, Ben set himself to escort his mother sociably around the room as she no doubt wanted. But she didn't move toward that and her tone was forgiving—he tried to think for what?—as she said: "Are your ears burning? We were just talking about you."

"And here I thought that was frostbite from the bus ride," he endeavored to make it sound teasing. "So," he watched his mother for a further moment to see where this might go, "what did you conclude?"

She had not expected that he would treat her remark as more than a pleasantry to warm him up for the meeting and greeting ahead. But then Ben was inadvertently dramatic tonight, the last healing traces of scrapes from that plane crash like character lines drawn strong on his face. "If it were up to me," she decided to venture, "I'd say that you look like you could use more than a night off. I'm worried about you, you've been all over the map without letup. Doesn't that strange unit of yours ever have furloughs?"

Ben drained the last of his drink. "The war doesn't take furloughs, Mother, so TPWP sees no reason to. I'm theirs for the duration, lock, stock, and typewriter."

She looked at him critically, hoping Carnelia Muntz didn't cross paths with him while he was like this. "Are you tight?"

"Sober as a gravedigger." The old saying fit his frame of mind, if not the moment.

"Ben." His mother's intensity broke the spell of debate. "I know you've had a hard time of it recently, but heavens, it's New Year's Eve. Can't you enjoy yourself for that long?"

The prowess of more than one small-town drama director rested on Cloyce Reinking's ability to use her voice the way a hypnotist uses a watch fob. The trouble was, the two men in her own house had built up a certain level of resistance down through the years. *I'm here, Mother. Your competition is on standby tonight or you'd really have a vacant spot where I'm standing.*

Smiling winningly, she slipped her arm in his. "Come on over and meet the Senator's daughter. Adrianna is in the service too. She's stationed in Washington. You'll have a lot to talk about."

So that was it. Glancing across the gathering, he picked out the significant young woman in the cluster around the Senator and his wife; no male of military age in sight there or for that matter anywhere else in the room. He nearly laughed out loud, wishing Cass were here to see what happened when good intentions met up with his mother's designs.

CASS TOOK A QUICK look at the moonstruck officer Della had left parked at a table to wait for her; another new one, chronically the case with Della. *Playing the field. I wonder what that's like. I hope to hell I never find out.* The question of Dan or Ben constituted as much choosing as she ever wanted to have to do in one lifetime.

"Tough night to draw standby." Della's sympathy did not sound overwhelming. Actually, Cass was unprepared for any at all from her after their run-in at Edmonton just before Christmas. On that flight up, Della had piloted like a Sunday driver, lagging the formation and straying off the radio beam. Luckily the group of planes hadn't hit heavy weather or Cass would have had a lame duck back there to worry about along with everything else. It had taken a monumental chewing-out and a threat to ground Della if she didn't shape up, but it had worked, for the time being. Right now she had her eyes modestly down on the blue air-letter paper Cass's pen rested on. "Catching up on your correspondence?"

"To my husband. Della, what's on your mind?"

"I'm thinking of putting in for a transfer. To ground duty."

Happy New Year to you too, gutless wonder.

THE ENTIRE PARTY seemed to somehow have shifted about a step and a half toward the far wall of the living room, leaving a pocket of expectation where he and Adrianna were left together to make the most of this chance to get acquainted. *The young people, herded together as if nature intended. You'd think the two of us were being bartered by our tribes.*

"I heard you on *Meet the Forces*," she was saying, wasting no time, "telling about your plane crash. You made it sound all in a day's work."

"They put anybody who can deal in consecutive sentences on that show."

"That's awfully modest of you." She studied the traces on his face as though they were gladiator souvenirs. "You maybe can guess—my folks have followed your doings ever since football. They tell me when you set out to do something, you're the best at it."

It took just a few such battings of the eyes for Ben to realize that she was being a good deal more than daughterly civil in making talk with him. And he had to admit, being around her was not hard duty. Adrianna was cute and a dash exotic in the same glance. Slender but substantial in the right places and in a snug maroon skirt and matching sweater that showed that off well enough. Caramel-colored hair that no doubt received a hundred brush strokes a day. Almond eyes and olive complexion. It was well-known that she was adopted, the senatorial couple setting an example of humanitarianism after that first inhumane world war. From somewhere on the Adriatic, or was he simply mixing that up with her name? She was a WAVE, that much he was sure of; the Senator had a practiced chuckle when he'd introduced her as his daughter the sailor.

For the next few minutes they kept on trading generalities—she told him she was just another of fifteen thousand Navy women serving in Washington wartime offices; he told her he was just a typewriter soldier being sent off on an overseas assignment early in the new year—until he came around to asking, "What do they have you doing?"

"I'm in the wire room."

Ben tried not to show any sign of the disputes he'd had with teletype clerks of many kinds down through time. Maybe she wasn't one of those, maybe she was in charge of changing the spools of telex ribbon. Which he immediately doubted; a senator's daughter would not be doing the chores.

"Keys to the kingdom, A to Z," he said guardedly.

"There's one bad part of the clerk job." Adrianna made a face. "Carbon paper. Our seersucker uniforms sop it up." She leaned a trifle closer, confidentiality coming with it. "Know how I get it off?"

"I have to confess I don't."

She looked around, then right up at him. "I climb in the bathtub with the uniform on and scrub the carbon off. It's kind of like using a washboard. Rub a dub dub." Hands in front of her chest, she surreptitiously pantomimed washerwoman motion on that handy part of herself for him. "Then drain out the blue water, take off the uniform and hang it to dry," she continued ever so innocently, "and go ahead and have my bath. It works."

"I'll bet it does." The back of his throat felt dry. There was a great deal more than a fleck of attraction in the thought of rub a dub dub. A debate had started up in him like dueling lightning.

When someone such as Adrianna handed herself to him on a platter, was he obliged to do his best to drop it? After all, you can cordon sex off from love. Soldiers did it all the time.

"THAT'S UP TO YOU," Cass was saying to the problem pilot across the table from her. Leave it alone, she told herself. Let her turn into a groundpounder if that's all she has the brains to do. And heard herself asking: "How come, Della?"

A flip of the blonde hair heralded the answer. "There's no room for me to move up in the squadron, is there. I'm always going to be Tail End Charlie."

Cass lifted her hands from the table and let them fall back.

"I'm not kicking about that, understand," Della hastened to say. "It's the way things are, seniority is something I can't do anything about. Buy you a drink, to show there are no hard feelings?"

THE ALASKA VODKA lesson staying with him, he sipped cautiously as Adrianna steered the conversation.

"TPWP is sort of hush-hush, isn't it." She treated this as though it were a secret between just the two of them. "You have your own code—it's off-limits to us."

"Mysterious are the ways of Tepee Weepy, I'm the first to agree."

"Tepee Weepy," she laughed low in her throat, "oh, that's funny. We have all kinds of those insane abbreviations in Washington. My father gets a charge out of saying the government is nothing but one big pot of alphabet soup."

Ben glanced now at that senatorial father, still holding forth to the other half of the room as inexhaustibly as if he were fili-bustering. *Sharp-cornered old devil. To look at him, you'd never know he's busy shopping for a son-in-law.* Right there in the fray, feeding the occasion in more ways than one, was the zealous hostess of all this. Ben had the passing thought that his mother should be the one writing a movie script. *Mr. Touchdown Goes to Washington,* by Cloyce Carteret Reinking.

UNCOUNTABLE DOWN through the terms in office—like a canine's, a politician's years measured differently—these home-state gatherings out away from that company town, Washington, were part campaign ritual and part self-schooling for the Senator. In the crisscross of conversations loosened by a bit of booze, he often picked up matters of interest that might otherwise surface unpleasantly on election day. He himself was a restrained drinker at these, as was Sadie, Adrianna a little less so. At the moment the daughter they had so fondly adopted and raised was, to his understanding eye, a sailor on leave, chatting up the pick of the evening, Cloyce and Bill Reinking's prize son. He and Sadie had needed to learn that Adrianna was rapid in her affections—at Thanksgiving it had been the Free French naval attaché. One of these times, something would have to come of these acquaintanceships sparked by the war. Gazing around the living-room party in apparent benevolence, the Senator marked Ben Reinking as one would a passage in a book worthy to return to.

THE DRINK OFFER was the only good thing Cass had heard out of Lieutenant Maclaine since she plopped down at the table. "Can't. Going on duty at midnight." Which, she figured, Della well knew when she volunteered to buy. *Why the hell can't she strut her stuff when it counts?* "It's a shame, though," Cass said as if the words were too stubborn to keep in. "You throwing away your wings." *Messing up the squadron just when I was finally starting to get you straightened out.*

Della checked her for sarcasm. "What do you mean, a shame?"

"Don't you remember?" Cass waved accusingly in the general direction of Texas. "From day one at Sweetwater, those bald old

coots who called themselves flight instructors said that about us.
'Most of you women won't stick around in that pilot seat,'" she
mimicked their seen-it-all drawl. "'Something will git on your
nerves and you'll take up being a pedestrian again.'"

That set off a blonde flare in the chair opposite. "Cass, that
is in no way fair. My nerves are perfectly fine and I am not most
women."

"It's rough," Cass led into, "to be low schmoe on the totem
pole, I know. I've been there." She drained the last of her lonely
drink and took a quick look at the clock. "But lack of seniority
doesn't last forever, if you keep on breathing." She mulled how to
say the rest of this, knowing she should be strenuously debating
with herself about saying it at all. *What the hey, bluff on through,
you have nothing to lose but a Tail End Charlie.* She honored
the fact that Beryl did not want her request for a transfer to the
Wichita bomber factory run bandied about, but a hint would
serve the same purpose, would it not. "There are a dozen slots in
the squadron, there just might be some turnover."

It changed Della's approach markedly. "I'd have a shot at being wingman?"

Cass rose to go on duty. "Only if you hang on to your wings.
Happy new year, Lieutenant."

ONE THING WAS leading to another more precipitously than
Ben wanted to be led, all signs pointing to a celebratory kiss at
midnight to start off the Adrianna era. He could wish dozens
of things for the coming year, starting with Cass and him in
circumstances that did not know war or inconvenient husband.
All that went onto the tosspile of dreams, however, if he got
involved with what was standing in front of him in snug maroon. "My father just gave me the high sign about something,"
he resorted to. "Let me get you a drink while I go see what's on
his mind."

"I'll hold out for champagne," Adrianna said with a wink. "Hurry back."

A sign of some sort, in fact, was what Ben had spotted across the room, the back of his father as he slipped away from the party hubbub to the quiet book-lined room upstairs. Hearing Ben step in, Bill Reinking turned from the window where he was looking out at the snow sifting down. "What's this, another absconder from the merrymaking?" He smiled faintly. "You needn't take after me in that bad habit."

"The merrymaking can stagger along without us for a little while, Dad."

His father nodded. Swirling his glass, he turned back to the snow scene of the window. "Vic Rennie," he said barely above a murmur. "I owe it to Toussaint to write a little something more about him." He chugged the last of what was in the glass. "Don't worry, I'll stay away from how he died. I'll keep to the soldier-from-the-reservation peg, although I goddamn sure won't make it heartwarming." He shook his head one more time. "Poor divvied-out kid, always caught between. What was he, half-breed, quarter—?"

"I don't even know," Ben answered. "When anybody would ask, he'd say 'Enough.'"

Bill Reinking grunted and moved off from the window-well to the bookshelves that walled the room. His son followed him with his eyes, the old feel of the words in wait enwrapping the two of them. Ben never forgot the touchable value of the books in this room, his boyhood times of running his fingers across the collected spines standing on the shelves like delicately done upright bricks. All the good-nights when he would pad in to find this bespectacled man deep into Thucydides or Parkman or Tolstoy, and there would come the brief contented smile and the adage, time and again, "History writes the best yarns." As Ben watched now, his father scanned the rows of titles as if reminding

himself there was this room to come back to after tonight. Thinking aloud, the older man said: "Your mother will nail both our
hides to the wall if we don't pitch in at the party pretty quick."

"Mine, anyway," Ben conceded. "I'm supposed to be down
there making out like mad with fair maiden Adrianna."

His father took down a book and put it back without looking
at it. "Peril is not confined to the theaters of war, son."

This from the man known to have put in as the filler at the
bottom of a newspaper column *The matrimony vine is also called
boxthorn.* Ben shifted restlessly. He had pieced together the story
of his father and his mother considerably beyond even the evidence he grew up around in this house. The opening scene: the
glamorous set of grandparents he had never met, Clyde and Joyce
Carteret, early Hollywood royalty, silent-movie producer and actress. In 1919 the Carterets had brought their film company to
Glacier National Park and the adjacent Blackfoot Reservation
to shoot a quickie movie full of Indians and headdresses. While
there, their teenage daughter Cloyce met and fell for the young
man on assignment from the *Gleaner,* Bill Reinking. They bedded
and wedded, in a hurry both times; natural inquisitive reporter
that he was, Ben long since had figured out that his parents' was
a shotgun wedding. And early in that marriage, the Carterets
of Hollywood and Beverly Hills were killed in a car accident on
location and Cloyce, reluctantly of Gros Ventre from then on,
was left with another of those utterances fit to sneak beneath a
column of type, "*God made the country, man made the city, and
the devil made the small town.*"

Family, the oldest argument on earth. Ben gazed across the
room at the male half of the one that endured under this roof.
"I'm open to ideas that won't put both of us in the doghouse,
Dad."

Bill Reinking paused in his roaming of the bookshelves as
if he had come to what he was looking for. "If you want to head

down to the Medicine Lodge," he said over his shoulder, "I'll cover for you. I'll tell your mother you just remembered you had to cadge some gas coupons, she really can't argue with those."

Ben grinned for the first time that night. "The daughter of a senator up for reelection can't afford to be seen trotting off to a saloon with a soldier, would you say?"

"I would. Don't forget the gas coupons."

7

⭐ THE PACIFIC WAS anything but pacifying as he picked his way along a shore completely foreign to him. To one side of his narrow line of march, giant logs gray as archeological bones had been tossed by storms into an endless pile he could not see over, while just beyond the driftwood barricade the forest came crowding in, thick and bristling as bear hair. On the ocean side, a short distance offshore towered dark contorted seastacks like the Great Wall of China fractured by eternal assault. The tide, thick cream-colored surf changing eerily back to milk as it slid up the beach, seemed particularly determined to hem him in; every step of the way he had to monitor the tide line from the corner of his eye or the hissing white water would flood over his boots. Meanwhile the footing shifted from gentle sand as black-gray as gunpowder one minute to rugged gravel the next and then to roundbacked rocks, without rhyme or reason that he could see. *And this is the easy part,* Ben reasoned with himself.

He had hiked his full share of the arch of North America, the high hunting country that crisscrossed the Continental Divide back in Montana, but this was his first time to explore any of the other national extremity, the coastal sill where the land-mass wrested itself from the sea. Out here in the state of Washington was the American shore at its most remote, dangling like a coarse fringe from the huge cape where the Strait of Juan de Fuca angled into the continent. Its isolation spooked Ben. He'd slogged the beach for three hours from the barely extant salmon fishing village of LaPush without seeing another living soul or even a footprint, and now nearly another hour from the pre-fabricated military hut where the Coast Guardsman he roused from off-duty sleep told him Prokosch was on patrol somewhere around the next big rocky headland. Somewhere translated to anywhere, Ben discovered as he neared the rugged point of rocks backed by a clay cliff fully a hundred feet high and there still was no least evidence of Prokosch.

"SIG!" he shouted again through cupped hands. "HEY, BUDDY, YOU'VE GOT COMPANY." The Coast Guardsman at the hut had warned him sentry duty here tended to make a person jumpy and it would be a good idea to yell out for Prokosch every so often. The problem with that was, the crash of the surf obliterated all shouts. Checking back at the crescent beach he had just crossed, Ben still saw only the solitary string of his own tracks, no other human sign, and with consummate dread he faced around to the headland. *It just doesn't let up.* Surf poured onto the outermost ledge of stone with a power he could bodily feel, the spray spewing into the air like a school of geysers. The cliff was too steep and slick to tackle, so the only route lay across jumbled boulders in avalanche repose at the base of the headland. He wiped from his lips the saltwater taste that clung in the air and took a swig from his canteen while he eyed the situation some more. The question remained whether he could work his way across that rockfield without the tide catching him there. This notorious coast frequently drowned entire ships, it wouldn't hesitate a smatter of an instant on him. Yet Prokosch somehow navigated this shore on foot, didn't he, proving it could be done. *Or maybe he's learned amphibious rock climbing by now.*

Feeling like a tightrope walker about to launch into space between tall buildings, he nerved himself up and was testing the first footholds in the rock mass when a voice and a growl broke out in startling duet close behind him. The growl was universal, but whatever the voice was saying, it was in Japanese.

A nest of saboteurs: that was the first terrible thought flashing into his mind. Followed by the immediate one that this was prelude to an invasion, the follow-up on Pearl Harbor by the Empire of the Rising Sun. Whatever trick of war he had stumbled into on this alien coast, the enemy language numbed him like a bite by something poisonous. Spread-eagled upright, he could do nothing but cling motionless there while, ever so slowly, a man-size form and a lower one crept into the edge of his vision.

"Sonofagun, Lefty," Sig Prokosch spoke in English this time. "You aren't a Jap at all. Come on down."

Unsticking himself from the rock face, Ben dropped none too gracefully to the beach sand. He turned all the way around to a strapping gray-helmeted figure much more bulkily outfitted than when they had been in football uniform together. A radio pack rode high on Prokosch's back and above that waved the antenna like a giant insect feeler; his field jacket bulged with other military items, including a .45-calibre pistol holstered on one flank of a web belt around his sturdy waist. Hooked into the other side of the web belt was a leash, with a copper-red Irish setter at its end.

The dog ceased its steady growl when Sig dropped a hand to it. Recovering his voice, Ben could only blurt: "You're a tough pair to find."

"Supposed to be," came the modest reply. By now Sig had slung his tommy gun around into proximity with the radio pack and had a hand free to shake with Ben. "Been me, I'd've waited at the hut."

Ben did not go into reportorial reasoning, which was that his previous piece on this old teammate happened to occur during the Coast Guard's version of basic training and amounted to a look at a taciturn block of young male trudging a treadmill of routine; in short, snooze news. This time around, he had come determined to portray Sigmund Prokosch, seaman second class, true-blue Coastie, on an unknown foreshore of the war. First question: "How'd you get so fancy in Japanese?"

"All it means, 'Don't move or I'll shoot.'" Sig shrugged. "They give us these phrase books."

"Well, it sure as hell did the job on me." With the indiscretion of acquaintances who had not laid eyes on one another since their world changed, the two of them traded extended looks. Not that the practiced sentry could be matched at that. One of Sig's traits was a prairie gaze; he seemed to blink only half as much as other people. Those pale blue eyes under wheat-colored hair, in a meaty mess of a face; a fairly alarming combination staring out from a football helmet or a metal military one. Prokosch had played guard next to Animal Angelides at tackle on the right-hand side of the line. Ben would not have wanted to be on the other team opposite those two, one a marauder, the other a boulder. Mindful that he knew the habits more than the person, he unshouldered his pack and searched into it. "Before I forget, I brought you some Hershey's."

The box of candy bars produced a bashful acknowledging smile on the recipient. During football road trips he'd had the reputation of practically living on chocolate sundaes.

"Thanks a bunch, Lefty," Ben received in return. He was going to have to get used to this for the next few days. The nickname applied to him by only five people in the entire world—three now dead—like a tattoo he hadn't asked for.

The candy transaction was watched by the Irish setter with keen interest to the point where his master broke off a square of chocolate and carefully fed it to him. As man and canine chomped in unison, Ben used the chance to ask, "What's the dog about?"

"I say 'Get him' and he gets you." Delivered with a straight face, this was either what passed for a joke with Prokosch or the stolid actuality. Another shrug. "Give you my guess, I think he's supposed to be company for us." The dog's back was stroked with a beefy hand. "Naw, though, Rex here is trained to sniff out Japs, aren't you, boy."

Catching Ben's skeptical glance at the untrodden shore, Sig laid it out tersely: "Fresh water. Their submarine crews sneak in on rubber rafts to fill up." His listener envisioned the possibility. Constant creeks with water the color of tea had intersected the beach all during Ben's hike to here, some he'd been able to scramble across on logs, others he had needed to ford up to his thighs. As he unsheathed his notepad, the thought that he could have stumbled onto Japanese submariners replenishing their drinking supply from this seeping shore made the whole place more creepy than ever.

What Prokosch was saying furthered the feeling. "Raft rats, I call them. If I ever catch them at it and they give me any trouble, I'll put Tom to working on them." He patted the stock of his Thompson submachine gun.

Ben took due reportorial care over *if.* "These rafts, Sig—ever laid eyes on them yourself?"

Prokosch indicated *Not yet.* "Just signs. The buggers can't resist taking a crap on dry land, for sure. Find piles around the creek mouths." His expression registering offense at that, he petted the dog again. "Rex here smells out that stuff and any drag marks that look like where a raft came in and so on. If the signs look fresh enough, we call in the depth-charge boys from the air base at Port Angeles. Done it a couple of times already."

"Have you." Ben groped for any certainty in this. If ever there was a coastline that would breed phantoms, it was this murky Pacific Northwest one. But Prokosch must be able to tell human crap from bear shit, mustn't he? Or was all this just classic jumpy nerves of an isolated sentinel? By any sum it was more than a notepad-carrying visitor bargained for. How would Tepee Weepy react to the story of a Supreme Team member in hide-and-seek with Japanese naval forces, genuine or imagined, in America's own backyard? There was one way to find out. "Any luck?" Ben inquired as he scribbled away.

"Never know," the sentry blunt as the coast he walked. "The flyboys think they spotted an oil slick after they bombed like hell one of those times. Could have been a decoy or from a sunk tanker." He kicked some sand as if his next thought might be hidden under it. "Those tin fish are out there, though. We got a report a while back that a Jap sub came up in broad daylight down in Oregon. Fired a few shells onto some beach. Just to prove they could, I guess." The contemplative Coast Guardsman scanned out past the curling white sets of breakers to the vaster ocean as if mildly daring the enemy to try that on his patrol route, then turned unblinking eyes to Ben. "About time to head for the hut. Ready for a hike, Lefty?"

IT WAS WORK every step of the way, trying to fathom Sig Prokosch those next days on the challenging coast. Trudging the hours of patrol with him, Ben would catch himself yearning for Jake Eisman's wisecracks or even Dex Cariston's high-flown sparring. Somewhere between shy and offhandedly mum, Sig went his route like a man who had left his conversation at home. Questions to him had to be doled out, circled back to, followed to conclusions somewhere down the road, and there were times Ben felt he would have better luck talking to the dog.

Gradually, though, the thickset guard gave out glimpses of himself unsuspected in four years on the football field and in the locker room. Sig liked to cook; at the hut it invariably fell to him to prepare any meal fancier than fried Spam with canned pineapple atop. He was a twin, a truly startling thought; his sister was a missionary in the Yukon Territory. *If she's anything like him, the natives will convert just to see what's on her mind.* The Prokosch family came from Devon, one of the depot towns sprinkled out of an atlas in the last century when the Great Northern Railway needed names for its stops in the middle of nowhere across the top of Montana. The wrong side of the tracks of Devon at that, Ben divined: the father had always worked as a common section hand, riding a speeder on the rails across the prairie to wrestle creosoted ties into place and disgorge brush and muck from clogged roadbed culverts. A modern coolie. Sig with his accounting degree aspired to one of those American human cannonball advancements in a single generation, a desk job at the railroad home office in St. Paul. Ambition, incentive, a path in the mind with sufficient byways: little by little, the personality practically buried under that gray Coastie uniform began to assume shape as Ben made notes. Yet something kept nagging about Sig's enlistment in the Coast Guard and Ben could not get at it. Phrase it every which way, no clear answer could be drawn as to why someone from one of the most landlocked towns imaginable had chosen to turn into a beachpounder.

Until it emerged that Prokosch had a girl waiting for him back home in Devon. Inasmuch as Sig would have been a serious contender in an ugly contest, this constituted news. It also prompted in Ben a sense of relief that he was not sure he could defend, that the not particularly imaginative man at his side had chosen, with marriage aforethought, to put in his military time away from the front lines. Back at East Base in the farewell round of beers at the Officers' Club, Jake Eisman had leaned back and shrewdly observed, "Benjamin, you're maybe just as glad some of us are stationed stateside." How deny it? Given the toll on overseas members of the Supreme Team, if any of the others could be hoarded to safer duty, so much the better. Obituaries were the dregs of writing; if he never had to write another one it would be soon enough. Now Ben took a fresh look at Seaman Prokosch and asked, "What's this wonder woman's name?"

This brought a bashful dip of the head and the smitten intonement:

"Ruby."

When Sig spoke it, the word glowed as if it were her namesake gem. Love and the salt taste of absence, old as Odysseus, thought Ben as they tromped onward up the beach with the punctual waves always at their side. Wide open at the heart now, Sig poured forth the life he and Ruby were trying to plan in the time to come, that touchstone of all soldiers, *after the war*. Look that in the face long enough, and you begin to question the current sorry state of things. Sig at length reached the point where he brought out:

"Been going to ask you something. You get around in the war. You know about those balloon bombs?"

Ben merely nodded, to see where this would go. As if in some final desperate frenzy, Japan on its side of the Pacific had begun launching slim long-range balloons with explosive devices attached. The aim was to set the forests of the western United States on fire. Some of the balloons, weirdly like miniature paratroopers, had drifted as far as the Rockies. No great damage had been reported as yet, but the devices were worrisome if, as intelligence estimates had it, they were launched hundreds at a time.

Sig indicated the oceanic sky. "We spot any coming, we're supposed to shoot them down, ha." His gaze dropped to the watery horizon and stayed. "Maybe Animal will get first crack at them—Marines are supposed to take the lead, aren't they." A considering tilt of the head. "Kind of funny to think of him at the other end of this water, somewhere." Ben noticed he did not include Danzer, on destroyer duty in what was equally the Pacific, in this musing.

Reflection evidently over, Sig fixed his attention back toward Ben. He for once looked bothered. "They tell us the Japs even have their little kids in school making those balloons. Think that's so?"

"I don't really doubt it."

Sig's expression changed for the worse, which was saying a lot. "There's no limit to what people will do, I guess."

Just then they were coming to a creek mouth, and the Irish setter tugged at the leash.

"Rex thinks he's got something," Sig murmured as he swiftly unslung his tommy gun. In the next motion he handed Ben the .45 pistol from his holster. "Just in case."

Ben took in the situation uneasily. Where the brown-colored creek snaked out of the forest, vegetation proliferated. The dense greenery, too thick to see into, could handily hide a rubber raft and a raftload of touchy Japanese. The American jungle: he had never expected to be going into combat here. Sig showed no such concern.

Weapons ready, the pair of them stayed out of sight as best they could behind driftlogs and approached the verge of the overgrown patch, led by the stalking dog. The question ran in Ben's mind, what armaments would Japanese submariners bring to shore with them? *Probably a hell of a lot more than one tommy gun and one pistol.* As he and Sig edged in, far enough apart not to be raked by a single burst of gunfire, the bloody path above the Bitoi River came back to him full-toned as a film on a screen.

In New Guinea the cover for ambush had been tall boonie grass; here it was salal, brush, fir forest. He tried to creep silently through the undergrowth that crowded the flow of water, watching the twisting creekbank ahead for any movement. Sig, with the dog now alertly obedient behind him on the leash hooked into the web belt, was in view one moment and then wasn't. Ben braced, reminded himself to blaze away with the pistol rather than sight in—the .45 would knock an enemy down if it so much as nicked him—and parted the last underbrush into a glade of grass.

Sig was standing there peering at the beaten-down vegetation. "Deer," he called over and shouldered his tommy gun. The dog wagged, awaiting praise.

It was when they resumed their line of march on the other side of the creek, raft rats receding back into the hypothetical, that Sig's line of thought circled around to:

"You got somebody like Ruby?"

"I do." Ben was surprised both by the question and his own answer. By any reading of law civil or military, Cass was anything but that definite in his prospect. And the war was not nearly done with either of them. Yet, for the life of him, he could not have replied other than he did. "She'll be in Seattle when I get there."

"Good for you."

So it went, those days of pounding the beach side by side with Prokosch. Bit by bit Ben absorbed the feel of the continental coast, the inevitable linkage of the Pacific to national destinies. *The ocean named for peace now rims the widest war in history,* his piece would begin. *The circumference of war takes in even those who lived farthest from the muster of the surf.* And Prokosch himself he liked in the way you like an oddball cousin met up with at a family gathering. Let him be vigilant against raft rats, quite possibly more imagined than real; it put a human boulder into place out here among the shore rocks, Ben could attest to that. For once he felt he was writing about duty without bloodshed hanging over it like a red cloud about to burst. Prokosch's modest odyssey, a saltwater watchman on watch, suited the coastal subject with the ease of a hearthside tale. So he thought.

"Lefty?"

On the last day, patrol nearly over, the hut within welcome distance, Sig had halted. He kicked at the sand, a sign Ben recognized. Then came out with it:

"I want to get up north. The Aleutians."

The grimness of a chronicler whose storyline had abruptly veered off the page took Ben over. *You and Jones. That makes two of you out of the entire human race, maniacs for the Ablution Islands.* He knew that a rain-quiet snuggery in which to read the Bible was not Sig's reason. He asked anyway:

"Why there instead of here?"

"Better chance to actually see what a Jap looks like before the war is over," Sig reasoned thinly as if still rehearsing this. "Instead of just their turds." He looked at Ben with gathered determination. "Sea duty on a patrol frigate, is what I'm thinking. Wondered if you could help any on that?"

"There's real war up there," Ben argued. The newsreel of the Japanese bombing of Dutch Harbor, smoke boiling above Alaskan soil, brought that home to America; he wondered if it had missed Prokosch. "Coast Guard service, though, that's still considered home waters, right? Won't bring you any overseas points toward discharge."

"Naw, it's not that." The unblinking gaze stayed on Ben. "I want to get back at them some for the other guys." O'Fallon, Havel, Friessen, Rennie. Three fellow linemen and everyone's favorite backfield teammate. The outsize loss that preyed on those who were left. The mortal arithmetic that nullified reason. The war did this to people.

Two men and a dog, they stood there in the surf sound, its grave beat upon the shore. Finally Ben said, "Sig, I don't have that kind of pull." Fully aware of his unsureness whether he would use it in this instance if he had it.

"You ever get some, Lefty," came the stolid reply, "keep me in mind."

8

⭐ "I HATE IT WHEN I'm late. What's on the menu here besides you, good-looking?" Scooting in across from him in the booth, Cass shot him a smile with the teasing little slot between the teeth like a central promise of mischief later.

Ben just sat there taking her in. The crush hat, pilots' cachet in its rakish touch of crumple and scuffed visor brim; only veterans of the air were permitted to wear it without the loop band in the top that way. Her hair casually cut to mid-length but nice as ever. The army-tan tie knotted just so, spacing the twin silvers of captain's insignia on her collar tabs. Standard-issue trench coat worn against the Seattle damp, over her light khaki dress uniform, both trimly tailored to the snug body he knew so well. This was essential Cass to him, managing to look both proficient and snazzy, and the smile added to it as she eyed him back. "What are you so busy grinning about?"

"You. And how baboon lucky I am to be with you."

"Hey. I'm not so sure I'm a lucky charm." Shedding the crush hat and coat with dispatch, she took in the weathered waterfront atmosphere of the eating establishment. "More like a busted-flush flier trying to wind down. What's to drink?"

"Beer by the pound." He indicated the generous golden schooner in front of him.

"Mmm, tempting." A little beat of deliberation before she said: "I need something stiffer than that, though, after fighting off the MPs."

"That's not funny, you know."

"I know."

No, the military police were not a kidding matter. Besides whatever "fighting off the MPs" meant. *Where did this come from, Captain Standish? Only one night together for who knows how long, and something already is in the way.* Resolutely he flagged down a gray-haired waitress built along the lines of an old workhorse, who creaked off to fetch a scotch for Cass.

"So tell me," he could not keep the apprehension out of his voice, "what introduces you to the MPs?"

"The uniform," she answered bitterly. "Those idiots didn't know what a WASP is." Recounting it riled her up to the degree of combustion the military policemen must have faced. "They stopped me down the street. I don't know what they thought, that I'd rolled some soldier for his getup or I was a streetwalker ready to play games or what. It burns me up, Ben. I've been in this damn war as long as anybody, and so have plenty of other women. And we still get chickenshit treatment like that. Why should we?"

He took a chance and gawked off in the direction where it had happened. "I hope there's not a couple of MPs bleeding in the street out there."

It raised her mood. "Close," she laughed. With a mock air of insouciance she touched the captain's bar on her collar. "It ended up I had them calling me 'sir.'"

Relieved, he signaled for another round of drinks in tribute to that. With lifted spirits, they locked onto what the rest of the evening promised. The waitress decided they were worthy of menus, and they teased each other into ordering oysters. Angels on Horseback, he picked out, how could he pass up a chance at something so grandly named? She would go him one better, she growled in her best poker-player guise, Oysters Rockefeller. The shambling restaurant was situated above the harbor, tacked onto the arcade and stalls of the public market, and out on Puget Sound ferryboats found their way back and forth with navigation lights that shimmered on the water. Seattle these nights had a military bearing, sailors in from the Bremerton fleet, soldiers unwinding from training at Fort Lewis, pilots from anywhere, and he and she for once sat comfortable as could be in the anonymity furnished by the surround of so many uniforms like theirs. The rouseful smells of things grown in the earth and things harvested from the sea clung to the old set of structures hosting the market. The two of them imbibed it all, wanting to be nowhere else and in no other company. *Why can't it be like this,* they shared the thought without having to say so, *on and on?*

Catching up on their weeks apart, Ben told of his time with Prokosch on coastal patrol. "I hope to hell he's imagining those rafts," he finished up, "and keeps his finger off the trigger. He's kind of like a jumpy sheepherder with a lot of gun. Spending all his time with himself can do funny things to a guy."

Cass in turn recited the latest twists and turns of keeping Lieutenant Maclaine in the air. "Last time up to Edmonton she was next thing to an ace, and this time we had to go on instruments and she was ready to quit by the time she found the ground. That's Della for you."

He sat back, reflective. "So you have one you're trying to keep in the war, and I have one I hope never gets near it."

"There are times life doesn't cooperate worth a damn. How's that, newspaper guy?"

"I'll pass that right along to my father for filler. Guess what, we pay off in angel morsels." He speared his last oyster wrapped in bacon and held it across for her, and she leaned in and royally ate it off his fork. They traded a gaze of love well-flavored with lust. Or was it the other way around?

"Christ, Cass, I'm glad you showed up." The mention of flying blind in Canadian weather reminded him he hadn't asked her about getting here. "Any trouble cutting loose from East Base for this?"

"No, I flew a hospital ship over," she tossed it off along with a gulp of scotch.

The startled expression on Ben said if that wasn't a definition of trouble, he didn't know what was. An aircraft flown back to the factory with something internally wrong was called that because the hospital was where you might end up from flying it. He helplessly studied this woman he wanted so bad it made his ears ring and who came with all manner of peril attached. First the MPs, now this news. He always had to be aware Cass was a good deal more complicated than anyone gave her credit for. However, he would gladly do without further surprises along this line tonight. "Don't give me that look, you," she fended, trying for innocence. "I'm not the one who cracked up a floatplane in high-and-dry Canada, am I. The hospital crate didn't give me any trouble. The engine didn't conk or anything."

He resisted saying what a good thing that was, inasmuch as P-39s had the reputation of gliding like a brick. "I'm no authority," he graveled out, "the only damn thing they let me fly is a mahogany desk. But I don't want you risking your neck for me, Cass."

"Look who's talking." She said it lightly enough, but there was stiff meaning behind it. "If I remember right, you're the one with the scar "

"The wound was only skin-deep, that isn't anything like—"

"Don't give me that, hero. Skin is deep enough, when it comes to a bullet. You got that scar from following your football buddies around to places where people mainly get shot at. And you're about to do a bunch more of it."

"Only partly. The next one I go to is having as nice and safe a war as anybody can." Omitting *the one after that isn't.*

If Cass was reassured by the semi-alibi, she didn't show it. Cocking her head, she looked across as if needing to memorize him. "So how long do I have to get along without you?"

"Until summer sometime," he came out with it. "Teepy Weepy keeps feeding more stuff between the Supreme Team stories. I'm going to be all over the Pacific."

Cass smiled differently. "Next you're going to say, 'Write to me.'"

"Took the words right out of my mouth, grabby." Ben put his own best face on it. "I'll be a moving target, but letters—"

She reached over and flicked a blunt-nailed finger against one of his knuckles hard enough that it smarted. "I'd just as soon you didn't call yourself that."

Shaking the sting out of his hand, he made a bid for truce. "Before I get any deeper into trouble, how about we have another drink and I show madame to our room?"

Playing along, she leaned her arms way out onto the table of the booth and propped her chin on her hands before purring: "And will the accommodations be up to madame's expectations?"

"I'll have you know," he gave back haughtily, "the hotel room, the last one available in Seattle, is actually larger than a closet. By a foot or two, at least. It even has a special feature. A Murphy bed."

She hooted. "One of those that folds down out of the wall? Genius, what's to keep it from folding back up into the wall just when things get interesting?"

"Murphy the bed has experience longer than a flatfoot's lunch hour," he gave it the tough-guy treatment, "at such matters as this. The first time Murph lays his mattress-button eyes on the likes of you, he's gonna say, This is a lollapalooza I could happily fold away with forever—"

"See!"

"—but she is too classy to do that to. No, I'm gonna keep my frame on the floor for her, just to show my respect. The second I seen her I says, Murph, this dame takes the icing—"

"That's Captain Dame to you and Murph," she snipped in, "or I'll call my buddies, the MPs."

"—and like I was saying, it ain't many femmes in the land of Murphy that's also an officer and a gentleman, in a manner of speaking. No, I tell you, Murph the bed has seen his share and then some, and this woman is like the royal jewels shined up. Like the Taj Mahal in a skirt. Like—"

"Like a lunatic about to be with the guy for the last time in a blue moon," she took over the formulation, voice husky.

"That, too," he conceded wistfully. "Let's make this drink a quick one."

Out in the night the ferries came and went, shuttles on the dark loom of water. The port city in its nightspots and unbuttoned privacies settled to the business of such places down through time, harboring lovers and warriors.

9

⭐ *WHY HAVE I NEVER been able to stand Danzer? Let me count the ways. On the team, there was no love lost between the Dancer out there at right end grabbing glory with his jersey clean and the rest of the linemen beating their brains out throwing blocks for him with never any thanks. The only good word he ever had in the huddle would be for Moxie. "Good call, Stomp," I can still hear it, as if a Stamper-to-Danzer pass play didn't take the other nine of us to make it work. Jake used to say Danzer was so stuck on himself he had gum in his fur.*

That was football, only a game, supposedly. Games have any number of outcomes, though, personal scores that are not settled. If the ground of chance that brought us together had been in England, no doubt I'd be remembering a cricket match with Danzer in the whitest pants—and it still would be called only a game and count as eternally as if the score was being kept in the Doomsday Book.

"YOU'RE SURE THIS is the only way to get there, Chief?"

Ben arrived alongside the USS *McCorkle* to find a chasm of disturbed gray-green seawater between it and him, with canyon

walls of ship steel on either side. Consistently the swell of the
open ocean lifted the destroyer, across there, atop a foaming crest
while wallowing the oil ship he was aboard in the trough of the
wave. The ships then would dizzily trade elevations. Between the
rising and falling hulls stretched the pulley rope that was supposed to carry him across. The line looked to him as thin as
spiderspin.

"The motor launch might get crushed between if we tried
that, sir," the oiler's bowlegged chief petty officer replied, unflap-
pably tugging the breeches buoy into place around Ben's hips like
an oversize canvas diaper. "Not to worry, Lieutenant. We'll haul
you across in a jiffy and you'll get a real nice reception on the
Cork—the mail sack is following you over. Ready, sir?"

"No, and never going to be, so let's get it over with."

Legs sticking out of the canvas sling and arms tight around
the ring buoy that the sling hung from, he was sent bobbing into
mid-air, dipping and soaring with the teeter-totter rhythm of the
ships, the line with its dangling human cargo above the viciously
sloshing water but not that far above it. The sleek gray hull of the
destroyer loomed nearer and nearer until he began to be afraid
the next toss of ocean would splatter him against it like a lobbed
egg. Then there was a powerful yank from the crewmen handling
the haul rope attached to the pulley and he spun up over the side
of the hull into a sprawling descent onto deck.

A helping hand came down to him, and an unmistakable
dig along with it. "Welcome aboard, eminent war correspondent.
You're just in time for the invasion of Europe."

*Great start. Looking at my reflection in the Dancer's famous
shoes.* Unharnessing himself from the apparatus, Ben got up off
his hands and knees and sought his footing, the deck of the destroyer livelier than that of the slow-rolling oil supply ship the
past many days.

Meanwhile Danzer stood planted like a yachtsman in an easy breeze. Even though both men knew it did not fit their acquaintanceship, he had put on for general show his languid smile, as if about to say something then disdaining to.

Already irked—*What was that Europe crack about?*—Ben gave back the briefest of handshakes. "One of us has his oceans mixed up, Nick. I was under the distinct impression this is the Pacific." Without taking their eyes off the new arrival a number of sailors went about rote chores around them, their faded blue work attire a contrast to Danzer's khaki uniform, crisp in every crease.

Elaborately considerate, Danzer drew him away from the rope-and-pulley rig. "Stand aside, Ben, here's the real cargo." The mail sack came zinging down the line to the cheers of the sailors, followed anticlimactically by Ben's travel pack. "Come on to the wardroom and catch the broadcast of how the war is being won for us."

He realized Danzer wasn't just woofing him. There in officers' country it was standing room only, those who were off-duty awakened by the news and joining the morning watch in listening to the transmission piped in from the radio room. The entire compartment fell silent as General Eisenhower's crackling voice, half around the world on the Atlantic side of the globe of war, addressed his cross-Channel invasion force. "You are about to embark upon the great crusade toward which we have striven these many months . . . In company with our brave Allies and brothers-in-arms on other fronts, you will bring about the destruction of the German war machine . . . The tide has turned. The free men of the world are marching together to victory." Ben furiously scribbled down snatches of it, needing to do something while history was dispensed without him. *D-Day somewhere on the coast of France and I'm out here with the albatrosses. Thanks a whole hell of a lot for the heads-up, Tepee Weepy.*

In the wardroom's explosion of speculation that followed the Allied supreme commander's brief pronouncement, Danzer murmured aside to Ben: "A gentleman's C, on that pep talk by El Supremo?"

You're the one who would recognize one. "You were spoiled by Bruno," Ben came back at that. "Halftime dramatics don't sound that good with real blood involved." This was not a time he wanted to be standing around trading smart remarks, however. Like a change in the weather sensed in the bones, he could feel the time coming when the dateline on what he wrote would read SOMEWHERE IN EUROPE. "Moxie's ack-ack outfit is in that invasion force," he thought out loud, "you can about bet."

Did he imagine, or did Danzer draw back a little in surprise at those words?

Ben shot him a curious look, but the Dancer was elusive there in his naval crispness. He still was as lean as when he lined up at opposite end from Ben and as apart. "You knew he was stationed in England, didn't you?"

"Merry old Moxie," Danzer said as if that constituted an answer. "You're bunking in the sick bay. I'll show you to it."

NICHOLAS EDWIN DANZER. *"Ned" when he was growing up in Livingston, but "Nick" as soon as he hit Treasure State University and figured out what rhymed nicely with "slick." His family has the Paradise Gateway Toggery, outfitter to moneyed tourists on their way to Yellowstone Park. The snappy Stetsons. The gabardine slacks, men's instant fittings by a male tailor right there on the premises, women's by a female one. The specialized cowboy boots with walker heels, which takes the nuisance of cowboying out of them. How it all must have rolled into the cash register, and out of that, the vacation home up the Paradise Valley, the fishing trips with the Governor, the high school football camp at the Rose Bowl while most of the rest of us were teenage muscle sweating through summer jobs at a dollar a day. Born with a silver shoehorn in his booties and he took advantage of it. Give Slick Nick the benefit of the doubt, allow as how it was okay for him to be the clotheshorse of the locker room and a mile around, for that matter. The more-wised-up-than-thou attitude he wore, that was not okay.*

It was Vic, rest his soul, who shut him off at the mouth. Sooner or later it might have been Jake or Animal or, I like to think, me, but Vic drew first honors. That day Bruno had run us ragged in practice, all of us were out of sorts, and Danzer made the mistake of pushing past Vic into the showers with "Move it along, Tonto." Vic hit him in the chest with the base of his fist the way a person would bang hard on a door and that finished that. From then on, Danzer's attitude still showed but he kept it buttoned.

And here he is, supply officer on the destroyer USS McCorkle, on station probably a thousand miles from the nearest Japs. As cushy an assignment as there is in a theater of combat, however he snagged it. He makes Dex Cariston look like an amateur at fore-swearing war. For once, I wish I had less knowledge of the person I'm supposed to write about.

But that's not how it is, or ever going to be, with the Dancer. I know him right down to his shoe size. Or in his case, to his shoe polish.

The story galloped among the former teammates, after Animal Angelides picked it up from a troopship navigator who went through officer candidate school at Great Lakes with Danzer. Inspections were ferocious in their barracks, a terminally picky commander stalking through the squad bays handing out gigs—demerits—for specks of dust imaginary or not. Always with one exception. Danzer's shoes dazzled the man, as well they should have; shiny as black glass, sheerly flawless as obsidian. It reliably drew Danzer an approving nod and a squint at his nametag, and everyone knew that the good regard of the commander was the one sure route around wading the chickenshit that customarily awaited an officer candidate. Danzer's shoeshine secret, whether he bribed it out of some crafty yardbird at Great Lakes or more likely devolved it from making those fancy boots gleam to best advantage in the show window of the Toggery, was to press the polish into the leather with a spoon made hot by a cigarette lighter, buff it, melt some more polish in, buff some more. It wrecked the shoes for wearing—Danzer had to hop into an ordinary pair when inspection was over—but could not be beat for display.

"Better have another pork chop, Ben. I had to practically buy out the hog farms of Queensland to get them." The gloss on Danzer these days shone up from the capacious plates the officers of the *McCorkle* ate off of. It had the reputation of a ship that fed exceedingly well.

"No thanks. My stomach still wants to be back on land."

Which he knew would take another week yet, before the destroyer put in at Brisbane. *And Slick Nick can keep on with the war effort by bargaining the Aussies out of groceries.*

Supply and demand were immaculately matched in Danzer and this ship, he had already determined. By whatever flick of fortune in the chain of command, the vessel was something like a palace guard to the commander in chief in the Pacific, General MacArthur, headquartered in the Australian port. Or as those less kind put it, driven into exile there by Japanese triumphs. MacArthur's war thus far had been an early series of ghastly defeats—Bataan, Corregidor, then the entire Philippines—now somewhat assuaged by amphibious invasions that had rolled back the enemy from New Guinea and a handful of other strategic map spots strewn down the South Pacific. The *McCorkle's* war this far along consisted of patrol duty and support chores here in the conquered waters central to MacArthur's realm. Ben didn't think he could get away with writing it, but the Southern

Cross in the night sky was a constellation of extreme luck for the crew of this ship.

"Lieutenant Reinking? I can't resist telling you"—this was on its way from a redheaded officer so young and junior in rank that he practically shined—"I read one of your pieces in JWP at Northwestern. The one where they held the wake for your team-mate in a bar."

Ben wished the junior ranker had resisted speaking up; there were too many faces in that messroom plainly ready to savor morsels beyond any found on the plates. "Kenny O'Fallon, that was," he reeled off to try to get rid of this. "Butte knows how to give a person a send-off." He sent a knotted look back along the table. "What's JWP?"

"Journalistic Writing Practice," the young admirer reddened as he said it. As he spoke, a white-jacketed mess attendant went around the table pouring coffee and dealing out fresh forks for pie. The Navy's ways made Ben feel at sea in more ways than one. Except for whoever was on the bridge the dozen or so officers all ate together at the one long table in obligatory lingering fashion, which meant the talkers got to talk endlessly and the listeners got to listen eternally. Cliques showed through the crevices in conversation; this nonfighting destroyer mostly was officered by a mix of merchant marine retreads, such as the gray slump-shouldered captain who sat at the head of the table regarding Ben without pleasure, and ninety-day wonders (example: Danzer) turned out by officer candidate school. All meal long, Ben had to behave like an anthropologist tiptoeing between tribes.

Right now, with more pluck than sense the redheaded one-striper was back at what he had read in college:

"I'm trying to remember, in that piece. Your football buddy—your and Lieutenant Danzer's—he was killed out here in New Guinea, wasn't he?"

Ben sat there struggling to measure out a more civil reply than *No, shavetail, that was another dead one of us.*

HE WAS AWARE OF being worn to a thin edge by the time he reached the destroyer. Ever since shipping out of Seattle in what seemed an eon ago, he had filed stories from latitudes of the Pacific theater of combat. The Pacific conflict was a strange piecemeal war, fought from island to island, mapping itself out more like a medieval storming of castles, if the castles had been of coral and moated by hundreds of miles of hostile water and defended by men committed to die for their emperor rather than surrender. Out here, a war correspondent's movements from one jungle-torn place to another were like continually journeying into the black fire of nightmare. He had seen things it took all his ingenuity to put into words that TPWP would let pass into print, and some that would never surface in civilized newspapers.

The dirt road at Rabaul, the dust carpeted with excrement, where the retreating Japanese had evacuated their hospital patients in some manner of forced march, the sick and wounded defecating while they walked like cows with the drizzles.

Constant corpses, the accumulations of death on every fought-over island, decay and flies always ahead of the burial squads.

The pilot who fell to earth—New Guinea again—near enough the American forces that a patrol was sent out to recover him. Ben was with them when the spotter plane dropped its flare where the dive bomber had failed to come out of its dive and they thrashed through the jungle in search of the pilot. No one had seen his parachute open for sure, nor did it. The lead man practically fell in the hole the body made in the jungle floor, three feet deep. Then and there Ben had been seized with a stomach-turning fear for Cass, the altitudes at which she did her job a deadly chasm as constant as the sky over him after that. No remedy in sight. He had tried to shake that feeling in his gut—he had enough of those already—but the thought of life without her refused to quite go away. It was going with him throughout this ocean of war, a hue of loneliness always accompanying him now, like another depth to his shadow.

SOLITARY IN THE company of the destroyer officers, he at last came up with a response to the question that had pasted O'Fallon's fate onto Friessen's. "No, you're thinking of another teammate of ours. We've lost more than our share."

Danzer had been watching throughout, gray-eyed as a stone visage. He showed no sign any of this fazed him. "It's strange how war has imitated life," he said as if mastering the philosophy for them all. "The middle of the line has taken the hits. Ben and I had the luck to be the ends." Smiling to take the edge off mortal matters, he knocked on the wood trim of the mess table.

"We're jealous of Danzer, you know," one of the older officers said in a joshing tone, if that's what it really was. "You're here to make him famous back home, and as dog robber he already gets to be the first one off the ship when we hit port."

"You wouldn't want the burden of being Slick Nick," Ben answered the officer oratorically enough to draw a laugh. Danzer joined in.

"Still, it's an interesting morale device, isn't it," the executive officer spoke up briskly. The exec was a Naval Academy man, and chafing at this becalmed post in his career climb if Ben did not miss his guess. "Giving people a periodic glimpse— not that your talents can be entirely captured at any one time, Nick—of someone all throughout the war. Rather like time-lapse photography."

Before the executive officer could hold forth further, Ben put in, "Right now I'm the one lapsing," barely covering a yawn. "If you'll excuse me, gentlemen"—he tried to intone it without irony and could not be sure he succeeded—"I'm going to have to hit the sack."

THE ONE ADVANTAGE of bunking in the sick bay was privacy, which he craved in the crowded confines of the ship. *Just me and the aspirin and the sawbones's slab.* Those and the unsettling sense of being cast backward in time.

Hands under his head, he lay there on the berth and mulled. It had been, what, nearly a year since his impatient period of mending in a similar medical compartment on the ship off New Guinea. The swollen thoughts of that time returned to him, as haunting as they were contrary. A main one, borne back by the dinner episode: why couldn't Carl Friessen have come out of the hand-to-hand combat on that bloodslick trail with just enough sacrifice of flesh to retire him from the war? The million-dollar wound, shrapnel in the back, a stray bullet in the lower leg, that sent a soldier home for good. His own encounter with a bullet seemed to him the two-bit variety, scarcely deserving of a Purple Heart or anything else, yet the twinge in his shoulder was a message of what might have been. At the time he was disturbed with himself for wanting any of the Supreme Team out of the war; Friessen, Vic, the others were in it of their own choice and who was he to wish carefully calibrated harm to any of them? With what he knew now, he should have called down the heavens in support of such a wish.

That and ten cents would buy a person a dime's worth of difference in this life, wouldn't it. He swung up off the bunk, determined to leave the mood there, and crossed over to his typewriter on the cubbyhole desk. First, though—another habit back from that other sick-bay stay—he flicked on the radio tuned to Tokyo Rose. As ever, the sultry voice was there, alternating between taunting American soldiers all over the Pacific and playing the likes of "Tuxedo Junction," the rhythm that began swelling out

now. The Japanese were good at such propaganda, he acknowledged; the German counterpart, Lord Haw-Haw, sounded like
P.G. Wodehouse construing Bertie Wooster. Swing music outdid
a drone any old night. Something to keep in mind, would-be
scriptwriter, he told himself. He turned the sound just low
enough to be background, and settled to his routine.

His things were laid out on the slablike medical table and
he reached over for fresh paper and rolled a page into the typewriter. He took his time at this, which would have astounded
Jones or anyone else back at East Base who had ever seen him
put a typewriter to work. On TPWP pieces he wrote as fast as
the keys could tolerate, never needing to glance down—one of
the blessings he owed his father was those boyhood sessions
at the training typewriter in the *Gleaner* office, with bunion
pads hiding the letters on the keyboard. But nights on his movie
script, which were many, he deliberately slowed to a sculptor's
pace, letting the imagination feel its way toward the shape of
trueness. The scene he was working on took place on the Letter
Hill. The character based on Purcell was the last player to reach
the whitewashed rocks—*Camera: the slope below him appears
steep and endless,* he tapped onto the paper—and others of the
football team sagged against the stone emblem trying to catch
their breath. His fingers resting on the keyboard, he tried out
dialogue in his inner ear, trying to catch words out of the air. It
was a pursuit that enabled him to stand the slow, slow passage of
military hours, the way some other man in uniform somewhere
might endure the duration by nightly reading in *War and Peace,*
and upon finishing it, starting over. (He made a mental note to
find out what Danzer did to pass the time, if he did anything.) It
was an abiding mystery, the script, that promised to reveal itself
only in the measured workings of his mind and his fingers. And
it was something Tepee Weepy could not reach.

———

HE LURCHED THROUGH the next days at Danzer's side, listening over and over to him regulate a cook here, a baker there, a
storeroom swabbie down in some gloomy chamber at the bottom
of the ship. All of it about as exciting as the derring-do of the
corner grocer. SUPREME TEAM MEMBER BATTLES ENEMY WITH
BISCUITS, he could just see the headline. Tepee Weepy would be
thrilled to the gills with this piece. Sure it would. As military
service went, what he was reporting on aboard the USS *McCorkle*
amounted to the essence of quiescence.

Meanwhile the long lean destroyer itself was never at rest. The
Cork was aptly nicknamed, bobbing with every bit of weather. Yet
that was the only discernible peril it faced. There were moments,
staring out at the methodical ocean, when he pined for a genuine
storm to shake matters up into something he could write about
with some life to it, before snapping back to his senses. *Think
about it, Reinking. Throwing up your guts doesn't help you do your
job. Just ask Dex.*

So, it seemed like just another helping of the idly floating
Cork's routine when Danzer turned to him over dessert one
dinnertime and announced for all to hear: "You can't deprive us
of your company this evening, Ben. It's movie night."

Well, why not? he figured. *Let's see if Slick Nick supplies pop-
corn and soda pop along with the main feature.* He trooped into
the wardroom with the topside contingent and the petty officers
invited up from below and sat there in tight quarters watching
Compromised with Edward G. Robinson and Bette Davis chewing up the scenery and each other. That soapy drama, however,
did not stand a chance of staying with him after what flickered
onto the white metal wall at the end of the room first. He should
have known Danzer had something of the sort up his sleeve. The
short reel, *Your USO on the Go,* blared into action standardly
enough, jaunty Italian music as the blondest of Hollywood
blondes entertained the troops on a woodsy stage somewhere

near the Anzio beachhead. The announcer had just begun to boom in when someone in the wardroom spoke up:

"Nick, I could look at Betty Grable's prow every night, but we did see this last week."

"Our guest didn't," Danzer grandly dealt with that from his presiding spot near the projector. "Humor us once-upon-a-time athletes for a little bit, if you'd be so kind."

Ben tensed, glad his face could not be seen in the dark. *Oh, goddamn. Here comes the load of crap.* Slouching down in his seat in a way he had not done since he was a kid captive to the screen back in Gros Ventre, he took in Bob Hope rattling off jokes and the McGuire Sisters spunkily harmonizing. Then the soundtrack music trumpeted off in the direction he was expecting and dreading, and here came the voice like hail on a tin roof, resounding back from the season of the Twelfth Man into the darkened compartment.

"Hello and a hurrah, for you fighting men and women everywhere! This is Ted Loudon with your USO sports report. Once again, the United Service Organizations and the man at the mike, yours truly, are in your corner as we bring you the events of—"

Loudon had the knack, Ben had long ago divined, of spreading himself like a weed. Newspapers, airwaves, celluloid, the so-called sportscaster was everywhere but the backs of matchbooks and that was probably next. Ben set himself to endure another kaleidoscope of clichés, still trying to figure out Danzer's purpose in thrusting this in front of him. *There's no football this time of year. Is he just throwing Loudmouth at me to see what will stick?* Meanwhile in close focus there on the wardroom wall, Loudon himself was grandiosely shepherding an over-the-hill heavyweight boxer onto a hangar stage at the big air base in New-foundland. In the space of the next breath, he was spouting his way through opening day of baseball season, replete with himself among the wounded troops in the box seats at the Washington Senators game.

Then the projector beam gave a wink of light between scenes, composed itself into gymnasium bleachers full of cheering soldiers, and onto a basketball court surged a pair of teams, one wearing no jerseys and the other wearing beards that reached to the chest letters on theirs. "For the troops at Fort Dix gathered in the USO field house, it's basketball, down to hide and hair!" Ben jolted up in his seat. "Yes, folks, it's the Carlisle 'Skins versus the House of Isaiah! These barnstorming teams have entertained America from coast to coast, playing a brand of ball that their ancestors would not recognize but they have adapted for their own." Eerily he watched five fleet ghosts of Vic Rennie racing up and down the hardwood floor, the Indian team in just its trunks running and shooting like boys let loose. For their part, the big bearded men on the other team set up passwork plays of geometric grace. In between the pure basketball there were stints of showmanship nonsense, as one of the bearded giants held the basketball in one hand over his head and a couple of the shorter Indians jumped and jumped and couldn't come close to reaching it, then in the next sequence the Indians sped upcourt passing to one another so swiftly through the windmilling House of Isaiah players that the ball seemed to be in two places at once. It was all circus to Loudon, who in his patter managed to ignore superb run-and-gun plays to concentrate on exaggerated pronunciation of names like Hunts at Night and Buffalo Scraper, and for that matter, Perlmutter and Rosenthorn. Numbly Ben blocked out all of that he could, summoning instead the intrinsic memory of Vic with his hopes set on the 'Skins, on the playing career beyond football that would take him anywhere but Hill 57. Until his leg disappeared from under him. And then his life.

I get it, Danzer, you bet I do. Luck looks after those with shiny shoes, not the ones in moccasins. You've got the recipe for cynical.

The instant the lights went up at the end of the main show, Ben ducked out. He didn't know what the movie-night protocol was, coffee and cookies and conversation afterward or what, but he didn't care, he simply wanted time alone. Sleep was nowhere in the picture, he was too worked up. No sooner had he closed the sick-bay door than he was across at the radio to flip on Tokyo Rose for some distraction. *Might as well make it a full night of propaganda.*

He settled to the cubbyhole desk and his typewriter as the Rose of Tokyo pleasantly promised doom ahead.

"Poor American boys. Your ships go up in flames every day and your planes are shot from the sky every hour of that day. There are too many islands where your death waits for you, while slackers at home sit out the war. Go home, GIs, before a bullet brings you the sleep that lasts forever." Out wafted the eternal strains of Brahms's "Lullaby."

"Sweet dreams to you too, Rosie," Ben mocked back but kept the music as he twirled a half-finished page of script into the typewriter. A warm awareness different from other writing nights kept coursing through him. As much as he hated to admit Ted Loudon could possibly amount to any kind of inspiration, that rapid-fire voice worked as a goad, evoking the Golden Eagles stadium, the cleated team poised to charge onto the football field, the gilded season that led to so much else. They probably didn't teach that in Journalistic Writing Practice. His fixated gaze at the waiting white space was just beginning to find the forms of words when a rap on the door broke the trance.

Oh, goddamn came to mind one more time, and he went to answer the knock hoping it would be any other of the officers, even the lecture-prone exec. Naturally it was not.

"You scooted out of the wardroom before I could catch you, Ben." Danzer stood there in the passageway as crisp as the cutout of a naval recruiting poster. "I thought we ought to have a chat, old lang syne and all."

"It's your boat, Nick." Ben gestured him in.

Gliding by, Danzer assumed a seat on the bunk and turned an ear as he did so. "Blotting out the war with Beethoven?"

"Brahms."

"Same difference?"

"Hardly. Beethoven's is music to move the universe, Brahms's is to move the heart." Ben reached over and clicked the radio off. "Sorry. I picked that up somewhere and it's always stuck with me."

"You were the word man among us and that hasn't changed," came the response from behind the held smile. "Our old friend Loudon hasn't lost his touch either, has he."

"Nope. Bullshit stays green for quite a while."

That did not appear to be the reaction Danzer had been counting on. He scrutinized his host briefly, then leaned forward, hands steepled together as if aiming a prayer. "I hope this isn't stepping on your toes, Ben, but I wanted to make sure you're coming along all right on your article. Two more days until we're in Brisbane, and you're off to wherever's next. It would be on my conscience if I haven't provided everything you need."

Ben studied the slick source of those words. *You're a provider if there ever was one.* Danzer, monarch of the cold storage locker and master of the cooks and bakers and servers; the story that really interested Ben was how he had cozied himself into this slot in the American logistical empire. Some alliance of convenience made back there in shiny-shoe OCS? Some influential Yellowstone tourist, togged out by the Toggery, who knew someone on MacArthur's staff? Pull was involved somewhere, Ben would have bet any amount of money. There was nothing wrong with

being a storekeeper. What rankled was Danzer being Danzer, his
every pore exuding the attitude that he was entitled to a free pass
through the war.

"Well, Nick, I'll tell you. It's a little tough to make the commissary sound like a knife at Japan's throat. I'll come up with
something along those lines, though. Bread knife, maybe."

That drew a chuckle of sorts. "I'm the first to admit, patrolling MacArthur's backyard is a tolerable tour of duty. There's a
nice amount of leisure." Danzer pronounced it as if it rhymed
with *pleasure*. "But don't forget it's a long war for me, too. They
also wait who only stand and serve." Ben could tell it was not
nearly the first time that line had been trotted out.

"By the way, how did you like the show, over all?" Danzer
switched to, as though it was considerate of him to ask. "Loudon's loud mouth aside, the bit of basketball was interesting,
wasn't it? I thought you would get a kick out of it." *Is that what
you thought. Somehow I doubt it.* Danzer steadied his gaze on
his reluctant listener. "I never had anything permanently against
Vic, you know. If his idea in life was to play shirts and skins, I'd
have been glad to see him do it," not quite saying *on the side of
the redskins, naturally.*

"Life never did cut Vic a break," Ben answered shortly. *Or the
other three who lined up with us in that stadium.* He did not want
to go over that territory, the team's lives taken by the war, in the
clammy companionship of Danzer. "Moxie's all right, by the way.
I checked. His outfit's dug in high and dry in a lucky pocket at
Normandy, not much resistance."

"Is that what that was about, the code traffic ahead of the
captain's morning messages," the other said blandly. "The skipper
thinks you have more radio priority than Roosevelt." He thought
to tack on, "Good for Moxie," before bringing the conversation
to where Ben saw it had been aimed all along.

"I have a bit of news of my own," Danzer delivered it with relish on the side. He looked off around the room as if gathering his statement. "I know where our buddy Dex is and the reason why."

Ben felt a lurch the ship was not responsible for. He shifted in the chair as he eyed his now truly unwelcome caller.

"Is that so. You're busier than you look, Nick."

Danzer spread his hands. "This fell in the family lap. A boot representative"—it took his listener a moment to translate that to traveling shoe salesman—"we deal with has a line of work wear he thought might interest the Forest Service. Just right for smoke jumpers, you know? The Cariston stores are one of his accounts too, so imagine his surprise when he paid a call to Seeley Lake and spotted Dex in there with the conchies. The rest of the conchies, I think it's safe to say."

Knowing what the answer would be, Ben grimly asked anyway:

"Are you spreading this around, back home?"

"Word might get out, I imagine. You know how these things are. People have no idea the heir to Cariston Enterprises is taking the yellow road through the war otherwise, do they." The offhand manner in which Danzer said it made Ben realize he had underestimated the man's disdain for the rest of humankind. He was the sort whose contempt you couldn't tell from the wallpaper. It was always there in back of whatever he said or did.

"That was one of your pieces I did happen to see, on Dex"— Ben stared back while Danzer delivered this straight at him— "and 'conscientious objector' did not leap out at me. At any rate, it might not reflect on him any too well, do you think? What with the rest of us putting in our tour of duty."

I get the message, you manipulating bastard. Make you look good or you and your Toggery bunch smear Dex and me along with it for covering for him. Silently Ben wrung the neck of the words he had just heard. Tour of duty. That's what Danzer was doing with it, all right, touring duty like a cynical sightseer for every spot of advantage it might offer him. The pampered tourist of the war who knew how to keep on pampering himself. The gleaming face confident it would never know doom until its allotted threescore and ten years, or more. For several seconds he did not trust himself to respond to Danzer, because the response he most wanted to give was to knock some teeth out of that smile.

"Nobody's perfect," he at last managed to keep it to, too much at stake not to, "but I do my goddamnedest to give everyone I write about a fair shake."

"Then I've been speaking out of turn about Dex and all, haven't I," Danzer provided with the grace of one who had won. "A man's best is all he can do." Showing every appearance of being pleased with that bromide, he made as if to go, but paused when the paper in the typewriter caught his eye. He cocked a look at the ragged margins of the typing, as when he had deigned to notice the classical music. "Writing poetry in your spare time?"

"If you have to know, it's a screenplay."

"Is it." Danzer seemed to weigh that information. "As I suppose they used to ask of Shakespeare, what's it about?"

None of your goddamn business. Something contrary sparked in the back of Ben's mind, and he gambled it on out.

"Purcell. The twelfth man. Football as we knew it, Dancer, war by another means."

Danzer's expression slipped several degrees of control. Ben thought he saw bleak surprise in those flinty eyes, something buried threatening to come out.

"It's about an accident of nature, then," the chiseled voice quickly recovered, at least. "Two of them. That freak kid himself

and what happened to him on the Hill. I'm surprised you can't
find anything more worthy of your talent, Ben."

You think you're surprised. Purcell does the trick on Slick Nick:
that's *a surprise.*

Sitting there gratified at discovering a way to get under Danzer's skin, Ben still was finding it murky territory to try to explore. True, in the famous '41 season Purcell became the most
glorified scrub there ever was, but still a scrub; he made the team
only posthumously. What was there about the raw kid from nowhere to upset, even now, the receiving end of that impervious
passing combination, Stamper-to-Danzer? "Stomp and Dance,
the touchdown prance." Ted Loudon always went nuts over that,
he had plugged it into his column all season long. *You had your
share of fame, Danzer, did you want Purcell's leftovers too?*

Something had colossal staying power from back then, but
what? The time since had changed the mortal balance in too
many ways that Ben had seen, but not in this case. The Dancer
was still scoring plentifully in the game of life, the Twelfth Man
was still dead. Whatever grasp the specter of Purcell had, let
Danzer squirm under it, he decided.

"Don't judge my script too soon, Nick," Ben flicked the page
resting in the typewriter. "Maybe it'll turn out to bring back
valuable memories for you."

Danzer regarded him stonily for a moment, then in turn
tapped the radio where the Brahms had been. "Do you know
your trouble, Ben? You let your heart be moved too easily. Dex.
Purcell. The list doesn't stop there, I'm sure. You're the type lame
puppies and roundheeled women sniff out, would be my guess."
That last was flicked lightly enough, but the lash was unmistakably there. "Whatever it is, you let it get to you too much."

"Is that what's wrong with me?" Ben acted surprised, although he had to work to hold it to that. *The sonofabitch can't*

know about Cass, too. Can he? "And here I thought it was an old pain from football acting up."

Danzer smiled that sterile smile as he got up to leave. "Those last on and on, don't they. Good night, Ben."

"GENERAL QUARTERS. ALL HANDS, MAN YOUR BATTLE STATIONS."

He woke up fighting mad at Navy games in the middle of the night and trying simultaneously to put on a light and his clothes.

Country club Sunday sailing sonsofbitches. If that captain thinks he is going to give me something to write about besides Danzer's pork chops by pulling a drill, he has another think coming.

The squawk box in a corner of the ceiling still was blatting the alarm when the compartment door flung open and the medical officer hustled in. He made a face at the clutter on the operating table. "I need that cleared," he said matter-of-factly, and with the sweep of an arm began gathering Ben's belongings and dumping them under the bunk.

"Hey!" Half-dressed, Ben lumbered across the room and protectively scooped up his typewriter and its carrying case. "What's all the rush?"

"A submarine is trailing us," the medico recited as if it were common knowledge. "You need to put your gear on and get out on deck, fast."

Feeling like he was in a severely bad dream, Ben in haste donned the helmet and life jacket he had been given and tumbled out of the sick bay into a passageway full of tousled sailors pulling on battle gear of their own. The general scurry conveyed him out onto deck, where the crew members spilled toward gun mounts and fire control hoses and other stations to which they were assigned. Pandemonium? Expertly drilled response to the worst of alarms? He couldn't tell which. The one thing he knew for dead sure was to stay out of the way, and he ducked off clear of any doors or deckpaths to let all the traffic pass. For whatever crazy reason he took notice of the full moon over the bow of the ship, like a searchlight barely on. In a rolling motion that made him stagger to keep his balance, the destroyer could be felt surging to a new speed and heeling in a fresh direction at the same time. He tried to think where in the maze of the ship Danzer's battle station might be, cursing himself for not having paid any real attention to that. Bolstering against the steel side of the superstructure while more figures in helmets pounded past, he was nearly knocked over by a crewman skinning down a ladder. He grabbed the man, recognizing him as one of the mess attendants. "Where's Lieutenant Danzer?"

"Chart house, should be, sir," the man stammered and raced off to pass ammunition.

Staying wary of anyone else plunging down the rungs from overhead, Ben climbed in spurts toward the bridge of the ship. There he slipped into a warren of tense officers and lookouts with binoculars pressed to their eyes. That frieze of unmoving figures glued to the night horizon could not have been more different from the scramble below. In the low level of light everything looked sepulchral. Out beyond, it was a perfect Pacific night, the water trembling under the stars. Catching himself on tiptoe as he tried to see everywhere at once on the moonlit ocean, he realized the futility of that; long before he ever could, the binoculars would pick up any deadly white streak that was the wake of an oncoming torpedo. *Too late then anyway. This thing can't outrun one of those.* The captain peevishly snapped out orders, and the orders went down the line of command into the nerve system of the ship, to what effect Ben couldn't discern. The destroyer was zigzagging, dancing with an invisible devil, but was that enough? He had to hope the *McCorkle*'s evasive action was as unreadable to a sub captain at a periscope as it was to him.

Not reassured by the scene on the bridge, he backed out to hunt up Danzer and found him in equally ghostly circumstances in the busy chart room, the combat analysis center. The dim greenish light etched ashen shadows beneath the battle helmets and into the hollows of cheeks. Here the executive officer was in charge, leaning over a translucent tabletop where the careening course of the destroyer was being plotted and exchanging aggravated questions with the strained-looking young communications officer and other distressed types crowded around the massive table. From what Ben could catch it amounted to an argument over whether to cut and run or turn and fight, and he didn't like any of what he was hearing or seeing. Faces that had not shown a worry in the world in the wardroom now appeared aggrieved, unsure. One person or another around that table swallowed hard too often. Fear not sliding down easily. Not ever. Now he had his own sudden taste of that lodged in his throat, the apprehension of dying in company such as this. *How'd they get us into this in the first place?* Among other things, a destroyer was a submarine-hunting machine. How had this one managed to become the hunted?

Danzer was off to one side, near the forward bulkhead, looking removed from the intense debate at the plotting table. Ben edged around to him. Danzer's duty station there, he deciphered, must have been to maintain the battle status board with code names and whereabouts of other U.S. ships in the fight. The problem with that was that there were not any, none nearer than somewhere around the Australian port in one direction and New Guinea in the other. Just the *Cork* and the enemy. *Different war than it was a couple of minutes ago, isn't it, Nick.*

Reaching Danzer, he whispered: "How are they going to shake us loose from this?"

"Your guess is as good as mine," Danzer whispered back, and for once sounded nervous.

"What's a Jap sub doing way down here? Who spotted the thing?"

"Who do you think? I was officer of the watch."

"No crap? You saw it?" Ben began surreptitiously scrawling in his notepad, trying to hear what was being said at the plotting table and listen to Danzer at the same time. Here of all things was the heroic piece on Slick Nick. If he stayed alive to write it.

"It's dark out in case you haven't noticed," Danzer muttered sarcastically. "Sonar picked it up. Can't you hear it?"

The pips registered on Ben then. PING *ping*. PING *ping*. Until that moment, the pulsations of sound had gone by him as some piece of the destroyer's equipment that might contribute to raising hell with the submarine. Now that it was identified as the pulse of hell coming the ship's direction, the pinging sounded louder.

Ben peered at the stiff-necked supply officer anew. If Danzer turned out to be the Paul Revere of the South Seas, the only thing to do was to write him up that way. "What then?" he resumed the under-the-breath interview urgently. "You got on the horn and ordered general quarters? On your own?"

"No, that's not by the book," Danzer said between his teeth. It was remarkable how nettled a whisper could sound. "There's a standing order to call the captain." Which in this case meant waking him up with maximum bad news. Danzer's drawn expression suggested it was an experience that stayed with a person.

Just then the exercise in exasperation around the plotting table broke up. "We're not shaking the bogey at all," the exec was saying, striding for the bridge. "We need to tell the skipper our only chance is to go at it."

Hearing that, Ben banged Danzer roughly in the vicinity of the collarbone for luck—he only later realized it was the old shoulder-pad slap the team traded before the game started—and bolted out onto the wing of the bridge to watch.

Sea air rushed by, there on the steel promontory into the dark. A mane of moonsilver flowed back from the destroyer's bow, and a matching tail of wake behind it. As his eyes adjusted, Ben could just make out the long narrow deck below, armaments jutting ready if they only had a target, faces of the gun crews pale patches foreshortened by helmets. Whatever discussion the executive officer had with the captain did not take long. The ship cut sharply to one side and kept on leaning like a skater fashioning a circle. Standing there witnessing the might of a fully armed vessel turning on its nagging foe could have been thrilling, Ben was duly aware, except for the distinct chance of being blown out of the water at any second. Drowned like a kitten in a sack. He tried to swallow such prospects away, down a throat dry as paper. The lack of any least sign of the enemy out there in the total surround of ocean seemed to him the worst part. On land he had been shot at by experts and never felt this much fear.

Determinedly not watching for a salvo of torpedoes except for moments when he couldn't stand not to, he strained instead to follow the burst of action at the *McCorkle*'s stern. He could just see the shadowy figures of the depth charge crew crouching ready, their barrel-like explosives neatly racked for firing. At some chosen point in the attack maneuver—he wondered whether it was decided by hunch, or some definitive echo out of the sonar equipment; on this ship, it likely did not come from combat experience—the commands were hurled out:

"FIRE ONE!"

"FIRE TWO!"

The firing kept on, each charge sprung into the air like a fat ejected shell, out away from the ship, then to sink to the depth that would detonate it. Nothing happened for long enough that Ben began to suspect duds. Then he felt the shudder up from the water. Astern, explosions bloomed white in the darkness. Knowing this to be one of the sights of a lifetime, he watched with an intensity near to quivering. Not often is it given to you to stare away death, see it go instead in search of your sworn enemy. There in the destroyer's wake, the geysers of destruction blew and blew. It was impossible to imagine anything human surviving in that cauldron of concussions.

Poor bastards. They'll never see the surface again. On the wing of the bridge, existence seemed benignly extended, stable as the feel of steel underfoot. Forgiving the *Cork* and its lucky-star crew all their sins of leisure, Ben raced back into the chart room to see how they marked the sinking of an enemy submarine.

He could have spared himself the effort. The jammed room was as still as a funeral parlor except for the pinging.

"It's still there, sir," the sonar operator called out, perhaps in case anyone's hearing had gone bad. In the greenish gloom, Danzer's face was a study in trepidation.

The executive officer at last spoke up. "Something's fishy about this. They can't shadow us that close after we blew up half the ocean floor." They must have taught logic at Annapolis.

Once more, the exec went calling on the captain. This time, their conference produced a marked slowing of the vessel. All hands stayed at battle stations as the sonar deepfinder was reeled in for inspection. Ben was there, scribbling like mad, when the sonar technician took a look at the sound head at the end of the cable and sourly gave his diagnosis:

"It's all chewed to hell, messed up the signal. A shark must have got at it."

Ben waited until general quarters was called off, waited while the decks emptied of cursing sailors and sheepish officers, waited as the medical officer vacated the sick bay, waited until he was alone in the soundless compartment. Then he put his hands to his face and laughed into them until he had to gulp for air.

Chortles were still coming like hiccups when he sat up to the typewriter in its restored spot. He was at full speed on the keys by the time the rap on the door came.

Danzer stepped in looking dazed.

"If it isn't the famous officer of the watch," Ben greeted him. "I guess next time you'll roust out the sonar tech ahead of everybody else, huh?"

With visible effort, the caller let that pass. He squared up as much as he was able and began: "I'm in a bit of a spot. The captain sent me to ask if you'll be writing anything about"—Danzer looked as if he would rather bite off his tongue than say it—"what happened tonight."

Ben couldn't help but grin and tap the typing paper in answer. "The case of the submarine that never was, you mean? Can't you see the headline? THE HUNTING OF THE SHARK. Beware the frumious Bandersnatch next, Lieutenant Danzer."

Danzer's face was a funny color, as if the ghoulish light of the chart room stayed with him. "Damn it, if you—"

Ben held up a hand. "Don't. As much as I'd like to, I'm not going to skin you in public. The outfit I have to answer to isn't going to let you look ridiculous, don't worry." He tapped the typing paper again, this time in a tired manner. "Oh, I could write it that way, hell yes, and it'd be red-penciled beyond recognition. So I'll do up tonight's stunt and then TPWP will take its turn. And in the end it'll come out as just one more unpleasant thing that can happen in war, Dancer."

10

★ THE WAR CHANGED tongues somewhere in mid-ocean as Ben hooked rides on anything that flew in the days beyond Australia. The spatter of sand and syllable where he eventually put down was a sparse island called Eniwetok, and out around it in the central latitudes of the Pacific were scattered other lingual odds and ends now synonymous with the battles on their beaches—Kwajalein and Tarawa, with Saipan and Okinawa and Iwo Jima and others yet to come. Eniwetok itself, Ben found, had been remade from the waterline up in the few months since being taken from the Japanese. Laundries, volleyball nets staked like flags, movie amphitheater, officers' club, enlisted men's canteen, chapel, library: it was all there, the practically magical portable platform of American amenities that materialized wherever U.S. fighting forces went. The skinny but vital island, key link in an atoll with a lagoon that went to the horizon, was surrounded by countless moored naval vessels; if a typhoon blew through, the yanking anchor chains would pull the plug on the Pacific.

It took some asking around, but ultimately he hitched a ride on a supply launch to the troopship that was his destination.

Confronted with Ben's orders, the deck officer made the usual face of discomfiture. "Ordinarily we could stow you in the sick bay, but we're crammed with assault force officers and there's no way—"

"Don't sweat it, I'll bunk below."

Below meant four decks down, each more fetid than the one before. The transport seemed cavernous after the destroyer. Ben's head swam a bit as he laboriously maneuvered his travel pack and typewriter case deeper into the sweltering hold of the ship. He wondered if he was coming down with something tropical. Three months in the Pacific had convinced him humidity by the skinful ought to be in the medical texts.

He came out at the bottom of the labyrinth of ladders and hatchways to a steel bay the width of the hull, where dozens of sweating men were stacked in racks of bunks that reached from deck floor to ceiling. Most were shirtless or in their skivvies as they tried to read or nap or clean their already cleaned rifles. Amid everything, a permanent poker game of the sort to be found in the countless coin pockets of the war was under way. Ben could tell from the cash in the pot it was too rich for his blood. He sidled through the alleys of bunks, his shoulder patch drawing quizzical squints, inquiring until someone pointed him past the toilets to the showers. "The large sarge, you mean? He's either smarter or crazier than the rest of us, he takes about half a dozen a day."

Leaning his pack and typewriter against the bulkhead, Ben stepped to the hatchway and called in to the naked personage camped under a drizzle from a showerhead: "Is that the usual Marine uniform in these parts, Sergeant Angelides?"

"I'll be go to hell, it's our recording angel, right out of nowhere," came the response just short of a shout. "How'd you ever find this stinking rust bucket, Lefty?" *That again. Remember it's me, not the nearest southpaw.*

Reaching behind to turn off the shower with one hand, Angelides grabbed Ben for a sopping handshake with the other.

"Somebody sent me your piece on Sig. Going right down the strong side of the line, are you."

"Danzer jumped in front of you this time," Ben manufactured a dismissive smile, "so I'll have to make it up to you by playing up your saintly side, Animal."

Angelides guffawed and began toweling himself rigorously. "Got your work cut out for you. So is the Dancer still defending Backtrack Mac with the gleam of his shoes?"

"Still is."

A shake of the broad-browed swarthy head and a glance so quick it was more like a glint. "What would we do without Danzer, prick of the month all year long." Angelides wrapped the towel around his hairy middle like a king kilting up. "Come on, we'll get you set up in a fart sack and you can see how Uncle Sam's finest live."

UP ON DECK out of the stifling quarters as soon as Ben's things were bunked in, the two of them found a sliver of shade beneath the superstructure to hunch under and talk.

"These tubs are the ass-end of the Navy," Angelides declared of life cooped up on one troopship after another. "The swabbies lug us around to wherever the Japs are holed up on the next chunk of coral"—he flipped a hand disparagingly toward Eniwetok and its recent past—"and we hit the beach. Never know how that'll go. Waipu was a breeze, we walked right in. Tarawa was total hell, they threw everything at us. One way or the other, it all counts toward getting our outfit's part of the war over." Shoulders set, he prowled over to the deck rail as he spoke, all the old impressions coming back to Ben as he watched that lithe restless motion. Indestructible on the football field, Andros Angelides had been rechristened "Animal" by the team for the fallen prey surrounding his spot in the line—offense or defense, it didn't matter, where Animal roved opposing players ended up strewn in the grass. To Ben's mind, Animal most resembled the creature of nature he had seen once on a high-country hunting trip. A ripple of tan against the timberline caught his eye and, by the time he blinked, had resolved itself into a cougar on the move. The resemblance was still there in the man at the deck edge. The extensive body, muscled everywhere that counted. The large rough hands, quicker than paws that size could be expected to be. The deep flicker of the eyes back under the bonebox of brow. All that taut animal vitality coming out now as the impatience of a fighting man ready to march into Tokyo and trapped amidships on a transport scow going nowhere fast.

Another of those glinting glances that Ben could practically feel as Angelides turned from the railing. "So what you're in for with us is the Marine Corps tradition of practicing a thing to death." He bared his teeth in a mirthless smile. "Next worst thing to Bruno and his stinking Letter Hill." He jerked his head for Ben to come have a look over the side of the ship. All along the hull a hefty web of ropes hung down from the deck to the water.

"You want to see a bunch of trained grunts who can climb down a cargo net in their sleep, that's us," Angelides was saying conversationally. "Samey same, over and over on maneuvers like this—the landing craft takes us in, dumps us in the water up to our peckers, and we storm the shores of Eniwetok one more time. It's a wonder the Red Cross isn't there selling us coffee and doughnuts when we drag up onto the sand." He fixed the kind of resigned gaze known as a thousand-yard stare on the practice island. "Aw, hell, it's pretty much necessary. A lot of our guys are cherries, replacements after Tarawa. Anyway, Lefty, you get to see this good stuff yourself tomorrow at 0500," the Marine topkick batted Ben's shoulder with the back of a hand as if to make sure he'd be awake, "and then the real thing whenever the hell some general makes his mind up."

"You sound like you can't wait, Animal."

Angelides cut him a telling look. "You know what, anymore I go by 'Andy.' It's just easier around the guys in the unit."

Ben seized the chance to trade. "Funny, that's how I feel about 'Lefty.' It's been a long time since I lined up at opposite end."

Angelides belly-laughed his agreement to the deal. "I guess this retires us from football for goddamn sure."

The squawk of a loudspeaker in some tuck of the ship broke in on them. Overhead came the shufflefoot sounds of sailors doing whatever sailors do. Ben waited for those to pass before testing out: "The real thing when it comes—you know where?"

It drew a shrug. "Scuttlebutt says it'll be Guam."

That was how Tepee Weepy figured it, too, Ben knew, or he probably would not have been on this troop deck with this particular member of the Supreme Team at this moment. No other target in the island-hopping campaign would rate bigger headlines. Guam had been surrendered in the war's earliest days when American garrison troops in pie-tin helmets found themselves facing a Japanese invasion juggernaut; there wasn't an admiral or a general in the Pacific who didn't want it back with a vengeance. Ben felt he needed to share his reading of the situation. "Andy? Say it is Guam. The big brass will pull out all the stops if it is. But the Japs aren't saps. They aren't about to say, 'So sorry, here, have your famous island back.' It could be a bloodbath."

Angelides looked at him solemnly and turned to go below. "I prefer showers."

AT BARELY FIRST light, the side of the troopship gray as a lingering shade of night, the Marines in full combat gear descended the cargo nets.

Below in the landing craft that kept bumping against the ship hard enough to jar him half off his feet, Ben craned up at the mass of humped forms as they came. Angelides was a marvel to watch. Somehow keeping an eye on the entire teeming shipside, he shambled down the mesh of rope rungs one-handed, reaching to any of his unit who needed steadying on the swaying net, injecting alacrity into those who lacked it: "Come on, you guys, you're slower than smoke off of shit. Move, move!" Only after the last of his men thudded safely into the boat did he swing free of the net and give the high sign to the coxswain at the tiller.

Ben's notepad could not hold it all. The bay was a serrated wall of troopships, the landing boats busy around each in the choppy moat of ocean, helmeted men collected in shoulder-to-shoulder embarkation as ancient as Troy. As soon as a landing craft was loaded to crowded capacity, it revved away into the coral shallows just offshore. Ramps flopped down like drawbridges and the Marines waded into the crotch-deep surf.

Ben piled off with the others, struggling against the weight of the water. Angelides, large sarge to the life, surged ahead while steadily prodding his outfit. "Everybody spread out. Six feet apart. Benson, don't you know what six feet looks like? It's the size of your goddamn grave if you don't spread out, meathead. Michaels, Krogstad! Haul that sonofabitching thing in closer, I don't give a rat's ass if it is bigger than you are." That pair was pulling a rubber raft, empty but still all they could handle in the surf swirl. The footing was treacherous on the sharp coral and more than once Ben had to catch himself from going face-first into the water. Around him by the dozens, and along the shoreline by the hundreds, Marines advanced at an encumbered gait with their rifles held high and dry. After about a hundred yards of this, the assault force clambered off the coral reef to the sands of Eniwetok. By all evidence visible to Ben the practice landing had gone as well as such things could. On the other hand, on the slight lift of land beyond the beach were situated volleyball courts rather than Japanese gun emplacements.

Panting and soaked to his midriff, Ben stayed close to Angelides as he lustily deployed his forces. When the order came down the line to halt the landing exercise, Angelides turned to check on him. "How do you like island-hopping so far?"

Ben squeezed water out of a pocket ruefully. "Why couldn't you have joined the ski troops or some other outfit that isn't half-drowned all the time?"

"And miss tropical paradise like this? No way." The big sergeant got busy again issuing orders, one of which sent a couple of men back down to the waterline to collect the small rubber boat, and Ben asked what it was for.

"What, that?" Angelides looked bemused to be asked. "You're looking at our hospital ship."

At those words, Ben felt the shiver of memory of his shipboard infirmary stay—the Purple Heart suite—after the shoulder wound. "Part of the Corps lore," Angelides was saying as if he had been asked that section of the Marine manual. "Get the wounded to shore with the rest of us. That thing's the best way I know how." He rumbled a humorless laugh. "A lifeboat for the wet-ass infantry, you could call it."

Ben gazed at the rubber boat, Angelides' seagoing ambulance. He thought of Prokosch, the width of the ocean away, on watch for the enemy floating in to a creek mouth. Rafts. In the middle of the most mechanized war in history. *What are the odds? Huck and Tom against the gods of war.*

BACK ABOARD THE troopship, the entire lower half of his uniform stiff with salt from the surf, Ben had barely made it to his bunk when a seaman stuck his head through the main hatchway and bawled: "Reinking? Lieutenant Reinking?"

"Over here, sailor."

"Message for you, topside."

DANZER PIECE A DANDY. WILL BE EXCELLED ONLY
BY YOUR NEXT, SPOKEN AS WELL AS WRITTEN: NEW
FIELD FOR YOU TO STAR, ARCHIVAL RECORDING OF
BEACHHEAD INVASION. LIBRARY OF CONGRESS ASKED
THIS FAVOR AFTER ARMY, NAVY AND AIR CORPS ALL
NIXED IT. TPWP KNOWS POSTERITY WHEN IT FALLS IN
LAP, THUS RECORDING EQUIPMENT BEING RUSHED TO
YOU. FOLLOW MARINES ASHORE AT WHATEVER ASSAULT
BEACH WITH EYEWITNESS ACCOUNT AND ALL POSSIBLE
SOUND EFFECTS. HISTORICAL RECORD, ORAL AND AU-
RAL, IS THE GOAL.

P.S. TECHNICAL AIDE ACCOMPANYING EQUIPMENT,
DON'T FRET.

Ben read it again with just as much disbelief as the first time
through. *Where do the Tepee Weepy bastards come up with these
ideas? They're turning me into the khaki version of Loudon. A play-
by-play of an invasion.* Starring, naturally, a certain keyed-up
sergeant and the outfit he would lead against enemy fire.

The ship's radioman and the code clerk both were watching
him with apprehension. "Any reply, sir?" the coder asked as if he
very much hoped not.

"Yes. Send: POSTERITY DOESN'T KNOW WHAT IT'S GETTING."

WHEN HE WENT back down into the hold to tell Angelides he
was going to be famous of a kind, the bunk compartment was
in such uproar he figured the poker game had drawn blood. It
turned out to be simply mail call. Squirming through clamorous
Marines clutching letters and packages from home, he worked
his way to his bunk hoping to hear his name called, but it was all
already there on the blanket, postal riches in a heap.

Flat on his back in the next bunk reading the sole V-mail
letter that had come for him—from his uncle—Angelides com-

mented: "You're a popular guy. I must have answered up for you twenty times."

"The stuff's been chasing me all over the Pacific, thanks for nabbing it," Ben rattled out his gratitude. As if fondling gifts, he sorted the pieces of mail into piles. The long-awaited treasure, Cass's letters. Weeks' worth of *Gleaners*, his father's fillers at the bottom of columns peeking out: *The only hope a person can be sure of is his own hatful.* Envelopes with his mother's well-schooled penmanship. A couple of blunt cheery notes from Jake Eisman done in pencil and beer. So many patches of his life, suddenly catching up with him. Almost reverently he slit open the letters from Cass and sped through the first one and the last, saving the others to savor more leisurely.

> Ben, love—
> How does a person write to a writer? I feel like a backward kid with a crayon. Maybe I can start by saying how much there is of you to miss. I can't turn around without remembering some crazy thing we did together. You've only been gone a week and I already have such a bad case, what is this going to be like from here on? . . .

> . . . Nine weeks gone, letter no. 9 to you, and I at least know you're okay so far by reading you in the paper. You look good as ever in print, but no substitute for the warm body. Must sign off for now, we take off for Edmonton in an hour. I'll waggle my wings toward Hill 57 as we go.
> > Keep low out there, you with the typewriter.
> > > Cass

HER P-39 MET the first of the rough air at the Sweetgrass Hills that afternoon.

It was an ordinary Edmonton run, although Cass long since had absorbed the cockpit wisdom that flying through thin air is never exactly ordinary. On a summer day of this sort, however, from fifteen thousand feet above these borderland plains between Montana and Alberta, usually you could see around the world and back again. But right now in the telltale tremor of air above the humpbacked hills her eyes would not leave the sight of the weather making itself, big prairie clouds ahead where none should be, building up alongside the Rockies over toward Calgary. *Who came up with that meteorology briefing we got, a blind man? "Clear and calm," my fanny.* Customarily the squadron could scoot in behind such weather cells before the cloud piles sucked the energy of heat from the prairie and rolled off eastward building into major thunderstorms. What was coming at the squadron looked major enough. *We get caught in glop like that, we'll be lucky to know where our own wingtips are.*

She checked around on her pilots. Beryl waggled her wings, showing she was watching the same cloud pattern. Off Cass's other wing, Mary Catherine made the universal hand signal as if pinching her nose against stinko weather. The plane in back of Cass was steady as if being towed, and she felt both relieved and guilty about that. Della Maclaine was on compassionate leave—a death in the family, it happened to everybody sooner or later. The TDY pilot filling in from the Michigan group was always on the mark, where Della as a rule was casually acquainted with the mark. Cass knew she should not be thinking about how much better the squadron flew without Della, but it was the kind of thing the mind does. Instinct was fully working during all this. She radioed the others and Linda's B flight and Ella's C flight farther back: "Instrument conditions, everybody. We need to try to bust through ahead of the worst of it."

The worst, however, was approaching at whatever a thunderstorm's top speed was, coupled with the fighter planes' velocity of three hundred and fifty miles an hour. In mere minutes the P-39s were bucketing uncomfortably in unpredictable air, and the cloud pile had closed in around and above. Within the murk, in the tight cave of the cockpit Cass constantly scanned her ranks of dials, flying the radio beam that would lead to the Edmonton airfield wherever the other side of this weather was, having to trust that her pilots one and all were doing the same.

She was straining to see if there was any sign of this box canyon of clouds giving way ahead, when blue crackles of light danced along her wings.

Whoa. This isn't so good.

St. Elmo's fire, playful static electricity, was known to forecast lightning. No pilot wanted a bolt of electricity sparking through the instrument panel. Already Cass was back on the radio: "Heads up, everybody. We're going downstairs to get under this. Prepare to descend to fifteen hundred feet, repeat, fifteen hundred." *That's low, but it's like the damn Fourth of July up here.* Down there, her hope was, lightning would be drawn to the ground instead of to P-39s. "Ride the altimeter real careful. Let's don't add to the magic number, hear?"

The magic number, sarcastically named, was a figure Ben had looked up when he wrote his piece about the squadron. One of the points of pride Cass and the others wore as openly as the WASP patch on their sleeves was that their safety record was better than the male pilots' in the chancy endeavor of ferrying unproven aircraft. Out of roughly a thousand WASPs, he found at the time, a total of twenty-two had been killed in crashes. Since then, of course, the so-called magic number had kept creeping higher as the women pilots' time in the air mounted up.

Like a bird flock seeking a pond of calm, the dozen airplanes nosed downward, shimmying and bucking in the turbulence of the storm. Accustomed as every P-39 pilot was to the ungainly torque of the engine mounted behind, this was like flying at the mercy of a cyclone. When her altimeter reading touched fifteen hundred feet on the nose, Cass leveled off, scanning right, left, and behind through the sheeting rain for the other planes. She could make out something that in all likelihood was the fuse-lage of Mary Catherine's aircraft and she had every confidence in Beryl off her other wing. *At least we're not lit up like neon signs.* The malicious upper-atmosphere wind reached down this far, however, and the sluggish progress was consuming fuel at a disturbing rate. Cass checked and rechecked the plasticine map strapped to the thigh of her flying suit. They would make it to Edmonton without dry tanks if they could feel their way down out of the headwind. The lack of contour lines on the map at-tested to flat country below. Even so. "All pilots. Descend to a thousand feet, we'll hold there if we can see the ground, repeat, if. Nobody get to thinking too much, just keep riding the beam. Edmonton is there, it always has been. Let's just damn do it and get this flight over with, officers."

This day, the magic number did not change.

THE HOURS OF the day in their circling of the earth returned now to the troopship. Spellbound by the immediate presence of Cass in the inked words, Ben read the letters over again, know-ing all the while there was another recipient of her lines of love or whatever approximated it.

Life was a sum of unlikelihoods, but in his wildest imagin-ing he could not have seen ahead to this, sharing professions of love from another man's wife. Were those letters to a long-absent husband somewhere at mail call on a jungle island like these? They couldn't be, the soul issued assurance. Why wouldn't they be? said the demons of the heart.

Only belatedly did he become conscious of being observed in his troubled séance with the set of letters. He tried not to show the extent of his embarrassment, and missed by far.

Angelides gruffly offered up: "This appears serious."

"I have to hope she is," Ben trying a doomed grin along with it.

Angelides waited, attentive to more to come.

"I'm in a fix, Andy. She's married."

The sentences escaped from him before he knew it. He hadn't told Prokosch when he had the opening. Never would he have told Danzer. He had not even confided in Jake, repository of life's complications that he was. Angelides in alert stillness on the next bunk he would have trusted with his life, but the confession he had just made came under another category entirely. *I'm not equipped for this.* Ben creased the letters closed. "Keep it under your hat, okay? I can't take any pride in being a homewrecker. If that's what I turn out to be, even."

"Sorry, I'm no help to you there," Angelides said as if it was a test he hadn't taken. "All I've ever been round is love 'em and leave 'em. I got left."

Ben looked over at him. One spill of guts for another. It seemed his turn to come up with something medicative. "You'll have better luck later on. Civvie life will be full of lovelies looking for Marines in shining armor, you'll see."

In an exceedingly swift motion Angelides no longer was flat on his back but sitting tight as a coil on the edge of his bunk. "Ben? Something you maybe better know. In case it affects what you want to write or something like that. When the shooting match is over"—that always meant the war in conversations like this—"I'm staying in." He worked up a rough grin behind the exchange of confidences. "True-blue to the stinking Corps."

Ben did not say anything immediately, confounded once again by a teammate he was supposed to know like an open book. War mocked the notion of some sort of order in the human race. The only sane route he thought he knew—it was also true of Cass, Jake, anyone he would lay down his life for and they for him—was to serve as dutifully as you could during the duration, then reconstitute yourself when peace came in whatever measure. Get on with the existence you were cut out for, or, in terms blindingly similar to the argument he would have made to Dex Cariston, we are servants of war forever. Yet here was Angelides, capability itself, turning his back on the TSU degree and probably married life, to stay on in uniform as a glorified groundpounder foreman, rewarded with stripes on his arm and little else. A garrison career for enlisted men was boredom with bad surprises sewn in; just ask the poor suckers stationed on Guam in 1941 when the Japanese imperial army showed up.

By now Ben's silence was saying much in itself. "You're sure," he tried with Angelides, "you just want grunt life to go on and on?"

The bared smile. "You can't tell by looking? It fits me like a cork in a virgin."

WORD CAME THAT a piece of cargo with highest priority and his name all over it awaited at the airfield, and when Ben went to fetch the dreaded recording equipment, it was attended by the wearer of the most disheveled uniform on Eniwetok.

"Hi, Lieutenant. Gosh, it's hot here."

"Jones!" Elated to see that familiar ugly puss under the crumpled fatigue cap, he fought back the impulse to ask a torrent of questions about East Base, especially the WASP side of things. "Old home week, right here in equatorial Eden. I can't believe Tepee Weepy took a fit of sanity and sent you along. I can use all the help there is." Saying so, Ben circled the recorder in its carrying case distrustfully. It basically resembled the bulkiest suitcase imaginable. He looked around the cargo shed for the technician whiz promised with it, then realized.

"Jones, I hate to take your name in vain, but please don't tell me you're the tech aide, too."

"That was the order that came down," this stanza of the enlisted men's repertoire practically sang from the bedraggled corporal. He puckered in contemplation and came up with a morsel of solace for Ben: "They did give me the manual and I read it on the flight over."

Oh, great. He can pray over the machine when it goes flooey. "Let's get this thing to the ship," Ben said in resignation. "Posterity beckons."

THE MARINE ASSAULT force command plainly regarded the TPWP pair and their recording assignment as a nuisance, and just as plainly had been ordered in no uncertain terms to put up with them. Angelides was mostly amused. "Seems dumb-ass to me—who needs more proof people are shooting at us out here?"

The machine when Jones opened its case and started trying to figure out its workings was not the Pandora's box Ben had anticipated, it was worse. It ran on a battery as heavy as a concrete block. It had delicate reels and a delicate needle. The cord to the hand microphone was scarcely longer than a dog leash. His brow creased, Jones at length looked up from the so-called portable recorder. "You know what, Lieutenant? If we're going to pack this thing from here to shore, what we really need is—"

"—a jeep," Ben admitted like someone coming down with a headache. "Excuse me while I beg my way through the Marine chain of command."

ACROSS THE NEXT couple of days, with Jones in earphones as he fiddled madly with the recorder's dials, Ben stood on the fantail of the troopship and practiced until his vocal cords were tired. Speaking into the microphone required an entirely different mentality from what he was used to at the typewriter. How did Edward R. Murrow do it? For that matter, how did that moron motormouth Loudon do it?

"Eniwetok's harbor is jammed with ships of the assault force," he stared around at the obvious and could only recite it in strained fashion. Wanting to say: *Cass, you should see this. You can't imagine the steel mills it took to do this, wall an entire island with ships.* "The Marines aboard this one say they are ready for the real thing after weeks of practice landings here." *They say it in the filthy language of war, naturally—pilots aren't the only ones with the vocabulary, Cass. Poor Jones goes around the ship looking like his ears hurt. Angelides these days has a mouth on him like a blowtorch. Invasion is a hellish thing to go through. Nobody is actually ever prepared to die, are they—it's not human nature, the imagination can't handle obliteration. And so the guys belowdecks talk tough, so the fear doesn't have a chance to speak up.* Again aloud: "Equipment of all sorts is in the cargo bays waiting to roll aboard the landing craft. Artillery, half-tracks, jeeps—"

"Sorry, start again," Jones muttered, repeatedly, from where he hovered over the temperamental recorder. *Oh God, Jones, so to speak. At Guam are we going to stick our necks out from here to Thomas Edison and only get a reel full of blank air out of it?*

When at last they got done with the rehearsal reel and played it back, Ben winced over his voice. He sounded dry and stiff as sticks rubbed together. As for the quality of what he was coming up with to say, if he had it on typing paper in front of him he would have been wildly crossing things out and scribbling in changes.

In the silence at the end of the reel, he gloomily turned toward Jones. "So what do you think, maestro?"

"Maybe it would help if you had some kind of a script?"

GUAM WAS ear-shattering.

Fiery salvo after salvo from the big muzzles of the American battleships and cruisers, more rapid fire from the guns of the rest of the convoy spread across the horizon of ocean, the bombardment ahead of the invasion was like all the sky's lightning dropping all its thunder at once. Explosions erupted onshore every few seconds, smoke and dust spewing as if from volcano vents. After enough of this the entire island looked like it was on fire.

While Ben struggled to jot the scene down amid the jostling swarm of Marines along the deck rail of the troopship, his memory tunneled back to the Salamaua beachhead in New Guinea. The advantage of darkness there. Friessen's temporarily lucky National Guard unit crawling ashore unhit. The worn-down Japanese defenders heading for the hills. A victorious landing if there ever was one. *And I still ended up shot, didn't I.* He looked out again at the island being smashed by shells and bombs from the invasion armada. Guam was an ugly lump in the ocean, rocky bluffs and jungle ravines looming behind the crescent of shore called the Devil's Horns. At least he and Jones did not have to follow on inland to the hand-to-hand fighting there, their task ended at the beach. *Look where the damn place is, though. This isn't anything like Eniwetok.* There the distance from where the landing craft disgorged the assault troops to the practice beach was about the length of a football field. Here, for real, the shore of Guam lay beyond what looked more like a quarter of a mile of coral shelf. The assault force would have to wade it all. Prowling through his riflemen as he checked over their packs and combat equipment hung all over them, Angelides looked ready to leap over the side and swim the distance. He had been through two of these to Ben's one. *You're the professional soldier, Animal. If the odds on this don't make you look bothered, maybe I worry too much about the difference between practice and the real thing. Shelling the living hell out of the place this way ought to even things up some. When we go in with the damn recorder, dead silence onshore would suit me.*

Struggling through the Marine mass toward him was Jones, a steel helmet somewhat lopsided on him. He had to shout to make himself understood to Ben a foot away. "They're telling us, 'Load up.'"

"Then let's go do it."

After a maximum of administrative runaround they had been allowed the backseat of a jeep assigned to Headquarters Company. It and a few others of a small motor convoy would follow—more aptly, wallow—in over the broad reef behind an armored half-track mounted with a 75 mm. cannon and a machine gun. Angelides' contingent wading in would be in clear sight off to the side. The jeep had nothing else to recommend it as a battle vantage point; a temporary steel panel had been installed where the windshield ordinarily was, with a slit for the driver to see through.

"It's still awful open, Lieutenant," Jones had pointed out when they looked over the vehicle in the cargo hold.

"Don't I know it. We'll need to crouch down until we're kissing the floorboards."

Now as they started to make their way below to get themselves established in the motor convoy's landing craft, the din of the invasion bombardment growing even louder overhead, a hand gripped Ben's shoulder. Startled, he in turn grabbed Jones to a halt and turned around. Angelides, looking lethal in his camouflage helmet, was there roaring in his ear: "Get in the half-track. You and Bible boy. Not the jeep, savvy? I fixed it with the loading officer and he fixed it with the trackie crew."

Ben hesitated. The half-track, which was half tank and half truck, would be in the lead crawling across the coral and draw enemy fire accordingly. "You're sure?"

Angelides winked. "One of us ought to keep his pecker dry in case fun in the sack ever comes back into style. Might as well be you." He slapped Ben on the shoulder, purposely right on the TPWP patch. "See you on the beach, recording star." Ben watched the big figure draped in ammunition bandoliers and grenade pouches recede back to his men at the deck rail.

All was commotion in the flotilla of landing craft bobbing against the ship. Jones had been down earlier to secure the recorder in the jeep, and now he and Ben wrestled the hefty equipment case out and into the back of the half-track and climbed in after it. The gunners there turned and met them with dubious looks. One cracked: "Hitchhikers, huh? That gorilla sergeant says we're gonna make history taking you along."

"That's the theory," Ben vouched. His voice sounded tight, and he rubbed his throat to try to relax it. Jones squirmed down beside the recording equipment, manipulating plugs and scanning dials as though they were compasses in a stormy sea.

The minutes of waiting before launch dragged by. The gunners slouched amid their stocks of ammunition and smoked, which maybe helped their nerves but not those of the pair at the recorder. At last the dispatching officer, lordly on the troopship, gave the signal and their landing craft and the one with Angelides' group of Marines putt-putted away like ducks abreast.

The half-track a metal box within a larger floating metal box, Jones and Ben could not see out during the short yet endless voyage. Engine noise and wave slosh and ominous clatter from the gunners as they made ready seeped through the crashing intervals of the bombardment. As best as Ben could tell, the shelling so far was all one-way, the naval barrage suppressing whatever waited on shore. At least the landing craft was not being blasted out of the water. Yet. "Waipu was a breeze, we walked right in," Angelides' recapitulations played unrelentingly within Ben, "Tarawa was total hell, they threw everything at us," the one experience against the other. Either outcome, he had to somehow summon into the microphone in his hand. Jones had traded his helmet for earphones—Ben hoped that kind of faith would be rewarded—and looked up expectantly with his finger over the ON switch, but Ben signaled him to hold off. "Not until we're on the reef. This is recess."

As soon as the broad-beamed craft ground to a halt against the shelf of coral and the landing ramp descended, everything

changed as if a single order had been given to every enemy soldier bunkered against the bombardment. Guam erupted back
at the invasion force. Geysers in the surf met the half-track as it
clanked down the ramp, the Japanese artillery opening up. Bullets pinged off the armored sides like terrible hail. "Inhospitable
bastards," one gunner grouched. Grimacing, Ben held the microphone out the back of the half-track to catch the sounds of being
under fire. When Jones gave him thumbs-up that the recorder
was functioning for sure, he climbed over the tailgate and slid
into the water to his thighs, holding the mike up out of the wet.

"War has many calibers," he began speaking from the shelter of the rear of the half-track. "The Marines wading ashore
here at Guam are getting an earful of the Japanese arsenal." A
nasty *sploosh* nearby punctuated that. When his flinching was
over, Ben reported: "That was a mortar shell, fairly close." No
sooner had he said so than a larger eruption sent jarring tremors
through the water and the air. "And that was big artillery, probably a howitzer in a shore emplacement. In the background you
can hear Nambu machine guns. Their muzzle flashes are red, like
Fourth of July rockets going off everywhere on the bluff above
the beach. The Marines make the joke, if it is a joke, that if you
listen enough those machine gun bursts sound like 'RIP RIP,'
although resting in peace is not how any man hopes to come out
of this day." Tallying such details in words as exact as he could
make them was crazily vital to him right then, something other
than fear for the mind to try to hold on to in the midst of battle.
Jones's suggestion of a script turned out to already exist in him,
accumulated from as many combat zones as the correspondent
patch on his arm had taken him to. The lore of war. An unsought
education. Spectator to himself in this, he talked on into a seeming abyss of time, the assault occurring in unreal slow motion,
infantrymen moving at a heavy-legged slog against the water and

the coarse shelf of reef. He clung to the tailgate with one hand to help his own footing, the half-track creeping over the rough coral at the same methodical pace as the wading Marines on both sides of him.

"Off to my left the rank being led in by Sergeant Andros Angelides is strung out wide. Bullets are hitting the water around them." So far, though, the rubber raft rode high and empty near the medical corpsmen as it was towed. Ben described that, the infantry lifeboat voyaging into the sea of hostilities. Leading the wave of men ahead, Angelides surged steadily along, turning sideways occasionally to present less of a target as he looked things over and bawled an order. Keeping up the running commentary with whatever arrived to him—the distinctive whumping sound of a Japanese mortar round; the carcasses of landing craft burning on the reef in back of the men in the water; the confused mix of smells, fine fresh salt air, stinking exhaust fumes, gunpowder odor from the half-track's cannon firing furiously—Ben consistently tried to estimate how far the first of the Marines were from the beachhead. By any measure it was too long a way while being shot at. While he looked on, soldiers near Angelides crashed over into the surf, one, two. All along the advance line of wading troops were other dark blobs of bodies in the water.

"Men are being hit as they come into closer range of enemy fire," he somehow kept the words coming, "too many to count. Someone's helmet just floated by upside down."

Just as he was at the point of describing the medical corpsmen splashing to the rescue of the pair in Angelides' unit but having to give them up for dead, an explosion close behind the half-track flung him against the tailgate. Breath knocked out of him, he cringed there as metal debris sailed through the air, miraculously holding the microphone up enough to catch the sound of it striking the water around them. Leaning out over the tailgate, a white-faced Jones had hold of him with one arm. Not knowing if the recorder was still working, beyond caring, Ben in a raw voice spoke into the mike for their own posterity if no one else's:

"That was the sound of a jeep blowing up in back of us, from a direct hit."

Jones vanished into the well of the half-track then came up nodding, twirling a finger to indicate the reel remained running. Wiping salt water out of his eyes and ears and the corners of his mouth, Ben groggily mustered himself and swung around in the surf to take stock, checking on Angelides and his men—*I owe you one, don't I, Animal, for stuffing us in the half-track instead of that jeep*—as the line of them advanced like walkers with lead in their boots. Halfway to shore. He gave the distance out loud, words tumbling from somewhere. The next ones that reached the microphone did not come from him.

"SARGE IS DOWN! CORPSMAN, CORPSMAN!"

The cry—it was more of a wail—arose from a young Marine near the leading edge of Angelides' outfit. Where the stalking broad-shouldered shape had been a moment before, there now was a sodden form facedown, and Marines on either side struggling to hoist him up long enough for the raft to come.

"Sergeant Angelides has been hit," Ben instinctively reported in a voice he would not have recognized as his own. "His men are bringing the rubber boat they use to carry their wounded." Even as he spoke that last word, he could tell this was no million-dollar wound, no ticket out of the war. He watched heartsick as the medics splashed their way to the big figure with a torso drenched darker than water would do, checked his vital signs, shook their heads at each other, and made the stark decision to leave his body to the tide. Numbly Ben told of this, finishing up:

"The life raft is there, but passing him by."

He choked up. One more time, death had won. Animal Angelides the indestructible, no more.

"Lieutenant?" A hand from somewhere, grappling away the microphone. "Lieutenant, climb in!" Jones was frantically tugging at him, trying to wrestle him upward into the back of the half-track. "It's over, Lieutenant. We're out of reel."

11

★ *I HAVE TO HAND it to you, Ben. You made it back here in one piece. From the neck down, anyway.*

In the ice-blue twilight that passed for illumination in the roadhouse, Cass drank him in from across the table. His months out there under the ocean sun had tanned him to a light bronze. The ginger hair was briskly cut in a way he must have caught from being around Marines, a curt bristle her fingers wanted into whenever they weren't otherwise engaged in the cabin out back a half hour ago. His face in its weary extent held both more and less than she remembered. Whatever else the Pacific trip had done to him, it had honed him down almost to thin, his every feature accentuated as if all excess had been pared away, bone truth underneath. *You were serious before, you're damn near drastic now.* The loss of his buddy at Guam was still with him any given moment, echoing off the stars and every surface between, but that was not all. Even when he was joking with her about the skunk juice the roadhouse passed off as scotch, there was a steady intensity to Ben, like a lamp flame trimmed low, burning through the night.

"Cass?" He spun his glass in the spot of condensation under it, as if studying the direction of the swirl. "Cass, how much longer do we have?"

She could tell he did not mean from then to morning. Her tongue caught on the words a little as she spoke back. "You could have talked all night, soldier, and not asked that."

"Just wanted to brush up on how things stand." He kept on watching the twirl of the glass as if it was going to do a new trick. "With us. The incurable ungodly galloping case of us, remember?"

They'd both had too much to drink, which still was not nearly enough. Right away their reunion had all but gone through the roof of that cabin. They climbed all over one another in the beat-up bed, fast and furious in their need. Their first lovemaking since Seattle, both of them went about it as if it was the last ever. Afterward, a bit dazed and winded, they adjourned out here to take a look at the matter of themselves through the comparatively cool reflection of drinks.

Carefully Cass steadied herself, both elbows on the table, chin up. Funny how a dive like this place was the one spot that didn't care how tangled you were, showed some mercy. The jukebox was turned low into a kindly monotony, "Deep Purple" swinging along invisibly for about the dozenth time. On down the long bar from their corner, the place was empty this far into the night except for the roadhouse bartender and a local codger idly taking turns at playing the punchboard. *So at least we don't have to make fools of ourselves in front of anybody that counts. Yet.* Braced, she looked Ben full in the face. "You're the one who's been out there in Tokyo's backyard, you tell me when the man I'm married to is likely to be told he doesn't have to invade any more islands."

Ben thought about it, showing the effort to get past the effects of the so-called scotch. Everyone in the Pacific theater of combat was betting MacArthur would try for the Philippines pretty soon. *That "I shall return" yap he let out in '42. As if he's going to come back to Manila and whip the asses of the Japs single-handed.*

Whenever the supreme general did try to retake the Philippine Islands, he would throw in all the troops he could find. Ben could not bring himself to tell Cass the overpowering likelihood, that jungle-veteran units such as her husband's would be used to mop up whatever MacArthur wanted mopped up. "It's anybody's guess what'll happen out there," he came out with, aware it was hardly worth it.

Cass looked away. "Dan's got overseas points, up the gigi, but his whole National Guard bunch keeps getting extended. He's on some wreck of an island called Biak, they let them say that in a letter finally." She paused to do some thinking of her own. "He wrote me that it's supposed to be a recuperation area now, but it's sure as hell no Australia or Hawaii—his outfit figures they're being held there for one last shooting match." She broke off to take a hard sip of her drink.

This was a moment Ben knew he should feel honorable remorse or worse for trespassing into Cass's life with another man. As far back as their first time as lovers, qualms of that sort were somewhere just beyond the edge of the bed. But stronger emotions would always push those away, if he and she had a hundred years at this. The nature of love is that it catches you off-guard, subjects you to rules you have never faced, some of them contradictory. All of the ones about fidelity of heart and life knotted him to Cass, and as far as he could tell, always would.

He scrunched in his chair, not saying it until he could no longer stand to hold it in. "What happens then? When he does come home?"

"I don't damn know. I do not know, Ben, how can I? I'm going to be faced with a man I haven't seen in two years, it'll have to decide itself from there." Watching her from across the table, he listened desperately, trying to determine if he was hearing ground rules of wingwalking again—*Never leave hold of what you've got*—or something more hopeful—*until you've got hold of something else.* Cass was gazing steadily at him as she finished up. "If you were him, you'd feel entitled to that much."

"If I were him, I'd hate me."

"Hey, don't get going in that direction." She shook her head in warning. "If anyone is going to be accused of messing up a marriage, start with me. Nobody held a gun on me and said, 'Go fall for that dishy war correspondent in the fleece jacket,' did they. I could have looked the other way and stayed in the rut I'm meant to for the rest of the war, one more pilot going nowhere."

"Come off that, will you?" he appealed. "Since when doesn't having a squadron count? *I* sure to Christ don't have one. You aren't anybody's idea of a pilot going nowhere."

"Not now. Wings on my brisket, bars on my collar, I'm a pretty good imitation of a fighter plane jockey on these ferrying runs, you bet I am. But what happens the minute the boys come marching home? Is the good old Army Air Corps going to treat WASPs like guys? No sign of it so far." Cass jerked her glass up to her lips, found it empty, and set it down disconsolately. "I want the war over as much as anybody, but the war is what keeps me in that cockpit. There's a pisser, isn't it? And Ben?—us, chronic us? How do I know I could keep up with you after the war? If we did stay together? You're probably going to be famous—what am I saying, you're famous or next thing to it already—"

"Only as long as bullets are flying."

"—and all in the damn world I'm good for is handling one half-assed kind of fighter plane."

He lurched his chair forward. "Cass, we can't put together life after the war until the sonofabitching thing shows us it's going to be over, but we can stick together until we can figure out—" Breaking off, he peered across at her and demanded, "Are you bawling? Because if you are, I'm afraid then I'll have to."

"Damn you, Ben Reinking," she said, fierce but snuffling. "I haven't had a crying jag since I was eleven years old." She wiped her eyes, then her nose. "Until you."

For some moments he gulped back moist emotions of his own. Why of all the people in this war did the two of them have to be on the receiving end of something like this? What was wrong with backing away from this and snapping up an Adrianna instead, sweetly available and nowhere near as troublous? What was wrong with him? "This is just crazy hopeless," he said at last, his expression pretty much fitting that description itself. "I'm stuck on you even when we're doing our double damnedest to have a fight."

"Swell," Cass sniffled, "that's me, too." She straightened herself up so sharply it jarred the table. "There's another kink to this, you know," she went on, wiping the tears away with determination now. "Dan's not the only one they keep throwing out there to get shot at, is he. I don't pretend to know squat about what the types in Washington have you doing. I just herd airplanes. The wear is starting to show through on those stories about the team, though, isn't it? I don't need to tell you that's getting to be an awful lot of dead heroes. Your guys are catching hell. And you're always going to be plunked right out there with them, Ben, you and just a pencil and paper, brave as anything—"

"I don't feel brave. I'm just doing it."

"—while every fool on the other side tries to draw a bead on you. Look what just happened to your pal the Marine. It could have been you. I am never going to be in favor of that part of your Tepee Weepy doings, you'd better know."

"Listen, they've got me under orders the same way you are, and I—"

"It isn't quite the same." She slapped the table for emphasis. "You've got some clout, you've got the name you've made for yourself."

"That works once in a while. And generally doesn't. I was about to say, if I ever get the chance to drop the supreme team stuff, I'll do it in the next breath. For right now, the worst thing I've got to do is cover Angelides' funeral." He tried to move along to a better face on things and did not quite get there. "Maybe it's just as well to have some practice at crying, hmm? Cass, the night's getting away from us. What would you think about seeing if the cabin is still standing?"

Her try at a better face at least came out better than his. "You haven't lost any of that ginger, is what I'd think."

He pretended a huff. "If you're not interested all of a sudden—"

"Didn't say I wasn't interested, preacher," she sounded much more like herself. "Pay the man again."

"Gladly. And just maybe I'll get us another drink along with it."

He headed up to the cash register, digging a few silver dollars out of his pocket as he went. *What a hell of a thing, that all we've got is sack time together. But at least it's something.*

The bartender, an older man bald as a peanut, was sitting there alone nursing a cigarette. He cut a squinty look at Cass, then back at Ben. "You and the little lady figure on playing a doubleheader?"

Ben pushed the money toward him on the bar. "That's what these nice round silver things are about, yeah."

The bartender still looked at him, one eyelid pulled down against the cigarette smoke perpetually drifting toward it. "Soldier, ain't you?"

Oh, please. Now the citizenry of Vaughn Junction is going to get picky about who it rents out hot sheets to? Crossly Ben indicated to Cass. "The both of us. Why?"

The man behind the bar plucked a shred of tobacco off his tongue, then asked: "Been overseas any?"

"I was in on Guam."

The bartender shoved the money back to him. "It's on the house."

When Ben returned to the table with both drinks and dollars in hand, Cass had the immediate question, "What was that about?"

"My guess is he lost a son in the Pacific."

They drank silently for a bit. Then he peeked over in the dimness at her luminous wristwatch. "Is it tomorrow yet, Captain?"

She checked. "Just past midnight. What's special about tomorrow?"

He made a satisfied sound. "I have a VIP coming in, although he doesn't know it yet. I don't know who they're going to get to stand sentry over the rocks and sand, but I sprung him for a leave to come to Animal's funeral."

Cass caught on. "The guy out on the Coast? The one you were afraid would shoot up everything in sight and himself with it?"

"That's him. Prokosch the tommy gunner."

"No crap?" Cass sat up in surprise and awe. "The guy isn't even kin and you hassled them into letting him come to the funeral? You must've had to pull strings the size of anchor ropes, all up and down the line."

He nodded pious affirmation. "Right to the top." If Tepee Weepy constituted the apex of things military. "At least it gets him away from submarine games for a few days, and he can see his girl along with it."

"WAKE UP, KID. Hey, hear me? Roust out, Coastie."

The off-duty sentry rolled away from the hut wall and with a groan elbowed up in his bunk. Two men with beach packs bulking on them were standing over him. The skinny sour-looking one was the chief petty officer from the Coast Guard station down the coast, the other was a peach-fuzzed seaman second class much like himself. "What's happening? The war over?"

"Dream some more, kid. Where's Prokosch?"

The off-duty man rubbed sleep crust from his eyes. "Sig? Out on patrol like he's supposed to be."

"Come on, I know that. Where the hell at?"

"How am I supposed to know, Chief?" Squinting at the twenty-four-hour clock on the radio table, he made an effort to concentrate. "He took off out of here this morning like his tail was on fire, him and the pooch. Must be up the beach quite a patch by now."

The other seaman was slinging belongings out of his pack onto Prokosch's bunk. "Hurry it up, Quince," said the chief petty officer. He glanced at the face of confusion trying to take this in from across the hut. "Quincy's his relief while he goes on leave, so get used to Quincy."

"Sig don't have leave coming."

"He does now. Something about a funeral. There's a plane waiting for him at Port Angeles." Waiting impatiently for Quincy to restow the pack, the chief petty officer ducked to the window facing the ocean and the rugged line of shore beyond, looked out, and rolled his shoulders. "Hell if I know what it's about, but I'm supposed to walk him out of here and put him on that plane. The way these orders smoked down the line, you'd think he was Jimmy Roosevelt."

The man still in the bunk looked more bewildered than ever. "You got to go after him on foot? Can't you just call him in?"

The chief petty officer turned from the window in final agitation. "Radio blackout. Jap sub sank a tanker, down off Oregon last night, the pricks. No transmissions that they might pick up until we get the all clear. Ready, Quincy?" He tromped toward the door whether or not Quincy was ready. "Let's go. Maybe we can catch him before he gets to hell and gone up the beach."

The off-duty sentry rolled back into his bunk. "You don't know Prokosch."

FARTHEST OUT ON the Pacific horizon from where Sig Prokosch happened to be patrolling, waves broke violently on a shelf of reef as if the edge of the world was flying apart.

Scanning from the distant mix of spray and drab rumple of the ocean, the Coast Guardsman strived to find a low-lying streak of white out there, a chalk trace on the greater gray, that would be the wake disclosing a periscope. He was keyed up, convinced this might very well be the morning he nailed the Japanese submariners. If not him personally, then the plane carrying depth bombs after he radioed in, blasting away beneath the surface in a relentless search pattern that would crack open the hull of the sub and give the damn Japs all the water they wanted.

Sig felt like winking at the oval moon, paling away as daylight approached. He was highly pleased at having figured it out, nights awake while waiting for sleep to catch up with him, gazing out the window of the hut at the moon furrow on the ocean—the enemy's evident pattern for those sneak raft trips to the creeks for their drinking water. The raft rats had to be using the lunar cycle. Not the round bright full moon, the obvious. Coast Guard headquarters had thought of that and orders from on high were for extreme vigilance along the coast during each such phase. But that had not produced anything except eyestrain among the nighttime sentries. No, the Japanese must be timing their shore excursions some number of nights either side of that, using the moon when it was just luminous enough to cast a skinny path to shore, Sig would have bet anything. That way the raft rats could paddle alongside the moonbeam glow on the water without having to use a torch and with less chance of being seen than during full shine. It made every kind of sense to him, and lately he had matched it up with times he found fresh crap at a creek mouth.

He cradled the tommy gun. There was reassurance in the highly tooled grip of it that one of these times he would jump the raft rats, the odds could not stay in their favor forever. On this coast he was the constant, they were the variable, and all those accounting classes at TSU had taught him that the basic determinant was to be found in constancy. One of these times, the raft would get a late start from the submarine or be held up by choppy waves on the way in or happen into some other inconstant circumstance, and he would have them where he wanted them. Maybe this fresh morning.

THE PAIR FROM the Coast Guard station slogged down from the hut to the strand of sand between waves rolling in and the tumble of driftlogs lodged against the forest. Awaiting them were bootprints of considerable size and the much more delicate scuffs made by dog paws. The tracks went straight as a dotted line the length of the sand and disappeared around the clay cliff of the headland ahead. The chief petty officer swore. "I hate to do it to you in this sand, Quince. But we've got to quick-march or we'll be chasing him all damned day."

ONCE MORE PROKOSCH scanned outward from the thin crescent of beach. Stirred up by some distant storm, the waves coming to shore tumbled themselves into sudden rolling tunnels, crashing apart moments after they formed. A froth of spume piled itself high at tide line, chunks of it flying off in the wind like great flecks of ash.

At his side the Irish setter nosed at one of the spume clumps and brought on itself a wheezy dog fit of sneezing.

"Bless you, Rex," Sig said as if speaking to an equal. "But that's what you get for not paying attention to business, isn't it. Heel, boy." He lately had written to Ruby that he figured it was okay to talk to the dog, as long as he didn't start hearing the dog answer him. He smiled to himself, thinking back to all the conversation during Ben Reinking's stay. Starting with Japanese, when he had come upon the figure that turned out to be Lefty spraddled on that rock face. Funny at the time, but good practice for whenever he got the jump on the—

The leash sprang taut in his grasp.

"What's the matter, boy?" Sig's voice dropped low, sentry caution even though no one, no sign of anybody, had appeared. Growling, the dog tugged toward the dark band of vegetation that fringed the outlet of a creek not far ahead.

Sig at once angled inland, steering the dog toward the bulwark of driftwood. The pair of them skirted along it, out of sight from the creek, until they were almost to the dunelike bank. There he silenced the dog with a whispered command and, tommy gun ready, cautiously took a look over the bank. Below, at the edge of the brush at the creek mouth, there were marks in the sand that looked as if a rubber raft might have been skidded up out of the surf. Excitement came with the sight. Plain as anything to him, the Japs had been here at low tide. An hour or two ago.

THE CHIEF PETTY officer clambered up onto the rocky snout of the headland and took a long look north along the shore. Below him, the light blue of ocean clashed against the chocolate brown of rocks covered with seaweed. Where the sand resumed, the crescent of beach bowed around for a quarter of a mile or so before a brushy creek came wandering out of the thick forest.

The young seaman panted up behind him, tugging against the pack straps that cut into his shoulders. "Any sign of him yet, Chief?"

"No, but he's got to be up around that creek somedamn-where—he didn't have any too much head start on us."

"How about we fire a shot?"

The chief debated with himself. "We don't want to spook him, if he's at all touchy around the trigger finger. Try yelling again. Put everything into it—with this surf you can't hear yourself think."

"PROKOSCH! WAIT FOR US! YOU'VE GOT LEAVE, BUDDY!"

SQUINTING OUT AT the ocean again in search of a telltale periscope wake, Sig was unshucking his pack to use the radio when the dog reared to the end of the leash, whining in agitation. "Rex, down," he hissed without effect. The dog was definite, straining now not in the direction of the creek but toward the salal and ferns and overhanging forest.

"Easy, boy," he whispered. "What is it you think you've got?" Alert to the possibility that the Japanese were still ashore, holed up there in the woods, he weighed his options. Using the radio was slow and cumbersome and they might hear him talking into it. On the other hand, if they hadn't spotted him by now, he had the advantage of surprise. He knew these woods, the raft rats didn't. If he left the radio pack, he could ease ever so slowly into the undergrowth and see what was what. Although there was the matter of the dog.

He hesitated. If he tied the dog here to a limb of driftwood, it might bark. Besides, the Irish setter's nose was the quickest guide to any Japs. Patting Rex's head and murmuring soothingly to keep him quiet, he hooked the leash into his web belt and crept toward the forest.

Sniffing constantly, the dog led him on the leash through the head-high barrier of brush and into the forest-floor growth, until shortly yanking to a halt. With his weapon up and every nerve afire for action, Sig even so was surprised, confused, by what awaited almost within touch of him. Not Japs at all, but a sizable wad of what looked like some odd kind of fabric. A pale shroud of it, crumpled in the salal. *Parachute,* he thought immediately. Before realizing it was balloon material.

In that fatal instant he saw the dog sniff at the explosive device tangled beneath and put a paw to it.

12

✪ "WILL YOU LAY OFF that damn hymn? You're driving me ape."

Jake Eisman's humming snapped off, but not his dolorous expression as he looked sidewise at Ben behind the steering wheel. "I for sure don't want to be trapped in a moving vehicle with a pencil-pusher gone apeshit, do I." He mopped at his neck with his hand. "Man, I hope sweating is good for the health. How about cranking the windshield open?"

"Now there's an original idea," Ben changed his own tune. "Let's give it a whirl, until we get grasshoppers in the teeth."

The pair of them were in a ragtop jeep, all that Jones had been able to snag for them out of the East Base motor pool, heading down the height of bluff south from Shelby toward the brief green ribbon of trees in the Marias River bottomland. Each man had shed the jacket of full-dress uniform, and the cloth doors of the jeep were tied back to let air in both sides, and still it was like traveling in an oversize oven. The fields along the shimmering highway the next couple of hours to Great Falls, they well knew, would be the cooked results of summerlong sun, the waiting grain baked golden, the mown hayfields crisp and tan, the distant dun sidehills further tinted with broad scatters of sheep. Behind them were a good many miles of the same. They had buried Angelides the day before five counties away, Prokosch that morning in the remote little railroad burg of his upbringing.

Jake rested a foot the size of a shoe box against the dashboard and slouched back in the confines of his seat. He yanked at his tie again even though it was already loosened. Honor-guard pall-bearer was not a role he was suited to. "At the rate we're putting people in the ground," he brooded to Ben, "you'd think the Japs had invaded Montana."

"I've noticed."

It was hard to say which funeral troubled the tired pair more, but Angelides' at Fort Peck yesterday had been the stark one. Only the bushy mustached uncle, off shift from the powerhouse at the monumental earthen dam, to see the casket into the clay. Towering among the five other pallbearers rounded up by the funeral home, Jake throughout looked upset and angry over the scant farewell in the scarcely populated cemetery among some Missouri River badlands. Ben knew the feeling. He said now, "You've had more than your share of lifting coffins lately, Ice. Any chance you can spring a weekend pass for yourself?" At some level they were aware they were making talk so as not to be alone with their thoughts.

"Hah. It's back to chauffeuring bombers to the Russkies again tomorrow," came the glum reply. "I have to make up for all this inspiring funeral duty, don't I. Aw, shit, what am I saying? Sig and Animal would've done it for me." Jake's gaze went distant, then came back. "Anyway, Benjamin, it was good to see your folks there this morning, huh? Your mother is a real pussycat."

Ben looked across. Jake did not appear to be kidding.

"Your dad didn't miss a lick of what was going on," the one-sided conversation from the passenger side of things persisted. "Figure he'll be writing about the funeral?"

"I'd bet my bottom dollar on it."

THE PACKARD CRESTED the long pull up from the Two Medicine River and slowed as if made shy by the sudden cliff-faced mountains—Jericho Reef, Phantom Woman Peak, Roman Reef— that stood up into view in the direction of Gros Ventre. It was considerably more car than Bill Reinking was accustomed to, and he drove in a skittish way that had Cloyce itching to take over. Montana men did not believe that a woman's grasp in life included the steering wheel. It mattered not that she'd had use of the family roadster whenever she wanted, at the country place among the orange groves, when she was sixteen. As her husband nursed the high-powered automobile around another curve, she told herself yet again this was only to be expected; a shopworn luxury car running on black-market gasoline, both provided by a saloonkeeper (and presumably worse), was just the sort of thing that came with Gros Ventre, with marrying the complete town when you wed its newspaperman.

They had not said much on this trip back from the packed foursquare church across the tracks from the Devon depot out east of Shelby, Bill busy in his head, Cloyce in extensive thoughts of her own. Try as she would, she could not get over the Prokosch boy's watery-eyed mother and father, in sagging funeral clothes that they looked like they'd been sacked into. There but for the grace of something or other—despite what the preacher said in the funeral service, she could not credit an all-wise divinity in charge of every life and death in this immense war—wept Bill and herself, if Ben had not survived Guam and those other places. Even yet she could feel fate narrowly brushing past, back at the start of this unnatural week. She had been out in the backyard coddling her roses with root food, the shade of the cottonwood trees pleasant in the already warm summer morning. Around the corner of the house came Bill, a telegram in his hand. If she had not already been kneeling, she would have been thrust to her knees by the sight of the yellow message form known for carrying the savage words: WE REGRET TO INFORM YOU THAT YOUR SON—

With his head dipped to make out the dappled yard through his bifocals, Bill did not spot her soon enough, then froze at the look on her face. He fumbled out the sentences in contrite haste:

"Ben is back from the Pacific, he's all right. He has funeral duty. Twice."

"Is he coming home"—it caught in her throat to say it—"as usual?"

"Not this time, for some reason. We'll go to him. I'll work it out somehow."

Attending the Prokosch boy's funeral had been better than nothing, she gave Bill that much, even though there had not been nearly enough time afterward with Ben before he and nice Jake had to start back to East Base. Back to the madhouse of war. How she wished Ben had gotten hold of himself and made the most of the chance she'd set up so perfectly at New Year's—

"Dear?" She jumped more than a little at the surprise of her husband's voice, after the constant miles of silence. "Take something down for me, will you? There's a notepad and Eversharp in my suit coat."

Now she really was startled. Bill never did this. His work was kept so separate as to be almost holy, done either at the *Gleaner* office or in private in his upstairs library, and they would be home in Gros Ventre in no time if he would floor the gas pedal just a bit. She twitted him, "Isn't the usual line, 'Get me rewrite!'? Whatever are you thinking, Bill, this isn't exactly the set for *The Front Page* and I'm not—"

"Cloyce, will-you-please-just-do-this."

Speechless at the steel in that burst, she reached around into the backseat for the writing materials in his coat.

"Ready?" His voice bristling as much as his mustache, he started dictating at a deliberate pace. *"You have seen the ready-made insignia of the home front all across our state, in our neighborhoods, on our ranches and farms, wherever there are window casements framing proud but anxious parents. The small satin banner no larger than a tea towel*—cross out 'small'—*hangs from the lock on the middle sash of the window. The gold-colored string, tasseled at the ends, holds a thin*—no, make that 'slender'—*dowel, and down from that the banner hangs like a quiet flag. Red-bordered, with a field of white, centered with a star. A blue star shows the world that a member of that family is serving in the military. A gold star testifies that the household has lost a family member in the war.*

"In the trackside house where Sigmund Prokosch grew up, the blue star—let me think a moment—*has been eclipsed by one of gold."* Working on the next sentence, he took his eyes off the highway only enough to make sure she was keeping up.

Cloyce was quietly crying.

Bill Reinking set his jaw. At the next turnoff onto a ranch road, he sideslipped the big car to a sharp stop. Resolute as a man with a mission from on high, he faced around to Cloyce. "You drive, while I write."

CONTRARY TO HIS custom, the Senator did not arise from behind the piles of books at his end of the table and plant a kiss on his wife's brow as she settled to her breakfast spot that morning. Suspiciously she peeked over at the reading material strewn around him to see if the Bible lay open somewhere there. His habit before an election was to thumb through until he found a pertinent verse about afflicting one's enemies, then righteously set out to do so by the lethal means known as Montana politics.

The rough-and-tumble of another campaign did not seem to be this morning's order of business, however, as the volumes surrounding his plate of drying egg yolk and bacon grease were the usual maroon tomes of military history and green-and-gilt biographies and memoirs of political figures. She looked on with fond exasperation as he pored over dense pages, taking notes in his leatherbacked notebook. Beaky old cowboy that the national press made him out to be, the husband and mealtime companion known to her all these years feasted on the holdings of the Library of Congress as no other member of the United States Senate ever did. Whatever was immersing him this particular day, she could be sure it was all part of the strong old scripture of seniority and power.

At length the Senator roused himself enough to rumble, "Good morning, Sadie, late-sleeping lady."

"Morning yourself, Luther. You wouldn't be so quick to hop out of bed either if knitting Red Cross socks with Eleanor while photographers watch was waiting for you." Such relationship as this politically apostate household had with the White House— scant—was by way of the Senator's wife. She held her tongue now as the broad-beamed cook marched in bearing her breakfast of soft-boiled eggs and crisp toast. As soon as the servant was out of the room, she arched a look at her still musing spouse. "And what is your own Christian mission this fine tropical day in Babylon-on-the-Potomac?" The honey she was trying to spread on the toast already was runny in the Washington heat.

"Roast an admiral or two," he anticipated, patting the volume *The Fate of Fleets*. "The fools still think they can yell 'Pearl Harbor!' and we'll forgive them any goddamn thing. The hearing may take a while before they're whimpered out. Don't look for me home till supper, my love."

As if reminded of the unremitting passage of time, he yanked out the dollar watch that had regulated his day through four terms of political infighting at the highest levels. There never were enough hours in the day, especially in wartime. Even so, he stayed sitting a little longer to dab more verbal ammunition into the cowhide notebook, his wife covertly watching. He still was riled up from Sunday when Adrianna was home on overnight pass and they had listened to *Meet the Forces*, the special broadcast of the recording of the Guam landing by Bill Reinking's son. That young man was quite something. He did the job there in the hellish water in fine style. It about took your heart out, particularly what happened to that Marine sergeant, but the Senator had also heard something gut-wrenching before that in the description of the quarter-of-a-mile wade from the so-called landing craft to the beach. He'd had his staff check, and that was as close in as those craft could maneuver against the reef. Accordingly he would peel the hide off the Navy at this afternoon's hearing—the gold-braid ninnies had taken half a dozen tries and most of the war so far trying to develop landing craft that could actually put men and trucks and tanks onto a beach instead of depositing them into the surf, and look at the Guam result: dead Marines thick in the water.

He clapped the notebook shut, ready for political battle even though it seemed unending. Targets in the military popped up almost faster than he could keep up with. He still steamed over those Air Transport Command nitwits who had spent taxpayer dollars training women to fly and then wouldn't let them take the planes as far as Canada; hell, you could spit into Canada from Montana.

"THIS IS SOME WAR. Our guys are knocked off right and left," Jake lamented huskily, "and I can't even talk my way past a paper-ass general to get overseas and drop bombs on the worst human beings in history." He sneaked a glance at Ben, rigid behind the wheel again. "You don't happen to be doing it to me, are you?"

"What, keeping you on the Eskimo run? You give me too much credit, Ice." *You're not alone in that kind of wondering, though. You flying nowhere but to Alaska, apparently ever. Prokosch turned down for sea duty before he got blown up anyway, poor luckless kid. Danzer's soft assignment to MacArthur's palace guard was handed to him from somewhere, such as from way on high? While Animal gets flung onto beachhead after beachhead until a Jap bullet finally finds him, and Moxie is over there month after month trying to shoot down planes that are trying to bomb him. It looks just random, the war cuts some guys unhealthier orders than others. But a setup would want to be made to look like that, too, wouldn't it. If Tepee Weepy is picking and choosing who is supposed to stay safe and who goes into combat—*

"I wish Grandpa Grady would get off my case," Jake was saying. "Hell, it was only one floatplane, it wasn't as if we—"

"We? I was only the sandbag, remember?"

"—wrecked the whole goddamn Eighth Air Force. Hey, watch it!"

Ben saw it at the same time. Just ahead, in the middle of the highway, a magpie was eating a skunk. The long-tailed bird took a last impertinent peck, then lifted into the air, stunningly black and white as if having intensified its colors with those of its prey. Steering with one hand, with the other Ben frantically tried to crank the windshield closed.

Not in time. As the wheels straddled the squashed skunk, the smell swept into the jeep like a stink bomb through a transom. "Yow." Jake was blinking the sting out of his eyes, as was Ben. "That was some ripe polecat."

"The Montana state flower, Dex always called one like that," Ben managed after gasping.

"Dexter the Dexterous. That sounds like him, let the peasants scoop those striped pussies out of his way." Still fanning at the linger of the skunk, Jake thought of something. "Hey, our secret-mission guy must be about due to get his turn at fame from you again, ain't he? Then the milk-run pilot Eisman, specializing in pallbearing? My ma's got her scrapbook open, waiting."

"Tepee Weepy has loosened up a little about that, so if you treat me right, I might squeeze you in ahead of him this time," Ben hedged, aware it was drawing him a deeply inquiring look. Hastily he skipped on past the situation of Dex: "That doesn't mean I'm going to fly into the cold blue yonder with you like last time. Besides, you've got enough company in Alaska without me." He was secretly relieved Jake was shelved there in the ATC icebox. *That's what comes of climbing into a Red bed, my friend.* "Fill me in, Yakov—how's the bewitching Katya?"

"Gone, is what she is."

"Say again?"

"She's vanished." Jake looked even more bleak. "I ask the other Russians about her and they just look at me and give the galoot salute." Illustratively he shrugged his more than sizable shoulders up around his ears. "Nothing I can do about it, Ben. Like everything else."

Governments and their coin tricks, with people instead of pocket change. Ben fell silent, into hard thinking about Tepee Weepy, as the jeep went up a rise from the Teton River bridge and there a couple of dozen miles ahead on the horizon stood the Black Eagle smelter stack, its plume dark against the sky. Off the western edge of the smoke cloud a set of specks separated from the smudge and kept on going, a flight of bombers setting out for Alaska.

"Home sweet home," Jake crooned. Somehow it came out pensive.

13

✪ "MORNING, CAPTAIN."

Yawning his way into the office, Ben met those words and looked back down the corridor apprehensively. No such intruding rank in sight. "You're getting absentminded, Jones," he chided as he came on in and situated into his desk chair for another day on the calendar of limbo. "The captain's the guy around the corner, runs the mess hall, remember?"

The next surprise of the morning was the corporal's wanted-poster face breaking into a grin that went halfway around his head. "'The worthy shall be risen,'" he quoted as if he had been waiting for the chance and passed across a ditto set of papers. "Your promotion orders came in today's packet. Congratulations, Captain Reinking," he delivered with nice emphasis. Leaning closer, Jones squinted around as if to make sure they were alone in the dinky office. "The personnel clerk let me in on something. General Grady is going to pin the new bars on you himself at next commander's call."

"Jesus ten-fingered Christ! What's he want to do that for?"

The expostulation turned Jones prim and enlisted. "No one shared the general's thinking with me."

"Any other surprises from our lords and masters?" Ben immediately went to, trying to sort by eye the thin contents of the daily TPWP packet spread in front of Jones. "Like maybe the Prokosch piece miraculously set in type?"

Jones shook his head.

Which caused Ben to twist his as if trying to relieve a pain in the neck. *You think General Grady's thought process is a mystery, Jonesie, what does that make Tepee Weepy's?* Leave it to the military to think up its own form of purgatory and then not define it for you. Ever since he alit back at East Base from the Pacific, life with the Threshold Press War Project was every kind of a puzzle. The unseen powers in Washington had done everything with his Guam recording but play it over loudspeakers in place of the national anthem, and the account he wrote of Angelides' burial on the loneliest of prairies had likewise been punched up into maximum headline treatment. And the subsequent Supreme Team treatment that he had cobbled together about Jake—steadfast service hand in hand with our stalwart Russian allies; the kind of thing his father called a Ph.D. piece, Piled Higher and Deeper—also went out and into newspaper pages across the country like clockwork. Yet the weeks since Sig Prokosch was blown to bits on American soil were turning into months, and that story still was spiked somewhere. Tepee Weepy was even less forthcoming, in Ben's baffled estimation, over Dex and Moxie. It was not a pure silence, the distracted kind, either.

WHAT DO? he had telexed in frustration at the point on the schedule where he was due to write about one or the other of them and had heard nothing, and a message shot back short and cryptic: TIME OUT IN THE GAME. ADJUST PADS ACCORDINGLY.

Well, by now he and Jones indeed were padding desperately, doing articles about scrap drives and Red Cross blood draws. Top off the situation with this unlooked-for promotion (major, lieutenant colonel: he gulped at the thought that there were only two more ranks between him and the ghostly brass who operated TPWP) and Ben could not tell whether it was the altitude or the servitude that was getting to him.

"All right, Corporal," he braced up with a deep breath, "what journalistic exploit do we face today?"

"A twelve-year-old kid here in town invented a military vocabulary crossword puzzle," Jones recited. "Tepee Weepy wants a picture and a thousand words."

"One across, an unexploded shell, three letters," Ben said tiredly. "Dud."

HILL 57 HAD ITS hackles up, bunchgrass stiffly trying to resist the wind, as Ben started down the rutted path at the end of that afternoon. In off-duty civvies, he had on the canvasback coat he had worn that time here with Cass but was wishing for the flight jacket at the rate the wind was breathing down his neck. As ever he had to be mindful of what the gusts might bring; Great Falls collected weather from all around. Over toward the Rockies, the waiting clouds were thickly gray and flat-bottomed as if ready to be sponged against the earth. The benchlands surrounding the leafy city were another picture entirely, with half a dozen squalls around the horizon, isolated showers that almost stopped at fencelines. By his estimate, the cylinder of none-too-warm autumn sunshine here between the storm systems just might last long enough for what he needed to do. *It better. Could be the last chance at this.* How many times now had he watched the zigzag route to the white rocks, here and on the Letter Hill, turn to mush in spring and twisted iron in summer and then utterly sink off out of sight into snow for most of the rest of the year? Come winter, there was no telling where he would be, either. Somewhere on the continent of Europe where Moxie Stamper was among those taking aim at the heart of the

Third Reich, if Tepee Weepy had any sense about Supreme Team assignments any more. *Big if. On top of all the others.*

At the base of the laid-out rocks, he squatted out of the wind temporarily in the shelter of the broad numeral 5. No Cass beside him this time with scotch and opera glasses handy. The sky equally empty of any P-39 piloted by her, spearpoint at the lead of a squadron turned phantom now. He tensed nearly to the point of agony against thinking about it. If there was a more lonely time in his life, he did not want to bring it to mind. Although that at most amounted to only a postponement; his nightly craving did not know what to do with itself, without her. *There's always the USO, right, Cass? The cookie-and-nookie crowd, as you liked to call it.* Every faculty in him from his loins upward jeered at the notion of any substitute for Cass Standish.

Turning his head from the vacant spot next to him in the snug area against the rocks, he sent his gaze to the interlinked letters of the butte across the way. He had devoted so many otherwise soulless nights to the script about the twelfth man that the Letter Hill was branded into his mind, yet he scanned the TSU again now as if, in the right light, it would spell out his hunch. He had tried the supposition out on Jake during that long drive on funeral duty.

"TELL ME IF THIS is too crazy, Ice. But out there on the tin can with Danzer, I got to wondering why he was so rattled when I brought up Purcell's name. Remember that last practice, when our mad genius of a coach for some reason yanked him and stuck Purcell in? What if that wasn't just some lamebrain substitution, what if Purcell was being seriously promoted to the starting team?"

"You figure Bruno was as tired of the Slick Nick act as the rest of us were?" Jake's jackrabbit mind took a moment to go back and forth over that. "Possible, I suppose. The Dancer could catch the ball and keep it, both, though."

"But Purcell could run circles around him, and if Bruno could knock the dropping habit out of Purcell he had something better."

"Yeah," Jake agreed without quibble. "The kid was a ring-tailed wonder except for that one thing."

"Then all that sonofabitch Bruno had to do," Ben savagely rewrote that central page of the past, "was not be so hepped up about his damnable Golden Rule and simply play it straight with Purcell: 'Hang on to the ball, Merle boy, and you're the varsity end for the season. You'd like to be our eleventh man, wouldn't you, kid? It's yours for the taking.' It shifts the whole thing, Ice. No twelfth man. No Supreme Team crap, then or now."

"Possible," Jake had allowed again. "I can't see Danzer running his heart out on that hill."

THAT HILL OFFERED no more answer today than ever as Ben drew his eyes over it. So be it, one more time. He stood up, the wind keenly waiting for him, and started down to the shoulder of the coulee between that mute slope and Hill 57's tar-paper collection of shacks.

Picking his way through the bunchgrass and prickly pear cactus, he approached the solitary shanty at the coulee edge with no real hope. Other than its usual jittery honor guard of gophers, half a dozen at a time constantly popping from their holes and then receding as he neared, the ramshackle place appeared as short on hospitality as it was on all else; dilapidation never welcomes company. No smoke from the chimney again, although a fresh cord of charity wood was stacked against the tar-paper siding. Every Hill 57 shack he could see had one, the firewood considerately chopped into sticks not much bigger than kindling so heat could be eked out of rusty stoves as long as possible. Even so the woodpiles would not last through the winter and the Indian families would have to scrounge or freeze. He marveled again at the pride of Vic Rennie, trudging down cold to the bone from this prairie sidehill slum for four years, never asking anything from the sumptuous university when there were any number of Treasure State football boosters who would have given him a warm place and other favors on the sly.

Ben walked up to the weather-beaten door and knocked strongly, the sharp sound like a punctuation of echo from another time and place.

"Catch her sober, after she gets over the shakes. That's the trick with a wino. Wait until allotment money's gone."

"End of the month, you mean?"

"Middle. She's a thirsty one."

Three months in a row he had made the try, and Toussaint's formulation notwithstanding, not even come close to catching the aunt whom Vic had lived with here. Rapping on the door was bringing no result this time either.

Well, hell, does she live here at all or doesn't she? He tromped around the corner of the house to see whether any firewood had been used from the stacked cord.

And practically sailed face-first into the mad-haired figure moseying from the other direction.

They each reared back and stared.

The woman looked supremely surprised, but then, so did he. Scrawny and askew, she swayed there all but lost in a purple sweater barely held together by its fatigued knitting and a dress that hung to her shoetops. The mop of steel-gray hair looked no less of a mess on second inspection. Fragile as she appeared to be, Ben felt wild relief he hadn't collided with her; in the raveled sweater her arms seemed no larger around than the thin-split sticks in the woodpile. The scrutiny she was giving him during this was more than substantial, however. She had eyes black as the hardest coal; anthracite is known to burn on and on, those eyes stated.

"Spooked me," she recovered a voice first. "Been visiting Mother Jones." She jerked an elbow to indicate the outhouse behind her. The coaly stare stayed right on him. "You aren't from here."

"No. From the base."

"Hnn: flyboy. What's a flyboy doing here? Looking for coochy?" She made the obscene circle with thumb and first digit and ran a rigid finger in and out. "Tired of white meat?" She chortled. "Long time too late for that, around here."

"I'm not here tomcatting," he tried to say it as though that were a reasonable possibility. The years of drinking had blurred age on her; she could have been fifty or seventy. "It's about Vic. We were friends, played football together across the way. You maybe saw us at it." He watched the woman closely as he said that, but the set face and burning gaze did not change. "I'm looking for Vic's aunt," he went back to ritual. "There's a thing I need to find out from her. It would have meant something to Vic."

She took her time about deciding. Finally she provided grudgingly: "Maybe that's me."

"Mrs. Rennie, what I came to—"

"Hwah, you crazy? If I had that name I'd cut my throat and let it out of me."

Too late, he remembered the family battle lines of the reservation. "Excuse me all to pieces, Mrs. Rides Proud. I just thought, because Vic's last name—"

"Not his fault he was named that," she conceded. Absently she primped the nearest vicinity of flying hair. "You can call me Agnes. Everybody and his dog does." With that settled, she eyed him in bright negotiating fashion. "You came for something. Got anything on you to wet the whistle first?"

"It just so happens." He produced the bottle of cheap wine from his coat's deep side pocket and held it out to her for inspection.

Belatedly he remembered "She don't much know how to read," but she was nodding appreciatively at the spread-wing symbol on the label. "Thunderbird. Now you're talking." She quick-stepped past him and wrenched the door open. "Come in out of the weather."

The prairie came inside with them, bare dirt of the floor except for a splotch of torn old flowered linoleum under the kitchen table. Boxes of belongings far outnumbered the derelict furniture. A drafty-looking back area that elled off from the one big room must have been where Vic slept and studied, Ben decided. As he glanced around from tattered bedding to cardboard heaps, the woman was fussing at the cookstove. "I'll make a little fire. Usually don't until it gets cold as a witch's tit." Vaguely she gestured toward the table and rickety chairs. "Make yourself to home."

Wasting no time, she fired up the stove with a shot of kerosene, from the smell of it, and joined him. A pair of jelly glasses clinked as she shoved them toward the Thunderbird bottle he had put in the center of the table. "Do the honors."

He poured her a full glass of the sweet red wine and without regret set the bottle aside. "None for me, thanks."

She would not hear of that. "You better have something so I don't drink all alone. Kool-Aid, how about?"

"Sounds good," he fibbed for etiquette's sake.

Grunting, she got up and navigated into the kitchen clutter to try to find the drink mix for him. To keep any kind of conversation going, he called over: "They told me you were at your daughter's."

"She kicked me out. Thinks she is somebody—like her grunny don't stink."

One binge too many, Ben thought. "There are people like that." Still trying to sound conversational, he asked: "Agnes, were you mostly here when Vic was in college?"

Now the anthracite eyes showed a different temperature entirely. "I never went nowhere when Vic was getting his learning."

She followed that statement back to the table and slid a packet of Kool-Aid to Ben. "Here you go." The water bucket and dipper were within reach from the table—a lot of things were— and he mixed the stuff for himself. She waited standing until he was done, then declared: "Bottoms up." Blithe as a bird, she alit into a chair and in the same motion leaned way forward and sipped from her glass where it stood on the table, touching it with only her lips. Not until then did he realize how bad she had the shakes.

Readying with a dry swallow, he kept his end of the bargain with a swig of the Kool-Aid. The flavor was grape, as purple as her sweater, and about as tasty as the wool dye would have been. He sleeved off the bruise-colored stain he suspected was left on his lips. Surprisingly, his drinking companion was sitting back watching him sharp-eyed instead of trying another guzzle. "You're not drinking up," Ben remarked.

She blinked at the extent of his ignorance. "Even Jesus stretched the wine."

This is getting me nowhere. He plunged in. "You remember when that fellow Vic and I played football with died on the hill, across the coulee?" He was not even sure what he was asking with this. "Just before the war?"

"That time." She shook her head, gray hair flopping. "They run that boy too much. I never saw that"—with both hands she managed to lift her glass and take a trembling drink—"before."

Ben felt his heartbeat quicken. "You saw him run up to the letters—the white rocks?"

"Used to watch all of you when I'd be outside. Wasn't anything before like that boy, though. They run him and run him. Made him do it."

"Made him? How?"

"The football boss kept making him run. He'd yell and wave his arm. You know, like when you're herding sheep and send a dog way around them?" She demonstrated the sweeping overhand gesture.

"Up and back one time, I know," Ben prompted. "But then on his own did the boy—"

"Hwah, one time? Where do you get that?" This shake of the head dismissed Ben's arithmetic as silly. "Crazy number of times. Up and back to that first rock thing." Agnes approximated a T in the air over the table. "Then up and back to—what's that next one?" She waved the notion of an s away, saying: "Then he runs up again, pretty pooped now, I bet, and touches the third one of those. That football boss, maybe he couldn't count so good?"

"He could, all right." Bruno. Coach Almighty making his point that last practice day. *I have to deal with a rube three-letter man.* *The bastard meant the ones on the hill. He was going to drill it into Purcell about no fumbles, once and for all.* Something else surfaced in Ben. "Agnes, you started off saying 'They.'"

"The two of them, sure. Football boss and, I don't know, little boss?"

"What were they wearing?"

"Raft hats."

Stumped, he labored to come up with the kind of hats people on rafts wore.

"George Raft," Agnes broke in, impatient again with his capacity for not understanding. "Vic took me to a movie when he had a jingle in his pocket, you know."

Snap-brim hats. The cinematic emblem of tough guys. Bruno and his copycat pet sportswriter. *Loudon was in on it, bastard number two*. Ben's mind was working furiously. "So you saw them make him run the hill three times. Then what?"

"After that?" Both hands around the glass again, Agnes sipped with shaky delicacy. "It was getting good and dark. I came in the house. The bosses maybe were getting tired of watching, they kind of were wandering off, but the football boss gave another one of those waves. The boy still was on the hill. I just about couldn't believe it. Think to myself, how many times they gonna run that boy?"

She jerked her head toward the Letter Hill. "I don't savvy white men's games."

Ben sat there unmoving, everything she had described passing in order behind his eyes like camera shot after camera shot, the full scene playing out into dusk. Merle Purcell struggling to the dimming rocks, legs and the organ in his chest pumping in determination that could not be told from desperation. Running one lap too many on the steep zigzag path, either from the command of a coach who then turned blindly away or from his own excess will to measure up. In either case, pushed to the brink of what a body could stand, before the lifeless collapse at the stem of the T.

"You told Vic?" It was as much an assertion as a question.

"Told him enough, you bet," Agnes vouched, draining her glass as if in a toast to the Hill 57 way of doing things. "Watch your fanny where those football people are involved, I said to him. End up like that white boy if he don't be careful."

Vic's silences. The scales of friendship are roomy, but nothing human is infinite. Ben sorted through the realization that the one person he thought he knew as well as himself had held back a thing this size. He could see the reason, seated as it was across the table from him. *In wino veritas?* Not in any court of law a half-bright defense attorney could find his way into. The word of Agnes Rides Proud did not stand a drunkard's prayer against whatever sworn version Bruno and Loudon would come up with.

Rolling the empty glass between her palms, Agnes looked over at the wine bottle and its neighbor, the Kool-Aid packet, in hostessly fashion. "There's more."

"Not for me," Ben murmured.

THE RAIN WAS moving in by the time he started back up the shack-strewn hill. As he climbed, his mind kept spinning with the facts of Purcell's pointless dying. *"They run him and run him. Made him do it."* It wasn't even war, although it was mortal contest. Then it became cult of the fallen hero. *"Merrrle! Merrrle!"* The stadium's roars, the whole Twelfth Man shenanigan. From that, the eleven teammates who were borne by it to two kinds of uniformed fame. Pelted by the chilly autumn rain and challenged by the slick trail under him, Ben fought his way up the slope, mindful in every nerve and muscle of Purcell's struggle on that other sidehill. *The Ghost Runner. Truer than the bastards knew.* He had his ending for the script about all that, now. If he lasted long enough to see it onto the movie screen, the fundamental bastard Bruno would know he had been found guilty in a venue beyond all the courtrooms there are, his accomplice bastard Loudon would know, a great many followers of the fortunes of Treasure State University's once-in-a-lifetime team would know. For whatever that was worth.

HALF-BUSHED AND WET through and through but oddly fulfilled, he reached his hotel room with daylight nearly gone, the rain gathering the gray of dusk to its own. He climbed into dry clothes and poured a scotch, just one, as his reward before settling to the typewriter. The night was his to write. Custom dies hard, and sometimes never at all; before going to the script, he instinctively checked his watch and with it the clock of war, the zone-by-zone whereabouts of the others, those who were left. Earlier by two hours in Fairbanks, whatever the weather waiting for B-17 crews between here and there; he hoped Jake was flying above the glop. Danzer smug across the date line in tomorrow. Moxie on Berlin time, not by German invitation. Dex operating according to his hourglass of conscience. All those were old habit in Ben, and it was the new that sought him out at all unexpected times of the day anymore. Cass Standish was on that clockface now.

"LISTEN UP, OFFICERS." She knelt to one knee on the wing of the aircraft, the opposite of the by-the-book briefing she was supposed to be giving, with schematic drawings and pointer in hand, in the ready room under the palm trees. She wanted the squadron's collective eyes, its combined capacities, zeroed in on the actual planes. "Remember we're pilots, not test pilots. Give these crates the same kind of going-over we always did with the Cobras, I don't give a rat's patoot that they're new and improved. 'New and improved' just means nobody's died in one yet." She paused, looking down at the faces that had pulled through all kinds of flying conditions so far. "Everybody got that?"

The P-63 fighter planes, poised as birds of prey, sat in a row of a dozen on the taxiway. To Cass and her pilots, the brand-new aircraft looked like a pepped-up cousin of what they had been flying. Four blades on the propeller instead of three, more bite on the air. A sharper tail, aid to maneuverability. Gone were the despised fuel tanks underneath that had made the P-39 a barbecue waiting to happen in a belly landing. Sensible wing tanks, added bomb racks, a nose gun almost twice the caliber of the old one: all of it added up, at least on paper, to a Lend-Lease attack aircraft that would give the Russians that much better chance of blowing up Germans and their implements of war.

Cass stayed kneeling a further minute, watching her pilots take in the P-63s that would be central to their existence from this day on. She could never get enough of this, the women in their canvas flying suits with manes brown, blonde, and black flowing over their purposeful shoulders as they eyed the new aircraft, keen as cats looking at available bacon. What needed doing—what was up to her to do—was to train these veteran fliers to take it slow with these hot planes. *Isn't that a joker in the deck—me ending up like those bald coot instructors at Sweetwater.* Holding in a rueful grin, she popped to her feet and gave a dismissing clap of her hands. "Okay, all concerned, find your tail number and go to work. Let's get with it."

The squadron members had drawn slips of paper out of a crush hat, letting chance decide who got stuck with a cantankerous craft and who ended up at the controls of a well-behaved one; it was a WASP article of faith that airplanes had personalities you could not change, short of the scrap heap. Cass walked around hers again for familiarity's sake, its unmissable 226323 stenciled large and white on the tail. *Damn the deuces and treys, following me around. Don't be getting superstitious now, though. No time for that.* She prowled the flight line, watching the eleven fliers comb the fighter planes. All of her pilots carried a lucky coin to unscrew the inspection plates. The hands-on testing started with that, reaching in and plucking each control cable to make sure it was hooked up to what it ought to be hooked up to. Up onto each wing next, take off the gas cap and stick a finger in to make sure the tank was full. Then into the cockpit, skepticism exercised on every gauge.

Spotting an opportunity, she eased her way over to where Beryl, with her swiftness of experience, already had the hood up on her plane. Cass clambered up next to where the tall matronly figure was studying the engine in back of the cockpit.

"The factory geniuses didn't get this off the back of our necks, did they," Cass joined the appraisal. Then, low enough so only Beryl could hear: "Sorry it's not your four-barreled bomber, Bear. I tried again on your transfer, but it's still hung up."

Beryl turned and gave her that veteran smile that said they both knew what the military was like. "I suppose they'll wait until they transfer Gene out of range of the bomber factory."

"Probably your paperwork is just sitting on the desk of some shit-heel punk officer in Washington," Cass gave her honest assessment. "Hang in there, I'll keep after the personnel dimwits to jar it loose for you."

She climbed down feeling half guilty, dreading the day she would lose Beryl as wingman. Della Maclaine's performance thus far today did not help that mood. Right now the blonde head was languidly scanning the fuselage of her P-63 as if ready to try it on for size. *Look down first, stupe.* Coolant and fluid leaks would evaporate fast in the dry desert air; checking for puddles should be as automatic as zipping up the flying suit. With no small effort Cass resisted the impulse to charge across the runway and deliver Della a chewing-out she would not soon forget. *Ration it out or Goldilocks will turn into even more of a tail-ender than she already is.* The lowball instrument rating she was giving Lieutenant Maclaine, which would seat her in a simulation trainer for a good many hours across the next week, would get her attention soon enough.

When Cass was at last satisfied with the walk-around inspections, she gathered the squadron under the wing of the first P-63 again. "Observations, anyone?"

"Just guessing," Mary Catherine spoke up, "but these things might have more prop slop than we're used to."

"Righto," Cass backed that up. "Stay to hell out of one another's prop wash until we get used to handling these buggies." *That especially means you, Maclaine.* Without making a show of it, she grazed a look down over Della, getting back a flip of blonde hair that might have meant anything. When everyone had had their say about the new planes, Cass slowly addressed the gathering:

"We all more than earned our wings on one of the most cockeyed planes in creation, the P-39, and we're about to again on the P-63, whatever piece of work it turns out to be. It's going to be worth it, let me tell you, it would be even if these things were box kites. Friends and officers," her voice dropped, "flying is the second greatest thrill a woman can know."

She paused, taking in the expressions on her audience, patently quizzical on some, borderline lewd on others.

"The first, you goofs, is *landing*!"

Over the groans and hoots, she threw a little salute of applause acknowledgment and gave the order, "Five times, everybody, touch and go. Linda's bunch first, then Ella's, mine last so I can be right here watching, pilots. Don't get caught up in the scenery, all it means to us is thermals. Let's go." As her aviators headed to their aircraft, she looked around once more at the strange terrain, the ash-colored mountains, the palm tree canyons. Only the military would put pilot training in the California desert for planes the Russians would have to fly across Siberia. Grimacing a bit, she tucked that away for tonight when she wrote either to Dan, wherever he was in the festering Pacific, or Ben, marooned lovelorn back at East Base. She made it a point of honor not to write the same thing to each of them.

"How GOES IT this fine filthy day of Great Falls sleet, Jones?"

"Uhm, morning, sir. We've got—"

"For crying out loud," Ben impatiently brushed wet tracks of the weather off his flight jacket, "how many times do I have to tell you not to call me—" The words swerved off in the direction Jones's eyes were trying to indicate, to the figure perched on the far corner of Ben's own desk.

"—sir," he finished numbly, staring in recognition of the all-too-evidently waiting personification of the Threshold Press War Project.

"Greetings, Captain." A touch of gray had come to the Gable mustache, and the crinkles at the corners of the commanding eyes appeared substantially deeper. Otherwise, the colonel from Tepee Weepy perching there on the desk edge, as tailored as a rajah abroad, appeared to be taking up in mid-session from two years earlier.

"Jones"—Ben held out a hand in that direction—"may I see this week's manifest of VIP arrivals again?" The corporal plucked up the list and passed it to him as if it was about to blow up.

"Spare your eyes," the colonel advised. "Officially I'm not here."

"Here or not, sir," Ben struggled with everything wanting to uncoil within him, "you're mightily in our thoughts."

"I believe I detect a tone of concern over your recent assignments in that," the colonel responded casually. In that same tone of voice: "Take a break, Corporal. Make it a nice long one."

Jones got out of there fast.

A puckish gaze from the visitor followed him. "Your clerk looks as if he stepped straight out of the homicide lineup, have you noticed?"

"Jones is washed in the blood of the lamb, sir."

"Admirable, I'm sure." The colonel went right to business. "One of your Supreme Team articles—very nicely done, let me say—has been conspicuous by its absence in the newsprint of the land, hasn't it, Captain. Your piece about Seaman Prokosch. We had to spike that piece, and I must tell you it will remain spiked."

"I didn't figure you were saving it for the gold-leaf edition."

"You have every right to be testy about it," the colonel granted. *Testy, my left nut. How about mad as hell? How about terminally pissed off, Mustache Pete?* "However," the practiced voice from

Tepee Weepy rippled on, "the balloon bombs are a classified secret and no mention can be—"

"Colonel?" If there was such a thing as whiplash inside the head, Ben suffered it now going from rancor to disbelief. "What's 'secret,'" he blurted, "about those? The Forest Service has people in lookout towers all over the mountains watching for the damn things, the air bases out on the Coast are trying to shoot them down, anyone out here with ears on his head has heard about Jap balloons. We aren't giving away a thing that a dozen states don't already know by saying a guy of ours met up with one."

"This was not a TPWP decision," the colonel's voice rose a notch for the first time. "It comes from highest levels—there is a complete news blackout, in all American newspapers and radio broadcasts, about the balloon bombs. Censorship has been applied for two reasons, we were told in no uncertain terms—to prevent panic by the public and to keep Japan in the dark about the balloons' effects." He favored Ben with an informative glance. "For what it's worth, Captain, the Japs' 'secret' weapon is not starting forest fires anything like intended—the incendiary devices appear to be faulty somehow."

"But not the explosive part," Ben cited darkly. "It worked just fine in blowing Sig Prokosch to bits. And why won't it do it every time some poor fool who doesn't know any better comes across a strange gadget on the beach or out in the woods? Somebody who hasn't read about it because we kept it from them?"

"That calculation, as I said, is not ours to make," the colonel uttered with the patience of bureaucratic practice. "Your understandably heartfelt article on Seaman Prokosch needs a bit of fixing, is all. Simply approach it from the angle that he was killed in a munitions mishap, let it go at that, and then—"

Ben broke in:

"Like the old newspaper joke of describing a hanged man as having been found dead under a tree, do you mean, sir?"

It drew him a look of mixed regard and reassessment. One more time, the colonel cautioned himself that these westerners were prickly.

THE CONGRESSIONAL hearing a few days before had been sailing along smoothly, the colonel concealed in plain sight amid the row of brass and braid and blue serge in back of the director of the Office of War Information as he testified, when a voice twanged out from down the line of senators.

"Mister Chairman, might I put in about two bits' worth of questions, just to earn my keep?"

"I yield to my friend, the gentleman from Montana."

"Thank you kindly." The Senator pulled at his weathered beak of a nose for a long moment as if tugging loose whatever was stored in his head, then addressed the OWI chief. "There's one setup here in the scheme of things you're in charge of that I'm a little curious about. It for some reason gets funded as a 'project'—year after year, I might add—instead of a line item. I think you know the one I mean."

The OWI man smoothed back his hair and made his bureaucratic escape. "The colonel, here with me, will need to address that."

"Trot the fellow on up to the witness chair," drawled the Senator.

Hastily tucking away the dispatches he had been skimming, the colonel took the seat indicated. He was barely there before the Senator was asking, "How about enlightening us on just what your agency does?"

"Glad to, Senator. At TPWP we—"

"Where I come from," the Senator interrupted, "big initials like that are only used on the hides of cows. Might we have the full name of your outfit for the record?"

"Naturally." The colonel cleared his throat. "The Threshold

Press War Project was conceived to disseminate news stories about our armed forces that otherwise would not reach the public. To fill a void in the home front's awareness, you could say."

"Why is the government in the business of dishing out news, through you?"

"If I may explain, Senator. The larger newspapers have their own war correspondents or the financial wherewithal to subscribe to the wire services. Our mission is to provide items of interest to the less prosperous news enterprises, primarily the smaller dailies and weeklies."

"That's all the newspapers in my neck of the woods," the Senator noted. "Would you say people in states such as mine get their picture of the war pretty much from you?"

"A decent proportion of it, Senator, if we're doing our job right," the colonel said carefully. "We want the folks at home to know the great service to this country their sons and daughters are providing—it's all part of the war effort."

The Senator leaned forward with a long-jawed smile, one old wolf to another. "Furnish them some heroes to help keep their morale up, would you say?"

"The genuine exploits of our fighting men and women deserve to be told, in our view," the colonel skirted that as wide as he could. "I would submit, Senator, that your constituents are as eager as any others for such news."

"In Montana we're a little leery of bragging people up too much ever since General Custer," the Senator stated, drawing laughter in the hearing room. He studied the colonel as if marking his place in a chapter, then sat back saying: "No further questions for now, Mister Chairman."

"LET'S HAVE A chin-chin about what's wanted of you, Captain Reinking," the colonel came out with now, still occupying a corner of the desktop in all apparent ease. He paused to tap one of the little Cuban stinkers out of a cigarillo pack and fire it up with a flick of his lighter. Considerately he blew the smoke away from Ben and at the same time fixed total attention on him. "You seem a bit bothered by the recent course of events in your war coverage. I sympathize, over Angelides and Prokosch—'the dear love of comrades,' as I believe a poet put it. But the war did not end with them. There are still your other teammates—"

"That's what's on my mind, sir," Ben could not stop himself. "The way it's turned out, some of the guys barely stood a chance of making it through while others—" He halted, not sure where the next words would take him.

"Share it out bold, Captain. It's just the two of us here."

Ben mustered it for all he was worth.

"How much has Tepee—TPWP had to do with where the ten besides me have ended up in the war?"

The colonel managed to look surprised. "Why think the fate of your teammates is any of our doing? I grant you, some have had the worst possible luck. Need I point out that war does not necessarily deal the cards fair?"

"Does that mean the deck has to be stacked? Sir?"

"The 'deck,' to call it that, is too much for any of us to get our fingers around," the colonel maintained.

"Maybe so," Ben said, unsatisfied. "But sir, whatever accounts for it, this whole thing with the Supreme Team has turned out way to hell and gone different from what you projected, hasn't it. I mean, why keep on with the series? Shouldn't we just scrap it now? Six men gone—I've tried, but for the life of me I can't see what's to be gained by serving up my buddies in obituary after obituary." He stared squarely at the colonel. "Dead heroes serve a purpose, do they?"

"We are not dealing"—the colonel stopped—"not trafficking in that sort of thing, Captain, what kind of cynics do you think we are?" Reaching down to a wastebasket, he mashed out the stub of his cigarillo, and treated himself to another. "Thanks to your talents," he resumed levelly, "the story of the eleven of you, whatever misfortunes have been along the way, is one of the epics of this war. So we are not, repeat not, going to scrap the series." The tone softened. "Modify it a bit, perhaps." He waved away a slight cirrus of smoke. "Let's proceed to the reason I'm here. I wanted to brief you personally on the war outlook as we at TPWP see it, to provide some needed perspective"—*needed by you to the point where you now shut up and listen or else,* his tone implied—"about your assignments from here on."

Ben did listen, with every pore. The colonel's briefing came down to saying he did not have to see himself as a war correspondent into perpetuity; there was optimism at knowledgeable levels in Washington that the war could be over within a year. *From their lips to God's ear, as Jake would say.* The colonel sprinkled in some pep talk about once-in-a-lifetime coverage chances as Germany and Japan, in whichever order, were ground down into surrender. *Depends on the lifetime, doesn't it.* By the time the TPWP view of things had been fully impressed upon him, not a word had been uttered about how he was supposed to handle the due pieces on Dex and Moxie, leaving him as baffled as ever. If that didn't amount to scrapping the Supreme Team, what did? What was "modify" supposed to mean?

"Now as to your next orders, Captain," the colonel had arrived at. "It may not surprise you that you'll be going overseas—"

Well, here it is, and with something strangely like the spin of a compass in himself Ben began trying to set his mind to it, *that ticket to Somewhere in Europe. Moxie, you win the sterling pencil-pusher for a change.*

"—you'll need to tidy up with your clerk, finish up any pieces you're working on, you may be gone a good while—"

Or a bad one, Colonel, given the history of this.

"—and when the time is nearer, we'll let you know your departure date—"

Oh, swell, let's add waiting to the game.

"—for your old stomping grounds, the Pacific."

Ben was floored. *What, again? Capital Y why?* Danzer had been written about not all that long ago, there was nothing sane to be said further about his cushy boat ride through the war. It just did not make a lick of journalistic sense that he could see, returning to— Wait a minute: return. *Oh goddamn, no.*

"Sir, begging your pardon, I don't want to seem out of line or anything, but damn it," everything in him blew, "are you sending me out there again just so Tepee Weepy will have an eyewitness when MacArthur wades ashore at Manila or Zamboanga or Leyte or wherever the hell he's going to do it? When that happens there'll be correspondents and photographers up the gigi, the general will have to wade through the cameras and reporters as much as the surf, and I don't see why I—"

"Calm down, Captain. Watching Douglas MacArthur walk on water is not going to be your primary mission."

"Then what is?" he asked dubiously, still suspicious that somewhere in MacArthur's entourage as the great man returned to the Philippines would be Danzer flourishing a white tablecloth and a feast of pork.

"The story is still developing, I'm not at liberty to tell you." Reaching into the attaché case at his side, the colonel extracted a file of clippings and dropped it dead-center on Ben's work place at the desk. He smiled just enough. "It might not hurt, though, if you were to do some bedtime reading about the Montaneers."

Beyond floored, this time Ben stared at the colonel in shock. The man might as well have said to him, "Learn the rules of dueling, you're going to Dan Standish's outfit." All else being equal, he could have understood that the regiment that had been un-

endingly fighting up and down the jungle hellholes of the Pacific
and now doubtless was destined for the invasion of the Philippines constituted a legitimate story to be written. All else was
not equal, not even close; bedtime reading had already happened
any number of times and it was indubitably the Braille of unclad
lover to unclad lover while a Montaneer was out there in the
jungle stuck with a matching wedding band. Still stunned, Ben
grappled with two instant convictions, that coming face-to-face
with Cass's husband in the Montaneers' next island assault was
by all odds a long shot, and that in the perversity of this war it
absolutely would happen.

He stood there stone-still, watched expectantly by the colonel, haunted in every direction he could look. The quantities of
death he had seen in the world of war. All the times of sitting
to the typewriter to turn teammates' foreshortened lives into
handfuls of words. Bruno's eleven, fingered by fate when the
coach's ordained list of varsity starters was drawn up at that
last practice. Loudon's eleven, damn his gloryhound hide. The
Supreme Team betrayed by the law of averages, with something
that amounted to a moving wall of oblivion hinged to the war
for them; a click at a time, it claimed life after life whatever the
odds said. It surpassed understanding, yet the circumference of
war plainly was different for these nearly dozen men. Until now
Ben had been able to tell himself life went on until proved different, trusting to the unbidden gamble of the flesh that was the
greatest and worst venture of his life, the love of another man's
wife. Now this.

"Colonel," he finally found his voice, "I've had it. I can't go
along with the way you want the war told, anymore. Kick me
out for 'nervous in the service' or some goddamn thing, I don't
care." His lips were so dry he could barely make them function.
He licked them to not much effect. "If it takes a Section Eight,
I'm ready."

"You don't want to do that," the colonel said with utmost civility. "A dishonorable discharge follows a person the rest of his life." He inclined his head as if regretting that fact, while spelling out: "In a lot of fields, a person won't stand a chance of latching on after the war if he's labeled as a bobtail soldier."

The veil on that was thin as could be. Anyone with a byline knew what fields were meant in that implied threat. Hollywood. Any influential newspaper. The by-the-book wire services. All of the messengers who tended to fall under question for their messages any time a hole in their patriotism could be found. None of those was going to want a wordsmith, no matter how good, with a military record that could not be held up to public light. A record of a soldier who quit.

Ben did not really have to say anything. The circumstances ahead, after the war, beyond Tepee Weepy but yet not, spoke it all. But he wanted the choiceless words inflicted on both of them in that room.

"Some decks are more stacked than others, aren't they, sir."

As the colonel departed the office, he gave Ben a passing pat on the shoulder, possibly a salute of sorts.

"So what's your secret?" Jake had just banged the hotel room door shut with his foot, one hand busy trying to undo the clumsy horse blanket the military called an overcoat and the other bearing a rattling sack of beer. "How do you get them to ship you overseas easy as falling off a log, while they confine me to the North American continent?" His big coat went on the bed, the beer onto the dresser, and he faced around to Ben rubbing his hands briskly. "Brr. Getting chilly out there. 'Frost on the pupkins, the poor curs.' What's that from anyway?"

"'Stars Fell on Alamogordo.' Tallulah." Ben put aside the week-old news magazine—news magazines were always a week old—he had been flipping through. "To what do I owe the unexpected pleasure of your company, Ice?"

"I thought it was sticking out all over me. *Au revoir* and all that."

Ben shifted in his chair as if caught. "They're keeping me in the dark about when I leave. I was going to look you up when I find out, honest."

"Yeah, with your seabag over your shoulder and ten minutes before you'd have to catch a gooney bird out of here—I'm onto you. Besides, I'm kissing East Base good-bye a while myself. A month on the Fairbanks-to-Nome run. The Russkies are getting short of pilots, so some of us are detailed to fill in on that last leg. Some detail, huh? You can about see Siberia from there. Anyway, I brought a proper farewell. Got a church key?"

"Bottom drawer."

Jake pawed out the opener, did the honors on the bottles of beer, and handed Ben one before settling onto the groaning springs of the bed. "This place makes me feel better about the barracks. How come they stick you here?"

"Where commanding officers are concerned, I'm a marked man."

Jake snorted. "Aren't we all, one way or another." They drank a couple of pulls of beer, looking at one another with the awkward affection of men who have become oldest friends in not that long a time.

"Ben? Where they sending you this time?"

"I'm not allowed to tell you, or I would suffer the death of a thousand paper cuts from a manila folder."

"Backtrack Mac country, no crap?" It drew a whistle from Jake. "He's going to take back everything Filipino from the Japs or know the reason why, ain't he." The big man drank deep, then pointed his bottle toward Ben. "I don't want you getting the shit shot out of you out there, hear?"

Ben took a sip of his own before finding the voice to parry. "Look who's talking—the guy who wants to deliver bombs to Hitler on his chamber pot."

"Notice I want to do it from several miles away, up above the flak," Jake said as if setting him straight on the rules of the game. "I think that's the way the Nazi pricks ought to get what's coming to them," he mused. "Just *blam,* something comes out of the sky and wipes them out of the human race."

"That'd be convenient," Ben found to say.

Jake leaned forward, adding gravity in all senses of the word. "Serious, Ben. Don't get fancy out in those islands. Things tend to happen around where you are. The time the Japs jumped you and Carlo," he took to reciting. "Then Animal getting it, damn near in your lap." Listening, Ben had to hear over the pounding of blood in the confines of his head. "That walk in the northern woods you took with me." Jake stopped, then said the rest as though it was the most natural of advice. "Bravery is just another way to die, my friend. Keep in the rear echelon for a change— who knows, it might be kind of nice there. The team is getting thin enough on the ground, without you crossed out."

"Ice, I intend to do everything I know how to stay on the living list."

"Good. We'll drink to that." Heaving himself off the bed, Jake fetched another pair of beers. In passing, he noticed the page of script in the typewriter. "You still tinkering with that? I thought you said it was done after you got the goods about Purcell."

"It is. I'm getting going on another one, I seem to be in the habit." Ben gazed at the waiting paper. "Vic and his grandfather, this is. You never met Toussaint. He's one they don't make anymore."

"Busy hands keep a guy out of trouble," Jake proclaimed piously. "Sometimes." They clinked bottles. "That's one more rea-

son you've got to keep yourself in one piece, you know—I've got
a date with that movie of yours." The big man grinned crookedly.
"I want to see you fry Bruno's nuts for him."

THE AUTUMN THAT everyone at East Base hoped would be the
last one of the war kept confusing itself with winter—a snow
squall for the first day of fall, then clouds that looked like they
were lined with lead chronically hanging low over October's advance across the calendar. He was late arriving to the roadhouse,
due mainly to weather delays of incoming flights with Very Important Persons aboard, Jones and his camera having needed
a final tutorial in brazening it out when generals and admirals
scowled at the presence of the lens.

*It's all yours now, Corporal old kid, Tepee Weepy be thy guard-
ian angel.* As for himself, he kept trying to think only of these last
hours with Cass before he climbed on the plane in the morning.
Kept trying and failing. These few weeks since she came back
from training her squadron to the new fighter planes had been
time after time of glimpsed and gone, the P-63s flying north with
the red star on their sides whenever he looked up, the stolen bits
of lovemaking with her here at the eternal roadhouse or in his
dumpy hotel bed too desperate and brief. All he had told her, all
he could stand to tell her, was that he was being shipped out to
the Pacific on assignments he would be filled in on when he got
there. He meant it as a mercy, in not saying anything about being tossed in with the Montaneers in whatever bloody pocket of
the Philippines invasion. Whether or not it was the right thing
for Cass, it cost him plenty of sleep. *You're quite the specimen,
Reinking. What are you going to do if you come face-to-face with
Dan Standish out there, stick out your mitt and say "Hi, I came to
cut the cards with you to see which of us gets Cass"?* He still was
trying to shoo away these thoughts as he dodged in out of the
blustery weather to the permanent blue dusk of the roadhouse.

No sooner was he in the place than the bald bartender leaned across and muttered, "You're in for a ripsnorting time. She's belting drinks down about as fast as I can pour them."

Ben approached the table at the back as if testing thin ice. Cass watched him mutely. She looked half-swacked. And the other affected half attributable to something other than alcohol.

"Cass, what in hell—"

"I lost one, Ben. First time."

He sank into a chair and reached across to cover her hand in his, which had the added effect of keeping her from hoisting another glass of scotch. That blonde number in her squadron, the one who always looked ready to climb a guy's leg—"Cass, don't be blaming yourself, if that's what you're doing. You said last time she's an ingrown tailender and the new planes weren't helping any. It probably was just a matter of time before—"

The wobbly sway of her head stopped him.

"Not her." Cass slipped her hand out from under his and clamped onto the glass, taking a gulp before he could react.

"Beryl," she said amid the swallow, choking on the name. "My oldest, best pilot. The landing gear folded on her and Beryl bellied halfway across Edmonton." Cass's head went back and forth again, her voice thickening. "She didn't stand a chance with that damn engine down her neck. Damn it all to hell, Bear logged hundreds of hours in that flying piece of crap, the P-39, and we get the hot new planes and right away I lose her." She clutched at the table to stop swaying. "Isn't that a pisser? We get the 'new and improved' goddamn planes and right away—"

"Cass, look at me." She made the effort, her gaze only approximate by now. "Listen up, you've got to. When are you on duty?"

She concentrated. "Tonight?"

"No damn way in this world are you flying tonight, I'll call the ops section and tell them you've caught the twenty-four-hour crud. I know it raises hell with the squadron, but you can't—"

"Who said anything about flying?" she said belligerently, all the drinks talking. "USO. Liaison officer to the cookie pushers, that's me. Can't lead a squadron worth a pork-and-beans' fart, so might as well herd bashful—"

"Just sit here until I come back, okay? Just sit, don't try to get up." There still was a modicum of scotch in her glass, and he downed it so she wouldn't. Swiftly he was onto his feet and headed to the front of the bar.

"Lit up like a church, whatever's got into her," the roadhouse bartender diagnosed as if a second opinion was needed.

Busy digging for silver, Ben specified: "That cabin with the whorehouse tub."

"No can do," the man behind the bar replied with a minimum shrug. "Don't get enough call for that one this time of year, so I shut down the water heater. Freeze your tails off if you was to get to piddling around in—"

"We're trying out to be Eskimos." Ben unloaded round dollars onto the bar until the bartender pushed them back, then returned to the matter of Cass.

She alternately tended toward limp and squirmy as he maneuvered her to the cabin. The massive claw-footed tub stood suggestively not that far from the bed, and he was able to prop her there on the mattress and keep an eye on her while he resorted to the cold water tap. He shed his clothes first, then advanced to where she sat wavering on the bed. "Ben, sugar," she greeted him glassily, "I don't feel so hot. I know you're always ready for a go, and so'm I, but—"

"Radio silence, Captain Standish," he blared, baffling her into shutting up while he went to work on her buttons. He had undressed her in a hurry enough times before, but this one was of a different sort of urgency. Off fell her blouse, the revelatory brassiere, her zippered skirt, the tedious shoes and stockings, the panties as ever the last prize of all.

What is love but random magic? It applies itself in unexplainable ways. Tenderly he swooped Cass up as if carrying her across a threshold, kissed her in the sweet spot between the breasts, crossed the space to where the water was running, and dumped her, squawking, in the frigid tub.

Gritting, Ben climbed in after her. It was all he could do to hang on to her, rubbing where he could to get the blood running, while she strenuously thrashed and gasped. Sobering by visible degrees from the shock of the cold water, she let herself subside quivering into his arms. "M-m-maniac," she chattered, gratefully or not, he couldn't tell.

When she looked clear-eyed enough, he helped her from the tub and wrapped a towel around her and then himself around the towel. As warmth began to return with the clasp of body to body, the towel was pitched away and they gave themselves over to the ancient powers of bare skin.

14

★ HIS DAY OF DEPARTURE, it was raining hard enough to concuss the gophers of Hill 57. Water was standing all over East Base, as though the Pacific had decided to come to him, and eddies of wind caught at his travel pack in his sprint from the ready room to the C-47 idling on the taxiway. Struggling aboard with him came a couple dozen other dampened officers and airmen, cramming the transport plane to Seattle. Beyond that, he was jumpily aware, awaited the interminable flight to Hawaii, and from there the hopscotch journey to speck after speck of captured island airfields that would ultimately land him to whatever awaited out there. As ever, the tight rounded confines of the plane cabin compressed such thoughts. The flying culverts that passed for Air Transport Command travel accommodations were his living quarters for these next days, and so far he was not lucking out at all, his bucket seat next to that of a talkative major.

"How do, Captain. Can't help but notice your flight jacket, it's a beauty. Pilot, are you?"

"The jacket," Ben conveyed, "has a higher cockpit rating than I do."

The major chortled, the kind that descends from the adenoids.

"You still have a sense of humor, you must be passing through this glorified cow pasture on TDY."

"No, I've been attached here. More or less forever."

"Well, you can have Least Base, as far as I'm concerned. I was sent here for a week of detached duty—dot and dash stuff, I'm in the code area—and I'll tell you, it seemed like Noah's forty days and forty nights. I'll be perfectly glad to get back to San Diego." Companionably he looked Ben and his travel pack over again. "And where are you being sent? Somewhere sunny and warm, I hope?"

It was to be Leyte. The news would be on the radio about now, a central island of the Philippines invaded in MacArthur's vaunted return. The coded travel order from Tepee Weepy had come in first thing that morning, and Ben had had to scramble to make this flight. He answered the inquisitive major minimally:

"I'm going to the tropics, probably not for my health."

The C-47's engines revved loud enough to drown out conversation, to Ben's temporary relief. The aircraft shuddered into motion and out onto the runway, lumbering along at the ungainly hopeful uptilt that had given it the nickname of gooney bird. He braced back a bit out of long practice, his mind already racing the war clock ahead to wherever the Montaneers were digging in on some Leyte beach, while the plane strained to build up enough speed for takeoff. Suddenly the major pressed a cheek against the fuselage window. "Oh my God, hang on."

Ben craned to see past him. Down toward the end of the runway, above the meat wagon, dropping through the murk was the comet tail of a red flare which meant *abort the mission.*

The transport plane lurched violently as the brakes were slammed on. Ben grabbed the seatframe and doubled over in crash position, all he could do to prepare if the aircraft was going to whirl into a ground loop on the rain-slick runway, buckle its landing gear, and set itself on fire from the friction of the concrete. Beyond that was the terrible acceptance that for him the war, and heartbeat and breath, could end right here, smeared against a dank strip of East Base.

The wheelskid seemed to go on and on, the plane whipping back and forth enough to scare the power of speech out of everyone in the cabin. When finally the aircraft did one last slow half-glissade and jerked to a halt, someone said in a hushed voice: "I hope we fight the next war entirely on foot."

The copilot surged out of the cockpit, boiling over. "Captain Reinking?" he demanded, his tone questioning why anyone of that rank was cause of this much concern. "The tower radioed. You're to get off this plane. Now." Ben could feel the indignant look from his neighbor the major.

"Here? In this?" Ben gestured in dumbfoundment, not knowing what motion was needed to indicate an obvious deluge. "Pal, it's coming down out there like a cow pissing on a flat rock."

"'Now' means now, the pilot says to tell you. Orders are—"

"I know what the chickenshit damn things are," Ben ground out, uncertainly unmooring from the bucket seat. "How are we supposed to do this in the middle of the runway?"

The copilot sandwiched past him. "I'll kick open the hatch and you'll have to swing down—we're supposed to make this snappy."

After as firm a hold as he could get on the bottom of the hatchway, Ben with a grunt dropped the slippery few feet to the runway, and his travel pack was swung down to him, followed by his typewriter case. With the prop wash of the C-47's idling engines spewing entire puddles his direction, he had the wild illusion it was raining up out of the ground at him. Hunched over, he duckwalked out from under the wing, around past the tail, and stood in the mud edging the runway as the C-47 taxied away to a fresh tangent of takeoff.

Welcome back from nowhere, pilgrim. What's next, leaving me out here to drown through my hide?

A jeep was coming toward him at more speed than it should have been on the wet runway, its wipers sloshing madly. Between swipes when it pulled up, he could make out the stumpy figure of Jones at the wheel. An isinglass window flapped open and the corporal delivered the non-news:

"They scrapped your trip, Captain. Better climb in."

So soaked he did not really want the company of his own clothes and skin, Ben squished into the passenger seat. "Tepee Weepy's orders—they sent the message in the clear, just put it on the wire," Jones was saying as if having been present at a miracle. "Boy oh boy, Captain, it's hard to figure these things out, isn't it?" He squinted back and forth from the windshield to Ben. "I went around to the clerk in the situation room and bugged him until he'd tell me what was up. You'd think we'd have heard about something like this, but Washington wanted the lid kept on the news, and so I guess we couldn't have had any idea of—"

"Jones, cool down and don't skid this thing into a parked plane. Now, in English if you can, what *is* up?"

"The Philippines. All heck is breaking loose out there."

15

✪ THE WAR LICKED its chops over the battle of Leyte Gulf, as it came to be called, with the inevitability from day one that history would speak of such a gang-fight of fleets in the same breath with the Spanish Armada, Trafalgar, Jutland, and Midway. Ben all but moved into the wire room at East Base to follow reports of the military struggle shaping up around the Philippine Islands. It proved to be like reading *War and Peace* standing up.

The battle unfolded across most of a week, dawning halfway across the world day by late October day as censored reports cautiously kept score of enemy vessels sunk versus the toll on the American fleet. The two American fleets, in actuality, for besides the aircraft carriers and battleships in Admiral "Bull" Halsey's task force stationed in that part of the Pacific as the U.S. Navy's trustworthy heavy weaponry, on hand also was Douglas Mac-Arthur's mongrel fleet. Consigned to the touchy Army general's command to protect his amphibious assault forces in the island-hopping invasions, this more plebeian navy consisted of battleships that had aged past being top-of-the-line; half-size "escort" carriers built on merchant ship hulls; and a pack of support ships from pesky destroyers on up. MacArthur's navy was going about its business of bombarding beaches and giving air cover to the

Leyte landing when spotty reports began to arrive that the Japanese fleet en masse seemed to be steaming toward those same Philippine waters.

In the end there would be a seaful of dead sailors from both sides, but first came the interlude between strategy and tactics as the navies formed up in modern warfare's unbelievable proportions. Ben had experienced those at Guam, but even so, the reports he grabbed out of the teletypes as the fleets maneuvered on the margins of the Philippines made him question the accuracy of his eyes. The same was happening on the bridges of the ships involved. Reconnaissance planes from Halsey's carriers bit by bit counted seven Japanese battleships—two of them the mightiest in the world, distinctive floating fortresses with toplofty superstructures like steel pagodas—thirteen cruisers, and nearly twenty destroyers in the oncoming battle array. Cloud cover and the labyrinth of islands and straits masked Tokyo's surprise fleet time and again as it kept coming, frustrating Halsey's intelligence evaluations. The one thing clear was the Japanese intent, to do away with MacArthur's navy and devastate the American assault force on the beaches of Leyte.

From the hour the Japanese fleet crept out of an archipelago maze into Leyte Gulf, the battle became, as these nautical epics have been down through time, a contest of seagoing monsters with dim vision. Halsey with all his battleships and heavy carriers chased off after a decoy of Japan's lesser ships. The Japanese battleship commanders dithered and wavered and failed to close the pincers on either the Leyte beachhead or MacArthur's outgunned fleet. That patched-together collection of assault support ships bore the brunt of the fighting, the mightier Japanese vessels slaughtering any escort carrier they found within range but torpedo attacks by the American destroyers and salvos from the second-rank battleships effectively crippling the Japanese attack. Ultimately the sea battle was won from the sky, with U.S. carrier planes hunting and killing enemy warships like exhausted whales.

Ben kept a reporter's habitual count, day by day, as he inhabited the wire room during this. His own taste of shipboard war clung in him as the reports of sunk ships rattled in on the teletypes. The carrier *Princeton,* gone down; someone he knew back in the distant days of pilot school was a liaison air officer aboard there. One Japanese battleship sunk, another put out of action. The destroyers *Johnston, Roberts,* and *Hoel* perished. Two more Japanese battleships and a cruiser destroyed. The escort carrier *Gambier Bay,* gone down; Ben himself had been on that one less than six months ago, a hop in the journey to Australia. Old visions of the gray mass of ships around him and Animal when they talked and joked at Eniwetok gripped him while he endlessly bummed coffee from the communications section clerks and sifted the constant combat reports. The five bells of a wire machine would go off again, and there were two fewer Japanese cruisers on the ocean surface. More clatter of the teletype keys and another chapter of smoke-veiled military engagement came in.

Throughout, he felt the hot breathing presence of history's proposition for a reporter, any true chronicler. The question is brought by Mnemosyne, goddess of memory, high priestess of knowledge, as she steps from the tall grove on Olympus with each hand cupped to you. In one is the grant of a long uninflected life, peace without pause to be looked back on. In the other lies the chance, issued only once per lifetime, to witness Waterloo from a spot within range of the guns. And in your most honest self, which would you choose? The oncoming shadow of the sea battle, not to mention the less-than-divine hand of Tepee Weepy, had done the choosing for him this time, in the shutdown of air traffic to the Philippines. Which hand of fate he would have chosen for himself, he was not perfectly sure. He prowled among the chatter of the teletypes vitally aware of having been spared one more time and conscientiously restless with not being out there when history pivoted on an obscure archipelago. In his reporter's vigil there was not even anyone to talk this over with, Cass back on track on the Edmonton run, Jake among the igloos, Jones scrambling to handle the office by himself. Alone with his insistent sense of something granted and something held back, he haunted the wire machines and drank coffee and waited for the next turn of the war.

It came on the fifth and last day of the Leyte Gulf battle, as the American victory became undeniable. With its fleet cut to pieces, the Japanese high command unveiled a fresh weapon. This lethal new contrivance would be launched more than three thousand times in the remaining months of the war, leaving carnage of an unprecedented kind when it struck, and even when it missed, it distributed terror into all who were anywhere in its way. It was called *kamikaze*—"divine wind," which in this instance meant fury aimed from heaven, consisting as it did of a sacrificial airplane with a bomb strapped under each wing and a pilot with glazed acceptance of a last mission. Its method was a suicide dive onto whatever American vessel it could find.

SLICK WITH SWEAT from the heat and tension of that Pacific noon, the officer of the watch stood clutching the railing on the wing of the *McCorkle*'s bridge, transfixed by the sight of the escort carrier *St. Lo* blowing up repeatedly in the near distance. His rational side of mind knew that each thunderous explosion was another of the *Lo*'s bomb and torpedo storage compartments going up, but the spectacle of blast after equally fiery blast erupting through the flight deck was beyond reckoning. In equal disbelief, the executive officer next to him cursed methodically while trying to figure out how the Japs had unobtrusively struck a ship in the middle of a victorious fleet; no sonar trace of a submarine had been reported. The gunnery officer now yelled out from the bridge something about a plane, although the destroyer lookouts had not spotted any aircraft overhead before the carrier began blasting apart, and the exec hustled back inside, leaving the watch officer alone in his spellbound state. None of the past hundred and some hours were supposed to go anything like this; the *Cork's* role at Leyte was to have been grandly ceremonial, delivering MacArthur into the bay for the historic moment of his promised return to the Philippines. The Japanese navy got in the way of that. Accordingly, the general found a lesser floating platform for his symbolic wade ashore while the *McCorkle* was scrambled into the battle formation with all other destroyers in the support fleet. In the ensuing near-endless days and nights, the man on watch believed he had done nobly—not heroically; that was a dimension he did not care to approach—at his post inside at the battle status board, keeping straight the tremendous number of ship names and their whereabouts during the constantly changing struggle. Now, sweaty and fatigued as he was, he felt entitled to a markedly more triumphant watch than this was turning out to be. By now Leyte Gulf was signed, sealed, and delivered for the American side, as would be the campaign ribbons and the commendations to go on one's service record. Yet there was the *St. Lo,* not that far off, still exploding like a gunpowder factory every few minutes.

Then he glimpsed the plane, in the low-hanging murk of smoke from the burning carrier. The half-hidden aircraft was skimming almost down onto the water, one of the carrier's own trying to ditch, he thought at first. But no, as it emerged incredibly low and fast out of the pall of smoke its wing markings flashed into view, the red ball of the Rising Sun bringing flame to the bridge of the *McCorkle,* the last thing Nick Danzer would ever see.

———

Your chum KIA confirmed. Sorry. Story needed soonest.

What was there to say? His first thought when the bells began going off on the TPWP teletype had been that surely it must be a case of mistaken identity. How was it conceivable that Danzer, of them all, would not maneuver through the war without so much as getting a toenail broken, until he came home a medal-polished version of the Dancer? But that notion or any other could not withstand a suicide plane.

Helplessly clutching the teletype message as if it had attached itself to him, it took him a little time to stop trying to outstare the blind numbers it brought with it. The Pacific war, its odds askew, now had chosen both Animal and Danzer for death out of what should have been statistical security. One wearing a uniform for what he could put into it, and the other for what he could get out of it, and it made no difference to the creeping wall of oblivion. "We've had the casualty figures from other wars run. . . . Many more soldiers survive than people think, and our figures merely back that up . . ." *Sure, Colonel, tell that to Bruno's eleven, marked down to four all of a sudden. When the hell is it ever going to let up?*

The job brought Ben out of that, the newspaperman's allegiance to the story. Faced with writing a farewell to Danzer fit for the world to read, he felt like a mechanic without tools. The task was there to be done, but how? The report of the kamikaze attack was coldly without details. There was not even a service record to cadge from, the grim file with the red tag on the upper corner; the war's initials for combat death simply were banged onto teletype paper along with reams of other military lingo quantifying the Leyte Gulf carnage. It was times like this when the making of words turned into frantic manufacture, and Ben started out of the wire room sickly dreading what it would take to bring an obituary version of Slick Nick out of his fingertips across the next some hours.

Behind him, the TPWP teletype bell rang five times again.

———

As Pacific amphibious landings went, Leyte was not as murderous as Tarawa and Peleliu and Guam had been, nor Iwo Jima and Okinawa yet to come. But murderous enough, predictably, where the hard-luck Montaneers were involved.

On Leyte the bloodiest combat moved inland a lot sooner than in most other island assaults, with the Japanese line of defense swiftly pulling back from the usual hellish beach to higher, even more horrendous jungle terrain. The day the sailors' long-range battle out in the gulf drew to an end, the Montaneers after most of a week of costly attacks managed to secure a strategic but otherwise worthless ridge called Dry Gulch Hill. Probably there was a Dry Gulch Hill on every Pacific island where the Montaneer regiment had seen action, but none had been more treacherous than this. This one was about as high as a football field is long, a desolate muddy hump that had been given an artillery haircut, leaving only palm snags and a general air of determined destruction. With a completeness like that of fog, the stench of corpses of Japanese soldiers rotting in the sun hung over the trails up the hill. The fighting had moved on, and high on the most recently battered section of slope the first two stretcher bearers to arrive were at work amid the wounded and worse than wounded under an embankment that had become an aid station. The one in charge glanced around as a second pair of bearers came slipping and sliding up the trail, cursing the red mud. "Where you been, sightseeing?"

"Stopped for cigars and caviar, what the hell do you think?" the lead man snapped back. "Murray's carry strap gave out and we had to pull up to tie the sonofabitch together. What's the picture here?"

"Couple for us, one for the body squad. The others can still walk, more or less." The man in charge turned to the last of the stretcher squad. "Hey, Murray, you're from Missoula, aren't you?" He pointed to a laid-out figure shaded by a poncho. "That one's Standish—conked out, loss of blood."

"Yeah, we played pool together," Murray reflected. "Dan's a live wire." He lowered his voice. "Is he going to make it, you think?"

"Got the tourniquet on him in time, he ought to pull through." The first man swung a bothered gaze toward a still body beyond Standish's breathing one. "One there that didn't. Their medic—always hate to see that. Don't know him. You?"

Murray stepped over for a closer look, shaking his head this time. "Never had the chance to. Poor devil didn't have time to get his boots broken in."

"Fish out his tags, Murray—the chaplain is getting finicky, doesn't like to touch guys when he does the mort report. Let's get at this."

The mortal remains of one more man in uniform no longer the business of the stretcher bearers, they turned away from the dog tag–marked body of Dex Cariston.

GOOD GOD ALMIGHTY, *Dex—if you ended up thinking anything like that. Why that conscientious? Couldn't you just sit out the war?*

He could only try to imagine the change of heart or mind or guts or wherever a conscience as restless as Dex's was seated.

"I'm doing what I can to keep blood in people," back there amid the warless parachutes of the smoke-jumper camp, "instead of letting it out of them."

Fine, well, and good, Dex, that was your decision, as large as life itself. But then? What got to you? The hundredth time some yokel along the Seeley Lake road shouted "yellowbelly" at you? The feeling of odd man out, nagging at you in those nights you struggled to sleep? You were made of stronger stuff than that, though, you could shrug those off even if they did get under your skin. No, it took something that hurt you down to the bone, and I was a witness to it coming. You died of gossip. Mere goddamn gossip.

Slumped against the wire room wall, the two messages crumpled and then uncrumpled in his helpless hands, Ben numbly added and subtracted elements in the weighing of both lives. Gossip was never mere if you were a mercantile prince, an heir with rivals to the prideful fortunes of the Cariston name, was it. And if you sliced conscience with a blade of disdain like Danzer's, there was nothing unnatural about skewering a rival not even going through the motions of serving in uniform, right, Slick Nick? *Talk about enemy action. The war didn't invent that particular one. Goddamn Danzer, I did what I could to head him off while I was on the ship. But all he had to do was wait until people forgot that shark piece a little bit and then have his wolf pack of haberdashers start the gossip about Dex, the conchie who would not serve his country in uniform.*

And Tepee Weepy fit into this—where? TPWP and the colonel, simply lost in the forest of good intentions? He felt entitled to doubt that. Yet as furiously as Ben searched for its red hand in it all, he could tell that Tepee Weepy's influence was not necessarily there this time. To his certain knowledge, it had kept hands off Dex all the while he was at the conscientious objector camp; if it had ever tried to push him into military service, the politically connected Cariston dynasty would have shown the Threshold Press War Project what real pull was. No, go over it every way he could find, it kept coming out the same: Dex surely must have enlisted on his own, and matters took their own course from there. A medic for the smoke jumpers, he offered himself as one for the infantry. Another Montanan built rugged enough to tackle jungle life, off he went to the next jungle awaiting invasion. All Tepee Weepy had to do was sit back and keep track, these past several months, and at the right time send Ben out to the Montaneers and there was the story, Dexter Cariston in change of uniform and conscience. It was heartless, but only heartlessly professional.

Feeling like he was in a vise the size of the TPWP teletype, Ben headed for the nearest wire room clerk. He grabbed up the paper pad, made two quick jabs with a pencil, and handed it over. The teletype operator blinked at it. "I can't just send a punctuation mark."

"You goddamn well will or you'll be peeling spuds until your thumbs fall off."

Sourly the operator hit the single key.

?

The reply came in a matter of minutes.

GOOD QUESTION, YOUR ANXIETY ABOUT PRIORITY UNDERSTOOD. FILE KAMIKAZE PIECE FIRST. CARISTON TO HAVE FUNERAL. NO REMAINS OF DANZER; YOUR STORY THE LAST WORD. SEND SOONEST.

He had to give it a number of tries, but by late that night he had a thousand words that managed to say between the lines that it had taken the largest naval battle in history to corner the Dancer.

THE ELEVENTH DAY of the eleventh month came white and gray in Helena, sticky snow in the early morning hours and sullen overcast for the afternoon. At the cemetery, Ben and Jake were encased in the coarse military overcoats besides their dress uniforms, but it was cold on the feet. They picked their way through the slushy snow toward the graveside where the Cariston clan and what looked like half of Helena were assembling, Jake grousing at the weather and the war and funerals and the Alaska duty he still was stuck with. "Nome sweet Nome, they ought to give the place back to the Eskimos," he was ending up with. "Thanks for getting me out of that frozen dump for a couple of days for this, I guess."

"Habit by now." The words came from Ben as chilly as the fog of breath around them, and Jake looked at him with concern. He didn't notice. He could feel everything about this day crushing in on him, this icy conclusion of Dex's life to be written, and what waited later. Armistice Day with the world caught up in an even worse war was in itself not anything to help a mood. Fingers stiff and unwilling, he took out his notepad and started with the inchwork of writing, details of the burial service.

Snow lay in the stone folds of the carved monuments in the section of old Helena families where Dex was being interred. The Cariston family plot was granitic in its standing stones. Oddly as if on perpetual guard, not far away stood the commemorative statue of the World War One doughboy, bayonet fixed in readiness. While Jake was at atttention with the rest of the pallbearers and the Presbyterian cadence of the minister went on, Ben was pulled to the statue to make sure of something that had caught his eye. The bronze plaque appeared to be out of proportion to the natural dimensions of the base and as he drew nearer he saw this was not simply an artistic misfire; the list of names of the county's World War One dead stretched so long the plaque barely fit onto the soldier's pedestal of sculpted patch of battleground. Death in war was thought to be a random harvest, but the outsize crop of young lives taken here made a person wonder. Bill Reinking had always said the so-called war to end all wars drained a generation of lifeblood out of Montana. About like this one, his son thought to himself as he turned back to the graveside service.

Grimly making himself function, Ben wondered what he was looking at in this funeral on this designated day. Was it a thumbing of the nose at any hearers of gossip, any doubters that there had been a brave man—brave enough to risk his life alongside other Montaneers—in Dex Cariston? Was it a salute to Dex's depth of conscience against war, burial on the day the world's guns stopped taking lives in 1918? The numerous Caristons with their set Scotch faces were not a family one could see into.

When the burial was done, they shook hands with the family and said their condolences. Jake showed surprise when Ben begged off the gathering at the Montana Club afterward, saying the two of them had something else they had to tend to in town before heading back to East Base.

"Something better than good whiskey at the fanciest place in Helena?" Jake asked righteously as they left the cemetery.

"You'll see," Ben said.

He took him along to meet Cass.

THEY MET OUT AT the edge of town in the Broadwater Hotel, which was not far from the Fort Harrison military hospital. Its landmark turrets and spread-eagle porches caked with snow, the elderly hotel looked under the weather in more ways than one, having seen better days and ritzier assignations. Cass, in uniform, was waiting in a faintly Victorian parlor off the lobby.

Standing to greet the pair of them, she led off with a pinpoint smile to Ben. "I see you brought some reinforcement along, good." She and Jake knew each other by sight from East Base life, but shook hands pilot to pilot for the first time. "Ben was just telling me about you," he said with ponderous neutrality.

Cass looked more worn-out than Ben had ever seen her. "I don't have as much time as I'd like"—she gazed at him and then included Jake—"I had the nurse tell Dan I was going to the drugstore. He's most likely asleep. He sleeps huge amounts since he was brought back."

They sank into the nearest plush triangle of chairs. In the awkward settling in, Ben went first: "What are they telling you at the hospital?"

Cass steeled herself and began. "Dan got shot through the shoe top. Doesn't sound like much, does it?" She looked at the two men who were sound of limb as if reluctantly translating this for them. "Wouldn't you know, though, the bullet caught the leg dead center. There'll need to be a bone operation and a skin graft and—we don't know what all yet." She shuddered a little, not just for effect. "No wonder they call the place Fort Hairy." Rushing now to get this part over with, she listed off: "As soon as he has enough life back in that leg, they're sending him to California. There's some specialist there—he takes a tendon from somewhere else and patches it into the leg. Dan will have to learn to walk."

The thought sat there, until it was Jake who rumbled, "That's a rough go, for both of you."

Cass tried to grin gamely. "I'll have time. They're kicking me out of the service, around Christmas." Seeing Ben's expression become even more tortured, she quickly went on: "All the women pilots, not just me. They're inactivating the WASPs." She toughed it out for a few sentences more. "The boys are coming home. Nobody needs the female of the species in the cockpit from here on."

Was there anything the war could not warp? After all of Ben's times of wanting Cass out of fighter planes with half a ton of engine riding at the back of her neck, now he sorrowed for her over this, too.

Jake gave a sympathetic murmur, and leaving the two of them with that, cleared his throat as if on cue and negotiated his bulk out of the depth of his chair. "I'm going to see if they have a beer anywhere in this mausoleum. Catch you later, Cass." When he had gone, Ben moved to the chair nearer hers, even though the difference was only inches.

"Hi, Scar," she said wistfully.

"How are you holding up?"

"Not so hot." She closed her eyes and knuckled each lightly, as if the strain had collected there. Then a sudden blink, and the straight-ahead hazel-eyed honesty that had been her hallmark with him. "Dan's a handful, with this medical rigamarole. The squadron is a handful, ever since our official boot in the butt. No morale, everybody's flying on empty, why shouldn't they be?" She lifted her shoulders a tiny bit, let them drop just as suddenly, one of her gestures Ben could have traced in his sleep. "End of report. How about you—the Tepee outfit show any signs of sanity?"

"Barely. They haven't come up with any new ways to kill me off yet."

"Please don't keep saying 'yet.'"

"Sorry. They're making noises that the war could be over by the end of the year. I'll believe it when I see it."

"Won't we all."

"Cass?" *What a privilege it has been to love you,* the words he did not dare to start saying denied him voice. *Even if you are going back to being his wife, what a privilege it will have always been.* He removed his gaze from her to the snowbound topiary of the hotel grounds until his speech steadied enough. "I—I came to tell you. At the base and"—he gestured in a way that took in everything from there to here—"so on, I'll stay out of the way. From now on. It's the least I can do."

"I'd say it's a lot more than that, Ben." Cass looked like a touch would send her to pieces. "If you don't go, right about now, I'm going to turn into a gibbering idiot."

"I'll drive," Jake let him know in no uncertain manner as they slopped through the wet snow of the hotel driveway to the motor pool sedan. "You look like you walked off a cliff and are still going."

Neither said anything as the car pulled out of town and headed up the long incline out of Helena's valley, past the scrub-forested Scratchgravel Hills, past the slow-flowing passageway of the Missouri River called the Gates of the Mountains, past the historic baronial sheep ranch with sheds broad and long as hangars. The road back to East Base and the war was winding into the bends of Wolf Creek Canyon shared between colored cliffs and gray river before Jake burst out.

"Call me cockeyed, Benjamin buddy, but you're the one who told me I was asking for trouble when all I was doing was getting my knob polished by a Commie. I guess you were more of an expert on the topic of trouble than I knew."

"Cass and I didn't set out to cheat on her husband." Ben couldn't speak beyond a monotone. "Just the opposite, at first—we gave each other the porcupine treatment. Then we got to talking, just stuff. Next thing we knew"—by now his voice was down to where pain comes in, and it hurt to listen—"we couldn't live without each other. It gets into your blood before you can turn around, Ice."

Jake seemed to gather his thoughts around that before finally saying: "Even porkies find a way to make love."

"I'll have to think about that."

"It takes two, Ben."

With Jake's words lodged in him he sat there lost in himself, seeing her in every phase of their time together—Cass over him, under him, clothes on, clothes off, making a face over coma cola, the long talks, the quick jokes, the wedding ring that only came off in the cockpit pocket of a P-39. "Her husband's outfit regularly got the raw end in the Pacific," he heard himself saying as if under ether. "There wasn't a whole lot of chance he would make it through the war. But I never damn once hoped he wouldn't. Not once. You can't and stand yourself." He halted. "There was no lifetime guarantee on me, either. The eleven of us haven't been any insurance agent's dream, have we. Why shouldn't she hang on to her marriage when every time she turned around I was being sent someplace where people were getting knocked off? I can't blame Cass."

The car moved on in the silence of the canyon, the cuts of the road hemmed to the river now with seams of snow. This was territory for black ice and Jake tapped the brakes a few times to gauge the road surface. Between, he asked:

"So I was the chaperone, back there at the hotel?"

"You guessed it."

Jake gave a large sigh. "First time I was ever picked for that part of the party." He was gauging Ben now. "What did you figure would happen if I hadn't been there?"

"We probably wouldn't have snatched the clothes off each other and gone at it in the lobby, but who the hell knows." He bit the inside of his mouth, a hurt that would shut off. "It doesn't matter now."

"Besides being Mister Priss, do I also get to be Uncle Jake and give you my two bits' worth of advice?"

"I'm in the goddamn car until we get to Great Falls, aren't I."

"You're not the first guy or the last to get in over his head where nature's better half is involved. For what it's worth, you chose an A-1 woman to fall for." The big dark head wagged back and forth as if sure of its ground here. "She's some piece of work. And I mean that in the nicest possible way, okay? So, go a little easy on yourself. Love is maybe meant to get the best of us. What's it for, otherwise?" Jake braked into a curve. "I'll tell you whose shoes I wouldn't want to be in, Cass's. She's got a tough row ahead."

"I didn't know the inactivation part," the words came out of Ben like the last of a bad taste. "She's as batty about flying as you are."

"Pilots are only barely of this earth," Jake said, seeming to mean it.

16

★ Days at East Base were a muddle after that. Ben avoided the flight line, the ready room, any flying-suited flock of WASPs in the distance, all the avenues of everyday that might conceivably lead to Cass. Putting in his time in the office and the wire room, he looked tensed up and narrowed in, like a man out on a limb that no one else could see. And he was.

Dex's death rattled him to his depths. What shook him even harder was that he found himself seriously questioning the amount of life he himself had ahead. It went against his nature. When you have not yet seen your twenty-fifth birthday you necessarily must feel you are unkillable. Why were you given all that vim if life was not meant to go on? Over and over he told himself to keep a sense of proportion. Eight men killed, when millions were being lost in this insatiable war. Yet from a group you knew best, it was a lot of dead men. And he had been counted into that hexed group from day one, hadn't he, back there on the TSU practice field. What kind of coach's witch's brew was it at that last practice, eleven names on a list jotted by Bruno to start the fate-filled season and sanctified by Loudon's Twelfth Man nonsense? Every man of them destined one after another, their lives

issuing out in the war like rain falling in an open grave? Ben did
not believe in omens and he did not want to believe in jinxes.
Statistical quirks were something else, though, if the war kept on
being so overpowering that it jiggled the odds on almost everything. Sure, you could believe for all you were worth that you
were too young and fit and lucky to be chased down by death,
but all of accumulated history yawns back, *Why not you?*

Ben did not have to struggle with the obvious any too long. *I
can't just go on being a target every place Tepee Weepy can think
up.* Already unstrung by Cass being gone from him, he did his
best to assemble his scattered self, knowing worse consequences
were out there waiting if he did not. *Any infirmary sawbones will
tell you there's no prescription that works on nervous in the service,
Reinking, so get a grip on yourself.* At least Jake had not managed
to wangle his way into the flak-filled skies over Germany and
remained stuck on the milk run—all right, ice-water run—from
Fairbanks to Nome. At least Moxie was in some anti-aircraft rear
echelon, getting to shoot first at any threats overhead. *I'm going
to give it a try, guys. Screwed-up law of averages or not, there's no
rule I can see that we have to end up with the others.*

He started what he knew had to be the last battle of words
with Tepee Weepy the day after Dex was buried.

The funeral piece he filed spared nothing about the highborn
Cariston name joining the oversize list of Helena sacrificial sol-
diery beneath the doughboy statue, but that was not the issue.
Apprehension behind every word, that next day he fed the block-
letter sentences one by one to the teletype operator.

END SUPREME TEAM SERIES NOW? GETTING LONELY, JUST WE
THREE.

The final line was trickiest of all to come up with, possibly
because it was hard to write with fingers crossed.

WHAT IF TOKYO ROSE AND LORD HAW-HAW KNOW HOW TO
COUNT.

"Don't you want me to put a question mark on this, sir?"

"It's not a question, soldier, it's a supposition. Just send it."

Nothing came back that day, no matter how much Ben hung around the wire room and mooched coffee and sprang alert every time a teletype bell went off. *Come on, you TPWP SOBs. Answer. Call off the damned series. Or are you going to tell me and the couple of thousand newspaper editors watching for this byline you set me up with that eight dead heroes aren't enough?*

The days after that, he sent Jones to check for a reply so many times that at last the corporal just gave him a funny look and started off before he could get the words out. Finally, at week's end, a wire room clerk stuck his face in the doorway and said there was a five-bell message waiting.

TPWP MINDFUL OF HAW-HAW AND TOKYO ROSE. FULLY INTEND ENEMY PROPAGANDA WILL NOT SCORE BIG ON SUPREME TEAM. SERIES WILL BE MODIFIED. DETAILS FOLLOW SOON.

Ben read and reread the sheet of wire copy for what it said and did not say. That damned "modify" again. The Tepee Weepy meaning of SOON was also clear as mud. He plainly enough had their attention, though, with that dig about what the master propagandists in Berlin and Tokyo could do with the obliteration of any more of the team. *So, okay, that does spook them and it's up to me to keep them spooked.* Immediately he holed up in his office and went back to block-letter work.

MODIFY IS MIDDLE NAME HERE AT EAST BASE. HOW ABOUT WRAP-UP PIECE ON STAMPER AND EISMAN AS SURVIVORS?

Again, a last line onto that was the hard stunt. Before deciding whether to send all three, he had Jones bring him the regulations to see what it took to be court-martialed for insubordination. Not that much. He sucked in his cheeks and had the third sentence sent anyway. FIRST THEY MUST SURVIVE.

Tepee Weepy's response practically jumped out of the teletype, the bells chorusing before he had even turned around to
leave the wire room.

WRAP-UP PIECE IS SHARED GOAL. YOU WILL GIVE IT SHINE
AND SHADOW AT RIGHT TIME, RIGHT PLACE.

Ben waited expectantly for the clerk to pass him the next
decoded sentences. The clerk shrugged and held up empty hands.

"That's it? It can't be, look again."

"I already did. That's all they wrote, sir."

Fuming, Ben stoked up on coffee and claimed a vacant desk
there in the wire room. He jotted and wadded three versions
before hitting on the one that upped the ante unmistakably
enough.

UNSURE I CAN TOUGH IT OUT UNTIL RIGHT TIME,
RIGHT PLACE. ILLNESS DISCUSSED WHEN COLONEL HERE
MAY RECUR. DIAGNOSIS NOT SO HOT, DETAILS MIGHT
HELP WITH CURE.

*Get it, Colonel and your partners in manufacturing the news?
I damn sure am sick of guys from the team turning into dead men
whenever the sonofabitching war feels like it, whatever the odds
are supposed to be. If you can't pull strings to save Jake's skin and
Moxie's and for that matter mine, then kick me out with a dishonorable piece of paper for refusing orders, see if I goddamn care. I
may be blackballed for life, but at least I'll be in one piece.* He sent
this message knowing he really was playing a thin hand now, but
gambling that Tepee Weepy had its own stake in keeping him in
the game.

ILLNESS UNDERSTOOD, the answer clattered back within minutes. PLAN IS TO HONOR STAMPER, EISMAN, YOU, AS SURVIVORS
OF SUPREME TEAM SAGA. FEELING BETTER?

Hovering at the clerk's shoulder, he sent right back:

SOME. WAITING TO SEE WHAT MEDICINE IS INVOLVED.

The wait this time stretched his nerves to the sagging point. It was growing dark enough outside for the five bells of the TPWP wire machine to constitute a vesper serenade before the return message began coming in.

MANDATORY BURN THIS AFTER YOU READ.

I guess I have their attention. "Loan me your lighter and nab a clean butt can for a bonfire." The clerk sighed and complied.

The whacking teletype keys seemed to spell out the message with particular emphasis now.

STAMPER IS FINAL STORY, BLAZE OF GLORY, ALL THAT.

"Quick, shoot this off to them." Ben was grabbing for the notepad.

"You want me to break in on a priority message from Washington?"

"You heard me." He jotted the words big and bold and handed them to the reluctant clerk. WHERE IS STAMPER, ANYWAY?

STAMPER STATIONED WITH NEW ACK-ACK UNIT AT HQ EUROPEAN THEATER. VITAL DRAMATIC STORY THERE.

Ben paused over that. Supreme headquarters where the invasion of Europe had been planned and carried out was in England. England meant London, and every correspondent from Ernie Pyle to Hemingway had a soft spot for London and the British, so dauntless under the bombing of the Luftwaffe in the first years of the war. He had learned to love the old city himself in his early stint of reporting there, and now the Luftwaffe bombers had been driven from the sky over Great Britain and even the rocket buzz bomb attacks were reported to have dropped off sharply. There was second allure in what Tepee Weepy was proposing; while he could not have put a name to her, Mnemosyne once more was gliding forth from the eternal grove with that double handful of tantalizing choice. If the Allied forces took Berlin by the end of the year, as everyone was saying could happen, London would be a fine place to write the one thing guaranteed to preserve Jake and Moxie and himself, the story that the war itself was dead.

Ben cast his lot. I'M LISTENING.

AS WE WERE SAYING, the TPWP teletype implacably resumed. STAMPER A SHORT-TERMER NOW IN ACK-ACK DUTY. HE WILL BE MUSTERED OUT WITH COMMENDATIONS AND APPROPRIATE CEREMONY, OVER THERE, THEN BRING HIM HOME AS HERO. EISMAN TO BE HERO BY THEN TOO, LONGEST-SERVING ATC PILOT ON ALASKA RUN, ALSO WILL BE MUSTERED OUT. SATISFIED?

It was a better bargain than he'd thought he could get: Jake would not be going to Europe, would not be at risk from Nazi flak and concentration camp. With a sense of relief, he sent back: FEELING BETTER ALL THE TIME.

GLAD CURE IS TAKING HOLD. WIND UP AFFAIRS AT EAST BASE NEXT FEW WEEKS. EARLY DECEMBER YOU WILL PROCEED FORTHWITH TO—

At first he thought the clerk at the Tepee Weepy end had garbled together some wrong keys in typing the ultimate word. Then he still had to think for a moment where Antwerp was.

17

✪ BELGIUM HAD BEEN a main road in two world wars, Ben knew that much, every schoolkid knew that much. It was notoriously easy for the Kaiser's army in 1914 and the Führer's in 1940 to rumble into the supposedly neutral low country where the port of Antwerp faced out alluringly into the entire maritime world. Back to Napoleon and Wellington, back greatly farther than that in the centuries-long swash of war as European monarchies contended for that foothold on the North Sea, the Belgians' lot had been to prosper cautiously during intervals of peace and to suffer foreign occupation as soon as the cannons were fired. Now, glory be to the dazed and half-starved little country, the four-year Nazi grip on Belgium had been wrenched free by a surprise British offensive after the D-Day landings. "Surprise" scarcely said it; Field Marshal Montgomery's tanks thrust north out of Normandy with such astounding rapidity that German forces emptied out of Belgian cities in mad haste. In particular, they unwisely abandoned Antwerp without taking time to sabotage the strategic waterfront along the River Scheldt and its mouth into the North Sea. There it sat, the prize port with its nicely intact docks and locks and cranes, and the Allied high command lost no time in turning Antwerp's dockland into the supply conduit for the final push on into Germany. Which, Ben could see, meant defending Antwerp against air raids as the Germans might seek to make up for their error of hasty evacuation. Which, also as far as he could see, meant duty as usual for anti-aircraft batteries such as Moxie Stamper's. *Keep your damn head down for a few weeks more, Mox, and we're home free.*

DAYS WERE HECTIC, nights were forlorn, as he readied to leave for Europe. There was a last quick visit home for Thanksgiving, his mother to be soothed, his father to be bolstered. The soldier's oldest ordeal before shipping out, how much to say to loved ones, how much not to say.

Afterward, expecting it day after day as he was, the message from TPWP finally came like a blurted order:

DEPART TOMORROW.

First, a farewell to Jones that they both found hard to deal with.

Next, in an icy December dawn at East Base, he boarded an eastbound C-47, acutely conscious he was carrying with him what little was left of the law of averages.

"BILL, IT'S NEARLY midnight, you know. Or maybe the time got away from you."

"You're not exactly tucked into bed yourself, Cloyce."

"I needed an aspirin." She hesitated at the doorway, then came into his lair of books and snuggled into the easy chair across from his desk, tucking the lacy hem of her nightgown under her knees. Unaccustomed as they were to this anymore, they glanced at each other a bit shyly and then out the window to the whitened town. Flakes were coming down featherlike, yet every so often the wind dislodged a branchload from the cotton-wood trees, producing a commotion like white dust rising back up, more clods falling within it. The all-but-silent crash of snow lent an otherworldly quality to this night, the first of many such the two of them were going to have to get used to.

"Where do you think he is by now?" Cloyce asked in a hushed voice.

Bill cleared his throat. "The Long Island field, maybe." All during the day he had studied Ben's route on the wall map of the *Gleaner* office every time he glanced up. New York. Newfoundland. Greenland. Iceland. England. Europe and whatever that portended.

"At least we did get to see him," she mused, as if still trying out for her role as mother. "Even if it was slim pickings as holidays go."

It was not a Spam Thanksgiving as she had warned Ben in his last-minute phone call that it might need to be, but it was venison pot roast, dry and gamy, procured by Bill in some manner that he would not divulge. The guests' dishes similarly tasted of improvisation: Carnelia Muntz's tomato-soup-and-olives aspic, without the olives; Mae Vennaman's dried apple pie, craftily achieved with saved sugar coupons. A decidedly mixed review, Cloyce told herself, but better than none. The duration sat right up to the table with them all, and the talk among the older people, which was everyone but Ben, kept coming back to whether the war would be over by the end of the year. "Sure," Ben had replied, "I just don't know what year." It had drawn a laugh from everyone except his parents.

Now Cloyce gauged her husband and what was stacked in front of him on the desk. "You've been reading it again, haven't you."

Nodding, he reached around and squared the pages of the script. "You're the expert, but I'd call it one hell of a movie."

"You're right, it's a wonderful work." She paused, the tip of her tongue against the roof of her mouth. "They actually did that to the Purcell boy?" It both was a question and not.

"They did. Ben has a firsthand source."

"I just wish he hadn't been so dramatic about leaving it with us," she murmured. "Mother, Dad," his words still were in the air of the house, "if I don't make it back, do what you can with this, okay?"

Bill Reinking smiled gently. Just sitting there in her night-gown, she looked ready for a director to sing out *Action!* "I can't imagine where he gets it from."

She gave back a soft laugh, then looked out into the sift of snow again. "I would give years off my own life to have kept Ben from being sent into danger all the time." She turned her gaze to Bill. "I did try, you know."

"How would I?" His head dipped as he looked at her through the very tops of his glasses. "You never said so, Cloyce."

She smiled the slightest bit. "That's what comes of living with newspapermen. If I'd told you, it would have gone right into his ear." The smile flicked off. "As you can tell, I couldn't get the job done. All those family friends in Washington, Bill? People my parents were thick as thieves with in the old days? Not a one of them," her tone deadly level, "would find a safe spot for our only son." It was not like her to curse, but she found the coldness of voice for it now. "The short-memoried bastards."

Bill touched the script again. "If—we have to do something with this, do you think you can?"

Her chin came up. "That's different, thank goodness. The Carteret name still means something at Zanuck's studio and some of the others." She nodded slowly. "I can get them to read *The Ghost Runner* and that's all it will take, I guarantee you. Ben's movie will be made, it's too good not to."

Cloyce saw her husband's mood uncloud just a bit and smiled

further encouragement to him. "Ben will get to tend to that himself," she said firmly. "I told him I was counting on him for New
Year's again."

HE WAS COOLING his heels in a few hours' layover in Newfoundland when a clerk tracked him down.

"Sir? Are you the TPWP captain? I'm from the wire room.
Message there for you."

Wondering *What now?*, he let the soldier lead him to the
communications building. The teletype sheet was ripped and
ready, waiting for him. He read it, went outside, and threw up in
the snow.

A WEEK. AND I didn't have so much as a goddamn hint about it.
Jake's plane had been missing on the flight between Fairbanks
and Nome for seven days, the official time for giving an aircraft
and its crew up for lost. Oblivion of the worst kind; it was not
known whether the B-17 bomber perished in the Alaskan mountains or the Bering Sea. Ben felt as if his soul had been operated
on, an essence of life cut out of him. *Why Jake? Why now?* There
in the Newfoundland cold, he tried to grapple himself together.
Back in to the wire room. Dull jots on the message pad, handed
to the clerk to be sent to Tepee Weepy.

I NEED TIME.

Tersely TPWP arranged a layover until the next morning's
flight to Europe.

HE SPENT A terrible day, wrestling the words out.

*Sky-high in his hundred-mission crush hat, loud as a good
takeoff, Lt. Jacob Eisman flew through life amending the laws of
gravity as he went. He was Jake to the world, and jake with us,
those who knew him in all his big ways.*

A line, two, would come, and then he would have to abandon the typewriter, go outside to clear his head in the elemental Newfoundland weather.

He came to this war from a thousand years of one-sided battles, his family becoming American—All-American in the finest, truest use of those words—out of a past ridden over by Cossacks too many times. And by one of the quirks war is so good at, he piloted bombers to Russian comrades waiting in Alaska, back door to Siberia, in the airborne supply line to the Eastern Front where the largest battles in history are being fought.

At the end, he sought out the base library to look it up.

"The dear love of comrades," wrote one of us who knew how to make words sing. Walt Whitman inscribed that out of his service as a nurse in the Civil War, another chapter of lost good men. Jake Eisman would have shaken his big, outrageous Cheshire-cat head over those words, but no man in uniform ever earned them more.

Late that night, he filed the finished piece to TPWP. In the morning, he was back in a plane, somewhere over the gray cold North Atlantic, descending the latitudes to the older world.

ANTWERP'S AIRDROME LOOKED like a military costume party. Ben understood that this rear-area supply sector was a joint command, with an American general serving under Belgium's liberator, the British tank tactician Montgomery. But Allied armed forces seemed to have proliferated far beyond that on this airfield. Belgian military types stationed themselves here and there, beaming in welcome but not notably in English. Over by the 'drome canteen a small herd of Free French brass was being met by an American liaison officer who looked overwhelmed. Elsewhere, coveys of soldiers in what appeared to be outmoded British uniforms were gabbling in some dour strange language; Ben at length figured out they must be Polish troops who until now had fought the war from England. Looking around futilely for any sign of a motor pool and a familiar U.S. Army driver to be conscripted, he wondered if he was lingually up to this. *So far, it's as bad as when Sig sneaked up on me in Japanese and I didn't know what the hell to—*

An officer, stubby and bright-eyed, stepped in front of him. Amid the wardrobe explosion of uniforms it took Ben a moment to identify this one as British, the sainted Royal Air Force.

"Captain Reinking, is it?"

The mellifluous accent issued from a boyish ruddy face with a nose on it like the round end of a hammer. From that ball-peen nose on down, the blue-clad officer was built about as square as a man could be without a loading pallet under him. "I trust you had a good flight? I'm Leftenant Overby. Assigned to you, it seems. Your liaison to the sector communications branch."

Ben did not like the looks of this. By this stage of the war, he had caught the enlisted men's aversion to fresh-faced lieutenants; that first syllable dangerously rhymed with "new" and green looeys were trouble in combat. He wasn't looking for combat, but he wasn't looking for whatever trouble might come with this British version of shavetail, either. "Lieut—Leftenant," he acknowledged this one with a dubious nod.

"I'm instructed to see to your needs," the pleasant tumble of words ensued again, "show you the ins and outs of the ticker room, and all that. Oh, and your mother branch—TPWP, if I have the alphabet mix right?—sends its regards. Let's see, I copied it off: 'END ZONE IN SIGHT. BRIEF TIME-OUT. HUDDLE UP, SCORING PLAY IS ON WAY.'" The RAF man glanced up at him with polite reserve. "A bit over our heads in the code department, I'm afraid, and we do hope we managed to decipher it correctly. Make sense to you, does it, Captain?"

Nothing they ever do does, but I get the gist. "It's their sweet way of saying hurry up and wait."

"Ah, well, then, military business as usual, isn't it. Shall we?" Overby swept the travel pack out of Ben's grasp, hovered the merest instant over the etiquette of grabbing the typewriter case too, and left that untouched. "I'll drive you to your billet."

Ben did not budge. "Let me catch up with what we're doing—where is it?" He was determined not to be dumped in some Antwerp hotel the Nazis had pillaged for four years.

"Not to worry, Captain, we're in bunkers," Overby replied patiently. "It would require a direct hit to do a person in, and there have been comparatively few of those here on the airfield."

Bunkers? Here? The inconspicuous airfield looked like a hastily transformed cow pasture—the runway the plane had trundled in on was composed of the metal mats that engineers could lay down in a hurry and the buildings were drab military prefabs— but now that Ben looked again, the open flat uncamouflaged terrain all around left the place as exposed as a beached aircraft carrier. Direct hits were a topic worth pursuing. "Comparatively few compared to what?"

"The city, of course." Overby indicated the low rough skyline of Antwerp barely visible through the gray air some little distance away. "Poor old Antwerpen town," his tone dropped to tragic, "is receiving a battering about like London's was."

About like—? Suspicious of being hazed as a newcomer, Ben fixed a dead-level gaze on the RAF officer. "You better spell that out for me, too. Where's the battering come from?" He knew any bombardment in this sector could not be from artillery, the German ground forces had been driven back nearly into Germany itself, the fighting front the last he'd heard was in the Ardennes forest over a hundred miles away. And while the German air command no doubt could crank up occasional nuisance air raids or Moxie's anti-aircraft battery wouldn't have been sent here, everyone knew Allied fighter planes ruled the skies of Europe by the time of D-Day. "I thought the Luftwaffe was supposed to be on its last legs."

"Quite," came the bland response. "The buzz bombs are ever with us, however. Fifty-some flying bombs in one day, in the worst of last week."

For a marginal few seconds, Ben wondered if it was too late to get back on the plane.

"Not that we censors," Overby raised an eyebrow a cautionary fraction, "like for that to become common knowledge, if you please, Captain."

"'We' censors?"

"I wanted to fly Spitfires, but someone determined a red pencil was more my speed." He hefted the travel pack again. "Ready, are we?"

"No, we are not. The billet can wait. I want to be taken to Captain Moxie Stamper's ack-ack battery. You're informed enough about why I'm here to know where that is, right?"

The lieutenant sent him a quick hard look. Down went the pack, and he took off his cap and ran a hand contemplatively over a dome of bald head. With the cap absent, Ben could see Overby was a good deal older and more seasoned than he'd first seemed. A lip was being chewed dubiously in the ruddy face. "It's a bit of a step—a fair number of miles, forth and back."

"I don't care how far it is."

"Not a problem, then." Overby set his cap as if aiming it on a compass heading and moved off with the travel pack, leading Ben to a hard-used jeep. "Away we go, Captain."

THE JEEP RATTLED along a cobblestone road so worn down that the Duke of Wellington's troops might have marched on it. Ben realized Antwerp was farther away than it had appeared from the airfield, the murky constant half-fog of the low country making it tricky to judge distance. Overby at the steering wheel seemed intent on making up for the lost career as a Spitfire pilot; every time he took a curve at a leaning angle, Ben missed Jones and his old-maid driving.

"The heater's up as much as it will go," Overby informed him as if he had asked. "Comfy?"

"Enough." Actually he felt highly uncomfortable with the weighty .45 automatic strapped on his right hip. When the Britisher or whatever he was proffered the weapon, web belt, and holster to him before setting out, he'd tried to turn it down with "I'm a correspondent, I don't pack a gun."

"I'm afraid you're in for a lot of bother if you decline to," Overby had launched into. "Top command's orders. The military police are instructed to pick up anyone off-base without at least a sidearm, and it must be loaded at all times. Of course, it is an individual decision whether or not one puts the gun to use, but that is a different cup of tea from whether one must carry—"

"Okay, okay," he had cut off the discourse, "give me the damn thing. You're responsible if I shoot my foot off." Now he was back to trying to figure out how much to trust this Overby. *Assigned to me in what way? To keep an eye on me for Tepee Weepy so I don't mess up their hoopla for Moxie? To lay down his coat for me every time I cross a mud puddle? To pull out his red pencil when I—*

Brakes screeching, the jeep pulled to a stop, facing a moving wall of military trucks and a frowning MP directing traffic. They had come to a ring road, at what looked to be a couple of miles out from the edge of Antwerp. "Convoys run day and night from the port," Overby raised his voice to be heard over the rumble of the trucks. "You're seeing the main supply line to the front." They watched the big Army 6x6s carrying food, fuel, medicine, and munitions roll by as if on an assembly line until at last there was a slight break in the traffic. The MP danced aside in the intersection and motioned hurry-up, and the jeep shot across.

"You were posted to England," Overby picked right back up, evidently duty-bound to make conversation, "earlier in the war, Captain? You saw something of the Blitz, then?"

"That's right, Lieu—Leftenant. Look, can we go by first names?"

"Assuredly, if you prefer." He tapped an attaché case lodged between the seats with Lt. MAURICE OVERBY RAF stenciled on it.

"Same song, second verse," Ben said. "Does that translate to 'Morris' or 'Moreese'?"

"Either, actually. Whichever I try to specify, half of the human herd get it wrong anyway."

"I'll go with 'Moreese,' it makes me feel like I'm in distinguished company." He still was trying to solve the RAF subaltern's mannerisms. "I wouldn't say I can always tell Hackney from cockney, but you don't sound like anyone I was ever around on bases in England."

"Oh, heavens no," accompanied by a scoffing chuckle at any trace of Englishness. Maurice was navigating past spates of Belgians on bicycles, men and women both and nearly all as thin as living scarecrows, close enough to reach out and touch. "New Zealand's my home—the real country, south of the Bombay Hills. Place called Christchurch."

"Well, sonofagun," Ben pulled his attention away from Belgium moving past on spokes and wheels, "Erewhon, huh?"

"You know of it? This is magical!" Maurice showed genuine enthusiasm for the first time. "Not many people can locate 'nowhere' spelled backwards, more or less. A devotee of the works of old Samuel Butler, are you then, Ben?"

"Not especially, read him some in college. Odd facts run in the family."

"I know it's only a book done where I was bred and raised," nostalgia wafted from behind the steering wheel, "but still, old Sam caught the country around Christchurch to the very blades of grass. To this day, freshets off his pages play against my pores."

"Maurice? Not to put too fine a point to this, but what in hell did you do in civilian life?"

"I professed," the occupant of the jeep driver's seat said as though it was perfectly obvious. "I was professor of rhetoric and argumentation there at Canterbury College. The war rather took care of that. The Japanese were closing in on Australia, and New Zealand looked to be next, so I joined up to fight for the homeland"—he looked aside at his uniformed passenger— "didn't we all. Naturally, the instant I had my commission, I was seconded to London. Plopped into the RAF, plopped again into the communications branch, put in charge of a pencil. Daft of the higher-ups, but there you are." He glanced over again. "You're a considerable word man yourself, as I understand it, the byline and all."

Ben shifted the aggravating .45 on his hip. "Tepee Weepy seems to think so or they wouldn't keep sending me to places like this."

"Tepee—? Oh, ha. Very good."

In what amounted to a blink at the rate Maurice drove, they passed one last open field and were in the city, aged three- and four-story housefronts with steep crenulated gables and tall skinny chimneys suddenly everywhere. An unwilling spectator to any more misery of war, Ben had to spectate nonetheless. Antwerp had gone gaunt during the occupation years, the German army had seen to that. The fresher depredation was even more shocking, cavities in the crowded-together streets of homes and shops where buzz bombs had found their target and taken out a building or two. At some such sites, hunched men in flat caps and women in flimsy lace kerchiefs picked through the rubble. At others, everything lay in a dead heap. From the doorways of scarred houses still standing, children so tattered and bony they looked feral jumped out toward the jeep and in Flemish accent shouted the universal "Hey, Andy, any candy? Any gum, chum?" Ben had steeled himself for this bomb-torn tour with the hope that it would be his last of the war. Even so, as the route wound through scene after scene of devastation he felt dismay to the pit of his stomach; Maurice had not been stretching the truth, this was sickeningly like London during the Blitz. The jeep twisted its way around a set of corners—there did not seem to be a straight street in Antwerp—into a neighborhood of sizable abandoned shops that seemed even more forlorn and tortured than others they had passed. "The diamond district, largely Jewish, before," Maurice covered a dazzling history of gem merchantry with the sad wave of a hand.

The streets began to show more life near the market squares in the center of the city. Ben stared up at the Old World guild-halls, ornamented to a frenzy. He couldn't tell if the architecture was meant to be baroque or rococo—perhaps baroco—and there were constant glimpses of a stone-lace cathedral spiked atop it all. Everything with the crust of centuries on it. "All older than dirt, isn't it," Maurice read his thoughts. "Just think," he expanded on that, "a hundred and fifty years before the first four ships made port in New Zealand and while red Indians still ruled over Montana, Rubens was in there"—another indicative sweep of the hand—"painting fleshy maidens and grazing as he went."

"What, there?" The tall-standing house with a stepped peak looked like any of Antwerp's others worn down by time and grime. "That was his passion pit?"

"Hypothetically," Maurice threw into the air, and drove onward through the petrified streets.

Shortly they were going past emplacements of heavy automatic weapons every few blocks, sighted toward the sky and crews at the ready. Ben recognized British Polsten guns, basic and lethal with the telescope-like barrel and prominent fin of magazine, from the air base outside London where he had last spent time with Moxie. *Two years ago already. If "already" means anything in this war.* He remarked on how numerous the anti-aircraft gunners suddenly were, and Maurice allowed as how there were quite a few assigned to Antwerp, twenty thousand or so.

Ben's head snapped around. "An entire army *division* of ack-ack troops?"

"Quite. It's about the port, of course." Maurice simultaneously blew his nose, steered through another avalanche of rubble laying in the street from a set of destroyed buildings, and talked on. "The Huns are damnably serious about putting it out of commission with their buzz bombs. So, the official thinking is, those must be shot down. However much gunnery it takes."

The anti-aircraft guns grew in size and number as Antwerp began to dwindle into villages and countryside. To Ben it all had the feel of a city-size castle, half as old as time, with catapults set at the outskirts to keep invaders at a distance. The strategy, as Maurice laid it out, was to have belts of artillery across the approach path of the flying bombs, which the Germans luckily were only able to launch one by one. If the first arc of ack-ack fire didn't bring down the rocket bomb, the next semicircle of guns a mile or so farther in still had a crack at it, and last of all, those swarms of heavy automatic weapons they had seen at the near side of the city. The gun battery Moxie commanded was in the outermost belt, the one that had to take on incoming buzz bombs headfirst—*oh hell yes, that's where he would be,* Ben resigned himself to. Open exposed country lay between Moxie's flak alley and the middle one they had just driven through, and Maurice considerately announced: "Hold on to your seat—we go flat to the boards here across this bit." He floored the accelerator and the jeep hurtled across the stretch of smudgy damp landscape.

In the rush of bitterly chill air Ben huddled in his flight jacket, wishing he had the horse-blanket overcoat on. Maurice Overby was burning red with cold but seemed unperturbed as he aimed the jeep at a roadblock out from a line of long gun barrels poking out of sandbagged pits.

They were looked over by tommy gun–carrying American GIs, obviously primed for business, and let through. Maurice parked the jeep in the shelter of what he hoped aloud was a parts shed and not a munitions dump. They had no more than climbed out when a figure with a certain familiar slouchy grace detached itself from the crew in the nearest gun pit and approached them.

Even when you knew it was coming, the voice went right under the skin.

"Well, well, the famous Captain Reinking. That what brings you here, Ben buddy? To be Rhine King when we whip the Krauts, write up the last chapter for the folks back home?"

Ben caught up with the other familiarities: the glint in the eyes as if reflecting off something hard; the complexion like steel dust; and Moxie Stamper still wore a helmet, albeit one meant to withstand falling flak fragments, the same way he had in football, tipped back just a trifle enough to look cocky.

"You know for a fact that we've about got them whipped," Ben refused to be nettled before they even shook hands, "do you, Mox?"

"I sure as shit don't," the voice momentarily lost its edge. On fuller inspection, Moxie looked as tired as a man could and still be on his feet. There was a tic where a dimple would have been on a face less sharp than his. Never one to fuss with clothes, he had let his uniform become a size too big for his war-worn frame. He jerked his head to the province of dim sky over the ack-ack guns. "It gets your attention that the SOBs in Berlin don't seem to run out of these overgrown fireworks."

Ben made up for lost time with a hasty introduction of Maurice, Moxie sizing him up from the brim of his tommy helmet to the shiny RAF blue trousers. He barked a laugh. "Overby, hey? So I finally get to meet the devil with the red pencil—the intelligence briefers about piss their pants when they talk about 'Baldy the censor.'"

Letting that sail by, Maurice said: "Ah, HQ's ignorance branch, also known as the intelligence branch. We do have our differences on occasion." He smiled at Moxie in a reserved way. "Better to be bald on the outside than on the in, I remind myself."

Moxie scowled. Ben jumped in with: "Before we all get carried away with teatime manners—do you know about Jake?"

The expression on Moxie darkened some more. "You start off that way, it doesn't sound like the Iceman is in good health."

"His plane—" When Ben finished the telling, Moxie turned away a step or two and gazed into the gray distance.

"Damn it all," he said over his shoulder. "Who would've thought the whole smear of us would end up you and me? I hope you're carrying a good luck piece, Rhine King. Because," he swung around to Ben, the gaze hardening, "you have more balls than brains for hauling yourself over here into this."

Thanks all to hell, Moxie. Remind me to try to save your life— okay, mine along with it—again sometime. Caught flat-footed by Moxie's accusing glower, he tried to read what was behind it and was not coming up with anything. *What, you don't get it that we're each other's ticket out of the war?*

Patient as pudding, Maurice had stood aside during all this, but now moved in before Ben could say anything. "Captain Stamper, I believe you're being beckoned."

A gunnery sergeant was poking his head out of the pit. "One incoming, Cap," he called out. "Five minutes."

Moxie took charge before the words were out of the air. "Acknowledged, Smitty. Get on the horn to fire control and the spotters"—Ben could not help but hear come into the voice the snap of cadence used for good effect in football huddles—"tell them smoke break and grab-ass is over. And chew out the loaders on Charlie gun while you're at it, yesterday they were slower than a three-legged race." He glanced at Ben and Maurice as though they were an afterthought. "It's time to shoot something down. If I was you two, I'd get my butt in back of those sandbags over there."

The pair of them hustled behind the head-high stack between gun pits, Ben asking: "They can track the things that far out?"

"Radar, yes, but it's not so much that," Maurice replied, checking his wristwatch. "When the Germans are at this, they launch one every quarter of an hour. They're quite Teutonic about that habit, in the worst sense. Oh, right, that prods the old memory box. Here," he dug in a flap pocket of his uniform for something, "as a healthy measure, carry this with you when you're out and about."

Ben looked in bafflement at what he had been handed. It appeared to be a pocket watch, but with only one hand and no crystal.

"It's a cocotte clock, in case you're wondering," the explanation was diplomatically put. "A chef's timer, actually, but French prostitutes use these to keep track of the various phases of their services. I have done the necessary research." Maurice paused dreamily. "Ah, Paris. What was that term you used—passion pit?" His brow cleared and he returned to the business at hand. "Set it for ten minutes after each buzz bomb. Gives you five to look around for shelter before the next one arrives."

"Swell, Maurice. I'll see if I can get used to kissing myself good-bye on short notice." Ben sagged against the sandbags to wait, and took stock. In the same opalescent Belgian sky that had looked down on the foot soldiers of Napoleon and the Duke of Wellington, a robot bomb was on its way. After it blindly fell and did its killing or not, the next one could be tracked in by a timepiece that ordinarily ticked off sessions of bed games. This was a war like no other. Or did writers always say that.

Ducking lower and yanking at Ben's sleeve for him to do the same, Maurice wordlessly pointed to a metal sliver cutting the sky. Unable to take his eyes off the object clipping toward them at six miles a minute, Ben had the sensation of everything in him pausing, waiting helplessly for the blind bomb with a tail of flame to pass over or not. Then the roars of the anti-aircraft artillery slammed through him.

FOR SOMETHING THAT sought its target by falling from the sky, a V-1 rocket was oddly nautical, built like an oversize torpedo and traveling with the rumble of a loud motorboat. When that throb stopped, terror began. Any V-1 in its silent dive to the ground brought with it a two-thousand-pound warhead primed to go off on impact. During the long weeks of V-1 ordeal, that feeling of the heart skipping its beats while awaiting doom or survival was the erratic pulse of Antwerp.

PUFFS OF BLUE smoke clouded the air over the gun pits, the long snouts firing, firing, firing as the crews worked madly. Flak bursts dotted the sky behind the flying bomb, then suddenly nearer as the gunners began to get the range and aim off in front of it, leading it as a hunter would a fast-flying duck. The ack-ack noise was unceasing yet somehow everyone knew to the instant when the throb, the buzz, of the bomb cut off and it began to dive. Right at that moment, a proximity shell exploded alongside it and the V-1 faltered in its trajectory, falling away into a field where it burst with a flash of orange flame.

One more time, Ben felt the moving wall of oblivion shift away, and with the tremor of the exploding buzz bomb, settle to a stop. At least temporarily. Another tug on his sleeve. Maurice was setting his cocotte clock and reminding him to do the same.

They scrambled out from behind the sandbags and over to where Moxie had emerged from the gun pit. Helmet off, running a hand through his thatch of wiry black hair, he looked drained. To their accolades of "Well done" and "Nice shooting," he simply stood there, all the swagger gone, eyes fixed on the distant bright spot of burning rocket wreckage. "We get nine out of ten of them," he said tonelessly. "About as good as can be done." He glanced down at his steel helmet as though it held something he did not want to see, then put it on and shifted his focus to Ben. "Night control takes over at 0500, it gets dark so Christly early here. I'll meet you at the O Club after chow. I've got a bone to pick with you, don't I." He turned his back on them and strode off, yelling for the ordnance sergeant to hurry up with the ammunition supply.

"Rough as guts, isn't he," Maurice Overby said mildly. "Shall we return to the charms of Antwerp?"

> Now you hear it, now you don't.
> The bomb, the bomb, the abominable flying bomb.
> If it hits you, then you won't.
> The bomb, the bomb, the bastardly buzzing bomb.

THE GATHERING OF British officers around the piano warbled more closely in tune than any Officers' Club songsters Ben had ever experienced. *Must be all those boy choirs.* Despite the Brit monopoly on the music, the crowd in the cavernous bunker had a more American flavor than the one in the airdrome, including an occasional heart-quickening note of feminine laughter from scattered flocks of Army nurses and such. Some wag had painted up an over-the-door sign in Germanic letters christening the place THE WONDER BAR. It made Ben wonder, all right. Sitting isolated amid the hubbub fifteen feet underground, wrung

out from the double journey through Antwerp's circles of buzz
bomb hell—*Why can't the glee club stay to "The White Cliffs of
Dover"?*—he felt as if this had been the longest day of his life.
Overlapping with that was the awareness that he had thought
the same thing trekking out of the Canadian woods with Jake.
And wading ashore at Guam with Animal. And healing on the
hospital ship off New Guinea after the ambush with Carl. The list
could go on, nearly as long as the war. *Not that anyone other than
you is keeping track, Reinking, but how many longest days can a
guy stand in one life?* Beer helped, luckily. Trying to force yourself
to relax is much like pouring into the wrong end of a funnel, but
sip by sip in the vaulted concrete room full of strangers' racket,
he took refuge in that sensation of a place where nobody knows
you're you. *Yet.*

He was on his second beer, and the Brits were going operatic
about how many balls Hitler, Goering, Himmler, and Goebbels
had in total, when Moxie joined him at the table, scowling toward
the piano crowd. "That pissant Noel Coward has a lot to answer
for, if you ask me—they all think they're him." He checked his
watch and slumped down into the chair opposite Ben.

"Here." Ben shoved across a bottle he had put aside for him.
"Beer is known to settle the nerves."

"Who said they need settling?" Well, thought Ben, the facial
tic, for one. Moxie in the old days had the nerves of a snake han-
dler. He was always the holder for point-after kicks, unfazed by
linemen half again his size hurtling at him as he delicately set the
ball in place for Vic Rennie's foot. He had commendations and
captain's bars to show for courage under those England years of
air raids. Now as he did quick damage to the beer and kept dart-
ing glances around the room, with a special dose of contempt for
the singing piano warriors, it was all too clear that what had been
Moxie's ornery bravado had turned into just ornery.

"Guess what, you're kind of grumpy, for a short-termer."
Ben's own mood was not one of his best. "What's eating you?"

"Short-termer," Moxie scoffed, "in an ass-backwards way.
I've been extended. But you know all about that from A to Why,
don't you."

The coldly spoken words sent a clammy sense of dread into
Ben. "Mox, slow down and talk sense, will you? I don't know a
rat's ass worth about you being extended."

Moxie studied him without so much as a blink. "Well, then,
let's just go over this, Ben old buddy." As usual, there was about
as much give in him as an ice pick. "The adjutant calls me in,
the first of the month. Says my new orders have just come in. I'm
standing there expecting the million-dollar handshake and the
plane home, and instead he tells me I've been extended indefinitely. Back I go, to the goddamn ack-ack and buzz bombs. Next
thing, you show up. You think I don't know when somebody
screws me over, Rhine King? Was it your own bright idea to get
me held until the Germans give up, so you can have your nice
story—the last of the team makes it to the end of the war? That
is just so shitty, Reinking, and I—"

Slamming a hand down on the table so hard the beer bottles
teetered, Ben put a period to Moxie's rush of words. "If anybody
is screwing you over, it's not me. I'm here because you were due
to get that handshake and a pat on the butt and be sent home,
goddamn it. If it was up to me, we'd both be out of here before I
finish this sentence." He was furious with Moxie and that mouth
of his like a cheap pistol, constantly ready to go off in any direction. "How'd you manage to mess it all up—smart off to that
adjutant? The general? Eisenhower himself?"

Moxie was sitting back out of the way of any more hand
forays. "Hey, not me. I've been keeping my nose clean, up the
ranks—no way did I want to queer that plane ride out of here."

With a mix of disgust and agitation he glanced around the cavernous bunker again. "I don't go for this living like a mole."

Tense as a harp, Ben took several strained seconds to decide he was on the level. Moxie had never smarted off to Bruno, even during the worst Letter Hill travesties of football practice. In the perfect season, game after game, the tougher the situation on the field, the more businesslike his quarterbacking became. It added up. In extreme cases—and Antwerp fit that, did it ever— the gambler side of Moxie Stamper was perversely capable of the oldest cardshark survival trick, win by not losing. "Okay, maybe it's not your doing. I'll—"

"Your pal Baldy," Moxie shot in. "Could be he knows what's up with this? One thing I learned around the Brits, it's hard as hell to tell when they're screwing you over."

"He's not—" Ben didn't pursue the issue of nationality. "I'll put it to him. If he doesn't have the goods about this, I know who does." He was half out of his chair before remembering Maurice was on catch-up shift somewhere performing what censors perform. And Maurice was his doorkeeper to the only other source, the wire room. "Tomorrow will have to do," he muttered as he sank back down. "Damn." Another set of hours with TPWP in touch only as a pain in the neck. *Time-out," right, you Tepee Weepy so-and-sos. Until when—the last goddamn buzz bomb is fired? Moxie will shrivel up so much by then he can be sent home in a matchbox. I won't be much of a specimen of humanity myself.*

Moxie was checking his watch again, and remembering Maurice's mild mention of an occasional V-1 straying to the airfield, Ben wondered if he should be setting the cocotte clock in his pocket. The weight of the war came down over him once more. "Mox, I'm going to have to get to the wire room early, so I'm calling it a day. I'll look you up tomorrow after—"

"Hang on a little while, can't you?" Moxie practically begged. "There's somebody I want you to—hey, all right, here she is."

An Army nurse, in off-duty khaki, was forging her way toward them through the packed tables. Busty and broad-beamed, she came with a fixed bedside smile on a square plain face.

Slick as a whistle, Moxie was on his feet and standing proud to greet her. "Hi, angel of mercy. This is my press agent I was telling you about," he allotted a foxy grin back and forth between Ben and her. "Ben Reinking, Inez Mazzetti." Moxie winked. "But that's all the *z*'s a guy ever catches around her, right, sugarpuss?"

"Knock it off, you," Inez gave him a tender swat on the arm. "Hi, Ben, gee, I'm glad to meet you." She kept the smile going as Moxie delivered her into a chair. "You can give me the lowdown on this Stamper guy—did he always have a vocabulary like a garbage can?"

"You should have heard him in football uniform—the Army has cleaned him up."

"Go right ahead," their subject of discussion grinned around at them again before embarking for the bar, "gossip about me while I'm hunting down beer for you, ingrates."

Left with no choice, they made small talk, Inez in a practiced way, Ben uncomfortably, until Moxie came back clasping bottles with both hands.

"To the oldest profession," he toasted as soon as he sat down, "nursing!" It drew him another little swat from Inez, smiling all the while.

Overflowing with possession, Moxie leaned toward Ben and divulged: "Inez is from Butte. Her old man worked with O'Fallon's in the mines. How's that for a small world?"

"Awful small," Ben vouched, hiding everything more than that behind a long swig of beer. *The damned odds again. Why can't the numbers just behave and quit giving out coincidences like card tricks?* In all likelihood he had crossed paths with that miner father at O'Fallon's wake, back at the start of all this. Back when one life subtracted from eleven was thought to be a lot.

In what passed for conversation from then on, Moxie kidded Inez as if he was playing with a kitten, and she all but purred in response. It would have been plain to a blind person, Ben summed it up to himself, that he was screwing her socks off at every opportunity. The undertow of desire lapping around the table made him want to wade away and flee to higher ground and at the same time dive in and let his imagination soak in it. He stayed helplessly there aswim in times with Cass. Cass curled beside him after making love in his hotel room . . . *I interrupted the greatest movie never made, didn't I.* Cass bright as her uniform buttons the giddy night in Seattle . . . *One of those that folds down out of the wall? Genius, what's to keep it from folding back up into the wall just when things get interesting?* Cass snuggling next to him in the shelter of the Hill 57 rocks, the Homecoming game losing their interest . . . *Do I have a better offer?*

"Hey, we're not hearing any fooling-around report out of you, Ben." Moxie was feeling better and better as the beer and the night went on. "Haven't you hooked up with anybody yet?"

Silence was no longer an option, with the two moony faces turned to him. "I did for a while. She's a," he swallowed hard, "a nurse, too—of a kind."

NINE TIME ZONES away, Jones was trying to make a readable press release out of East Base's announcement of another one thousand Lend-Lease aircraft successfully transported into Russian hands. He hummed a snatch of hymn when he was alone and bored, and he was humming now; there were six previous announcements of this sort and even he did not regard this as the freshest of news. He was trying to decide whether it was worth it to change *seven thousand* to *the seventh thousand* when he became aware someone had paused at the office doorway.

He glanced around, and for this officer rose nicely to his feet as he had been taught to do at home.

"Help you with something, Captain?"

"If you're feeling full of Christian charity," said Cass with a lump in her throat.

THE LIGHTS BLINKED in the Wonder Club bunker. The whole place went momentarily still, then the electricity steadied and the usual Officers' Club din of conversation came back with a rush of relief. One of the music-hall wits at the piano began to belt out, "I'll meet you at the Underground, you'll know it by the rumbly sound, and we will slip away, for a cozy day . . ."

"It's hard to get used to, the rocket SOBs see to that," Moxie addressed the tight look on Ben's face, his own expression more constrained than before. "That one must have hit near the power plant by the river. The night gunners have a tough time of it," he defended the ack-ack brotherhood, "they have to hope the searchlight crews get a fix on the goddamn buzz bomb before it cuts off." He shook his head and went back to, "It's hard."

"You know what, I'm going to go freshen up while there's light to see by," Inez said with practicality and headed for the toilet.

Moxie watched her wend her way. All at once he was talkative again. "Funny how things turn out. Back in high school, a carload of us would head into Butte to visit a cathouse and we wouldn't get parked before the Butte kids spotted the Dillon license plate and ganged up to beat the crap out of us. 'Come and get it, sheepherders!' they'd yell." He laughed, more bark than amusement in it. "And we would with our dukes up, and more often than not get our butts kicked good."

Ben knew Moxie was from a sheep ranch in the Dillon country, but he had not known he ever came out second in mouthing off. "That's Butte for you," he contributed, thinking back to the boisterous wake.

"And look at now, me and her—" Moxie held Ben in his gaze. "I know what you're thinking, I'm just using her for reconnaissance in the dark. But she keeps me sane, Ben. And she gets something out of it besides a good time in the sack." He leaned in to drive his point home. "Inez is not the greatest looker, unless you like them on the hefty side. But getting herself seen with me, and now you, gives her a lot of brownie points on this base. There are plenty of guys in this room right now you could shake awake in the middle of the night and they'd know how many touchdown passes I threw and how many you caught." He knocked wood. "Like it or don't, we're not nobodies. Even here."

No, that's been the trouble. Ben sat up to pursue that. "Listen, Mox. I found out something about Purcell—"

"Purcell? Haven't thought about him in years," Moxie was shaking his head, "dumb-ass kid." The head shake slowed into solemnity. "All the guys on the team. All the tickets to the marble farm," he said bitterly. "You know the one that really gets me?"

I'm afraid I do. Ben would have bet six months' wages he was about to hear a halo put on Danzer, courtesy of the Stomper-to-Dancer mutual admiration society.

"Jake." Moxie choked up on the name. "It is just a goddamn shame he didn't have the last laugh on the Nazi sonsofbitches."

Too much had welled up in Ben for him to say anything. Inez came to his rescue by returning, and he used the chance to exit the drawn-out day. He left the flirtatious pair with "Have fun, don't do anything I wouldn't do," and wove through the obstacle course of tables. He stepped outside to the long sunken row of concrete archways topped with more concrete and several acres of the sod of Belgium. It was starting to snow, the first natural thing he had found since arriving to Antwerp. He stood there a minute in the night gone quiet with the weight of snow as the storm came in off the Atlantic, general as the pattern of winter across the war-linked pair of continents and the cold ocean between, the hypnotic flakes accumulating as patiently as the passage of time.

18

⭐ THIS WAS A DRY snowfall that would not cling long, but Gros Ventre, which had not tasted paint since the war effort was born, appeared grateful for any fresh coating. Behind him he heard the grind of gears as the bus pulled away in the night to other towns too modestly populated to have a depot, a familiar accompaniment as he walked in so many years of his footsteps toward the newspaper office. The burden handed to him by the bus driver seemed heavier as the war went on, although he knew that was fanciful. Even so, carrying it in the new-fallen snow he took extra care, stomping every so often so his shoe soles would not cake up and grow slick. Shortly he came to the only other lighted enterprise on the whitened main street, two blocks up from where the *Gleaner* office cast its square of light. He thought to himself he really ought to write a piece about this, how in the ever-changing bargain with time one way-spot of civilization would offer up a cathedral while another would answer human yearning with something as homely as this, a place that could be counted on to be open in the snowy dark, a saloon like a book known by heart. What was the saying? Ancient faith and present courage. He smiled at himself a bit crookedly. Tonight he could stand a glass of courage.

"Haven't seen you in here in a hell of a while," he was greeted as he stepped into the Medicine Lodge. "I'd about given you up for lost."

"A man can't be in two places at once, Tom," Bill Reinking replied, slapping snow off his cap and coat. "I'm supposedly running a newspaper." *Or as Cloyce would say, it's running me.*

Toweling the dark wood to a trail of gleam as he came, Tom Harry mopped his way down the bar to him. "Liked what you said there in the gizette, back before the election. Franklin D. showed them his rosy red one again, didn't he." Beaming as if in response, Roosevelt presided larger than life on the whiskey-laden breakfront behind the bartender, the campaign poster accurately predicting FOUR MORE IN '44! Bill Reinking noted with bemusement that right next to it was pasted a faded placard spelling out, in the biggest letters to be found in a printer's jobcase, FORT PECK—DAMN! Momentarily he was taken back to before the war when those unlikely allies of the time, the President and the Senator, blessed into being the huge Fort Peck Dam and put Montana back to work. There was something to ponder there. Was it possible that the depths of the Depression, so daunting at the time, were no kind of a challenge compared to finding an end to this war? He knew the world was more complicated now, but he also knew that every era makes that excuse for tripping over itself.

Pulling himself away from that train of thought, he looked from Roosevelt and the exclamatory placard to Tom Harry as if giving the matter full consideration and said: "Politics is the art of turning ice into ice cream."

"I think maybe I read that in your paper one time," the bartender snorted. In practically that same gallop of breath, he came out with the essential: "What's the word from Ben?"

Bill touched the week's Threshold Press War Project bundle fresh off the bus. "I hope I'm about to find out."

"Then I suppose I ought to be getting you something to go with that," Tom Harry said as if they were both falling down on that duty. "What'll it be—you still drinking that scotch cough syrup?"

Looking longingly at the row of whiskey bottles with plaid pipers on them, Bill stayed resolute. "I have work to do tonight. Your glorified tap water, please."

"Turning unpredictable on me, are you." Tom Harry shook his head over serving a plain glass of beer, just as if the Medicine Lodge didn't practically run the stuff in its plumbing. Before he could step to the beer tap, a voice accented with Oslo or beyond quavered from the end of the bar:

"Mister 'tender! When you isn't busy, we gunna have some of t'ose jar weiners."

Bill's newspapering instinct of keeping track of things took a moment to put a name to the face of the latest keeper of sheep blowing six months of wages—Andy Gustafson, an old snoose chewer who herded for the Busby brothers on upper English Creek. Perched elbow to elbow with this splurger was another herder recognizable as practically a fixture in here, Canada Dan, sending down the bar an eager freeloading nod and a mostly toothless grin. Bill pursed back a smile. Some things you could count on.

"Catch the faithful, too," he capitulated, trickling more money onto the bar.

"You hear that, Gufferson, or something wrong with your ears?" Tom Harry called out, heavy with hint.

"Yah, t'anks!"

"Here's to lookin' bad and feelin' good, mister!" Canada Dan mistily chimed out.

"I should've been a milkman instead of a bartender," Tom Harry groused as he drew Bill's beer before moving on to the jar of whatever preservative the Vienna sausages swam in. "I'd only have to look at one horse's ass at a time."

Left in peace as Tom Harry marched on the other end of the bar, Bill took out his jackknife and carefully slit the bundle along one side. He turned up his nose as usual at the hefty halves of boilerplate that were the bulk of the parcel. For an honest editor, patriotism that simply bolted onto the printing press was not true news and he never used the ready-made stuff. Reaching into the middle, he slipped out the packet of TPWP handouts and skimmed, head poised at bifocals angle, until he found the words SUPREME TEAM.

He froze at the next word that caught his eye: *Jake.*

In a sick trance he began to read Ben's piece. When he was finished, he sat looking past himself in the dark mirroring of the saloon front window. This was Cloyce's canasta night. Jake Eisman had been her favorite of Ben's friends from the team. He would have to tell her when she came home, it would be no mercy for her to read it first when the paper came out tomorrow. He himself had the helpless feeling of time rounding on itself and unleashing the same bad news again. As a punk kid reporter in 1917 and '18, underage for military service, he had written obituary after obituary of the same sort as the so-called war to end all wars drained a generation of lifeblood out of Montana. About like this one.

"Well?" Gruffness serving as apology, Tom Harry disturbed both past and present.

"A deep subject, Tom." Bill resorted to his beer, a very long swallow, to gain time to compose himself somewhat. "What's on your mind now?"

"Well, do you need the goddamn Packard for anything?" The bartender sounded shy and grumpy at the same time. "You look like the dog ate your supper, and so I just wondered if the car and some gas rations would help you out any." Tom Harry bunched his shoulders. "Take the wife Christmas shopping in Great Falls or some damn thing—how do I know what you're supposed to do in maddermoany, I never been in front of any preacher."

Bill Reinking dispensed some more money onto the bar and indicated another round for the hopeful denizens at the far end. "Thanks for the offer, Tom, you're a prince among publicans." Rising to go, he hefted the bundle as if it had grown heavier since he came in. "But I have business to tend to at the word shop."

19

★ *ALL RIGHT, REINKING, think, damn it, think. Since you can't get your hands on the neck of that colonel or whatever other Tepee Weepy creep is screwing us over—Moxie is right about that much—you have to twist this the other direction somehow. Don't pitch a fit, won't do any good—they've got cast-iron butts in Washington, they can sit on our orders home until they're good and ready. Let's just try the old innocent start-the-show approach and see if that reminds them to be human beings.*

"As you see, Ben, the ticker room is quite the odd collection, your lot and ours squidged together rather like strangers on a trolley." In the bunkerful of teletypes and other message apparatus where Maurice was showing him around, the British uniforms of blue hue offsetting the khaki drab of American clerks did resemble a rush-hour swatch of contrasts. "I suppose the miracle is that it works at all," he gestured broadly, "separated as we are by a common language."

Ordinarily Ben's smile nerves would have twitched at that, but not today. "So how do I send smoke signals to Tepee Weepy, with everyone in here busy running the war?"

"Right. I've secured you a ticker, where you have utmost priority—that set of orders that follows you around, Ben, is quite magical—"

Sure, except when Tepee Weepy uses it as black magic and extends Moxie and leaves the pair of us dangling in the buzz-bomb capital of the world.

"—and I have authority to snaffle a clerk for you as wanted." Maurice meditatively tweaked his ball-shaped nose as if turning the knob for the next idea. "I thought perhaps a glamour-pants WREN, to add scenery to duty? The Women's Royal Naval Service has some lovelies bored with typing weather reports."

Ben could readily imagine that seersucker was not the only shapely uniform that sopped up carbon paper, and that an eye-batting invitation to join a scrub in the tub was not unheard of here, either. If Moxie and Inez were any indication, life under buzz-bomb siege tended to concentrate minds, downward. But the object of desire he needed to concentrate on was the earliest possible plane out of here. "No go, Maurice, thanks anyway," he committed to. "No WRENs or sparrows or cuckoos or anything else except a wire clerk in an American uniform that I outrank all to hell."

Maurice felt at his nose again, pondering. "It shall be done. Have yourself a cup of mystery beverage"—the lore was that when the Antwerp commanding officer tasted what was in the hot-pot urn over in the corner, he sputtered, "If this is coffee, bring me tea. If this is tea, bring me coffee."—"while I sort out a clerk of that mode."

Claiming a spot at a momentarily vacant desk, Ben took gulps of the stuff, figuring it went with Antwerp hardship duty, while he labored over a message pad. He crumpled several versions before the penciled words had the right nudge to them. When Maurice turned up with a bewildered U.S. Army private first class in tow, Ben barely caught his name before handing him the message to be sent.

READY AT THIS END. STAMPER WAITING ROYAL
TREATMENT. SOONER BETTER, SOONEST BEST—THIS IS
HOME FIELD OF BUZZ BOMBS.

The wire clerk, with prodigious eyeglasses and eyes almost
as large behind them, scrutinized the lines. "Sir, I'm supposed to
put it into code. Did you want to do this in plain English first, so
the other end won't misunderstand what—"

Ben hung a look on him that answered that. "Right away, sir,"
said the clerk, his rear end practically scorching the seat as he sat
to the wire machine. "The two of you seem as happy together as
a box of birds," Maurice said blandly, "so I shall leave you to this."

TPWP's reply clattered out in a surprisingly short time.

TIME-OUT NOT OVER YET IN HOMECOMING GAME. WORTH
THE WAIT.

Two quick darts of Ben's pencil and he held the message pad
over the keyboard. The clerk started to ask where the rest of it
was, encountered the just-send-it look again, and fired off:

Y?

This time the response from across the ocean came in a long
salvo of clacking keys.

YOU SOUND ITCHY TO BREAK HUDDLE, SO HERE IS
GAME PLAN. STAMPER BLAZE OF GLORY SCHEDULED FOR
USO HOLIDAY SHOW DURING TEN DAYS OF CHRISTMAS
TOUR, LONDON, PARIS, ETC. ANTWERP SHOW FIRST IN
LINE. FULL CHEERING SECTION FOR END OF SUPREME
TEAM SAGA—NATIONWIDE BROADCAST STATESIDE,
"YOUR USO ON THE GO" NEWSREEL, TED LOUDON
IN PERSON TO DEVOTE ENTIRE "SPORTS REPORT" TO
STAMPER AND—

It sunk in to Ben like a stab that kept on penetrating. Tepee
Weepy and Loudon. The unholy pair that manufactured the Su-

preme Team in the first place. Now an entire week of hanging around with the buzz bombs, just so Loudon could mouth off nationally, hell, internationally about—

"Break in, quick," he instructed the wire operator while frantically scrawling. The young soldier apprehensively but bravely looked up from the message. "'Loudmouth,' sir?"

"Sorry, that got away from me." Ben grabbed back the paper, cursing and fixing the name at the same time. Off the message went.

CAN'T WE DO THAT STATESIDE, AT TSU STADIUM
FOR INSTANCE, SITE OF INITIAL GLORY, ETC.? LOUDON
NOT A HABITUE OF EUROPE NORMALLY.

There was a pause, giving Ben some faint hope that logic might register on TPWP. Then:

NEGATIVE. LOUDON TO USE ANTWERP OCCASION
TO ANNOUNCE THAT THE TREASURE STATE GOLDEN
EAGLES OF 1941—'ELEVEN MEN AS BRAVE ON THE
ULTIMATE FIELD OF BATTLE AS ON THE GRIDIRON'—ARE
HIS ALL-AMERICAN TEAM FOR 1944, IN MEMORIAM.
YOU AND STAMPER WILL BE HIGHLIGHTED AS THE
SURVIVING TEAMMATES, THUS PRESENCE IN ANTWERP
MANDATORY UNTIL AFTER USO SHOW.

Ben could not take his eyes off the words. *You goddamn grandstander, Loudmouth. You never miss a chance to pluck the patriotic harp, do you. All-dead is closer to the truth.* Maximum urges contended in him, to sink into a corner laughing insanely or take a kicking fit against the TPWP wire machine. The owl-eyed clerk watched him skittishly.

Pulling himself together, more or less, he gripped the pencil and pad, and with concentration as slow and forced as a grade-schooler's put into block letters the next message.

> STAMPER COMING DOWN WITH NERVOUS IN THE
> SERVICE. SUGGEST IMMEDIATE LEAVE TO TIDE HIM
> OVER UNTIL USO SHOW. IF HE CRACKS UP, LORD HAW-
> HAW WILL HAVE PLENTY TO HEE-HEE ABOUT.

Parsing it to himself, he added, sardonically wondering if he had better get a rubber stamp of it made: SOONEST BEST.
Tepee Weepy got the message in more ways than one.

> SOON IS BEST THAT CAN BE DONE THROUGH
> ANTWERP HQ CHANNELS, BUT WILL HAVE STAMPER
> PULLED FROM ACK-ACK DUTY, DON'T WORRY.

The teletype machine fell silent for all of ten seconds or so, then burped back into action.

> NOW TO BUSINESS AS USUAL: EXPECTING
> THOUSAND-WORD PIECE, CLASSIC REINKING STYLE
> OF SHINE AND SHADOW, ON LIFE IN COMBAT ZONE
> 'SOMEWHERE IN EUROPE.'

"HAVE YOU GONE out of your gourd, Ben? They're supposed to give me leave here in a combat zone?" That evening in the Wonder Bar, Moxie was so incredulous he was neglecting his beer. "I'll believe that the day after it happens."

"Fine," Ben said tiredly. "You can test your faith when the general calls you in, first thing tomorrow. Maurice set it up." He started his bottle to his lips, then thought to check on Moxie's facial tic. It was active. *Good, that'll help.* "By the way, I had to make you out to be the next thing to a nutcase. So if people look at you a certain way, that's why."

Moxie laughed, short and sharp. "Rhine King, you never did think I threw you the ball enough."

THEY HAD TO KILL seven days waiting for the USO show, every one of those a blank-walled twenty-four hours of tedium with a concrete lid on it. It did not help that they both thought their underground quarters smelled like Montana earthen cellars where potatoes and rutabagas were stored. Moxie, restless as a sidewinder even in the best of times, had a particularly hard time with enforced leisure. "If I wanted to be caged up, I'd have been born a goddamn canary." Growly and still ticcing, he devoted himself to reading Philo Vance mysteries during the day and romancing Inez in the Wonder Bar at night.

For his part, Ben prowled the bunker maze of the base with a simmering case of deadline fever, searching for some way to write about Antwerp's deluges of death from the sky without ever mentioning buzz bombs. "What if," he tried out on Maurice Overby, "I just say it's a mystery weapon the Germans call a *Vergeltungswaffe*?"

"Rather a nice try, Ben, but I'm afraid not," came the prim response. "There are without doubt some among your American readership familiar enough with the German language to connect '*waffe*' to '*Luftwaffe*' and draw the pertinent conclusion, wouldn't you say? No, I realize it's a hard go, but HQ requires that you keep whatever you write about Antwerp"—the squarely-planted censor gestured off generally—"general."

Great, Maurice. I can just say Antwerp has an unusual share of funerals, can I? You should work for Tepee Weepy.

When he grew tired of beating his head against a story he was not allowed to tell, he holed up in the windowless concrete room with the scent of root cellar and made tiny editing changes in the *Ghost Runner* screenplay, aware all the while how geographically ridiculous it was to be conjuring the Letter Hill in waffle-flat Belgium. All in all, distance maybe lent something, but it did not smell like enchantment. And when he ran out of things to fuss

at in the script, he emulated Moxie and read, napped, brooded
some more about the piece that couldn't say anything. All the
while, the clock slowed to eternal Old World time. Another day
in the war. What was the count up to by now?

He was marking the fourth day of the wait by reading a
much-passed-around news magazine that grandly speculated
the war could be over by Christmas—*Yeah, right, has anybody
told the Germans?*—when Maurice rapped on the doorway in a
grand announcing fashion. "A communiqué for you, in the priority packet." He held up the envelope by the tip of one corner.
"Inasmuch as it's addressed in a feminine hand, I thought it wise
to deliver it forthwith."

Eyes widening, Ben reached out for the letter. Maurice coughed
discreetly. "I shall leave you to it. See you in the dining hall."

Dear Ben, wherever you are, Scar—

Already Cass's words had him aching for her. Quickly he
turned the letter to take in a line written sideways along the margin near the top:

Your Holy Joe corporal looked like I was about to set
his Bible on fire, but he took pity and said he could sneak
this to you somehow.

Bedazzled as a kid with a kaleidoscope, he spun the full page
of inked lines back into reading position.

This set of scribbles may surprise you as much as it does
me. But I can't hold back—I've been writing this in my head
for days on end and the only cure is to put it on paper. So
here goes. Remember we used to talk about the million-
dollar wound?

He remembered in all ways. The heart never forgets anything; the flesh remembers indiscriminately.

There were all those times I caught myself wishing you'd get a tiny one—just another scar—and be out of the war for good. But if Dan's is any indication, the price is awful damn high. I take him over to Fort Hairy once a week for the bone doc to test how his leg is coming along, and he hates that routine. He's on crutches in between—he hates that, too. Sometime after the first of the year, they'll ship him to the specialist who'll patch that tendon in and then all the time in rehab, as they call it.

We go around and around about whether I stay with him in California for all that. I say of course I will. He says like hell I will, he can be a cripple just the same without me around, go do something useful with myself. In some odd way I think he wants to be with other Montaneer guys— you know what a bloody mess Leyte has turned out to be, bunches of the worst wounded from his regiment are ending up there in San Diego—more than with me. I'm not crying on your shoulder, Ben, I just needed to tell somebody who knows up from down when it comes to a man and a woman.

Enough of that. This is the last time you'll ever hear from Capt. Standish—

His eyes misted instantly at that.

—in WASP uniform. They're inactivating us the middle of the month—happy holidays, P-39 birdwomen, huh?—and the squadron will scatter to the winds. Mary Cat is going into schoolteaching. Della has her hooks into a major in ops, and he's gaga enough she'll probably get him to marry her. I have my hands full with Dan, but I've been wondering whether to try to get on with the Forest Service after a while, flying smoke patrol. It'll be the same old thing, though, will they hire a woman pilot?

Maybe it'll all sort out okay after the war. But that's too far away to think about.

He pinched the bridge of skin between his eyes waiting for
the worst of the thought to pass: if there is an *after*. Then he
blinked back into reading the last of the letter.

> I suppose I could tell you I miss you something
> awful. But too much truth is maybe not a good idea,
> given the situation. You are always going to be a
> part of me, despite the gold string on my finger that
> ties me to Dan. I couldn't Dear John him while he
> was out in the Pacific, and I can't do it to you while
> you're over there. I think of you more than is healthy,
> and I just want you to know I regret not one damn thing
> of our time together.
>   It is getting late, and it's snowing like sixty—the O
> Club windowsills look like igloo territory—and I have to
> get back to the apartment. Now all this is off my chest—no
> wisecrack about that sort of thing, you—and on its way to
> wherever you've ended up. Take care, Ben—I don't need
> another hole in my life.
>
>   Hugs and tickles,
>   Cass

Back and forth, he walked the narrow confines of bunker
room, holding the letter as if memorizing it. For all his skills at
what was said between the lines, supposition resisted him here
as he read the sentences over and over.

In her feisty Cass way she wished him well, and maybe cast
a major wish beyond that, but nothing under the ink had really
changed, had it?

There still was Dan Standish.

There still was the war.

And the creeping shadow of fear, always there, that oblivion
was not through with the Supreme Team yet.

Even so, he felt distinctly better about life with lines from Cass in his hand even if they led to nowhere.

He figured he must be misunderstanding something.

IN THE DINING bunker he found Maurice poking a fork at chipped beef on overtoasted toast. By a grave misjudgment of joint command, the British had been put in charge of the food and the Americans in charge of the beer. "Saved you a spot," Maurice indicated across the table, "although you may not thank me when you taste this. No bad news from home, I hope, arriving in the fashion it did?"

"Good enough. No news would have been bad news." With the ghost of a grin Ben let the allusion hang in the direction of his host and censor.

"Ah, well, spoken like a journalist. Other than that," Maurice took a sip of tea or coffee, whichever it was, "still passing the time working on the hemstitch of your straitjacket?"

"You nailed it, Maurice," Ben responded with his first outright laugh in days. He couldn't help it, he liked the company of this man who talked as some people sing.

"I do have some allowable news, just between thee and me and the cocotte clock," Maurice brought out. "Intelligence estimates, to flatter them with that, indicate the Huns may be giving up on buzz bombs. It has been most of a week since that last batch. And no matter how many they've sent, they haven't managed to cripple the port at all. Hitler's rocket men may be out of business for lack of results—the German high command putting all that fuel into keeping the rest of its military machine alive, the thinking is."

"The lights aren't blinking and the ground isn't shaking," Ben said gratefully, "so I hoped something like that was happening."

"Absence of anything in the air at the moment may be the

intelligence wizards' full evidence too," Maurice offered his own airy speculation. "We shall have to see." Furrowing his brow and on up into the bald outskirts, he stated: "I have been thinking. As things now stand, it might be possible to get out and about a bit, if that would help with your TPWP matter?"

Ben tossed his fork into the gluey meal, ready to go that minute. "Christ, yes. It'd put legs under the piece."

"We need to be quite cautious," came the voice of prudence across the table. "But the Antwerp outskirts have been less dangerous than the city proper. If there's an all clear in the morning, we might judiciously explore some area of interest to you." Maurice sent him an inquiring look. "Ben, I have forgotten to ask— which are you, bars-and-brothels or castles-and-cathedrals?"

On the spot, he thought it over. "Somewhere between."

"Wise choice. All horizons kept open, that way," the man from Nowhere spelled backwards declaimed, bouncing it word by word. "I should leave to you any excursions in the direction of sin, however, personal taste and all that. What would please you in the other direction?"

"What I really want," Ben was somewhat surprised to hear himself say, "is to go to Waterloo."

20

⭐ THE NEXT DAY the two of them set off as soon as there was light enough to see by, before the fog was up. The stonework of Antwerp receded behind them in the thin winter dawn as the jeep passed through the successive belts of anti-aircraft gun pits, the ack-ack suburbs, and then out onto the main road in company with the around-the-clock line of trucks from the port. Squeezed in between the big six-wheeled cargo carriers, Maurice steered with the patience of a man whose reward was coming. "There are farm roads once we're out a ways—those will swing us around Brussels and this clot of lorries." He patted the plasticine map case atop his briefcase. "You're the navigator."

Before long Ben spotted the first of the rural roads and they turned off into a landscape white and quiet. Low ruined houses and sheds stood skeletal every little distance, and even the few farms that the war had not ravaged sat empty in a spectral way. Wrapped in his horse-blanket overcoat and glad of it, Ben blew on his writing hand whenever he jotted in his notepad. As the stark farmyards went by, he noticed there were no animals in the fields and then caught up with why—all had been eaten during Belgium's starving years of Nazi occupation, including the horses.

The graying snow on the farmyards and fields like a table-cloth on an abandoned empty table, they drove on into the flat midland of Belgium. In that world with all the noise smothered out of it, he and Maurice could talk comfortably. Moxie had told him they were goofy for going out on this. "You haven't seen enough battlefields to last you for one lifetime, Rhine King?" Not enough ones gone quiet. "I don't know if these are the same roads Wellington and Napoleon had," Ben remarked as he pointed out the next turnoff, "but you're sure as hell making better time than they did." Maurice handled the jeep as if captaining a yacht, swinging wide on the curves and making up for it with unfurled speed on the straight stretches.

"Ah, well," the figure presiding at the wheel said loftily, "one likes to get there in timely fashion, forth and back."

Not for the first time in honor of the New Zealander's locutions, Ben chuckled. "Is that a Southern Hemisphere way of looking at things, like the bathtub draining the opposite direction?"

"Hmm? Not at all, it's simple logic. One cannot, Ben, go *back* before one goes *forth*, therefore—"

Ben pursed a smile. "Spoken like a professor of argumentation."

"We shall see how I am as a battlefield muse." Maurice patted the attaché case between them. "*The Trekker's Guidebook to the Historic Battle at Waterloo.* Gift from my father, right off, when he learned I'd been posted to Belgium."

"He sounds about like mine," Ben mused. "Spends his nights in history up to his ears."

"Up to his rifle shoulder, in my father's case," came the response to that. Ben glanced over, sensing why it was put that way.

Maurice stayed staring straight ahead over the steering wheel as he spoke, the words suddenly less clipped. "Reads all the military history he can, the old fellow, says he's going to keep on until he finds the one that gets it right. He was at Gallipoli, in the first big go. Caught fragments from a Turk grenade in that shoulder, invalided home by Christmas of 1915. He never afterward could lift that arm enough to comb his hair. Mum has combed it for him for thirty years." A light of remembering, distant and wintry, had come into his eyes. "Even so, he counted himself one of the lucky ones. Some ten thousand New Zealanders and Australians did not make it home from that beachhead, ever." He paused. "My British colleagues can cite chapter and verse about their 'lost generation' in the trenches here, but they shrug off Gallipoli. As though there were a different set of numbers for those of us in the colonies." Breaking his spell of recital, Maurice sent a considerate look to Ben. "But why am I carrying on to you about unjust numbers? Sorry about that."

They drove on in silence, in the white iron winter over the northern half of the world.

THE SNOW GLARE on the buttes against the clear morning sky lent Great Falls a rim of dazzling ivory. *Wouldn't you just damn know. Perfect flying weather and we're grounded for eternity.*

Signing her way through last-minute paperwork, Cass every so often sent a pining look out the ready-room window. Around her, her pilots restlessly filled the wait as best they could, some jokes, some bitten lips to clamp emotion away. Taking extreme care not to show it, she herself was having to fight a case of trembles. So enormously much that was ending today. Everything else that was not. She had survived the war, the P-39, the P-63. Now to survive the situation with Dan. He was a bear some days—a lot of days—in the recuperation that sometimes he did not even seem to want. Other times, his old carnie self came through, he was full of plans, the old notion of barnstorming, flying, wingwalking. She was not sure wingwalking had survived the war.

And when I'm not sure, I start dreaming about Ben, don't I. If wishes were fishes, I'd be Jonah.

One more time, Cass strung herself together. She glanced at the clock next to the flight board, coming onto the hour. "All right, officers, let's get outside and form up."

The eleven women lined up in three ranks at the edge of the long runway. They were in Sunday uniform, white shirt, tan slacks—except for the leather flight jackets worn against the Montana cold, the same dress uniform each of them had worn at graduation from pilot school in Texas, hundreds of flying hours ago. Deep-creased crush hats crowned manes of hair; Cass could have picked every member of her squadron out of a thousand by the way the hat sat. She inspected them one last time as they stood at attention.

"Della, half step right. M.C., half step left. That's Beryl's spot between you."

With a deep breath she gave the command, and the squadron marched along the flight line to the hangar where the inactivation ceremony would be held.

Work on the unpainted bombers and P-63s stilled for a moment as the women mechanics in hairnets and overalls looked around from the wings and platform ladders they stood on, to the WASPs crisply saluting the waiting general. The gathering was not large. A perfunctory honor guard, rifles at rest and flag drooping in the still air of the hangar. The fresh-faced Canadian liaison officer, down from Edmonton for the occasion. Jones with a Speed Graphic camera, blazing away with flashbulb after flashbulb; he had worshipfully let Cass know there would be a set of photographs for each pilot.

The general at the portable podium his aide had set up shuffled his papers as if this were one more chore, glanced up at Cass as if she were personally responsible for his being saddled with Grady's Ladies all this while, and gruffly began.

Standing at attention determined to show him not so much as a quiver, she wondered if there would have been a ceremony at

all if the general hadn't had to read out the special letter of commendation—*the renowned flying women of East Base . . . service
above and beyond the call of duty*—from the Senator.

RISING FROM HIS chair like a gallant of old, the Senator came
around the table and delivered a forehead kiss to his wife as
she settled in her seat. "Good morning, Sadie, light of my life."
He stayed standing, looking out the lead-paned windows of the
breakfast nook at most of a week's worth of lazy flakes still descending on Washington like tired confetti. "Isn't this town the
damnedest place? It doesn't even know how to have a proper
blizzard."

His wife helped herself to what little coffee he had left for her
in the pot. "I hope, Luther, you aren't going to put yourself in
charge of the weather next."

"Not hardly," he drawled. "The Pentagon no doubt will be
enough of a snow job, as our daughter the sailor would say." Despite his words, his wife knew he was relishing this lame-duck
session of Congress, inasmuch as he was preeminently of the opposite species. The war having spawned so many military bases
in the western states, the region at last was in line to seat a formidable old cuss of its own in the main chair of the committee
that held the purse strings in such matters, now that the vener-
able chairman had retired to his peach farm. With his whopping
reelection, the Senator fit the bill and he intended to fill it. His
plateside reading these mornings was a tome titled *Bureaucracies
and Their Foibles*.

Her busy day of holiday chores on her mind with Christmas
coming fast, his wife somewhat absently waited for him to pull
out his dollar watch, his signal of leaving for the Capitol. Today
he made a show of consulting its Roman numerals, but a govern-
ing instinct of a murkier sort had taken hold of him as it sometimes did. "First thing, I need to futz around in the mail room

a little." His wife made a face as he left the table; she didn't like
futz.

Nor the mail room, for that matter. She never set foot into the
alcove library where he felt most at home in the otherwise wom-
anized house. And the colored maid was not let in the room, not
since the time she tidied by stacking everything together. With
the satisfaction of familiarity the Senator again gazed around
at the musty bookshelves, the favorite framed *Chicago Tribune*
political cartoon showing him as a bowlegged wrangler roping
a runaway bull with the head and face of President Franklin D.
Roosevelt, and last and most comforting of all, the outmoded
military trestle tables waiting with seven batches of newspapers,
eight to a pile. The weeklies from all fifty-six Montana counties, right here in the Potomac swampland ready for his perusal
whenever the spirit moved him. Of all the senatorial perquisites
there were, this one especially tickled him. He knew his staff
drew straws to see which of them, at the dawn of each week,
would have to take a taxi down from the Hill with the bulging
mailbag of newspapers and lay them out in prescribed order, and
the fact that they despised the chore only made him snort to
himself in amusement. Montana was big as hell and just as tricky
to represent, and he long since had figured out that having the
local view of things fetched into this room for him beat trying to
chase down the moods of constituents across a six-hundred-mile
swath of earth.

Actually, there was more to it than that. In dismal bunk-
houses and drafty line cabins when the century and he were
unconquerably young, this gaunt old bone-sprung prairie Cae-
sar had read his way up in the world via weekly compilations of
community happenings just such as these; somehow even then
he savvied more than was on the page, and the Faustian skills
of small-town editors—recording angel one paragraph, gossip-
monger the next—he had been careful to reckon with ever since.

If nothing else, it appealed to him as cheap insurance for a man in his position. He could see no sign in the insane modern world that the pen was mightier than the sword, but it was damn sure stronger than most campaign speeches.

As he worked through this day's stack of newsprint about livestock prices and the latest run of bad weather, he checked his watch again. The new power that was coming to him with the gavel of the committee needed judicious exercise in the halls of the Senate and he had to allow time for that. He at last was in a position to do something about alphabet-soup wartime projects that did not point straight to victory and he was not going to waste—

The bold line of type caught his eye as he was paging through the *Gros Ventre Gleaner*.

THOSE WHO GAVE ALL.

At these words something occurred, like a catch of breath but much deeper, in the hardened Senator. He blinked and looked again. He had not seen that heading since World War One. His kid brother had been one of those listed then, mortally wounded in a barrage at Château-Thierry in 1918.

Staring, he bent closer over the column of names of young ones grown to military age in the quarter century since.

> Adamic, Stefan, killed in action in New Guinea.
> Baker, Raymond, died in military hospital of wounds suffered in the Anzio invasion.
> Cooper, Samuel, sailor on the USS *Yorktown*, missing in action.
> Copenhaver, Theodore, killed in plane crash during training at Sweetwater, Texas.
> Crosby, Vern, killed in action at Leyte . . .

With a chill he ran his finger on down and down the alphabet of death. *Godalmighty, that many? In one county? A county—*

and an editor—he thought he knew like the back of his hand. In their span of political alliances of convenience he considered Bill Reinking a bit soft on Roosevelt, but rock solid other than that. The list broke at the bottom of the newspaper column, and started anew at top of the next.

> McCaskill, Alex, killed in strafing attack in Tunisia.
> Peterson, Morton, died as prisoner of war in Bataan death march.
> Petrie, Laura Ann, Army nurse, killed by artillery barrage behind the lines at the battle for Avranches.
> Quigg, James, shot down over Germany, missing in action.
> Rennie, Victor, died in England during a bombing raid . . .

He felt as if he was reading something direly biblical. Old family names of the Two Medicine country, the soul of the state. Heavy loss in more ways than one, and the *Gleaner* editor must have been driven to do this by its unavoidable weight.

The Senator rubbed his long jaw and rapidly riffled through the rest of the weeklies in that stack. The *Choteau Acantha* also listed its county's war dead, as did the *Lewistown Argus,* the *Sidney Herald,* the *Dillon Herald-Examiner.* He hesitated, then started going through the next batch of newspapers from the eastern part of the state. Lists of the war dead showed up in several of the papers from there too, so whatever Bill Reinking had caught was still breaking out elsewhere.

Something else, too. Like father, like son. The Senator went back and counted. Of the sixteen weeklies in the two batches, nearly all had run Ben Reinking's story on the last flight of the Supreme Team's ninth man, Lieutenant Jacob Eisman.

The Senator stalked out to the telephone on the hallway stand and dialed as if incising the numbers.

"Mullen, get me the goddamn figures on how many Montana soldiers have been killed in this war. And then compared to the other states."

AS THE GENERAL finished up and presented the Senator's letter to Cass, his aide stood ready with the bright-colored service ribbons for her to pin on the chests of her pilots. She hoped her hands would be steady enough; she set her mind to making them steady enough. The women mechanics on the wings of all the planes stood watching now. Someone started it by clanging one wrench against another, and then the others began banging their tools, the thunderous metallic applause filling the East Base hangar and rolling out to the glistening buttes.

THE HILL, WHITE and pyramidal and alone of its kind in the spongy Belgian countryside ahead, sent a chill through Ben as the jeep wheeled through the village of Waterloo to the actual battlefield. When he hastily checked, Maurice's guidebook described the area as gentle farmland when the armies of Europe massed there on a midsummer day in 1815, and the out-of-place hill, so artificially perfect in contour, as a mound of earth built to honor one of Wellington's Dutch generals, the Prince of Orange, wounded in the battle but of the kind he could heroically write home about that night. Ben already was jotting—*the Butte du Lion, name piled on it as sod was heaped in homage to a royal wound*—when Maurice proposed as if on cue: "What do you say we take the high ground, Ben? If glory does not await us there, luncheon does."

From up there, the winter rumple of the land for a few miles around was hard to read as history written in blood. Not much had been made of the battlefield. A modest museum across the road from the mound, not yet back in business since the Germans pulled out. A plaque there on the hilltop diagramming the battle, and a colossal cast-iron lion on a pedestal, supposedly emblematic of the Prince's courage, gazing implacably over the sleeping landscape. Otherwise, the mildly rolling plain of Waterloo looked unaltered since the sea gave it to the land. Yet down at the bottom of the manufactured hill lay the otherwise insignificant low ridge, the Duke of Wellington's high ground, where Napoleon's legions battered themselves to death in charge after charge. Ben measured off a mile with his eye, then another, then a third; incongruous as it seemed, that bit of countryside scarcely big enough to pasture a restless band of sheep had held the army of France, Britain's and armies of other nations scared stiff of Napoleon remaking the map of Europe, and thirty thousand cavalry horses. The only surly aspect at the moment was the weather, low-rolling clouds starting to spit snowflakes, and the forest near Waterloo village that had stood out dark against the snow when they arrived now was gowned in fog. Maurice had brought a thermos of hot drink—it was actually identifiable as tea—and they munched twists of bully beef and squares of chocolate along with it as they deciphered the battle site from the *Trekker's* guide. Then Ben began to write in the notepad and Maurice circled the tight top of the mound clicking photographs to send home to New Zealand.

When the chill began to get to both of them, Maurice at the other end of the lion's parapet sent Ben a look that politely inquired whether he about had enough for his TPWP piece. He did. The notepad held nugget phrases he could refine in the typewriter tonight. Belgium as the unwilling crossroads marched over by contending armies so many times, Waterloo as the sole crossroads in Belgium that counted on a reddened day four generations of soldiers ago. A high-ranking officer on Wellington's general staff who had a mania for resorting to rockets, buzz bombs of the day, although he would have to somehow get that across between the lines. The nearly permanent battlefield dateline, *Somewhere in Europe,* in 1815 here amid fields of Belgian corn and rye, at the moment in the forest and genuine uplands of the Ardennes on the border of Germany. That was part of the hell of war, you could so readily trace it from the past to now in an undiminished bloodline.

"I've had enough if you have," he called across the mound top to Maurice and they descended the steps of the hill to begin the journey back to Antwerp.

No sooner were they on the road along the foggy forest than the jeep popped around a corner near where a telephone line crossed and on the roadside just ahead were three American GIs, surprise all over them, arrayed at the closest pole. The pair in pole-climbing gear were about halfway up while the third one, carrying a rifle, stood guard.

"Minions of your Alexander Graham Bell at Waterloo," Maurice remarked, "what next?" He and Ben saw the guard call up to the others, then wave urgently for the jeep to stop.

As they pulled to a halt, the GI on guard stepped in close to the jeep and saluted. His winterweight field jacket and olive drab pants showing the grime of duty, his tone carried customary soldierly complaint. "Sure glad to see you, officers, isn't this weather crappy? They"—the universal infantryman's code for those in charge—"dropped us here to fix the line. Can you give us a lift, to catch up with the other fellows?"

"Willingly," said Maurice, elegantly courteous beyond what the soldier seemed to have expected. Ben looked at the reddened hands clutching the rifle. He chipped in some down-to-earth sympathy over standing around in the snow guarding Signal Corps handymen. "They've got you riding shotgun on the spool crew, have they. That can't be fun. Who's going to be around here except tourists like us?"

The soldier, no youngster, glanced around nervously. "Sir, looking out for infiltrators. Strict instructions, sir."

Maurice lifted an eyebrow skeptically. "This far from the front? That would be ambitious of the Huns." Overhead, Ben could see the pair of linemen feverishly squirreling into work position at the top of the pole, apparently eager for the jeep ride. The one leaning back in his climbing belt at the top said something to the lower one, who fumbled in the tool bag at his waist to hand up a set of wire pliers. It occurred to Ben, under the circumstances, to make conversation with the soldier at the side of the jeep. "What did you think of the Army-Navy game?"

"Army beat them good, hah?" the GI responded appreciatively. "Twenty-three to seven, right, sir?"

"Navy never stood a chance against guys who can run the ball like Pilchard and Travis," Ben offered his analysis. Drumming his fingers on the steering wheel during this football talk, Maurice looked over at him with abstract curiosity. Ben breezed on, "I didn't get to hear the game, so I missed out on the details— who got the touchdowns?"

The soldier worked at remembering. "Pilchard and Travis had one each, I think, sir."

Ben reached casually to his side and pulled out the .45 pistol. "It's Blanchard and Davis, *kamerad*." Then shot the man in the shoulder before he could yank the rifle up into action.

With that one crying out in German as he writhed on the ground, Ben for good measure fired a couple of shots up at the phone-line saboteurs. One hurled the tool bag and hit the hood of the jeep as Maurice jammed into reverse, while the other sought the skinny shelter of the pole as he tried to pull a pistol from the unfamiliar American holster with a flap. The jeep careening backward was well out of range down the road, when Maurice swung it around and tromped on the accelerator.

As the jeep roared its way back to the main road, they could already see a confusion of American and British military traffic ahead, armored vehicles streaming toward the German breakthrough on the Ardennes front and ambulances forcing through in the opposite direction. It was mid-December, and the moving wall of oblivion that Allied troops would call the Battle of the Bulge was set into motion.

21

(TPWP priority dispatch—Antwerp—byline Reinking)

German armored columns pierced the Allied lines in a surprise counterattack today along the Ardennes front. The offensive, spearheaded by tanks, took advantage of a ghostly infiltration by English-speaking Germans in U.S. Army uniforms who cut phone lines and changed road signs, sowing confusion behind the lines from the Ardennes forest to Antwerp.

Royal Air Force Lieutenant Maurice Overby and I witnessed this dark art of sabotage at a place haunted with history's bloody joust of armies, the battlefield of Waterloo. Our jeep was hailed by a rifle-carrying soldier, his GI uniform appropriately grimy and a footslogger's usual complaints ready on his lips. . . .

★ APPREHENSIVELY, Ben watched while Maurice read the piece, as if chewing every word and letting it digest. The wire clerk, bored, took off his glasses, polished them, held them up to the light, polished them some more.

Finally Maurice issued with a polite but firm frown: "Sorry, Ben, but this simply cannot be let pass."

No, no, goddamn it, Maurice, oh please. My biggest story of the war and you're going to sit on it. Why couldn't you tell me that before I busted my butt writing it? Anguished words building in him for what he knew would be a futile protest, he was stopped by the censorious finger significantly tapping the first sheet of copy paper.

"Flattering as it would be to have my name entered in posterity in this fashion," Maurice was holding forth, "you must strike it. Regulations." He handed Ben the full set of pages.

"That's it? That's all?"

"Right." Unmoving as a crate, Maurice stood watching Ben's pencil slash out his name and dab in substitute wording. He nodded in satisfaction and walked off as Ben thrust the pages to the waiting wire clerk.

> (New lede—byline Reinking)
> Allied forces are trying to regroup along a shattered Ardennes front, where German tank columns shadowed by Wehrmacht foot soldiers in snow-colored camouflage uniforms have advanced nearly a quarter of the way to Antwerp. The surprise breakout, bulging 25 miles into Allied lines, was aided by German infiltrators who snarled communication lines before the armored attack. (Pick up previous piece as follows.)
> A Royal Air Force officer and I witnessed this dark art of sabotage at a place haunted with history's bloody joust of armies, the battlefield of Waterloo . . .

As transmissions of combat reports filtered in to the wildly clattering wire room, Ben pieced together the picture and updated his story time and again. He eyed Maurice warily each time he handed him a new first page, but invariably it was handed back with that benign nod.

All that night and into next day—Ben had lost track of time—as the German attack careened through surprised Allied forces, the only interruption to his flow of story was the periodic message from Tepee Weepy: GREAT STUFF, KEEP SENDING.

> (6th new lede—byline Reinking)
> The bulge in the line of fierce fighting along the
> Ardennes front has grown hour by hour, as Allied
> forces fall back from the brunt of the desperate German
> counterattack. Smoke arose outside abandoned command
> posts as Christmas mail not yet distributed to American
> troops was burned to keep it from falling into German
> hands. Communications among Allied forces still suffer
> from the snipped phone lines and misdirected road signs
> inflicted by infiltrators. (Pick up previous piece as follows.)
> A Royal Air Force officer and I witnessed this dark art
> of sabotage . . .

"That's it, I must tell you, Ben." Maurice was just back from the command bunker. "HQ has had orders from Supreme Headquarters to halt all news reports except official releases. Which is to say, no news."

"Take a break," Ben blearily told the slumped-over wire clerk and saw him off to the beverage urn. He turned around to Maurice, rubbing his eyes and trying to work the kink out of his neck from all the hours bent over teletype machines. "Just between you and me and the red pencil that didn't come out of your pocket, why did they let me get away with what I sent?"

"Interesting situation," Maurice mused over it as if it were a problem in chess. "Our general was quite firm about making it known to the world this German breakthrough is a nasty business for us. What is the American term, to set up a howl?" His tone turned solemn. "All the combat reports indicate the bulge, so-called, is aimed directly here, to retake Antwerp. Shut down the port, cut our forces in two at the same time," he made a sweeping gesture to illustrate the extent of the strategy, "it makes quite good sense from the Hun point of view, doesn't it. Therefore HQ here thought wise to put the word out—your words, actually—before Supreme Headquarters clamped down on the embarrassing news that the Germans caught them with their trousers very much down."

Practically dead on his feet, Ben moved off from the TPWP teletype, clapping Maurice on the shoulder as he passed. "Tepee Weepy and me, always glad to be of service."

MOXIE WAS TAKING the Battle of the Bulge personally. Wound tight, he sat on the edge of his bunk as if about to spring. "Those sneaky Kraut SOBs. They're going for broke." It was the best military analysis Ben had heard yet. "Goddamn it, Reinking, are we still going to get out of here tomorrow?"

Propped in the doorway, Ben answered with each sentence taking effort. "If the USO bunch gets here, I don't see why not. The brass will have to get them back out, and they can squeeze us onto the plane. Maurice keeps checking, the flying looks Okay— the Luftwaffe isn't so much in this, it's more a hell of a ground attack." He looked at the man rooted to the bunk and before he knew it heard himself saying what he was thinking: "You know, Mox, there's no law that you couldn't get off your duff and see what you can find out—"

"I am. I have." Moxie shifted to one side on his perch, then right back. "I was about to tell you. I hunted up our ack-ack intelligence officer, we go back a long ways together. They figure when Supreme Headquarters gets its head out of its butt, they'll be able to stop the Germans about halfway here. Ten days or two weeks. It's going to get worse before it gets better." He gnawed his mouth at the next news. "Ben? They're pulling my crews and some of the others to throw them into it as anti-tank outfits.

Those ninety-millimeters can knock the turret off a Tiger tank. But it's frontline fighting, they could get overrun awful damn easy the way the Germans are rolling."

"Then aren't you lucky you're here and not there." Ben tee-tered away from the doorframe. "I need chow and sleep. Hold the fort, Captain Stamper."

HE WAS FORKING down scrambled powdered eggs and sausages that tasted like sawdust when the wire clerk came looking for him.

"Sir, the Hollywood major wants to see you."

"The which?"

"The rec officer. He's big on USO shows and the bigger the movie star"—the clerk's glasses glinted as he cupped his hands in front of his chest to indicate the category of big—"the better he likes it."

Food and fork forgotten, Ben tried to see past the opaque gaze of the clerk. Was this the ticket home? Or the next thing the war had up its sleeve? "Does that mean the USO troupe is here? On the ground?"

"Yes, sir. Landed from Prestwick about an hour ago."

Now Ben was halfway up out of his chair. "Where do I find this major?"

Giving him a *where else?* look, the clerk answered: "In the Wonder Bar, sir."

THE BUNKER CORRIDOR near the Officers' Club looked like a backstage that had dropped into a theater basement. The black pebbled leatherette cases of musical instruments were arrayed along the concrete base of the wall. People not in military olive drab, standing out like peacocks, bustled in and out of rooms. Passing one, Ben glimpsed the movie actress famous for choosing the shyest fuzz-cheeked soldier in the audience for the honor of sprinkling delousing powder down her back. Elsewhere, several band members were in a card game with the comedian whose jokes fed off how skinny he was. Picking his way in through the clutter of the USO troupe, Ben found the Wonder Bar all but unrecognizable—a temporary stage across one end and tables and elbow room banished to make space for wall-to-wall rows of folding chairs. Trying to tally it all, he felt cocooned in a weird mix of silly dream and nightmare. Not a hundred miles away soldiers were dying in droves in the German surprise attack, and in here was show business as usual, setting up to manufacture songs, patter, and jokes. Half-heartedly he tried a pep talk on himself: just get through this travesty of Antwerp's war; the Duke of Wellington had danced in Brussels a few nights before Waterloo, hadn't he? Morale of the troops, what antics are committed in thy name.

"Good, good, you're here. Ted has been wanting to see you." The major who had materialized and was patting him on the upper arm had chalky eyebrows and the hatchet face of a deacon. Amid the semi-chaos of entertainment being set up he was looking as pleased as could be. "I'll take you over and introduce you."

"That's okay, sir. We've met. Long ago."

Ben steeled himself and headed toward the familiar snap-brim hat in the small huddle near the stage steps. Bareheaded bored newsreel technicians stood on either side of Ted Loudon. The taller one, evidently a cameraman, was saying reluctantly: "All right, we can shoot that if we have to. What's the name of the damn place again, the Roxy?"

"Where do you think you are, back in palookaville?" Even in what passed for conversation, the sportscaster's pace of talk anymore was the fastest an ear could keep up with. "It's the Rex, you're in a country with a king, get it? So what I want is—" He caught sight of ginger hair and an impassive longitudinal face. "Ben Reinking! Captain Reinking. Captain on the gridiron,

captain in the service of his country." The idea seemed to enter-
tain the contriver of the Supreme Team and much else. "What
a piece of luck you're here to be on the show with Moxie, two
heroes for the price of one." He waved off the newsreel crew. "You
know the drill, boys. See you when you get back. Ben, you still
look like you're in great shape. Bet you could still run down one
of Moxie's passes. Hey, I wonder if—"

"Ted, no funny stuff with a football for the show. We're in
a goddamn war zone and Moxie and I both are on our last legs
and—"

"Sure, sure. Anyway, how's it feel to make All-American?
Catches you up with Eisman." Loudon's flat inexpressive face did
not match the voice. "Hell of a thing with him and Danzer, isn't
it—beyond dead, turned into part of the atmosphere." It took
great effort, but Ben did not respond to that. "You guys as a team
were something else," Loudon was going on, exuding sincerity.
He did a slight jerking motion of his head to one side as if making a check mark with his chin. "Something else."

Ben jammed his fists in his pockets to hide their readiness.
"Look, Loud—Ted, how about showing me what pony trick you
want me to do on the broadcast, so I can go get some rest."

"Sam?" Loudon yelled across the room to the show director. "Doing a walk-through with my guest star. Come on up,
Ben." The singing-and-dancing sister act was rehearsing on the
stage, in gowns that looked spun from cotton candy. "Excuse
us, ladies," Loudon pushed past with Ben following, "All-American coming through." At the far end of the stage was a folding
mockup of a stadium broadcasting booth, pennants painted on
and THE LOUDON LOWDOWN lettered large amid those. Rapidly
the sportscaster rehearsed Ben in coming onstage when the Supreme Team cue was given and slipping into a seat behind the
microphone in the fake booth. "It's tight for three," he jabbed
a thumb at the empty seat on the other side, "but we'll make it

work. Moxie'll be along later, he's getting dressed up. Hey, wasn't that tough about Bruno's team not making the Rose Bowl? One lousy touchdown short in the Stanford game."

"Tough."

"Anyway," Loudon thrust a copy of the script at Ben, "look over my questions so there're no surprises. Keep your answers short. Hell, I don't need to tell you the ropes—you're a star in your own right." The check mark with the chin again. "That Guam broadcast. Whooh."

Ben as if by instinct had zeroed in on the nub of the script.

> The unbeaten Treasure State Golden Eagles of 1941
> were a football team without precedent, and tonight I wish
> to honor them in a way befitting that. That gallant eleven,
> with every starting player enlisting in the service of our
> country after Pearl Harbor, went on to another peerless
> record, in courage. Nine of those football heroes gave their
> lives in this war, and in honor of how they gave their all,
> tonight I am naming that Supreme Team who so bravely
> traded football uniforms for military uniforms my All-
> American team for this year. We are lucky to have with us
> tonight the two surviving heroes . . .

Ben's temples throbbed. *You never spare the schmalz, do you, Loudon.* Script gripped in hand, he rose to get away from the man.

Loudon looked up at him expectantly. "The show's at midnight, remember, we have to do it that late to hit prime time back home. You're going to catch some rest, you said. Got an alarm clock?"

"In my pocket."

Ben left the Wonder Bar with Loudon staring after him in puzzlement.

———

HE FLOPPED DOWN on his bunk with the cocotte clock set to go off in half an hour. He knew better than to drop deep asleep for an extended time, he would still be groggy when it was time for the show. He had lived with the clock of war for so long, with its unending hours and split-second dangers, that rationing his time for one last night was worth everything. Tomorrow a plane homeward out of the war. In some other tomorrow, a script made into a movie that would reveal Loudon and Bruno for what they were. His tired mind traversed from the one thought to the other, forth and back, as Maurice would have said. He dozed off that way.

WHEN THE COCOTTE clock dinged, he cracked his eyes barely a slit and closed them again against the corridor lighting pouring through the doorway. It was the most welcome indulgence in days just to lie there with the faint rosy nothingness behind the eyelids. The nothingness dimmed for a moment.

He opened his eyes, unsure.

Then the tossed-off words came back. *"Moxie'll be along later, he's getting dressed up."* Moxie hated dressing up. He had barely managed it for Purcell's funeral. His deliberately careless fashion was that of an unmade bed.

Ben jerked upright on the bunk, put his shoes on in a hurry, and went out into the bunker corridor. He asked the officer next door: "Did the lights blink just now?"

"Same like always," came the reply in a used-to-it voice. "The buzz bomb dimmer switch."

He hurried down the corridor to Moxie's room. Empty. *Okay, he must be hanging around the Wonder Bar watching them set things up, is all. Showing Inez the glamorous life.* He couldn't quite convince himself. Moxie was not the kind to sit in a corner watching other people be in charge.

This time he stuck his head in the room across the hall, the senior enlisted men's side. A grizzled gunnery sergeant at the

wall niche desk writing a letter home looked around in surprise
and started to get to his feet. "At ease, Guns," Ben said quickly.
"Any idea where Captain Stamper's wandered off to?"

"Sure thing. Him and that nurse went to the flicks, in town.
Some newsreel guys wanted shots of his squiring her somewhere
and you know him, he wouldn't pass up—"

Ben set off for the wire room at a run.

The entire section was a din of teletypes clacking and phones
jangling. WRENs with messages in hand scurried off into the
HQ staff's warren of offices. Forging his way through the traffic of messengers, Ben latched on to the owl-eyed clerk blinking
up at him in alarm from his keyboard. "Sir, we're on emergency
priority, we can't send to TPWP without the commander's—"

"To hell with that. The buzz bomb that hit—where?"

"In the city, right in the center. Bad one, sir. There's a call
out for ambulances from units all the way to Brussels." The clerk
skimmed the message pad he was transcribing from. "The Belgian authorities keep calling the place a 'cinema' but our regs say
'movie'—"

Ben whirled, searching the room. Where was Maurice with
the damn jeep when needed? *Up to his tonsils in there with the
commander and the intelligence dummies who blew this, that's
where.*

Abandoning the wire room, he wove his way back to his
quarters at a trot, grabbed his flight jacket and crush hat and
the pistol belt, and plunged out into the long maze of corridors
to the hospital bunker. The scene there was the confusion of the
wire room multiplied. Stretcher bearers were bringing in a steady
bloodied stream of men, women, children—some so blackened
with blast dust and dried blood you could not tell which they
were. Army doctors and nurses swarmed around the stretcher
cases, scissoring off clothing, shunting the prone patients into
surgery or wards. Constantly dodging out of the way, Ben hunted

down the medical staffer keeping track of the military wounded
and dead, learned most of the victims were Antwerp civilians so
far, and Moxie's and Inez's dog tags were not among those the
staffer had copied onto his clipboard list. *Okay, they're among the
missing,* Ben tried to reason himself into, *that's a different list.*
They could still be at the theater, Moxie by nature would take
over any rescue task he could, she was a nurse—

The decision churning within him, Ben zeroed in on an
ambulance driver outside under the archway smoking a cigarette. Throat dry—*Comparatively few direct hits compared to
what?*—he stepped out into the wintry Antwerp night, calling
to the driver: "Sarge, the movie theater that caught it—are you
going back in?"

The driver stiffened but the cigarette stayed cupped in his
saluting hand. "Probably all night, Captain, why?"

"I'm riding with you."

The driver shrugged, not wanting any more trouble on the
night. "If you want, you can hop in back. Hang on to something,
we give it the gas going in."

OUT THE BACK windows of the jouncing ambulance he could
see spikes of light driven into the blackness, searchlights on the
hunt for buzz bombs. Whenever one was found, tracer bullets
streaked toward it, the flaring bursts of larger ack-ack following,
the sky over Antwerp like some hectic mosaic of fireworks. All
through the careening ride he clung to a support of the triple-
decker stretcher rack, watching through a porthole of the war
that he knew might be his last view.

As soon as the ambulance stopped alongside others waiting
to be loaded, he piled out. Unexpected brightness hit him. The
market square with its avalanche of rubble, he saw from under his shielding hand, was like a movie set done by madmen.
Huge arc lights illuminated the void in the line of gabled facades

where the movie theater had been. Under the glare of the arcs, the mountainous spill of brickwork and rafters, framed by the pale wall of the neighboring building the theater had torn away from, lay at rest in either stark light or grim shadow.

Rescue squads were prying up beams, military policemen were trying to direct the erratic traffic of ambulances and trucks bringing more squads. As if sleepwalking, Ben trudged farther into the scene where Hitler's rocket men had done their worst. Off to his left on the side of the square lay blanketed figure after figure. He helplessly counted as he passed the line of corpses; he quit at fifty.

It was cold in the blast-strewn square, his breath smoked from him in ghostly wreaths. Reaching a bit of open space where he could see all around, he scanned the chainlike ranks of rescuers on the rubble heap for Moxie's lean form, Inez's broadset one.

Suddenly, across the street from what had been the marqueed front of the theater, he spotted the tall newsreel cameraman from the troupe.

As fast as he could reach there without slipping on the blood on the cobblestones, he came up beside the man as he was busy reloading the big shoulder camera. "Where's Captain Stamper? *Where's Captain Stamper?*"

The cameraman turned and gave him a foggy look. Then realization came, and the eyes begged. "You didn't hear? Hell, I'm sorry, Mike must have missed you, I sent him back to the base for more film, he was supposed to tell Loudon. I've got to stay here and keep shooting—"

Ben grabbed him by the shoulders and shook him. "Just tell me what happened, goddamn it!"

The cameraman blanched, backing off to his small stack of equipment. He tenderly put down his camera and picked up something from the pile. "Maybe you better see this for yourself." He held the thing out to Ben.

It was a peaked officer's cap with leather brim, the kind that went with dress uniform. Taking it from him, Ben grasped the cap in both hands for a moment and then slowly tipped it over to look inside, already knowing. In the garish light cast by the arcs he could make out the inking on the hatband:

LIKE HELL IT'S YOURS. THIS CAP BELONGS TO CAPT. MOXIE STAMPER SERIAL # 19071353.

He looked the only question left to the cameraman.

"All we wanted were a couple of shots of him and her going up to the ticket window holding hands, like they were out on a date." The cameraman pointed across to the collapsed front of the theater, a chunk of the marquee with the enormous maroon letters REX sitting in the street crookedly but otherwise strangely unharmed. "They weren't even going in, the movie had already started. These old buildings"—his hand shook as he motioned up at the ornamented guildhall gables—"Loudon had that major scout these out, he told us it would make a terrific backdrop. So, we were just doing a second take, everything going fine, when the bomb hit."

Ben stared into the empty air where the balcony of the theater would have been, the projection room, the offices above, and then to where it had all fallen into a crumbled heap of bricks and broken wood and bodies.

The cameraman followed his gaze and hesitantly told the rest. "We were across the street here, it made a nice angle shot, the marquee there . . . Mike's my soundman, he was knocked over by the blast. I got thrown around pretty good myself. Just as everything started to, to come down"—the man wiped his lips with the back of his hand, and managed to speak again—"the captain grabbed his cap off and threw it to us while he pulled the nurse to him with his other arm and covered her with himself. I don't know how he did both at once."

"He was an athlete," Ben said dully. The cap in hand, he turned and walked off to catch a ride to the base in one of the ambulances.

"Hey, Captain, uh, sir?" the cameraman called after him. "Do me a favor? Lug this film back for me?" He gestured up at the night sky, quiet at the moment, tracer-lit a minute ago. "In case something more happens here?"

Ben took the film can and kept on walking toward the ambulances.

CLIMBING OUT AT the hospital bunker, he handed the cap to one of the medics. "Give this to the guy taking down names. Tell him Nurse Mazzetti was with the captain."

The long tunnel of bunker corridors resounded to his footsteps as he headed for the Wonder Bar, his mind cold and clear. Inevitability was claiming him. The wall of oblivion had moved closer one more notch, its tenth, Moxie the next to last off the living list. The others, back at the start—O'Fallon, Havel—and on up the black climb of odds—Friessen, Vic, Prokosch, Animal—and off the chart of any foretelling—Dex, even Danzer, Jake—teamed one final time in his resolve. He was giving himself over. With Moxie gone he was the eleventh man, the perverse odds now solely out to get him and they would, he could see them piled overhead as if he were in the bottom of an hourglass looking at the deathly sand above. He knew it would happen according to the war's whim of time, when he would go out into the Antwerp night after doing this. If a buzz bomb did not find him this night, something else ultimately would. A leftover booby trap in whatever hiding place he sought out. A guildhall wall, wearied by the constant return of war, collapsing on him. The Germans barreling into the city, if the Bulge was not turned back, and dooming him in their pogrom of able-bodied defenders. He accepted, he couldn't not, that the war would see to him, one fatal way or another. But first, this. He could find no reason in himself not to rid the world of Loudon. The .45 still had bullets in its clip.

Ben entered the hubbub of the Wonder Bar. Several members of the USO troupe were beside the stage signing autographs for early-comers, the confectionery colors of the singers and dancers glossy against the olive drab of the GIs. Loudon and the major, in conference at the show director's desk, spotted him and waved him over frantically.

"Ben! We've been looking everywhere for you." Loudon's words came faster than ever. "It's Moxie, he's—" The expression on Ben stopped him. "You heard. You're upset. Can't blame you."

Ben dropped the film can on the desk with a clatter.

"This is what's left of him."

Beneath the snap-brim hat the eyes guardedly darted down, then back to Ben. "Awful, what happened. We've got to make this into a tribute to him. Sit down, why don't you, we'll work over the script with—"

"I need a few minutes with you, Loudon. Just us. Now."

"Use my office," the major offered, all solicitude.

As soon as the door was shut, Loudon started again. "My God, who could have imagined this. Moxie the tenth one, I mean, there's no story ever like it." The chin doing the check mark, confirming to himself the Supreme Team saga. "You and me—well, no way it can be called lucky, watching it happen to all those poor guys, but at least we saw to it that they'll always be remembered." He sat down at the major's desk and beckoned Ben over. "Okay, the script, we have to make changes." The undercurrent of excitement still was in his voice. "Got your copy?"

Ben made no move toward the desk. As much as he had always despised the sportswriter, he at last realized Loudon in his darkest unacknowledged self wanted the whole team dead. Dead and buttered. Fit to serve up in his radio show, his newsreel, his newspaper column, probably a book. *The Eleven Who Donned the Uniform,* or something worse.

"Ben? We need to get going on this script. It's less than an hour to airtime and—"

"Shut up, Loudmouth." Ben's hand twitched against the pistol holster. He did not care whether Loudon noticed or not. "You're poison, you and your goddamn airtime and the rest, you're the death of the whole team. All the way back to Purcell."

Loudon looked at him, blank as a flatfish. The automatic velocity of voice started up: "Hey, let's not say anything we'll regret, I know it hits you hard about Mox—" The yammer stopped as suddenly as it started, something coming into Loudon's eyes now. "Purcell? Why bring that up?"

"You were in on it. You stood there with your hands in your pockets and watched Bruno run him to death."

"Ben, listen, you got it wrong. Bruno didn't have it in for Purcell, he had big plans for him on the team if he could turn him into enough of a man."

"He turned him into a dead kid."

"Sometimes things get pushed harder than anyone intended." Whatever it was in Loudon's eyes was matched now by the insinuation in his words. "It still bugs you that Bruno was turning Purcell into a starter, doesn't it. The team would've looked pretty different to you then, hey, Ben?"

"You slippery bastard, where did you come up with that, Purcell on the starting team? We had almost a week of practices yet before the season, Danzer had plenty of time to get his act—" Ben halted.

"In for Reinking at left end, Merle Purcell," Loudon maliciously mimicked broadcasting the substitution.

"What the hell are you talking about? I was captain of the team."

"That would have changed in a hurry if you were on the
bench." The words came out of Loudon as if he couldn't resist
the taste of them. "Bruno was going to bump you to the scrub
team before the opening game, like that." He snapped his fingers.
"Told me so, had me hold the story until he could put football
religion into Purcell, on the Hill. He'd never give up on Danzer.
Danzer was one of his. You weren't, sucker."

It reached all through Ben. "Then I'm not—" Purcell was
the eleventh man. The famously hexed varsity lineup picked by
Bruno at that last practice—*I'm not on the list.* The freedom from
the odds built upon that jinx day dizzied him. Death had made
its clean sweep. The skew in the law of averages brought on by
Bruno's manipulations on the practice field and Loudon's at the
microphone, that entire fatal scheme of things was not necessarily meant to have a place for Ben Reinking. He was odd man out.
Am. The inevitability lifted from him. From here on, if the war
claimed him, it would have to do it on its own terms, not by the
Supreme Team's wholesale bad luck. A crazy laugh broke from
Ben. No, he realized, the sanest one in a long time.

"Okay, we both have it out of our systems," Loudon was saying, nervous at that laugh. "Now let's forget all that and get busy
on the script, airtime will be here in—"

"I'm not going on the show."

Loudon gaped at him.

"The Supreme Team is yours, it always was." Ben found he
could say it calmly. "Give it a funeral any way you want."

"Listen, Reinking—Ben." The famous voice rose. "We don't
have to be pals about this, we just have to do the show. You'll get
your gravy from this as much as I will. Everything's set up for
us. The network time. The news cameras. The whole USO—"

A rap on the door and the major was in the room almost
before the sound. "I couldn't help hearing the ruckus. Something
I can help with?"

"It's him," Loudon flared. "Says he won't go on the show. Drive some sense into him, Major."

"You most certainly are going on the show," the major scolded Ben as if he were a Sunday schooler. "I've looked over Ted's script, you're everywhere in it. Let's not complicate things for him."

"Let's."

The major took another look at Ben. "Captain, I order you to pick up that script and prepare for the show." Loudon at the desk whacked his hand down on his copy to second that.

"Not a chance, Major," Ben said, stepping away. "I am a TPWP war correspondent, I have a story to write about what killed Moxie Stamper, and I am going out that door now and write it."

Commotion had spread to the other side of the door, from the sound of it. The major raised his voice, "Quiet, out there! We're in conference in—"

He stopped short at the sight of Maurice Overby striding in, military policemen in white helmets and white spats on either side of him, two more taking up a station at the door.

Maurice paused, glanced at the major's angry face and Loudon's angrier one, and raised his eyebrows at Ben. "Have we come at an inconvenient moment?"

"I don't know how you got wind of this, Lieutenant, but you're right in time," the major recovered. "Have your MPs ready." He leveled a deaconly finger at Ben. "How does arrest for disobeying an order from a superior officer and a Section Eight sound to you, Reinking? If you don't—"

"Actually, sir," Maurice broke in as if to save the major the trouble of saying more, "I'm here on orders from considerably higher up. I speak of the general. We"—Maurice swept his hand around graciously to indicate the military police contingent—"are to place Captain Reinking aboard a plane. In the word from HQ command, 'soonest.'"

I hope I heard that right. I hope I'm not dreaming this.

Loudon's face went from bad to worse, a good sign to Ben. "This man can't go anywhere," the major protested. "He's to be on the show or else—"

"I beg to differ, sir." Not without a bit of flourish, Maurice produced a set of paperwork. "He is being sent forthwith 'stateside,' again in the phrasing of the order. I have that order here should you wish to examine it, Major." The major did not touch it. Maurice nodded to the MPs, who moved in around Ben like bodyguards. "So. If you'll make your farewells, Captain, we can be on our way."

Ben looked straight at Loudon and said as if it was a vow, "See you in the movies, sucker."

Within the wedge of MPs, the blue-clad RAF officer and the flight-jacketed American cut through the gathering crowd in the Wonder Bar and swung out into the long bunker corridor where the footsteps were their own.

"Maurice, am I completely wacko," Ben asked urgently out the side of his mouth, "or were you bluffing back there?"

"Not at all," came the benign reply. "I might admit to providing a pinch of dramatic effect in the matter, but that's all. No, you are in mightier hands than mine. Your TPWP people had to come clean in their 'urgent' message a bit ago to convince HQ command you're worth high priority. A home-state senator—is that the phrase for a political old tusker in America?—raised rather a ruckus about the number of soldiers' lives your Montana has contributed to the war. I believe you know whereof I speak." The New Zealander turned a solemn gaze on him, then resumed. "All in all, it has become in Tepee Weepy's best interest to fetch you back alive and in one piece as speedily as can be." Maurice patted the side pocket of his uniform jacket. "I procured you a copy of all that, it should make pleasant reading on the plane. I don't mean to take the cherry off the top ahead of you, but I do think you'd like to know, Ben—you're to be mustered out as soon as you're back at that base in Montana and write the piece about Stamper."

At the mouth of the bunker was a stocky MP with a two-way radio clapped to his ear. He held up a hand like the traffic cop he had probably been in civilian life. "Hold it here, everybody—ack-ack is tracking one in."

In the shelter of the concrete archway, Ben and Maurice and the armbanded soldiers watched the sudden cat's cradle of searchlight beams over Antwerp. The arcs of white frozen lightning swung and swung, hunting, until fastening onto a glint far up in the black sky. Flashes from gun batteries pulsed on the low horizon, and as the flying bomb seemed to slow and hesitate, tracer bullets converged toward it like the ascending lines where the arches of a cathedral meet. Then the buzz bomb lost course, faltering off in a drifting glide, away from the battered durable old city.

"One less to worry about," Maurice pronounced briskly. Turning to Ben, he tapped his watch. "Fifteen minutes. The plane can take off in ten." Choked up, Ben could only shake hands wordlessly. The stubby lieutenant gave him an unreserved smile. "Fare thee well, Ben Reinking. Happy ride home."

The jeep thrummed under him on the steel grid of runway as it sped toward the plane, the guardian MPs riding shotgun front and back, the war behind him in the darkness. With luck—it was an amazing feeling to trust that word again—within three days the hopscotch of flights would deliver him back to East Base. Back within reach of the woman he would never get over. In the whirl of his thoughts the memorized lines of her letter danced to and fro. *"I think of you more than is healthy, and I just want you to know I regret not one damn thing of our time together. . . . Maybe it'll all sort out okay after the war."*

Flooded almost to tears with the rapture of survival, Ben un-loaded from the jeep the instant it screeched to a halt and raced

toward the hatchway of the revving plane. *You're getting giddy,
Reinking. If not now, when?* With his war over, in his every heartbeat he could feel the surge of his chances with Cass. A woman
with no regrets, two men—

He did not even have to calculate. All the rest of his life,
should he live forever, he gladly would take odds that good.

ACKNOWLEDGMENTS

THIS IS A WORK of fiction, and so my characters exist only in these pages. There is, however, a breath of actuality to the plot premise of World War Two's disproportionate toll on a given number of young men who had played football together: by the accounts available, eleven starting players of Montana State College in Bozeman did perish in that conflict. I am indebted to my late friend, Dave Walter of the Montana Historical Society, for providing me the pieces of that quilt of lore. Research virtuoso of the state's past that he was, Dave also furnished a vivid sense of conscientious objector life in the Montana woods during the war in his history of the Civilian Public Service Camp at Belton, Montana, *Rather Than War*.

Montana's war losses are summed up in another key historical study, *Montana, A History of Two Centuries* by Michael P. Malone, Richard B. Roeder, and William L. Lang: "As in World War I, Montana contributed more than its share of military manpower—roughly forty thousand men by 1942—and the state's death rate in the war was exceeded only by New Mexico's."

A number of the women who piloted miltary aircraft in 1942–44 as WASPs—Women Air Force Service Pilots—learned to fly in the Civilian Pilot Training program before the war, as

I had Cass Standish do. There were 916 WASPs—141 of those in the Air Transport Command, as Cass's ferry squadron would have been—when their branch of the service was disbanded ("inactivated") in December 1944. Thirty-eight women military pilots lost their lives in the course of duty. While East Base in Great Falls, Montana, was indeed a hub of ferrying Lend-Lease fighters, bombers, and cargo planes north to Alaska and Soviet Union air crews waiting there—the total is listed as 7,926 aircraft—the presence of Cass's flying women at East Base and on the route to Edmonton is my own creation.

Similarly, I have taken literary leeway with a few settings in the book. Citizens of Great Falls will find that I have put nonexistent Treasure State University on about the site of C.M. Russell High School, and the Letter Hill in back of it. Hill 57 did exist. The Reinkings' town of Gros Ventre and the Two Medicine country remain as I originated them in my Montana Trilogy, imagined versions that draw on the actual geography in and around Dupuyer, the hospitable armful of town of my high school years.

The Office of War Information from 1942 until 1945 had various sections involved in war news for domestic consumption, but the Threshold Press War Project, "Tepee Weepy," was foisted on it by my imagination.

In my characters' combat experiences, I have sometimes drawn on oral history accounts, memoirs, and unit histories for touches of detail. One source in particular I would like to single out, my late writing colleague and friend, Alvin Josephy. When we coincided at the Fishtrap "Writing and the West" Conference at Wallowa Lake, Oregon, in 1994, I heard Alvin's recording of the amphibious landing at Guam, and his memoir *A Walk Toward Oregon* has a further account of his wading the bullet-pocked surf with that microphone as a Marine combat correspondent. Ben Reinking's narration and specific experiences of the Guam invasion are invented by me, but the spirit of Alvin Josephy surely goes ashore with him. As to a few other military instances of where actuality leaves off and the author begins:

—Many Montana soldiers did serve in the long and terrible jungle fighting in New Guinea, Biak, and the Philippines. The Montaneers regiment that held Carl Friessen, Dexter Cariston, and Dan Standish is my own version of such a unit.

—The U.S. Coast Guard in the middle years of the war did patrol the Olympic Peninsula coastline with dogs. The balloon bombs launched by Japan occurred a bit later in the war than I have portrayed; the first of the 32-foot balloons with an incendiary device was reported in November 1944, and across the remainder of the war an estimated one thousand of nine thousand launched may have reached the American mainland. At least six persons were killed, although I know of no instance of a Coast Guardsman encountering a balloon bomb as Sig Prokosch did.

—Antwerp in the last autumn and winter of the war did suffer attacks of a severity reminiscent of the Luftwaffe's earlier bombing blitz of London: more than five thousand buzz bombs were launched against the Belgian city and its strategic port in 154 days. The casualty figures are given as 3,752 civilians and 731 Allied servicemen killed. Behind a screen of heavy news censorship, a combined Allied anti-aircraft artillery command of 22,000 personnel was deployed against the V-1, and later V-2, flying bombs.

In this novel's inflections of life in uniform, certain phrasings and observations are drawn from my own military experience as an Air Force reservist on active duty during the Cuban missile crisis.

Lastly, a considerable community of friends, acquaintances, and research institutions provided me information, advice, or other aid, and I deeply thank them all: the University of Washington libraries, and Sandra Kroupa, Book Arts and Rare Book curator; the Coast Guard Museum of the Northwest, and director Gene Davis; the Montana Historical Society, and Molly Kruckenberg, Brian Shovers, Lory Morrow, Becca Kohl, Jodie Foley, Ellie Arguimbau, Zoe Ann Stoltz, Rich Aarstad, Karen Bjork; Marcella Walter, for shelter, conversation, and half the laughing again; the University of Montana library, and archivist Donna Macrae; the Great Falls Public Library; Curt Shannon, director of the Malmstrom AFB Museum; Judy Ellinghausen, archives administrator of the High Plains Heritage Center; Christine Morris, executive director of the Cascade County Historical Society; Les Nilson; Bradley Hamlett for providing me with his memoir of missions against the bridge on the River Kwai, *Bombing the Death Railroad*; Wayne and Genise Arnst, for hospitality and friendship as ever; Jean Roden, and John Roden for advice on flying and parachuting; Diane Josephy Peavey; Betty Mayfield, super-librarian and savvy friend; Paul G. Allen's Flying Heritage Collection, for letting me hang around its World War Two planes; Rex Smith; Laurie Brown, David Hough, Linda Lockowitz, and Tom Bouman, for their customary literary wizardry; Liz Darhansoff, for magic in the clauses; and my wife, Carol, first reader for the dozenth time.